THE ENGLISH CLASS

OUYANG YU

transit lounge

First Published 2010
Transit Lounge Publishing
95 Stephen Street
Yarraville, Australia 3013
www.transitlounge.com.au
info@transitlounge.com.au

Cover photograph by Luo Hao (cheerycock@gmail.com)
Design by Peter Lo
Printed in China by Everbest

Australian Government

Australia | Council
for the Arts

This project has been assisted by the Australian government through the Australia Council for the Arts, its arts funding and advisory body.

Transit Lounge is a proud member of the A.P.A.(Australian Publishers' Association) and S.P.U.N.C. (Small Press Underground Networking Community)

National Library of Australia
Cataloguing-in-publication data

National Library of Australia Cataloguing-in-Publication entry

Ouyang, Yu, 1955-

The English class / Ouyang Yu.

1st ed.

9780980571783 (pbk.)

A821.3

For Lindesay,

With my best wishes,

from [signature]

THE
ENGLISH CLASS

[signature]

2012. 3. 17

To Zuo Zhen who gave me the tongue

to create a second tongue.

At night he stands up, the distant call of birds
already deep inside him; and feels bold
because he has taken all the galaxies
into his face, not lightly—, oh not like someone
who prepares a night like this for his beloved
and treats her to the skies that he has known.

Rainer Maria Rilke
The Selected Poems of Rainer Maria Rilke

to have lived
through one solitude to arrive at another,
to feel oneself many things and recover wholeness.

Pablo Neruda
The Poetry of Pablo Neruda

I couldn't make love in English.

An unnamed interviewee
Quoted in Kachru, *Asian Englishes*

So much takes place in the head, so little is known and fixed.

Jonathan Raban
Soft City

PART I

The Little Aristocrat

1

At twenty-three, Jing was not married. He had not done anything great in his life. Probably the only great thing he had ever done was to survive the Great Proletarian Cultural Revolution like hundreds of millions of his fellow countrymen, contrary to the Western belief. He was a small man, with a large square white face shaped like the Chinese character for 'nation'. It tanned easily in summer but went back to its creaminess in winter, a feature that would often draw comments from people behind his back: 'How come he is so white?' Or 'Did he originally come from the cold North?' Or 'Was there a foreigner in his family?' He had ambitions but did not quite know what they were. When he was an educated youth in the countryside, he had wanted to go to school so that he could spend his days reading books instead of planting rice and wheat in spring or carrying the back-breaking rice stocks on a shoulder pole from the fields to the village in summer and autumn. Now that he was a truck driver, after graduating from the wrong school, a driving school, the urge to learn more, to know more about the outside world returned.

The Great Cultural Revolution was virtually at an end and China was beginning to open up. For the first time, the university entrance examination, suspended for many years, was reintroduced, bringing a ray of hope for an aspiring youth such as Jing, who had spent years living with peasants in a mountain village by a nameless creek and had, as luck would have it, become a driver in the Truck Team attached to the shipyard in White Sand. Apart from his whiteness, there was nothing to suggest what this small man, standing in his blue overalls wearing a coat with a badge that showed he had received training from a driving school, was capable of. No one paid much attention to him in the team. They had seen the likes of him in the past: kids sent by their powerful parents to stay in the team as a jumping board to launch them somewhere else when opportunities arose. No one stayed long enough to strike roots. As Old Canton, an experienced mechanic who had been demoted from his position of professorship in a university for his overseas connections, said, in his heavily accented Cantonese Mandarin, the team was a temporary haven for the well-connected 'bastards' before they got better jobs. Few in the team questioned the legitimacy of this practice. All took it for granted that if one had power, one would naturally take advantage of it before it was too late. As Whooping Xu – he had earned the name because he was suffering from chronic bronchitis – aptly put it, *youquan buyong, guoqi zuofei,* use your power while you have it.

Jing had no powerful parents, although he did have some connections. His aunt worked for the Bureau of Transportation Administration. Over the phone, she told him he had two choices; he could either get a job with the Transportation Team or go to a shipyard. It did not take Jing long to make up his mind. The Transportation Team was a hell of a job, driving trucks around the provinces, rising before daybreak and going to bed at midnight; sometimes you had to drive overnight to avoid the busy daily traffic or the overwhelming summer heat. The wage was good but the risk was great. Some guys Jing knew had come to early grief, breaking their backs or necks as a result of head-on collisions or overturned trucks. The shipyard did not sound too bad a choice by comparison. If there was not much work, he could then do his own stuff. He enjoyed reading. Secretly, he thought of going to university one day. So, it was with some expectation that one spring day he came to the shipbuilding factory and registered with the Truck Team.

At White Sand, the shipyard consisted of three parts: a dry dock with a half-finished ship sleeping in it, surrounded by heavy lifting equipment that scarred the sky; the central part with a row of black-tiled, white-walled office rooms and, to the side, a stand-alone two-storey building wrapped in rusty sheet steel salvaged from sunken ships. From the dock on the water's edge of the Yangtze River, Jing could see, miles downstream, the bridge across the river between Snake Mountain in Wuchang and Turtle Mountain in Hanyang, and the river itself lined with ships of all kinds. At the sight of the surrounding weeds turning green in the cracks of the mud left from last year's flood, Jing's heart gave a leap. This was where he was going to spend the next instalment of his life. And, when the shrill siren of a passenger ship of five storeys pierced his ears, his eyes were drawn towards its familiar sky-blue shape with three red Chinese characters on its bow: The East is Red, chugging away against the stream on its way to Chongqing. Outside the walls of the shipyard was a flat land green with river growth, willow trees and soft hair-like grass and small pond-like industrial lagoons. His loneliness was relieved by the reassuring thought that he could come here in the evenings if he found being alone with himself too much to bear, as he had experienced in the past.

When he went to the Truck Team the next day, Jing was disappointed. It was not just the ironclad ramshackle affair that assaulted his eye. Added to that was the stark realisation that the team did not even have a proper parking site next to its repair shop, shaped like a box open on one side beneath the steel structure. In front of the open side, there was a strip of muddy ground strewn with sand and cut with deep dry ruts where the assorted vehicles were parked, some head first, some tail first, depending on the driver's whim. Nothing like the ones he had seen in the Transportation Team, where hundreds of dark-green Jiefang, Liberation trucks or semitrailers occupied the expansive old Racing Ground in neat military rows – these vehicles were the inferior stuff of unknown brands. One bulgy-headed four-tonner resembled a Jiefang but turned out to be a Hubei, a brand that Jing's mates in the driving school would sneer at. A paint-peeled Fiat perched over a black hole with one wheel gone. An elephantine truck stood in his way, dwarfing him. Next to it was a tiny little specimen that could neither be called a car nor a truck as it was too small for either but resembled both in its shape, all its paint gone, looking like a poor little joke.

All told, there were less than ten vehicles.

When he stepped inside the workshop, it was like stepping back a century into a darkened cave. Jing was astonished to see a cave painting. A room of tools lined the walls, hanging from the ceiling and carpeting part of the floor. Spanners, pincer pliers, boxes of screws, screwdrivers, crankshafts, crankcases, ignition plugs, and a lingering smell of grease and oil assaulted his nostrils. Sitting in this cavern was a group of people, frozen, as if painted, in various postures: Old Canton perched on a tool box covered with a clean towel, scowling at this nondescript newcomer, a smoking cigarette in his right hand and a large mug of tea in his left, hovering above it as if over a fire; Whooping Xu coughing and turning his thin chin around as he reached to open his cabinet to fetch a spanner when he noticed the student-faced Jing; Old Zhu quickly suppressing an abusive '*wo cao* (fuck), another one of them' by presenting a smiling face with an 'Oh, that's good, that's good', in response to Ba, the Team Leader's introduction.

In as few words as possible, Ba told Jing what he was supposed to do. He was to act as the replacement guy for anyone who couldn't come to work due to illness or family commitments. Otherwise, he was to stay around and see if there was anything he could help with.

*

A few days after his arrival in White Sand, Jing put down his impressions in his diary:

For some reason, the people I encountered here are not very friendly. Old Canton, for example. This man is so fastidious that he does not allow anyone to touch his tools, let alone use them, and he keeps his own little space shiningly clean, even though rubbish accumulates around him with engine oil or chunks of yellow grease. When he finishes his work, he uses a big mop to wipe his dark greasy hands and lights his cigarette. He has a pea-size mole on the right side of his chin, just the opposite to Mao's. He never says a word to me. He does not even look at me. He just sits there, his left leg thrown over his right while his right knee constantly jerks up and down as he makes a sucking noise through his big-holed nostrils, looking grave. I have never seen him smile once.

Master Tong must be over eighty now. He's the only one who smiles his almost toothless smile towards me and makes a welcome noise in his throat. Reputedly, he is the top mechanic here. Is Old Canton not happy because he regards himself as superior? Tong is so happy-go-lucky that no one seems to take him seriously. Even when they ask him for advice, they do it in a way that makes you feel it is they who give advice to him, not the other way round. If something is not properly done, they'll tell him off and say, 'Master, what's the problem with you? You are supposed to know better than all of us put together!' But you won't see him get upset. He'll smile, showing the dark hole of a mouth with countable teeth and say he'll fix it. Then they'll bully him into buying them a lunch or lollypops. 'He's our highest-paid man. Get him to buy us lunch!' Hu, an otherwise morose mechanic with an overcast face more due to grease than anything else, would often say this to goad others into action.

There are others but I'll write about them as I go. Life here seems endless, with them always talking about safety, women and money. I'm looking forward to going out on my first assignment to get away for a while.

*

It was not long before Jing got work from Ba, the driver of the huge truck they called *yu li ke* or Unique, as he had other commitments. Like the silvery Unique he was driving, Jing was driven by tasks assigned by his Truck Team, to go to Lion Mountain to haul truckloads of blasted gravel or to go to a cement factory in Puqi County for loads of cement. Puqi, a city by the Yangtze, about a hundred kilometres upstream, was famous for its bamboo products such as beds and chairs and, on his trips there, his workmates would often ask Jing to bring back a few for them. When Jing climbed into his cabin, high above the ground, his mind was at peace, although the muscles in his face jumped with the terrible vibration of this diesel-driven monster that must have been left behind by the Americans in the 1940s. He took out scraps of paper bearing English words, one at a time, inserting them between the windscreen and a piece of iron bulging on the dashboard. He was pleased with this way of learning, his own invention. As the truck floated down the asphalt road like an oversized boat, trees on the riverbank swiftly flowing backwards, Jing quickly shifted his eyes to the words and back to the road, in time to break for a set of lights or some arsehole speedster who was trying to overtake him, honking like mad. He was not concerned that the words might be jostled out of his memory by the large animal he was riding.

With no power steering, the wheel was so hard to turn that he was often seen standing up from his seat as he forced the iron elephant to turn into the curved driveway leading to the factory gate, the top of his head sometimes hitting the roof of his cabin. He kept going over the words in his memory, words that he had picked up from an English-Chinese dictionary, alphabetically, 'aback: *take aback*', 'abacus: *use an abacus*', 'Abaddon' and 'abandon'. The task that he had set up for himself was to commit to memory 100 new words or more a day. Jing was voracious. He wanted to amass a learning so huge that it would stand him head and shoulders above the rest of them in the team: the young Zhu whose only wish was for his child to become rich and famous when he grew up, who having spent years in the country as an educated youth resigned himself to the fact that he could never be anything more than a truck driver; the moon-faced Tann whose little joke sickened Jing whenever he referred to his wife as his *qingren* (mistress) in the morning study sessions before any trucks were allowed to move out of the factory; and Ba, the team leader, a Malaysian-Chinese whose family returned to China after the anti-Chinese violence in 1969 and who had such a fiery temper that he would yell abuse at anyone doing work that was not up to scratch.

Jing did not know where these English words would eventually lead him. He had only a vague idea that he would one day go away and leave this crappy little place behind, this place crisscrossed with intricate human relationships, a network of invisible intrigues and infighting for petty gains, where Jing felt a total stranger, was treated like a tool, picked up when needed and thrown down when not. Without a decent vehicle assigned to his name, he had to drive other people's trucks in their absence, sometimes the Unique, sometimes the Fiat and at other times the dark green Hubei, held in the lowest regard by drivers and mechanics alike. For him, English seemed to be the only escape to a world beyond this reality. And it was when he was out on the road, with vehicles assigned to him temporarily, that he felt truly free.

2

Jing's roommate was Li, a porter who assisted the truck drivers
to load and unload their trucks. From a brief talk with him,
Jing understood that Li was a local, but he never went home
on Sundays like his other workmates. Between their beds, Jing
and Li shared a window of six panes that opened in the middle
with a latch. Jing could not go home because his home, Yellow
Town, was about a hundred kilometres downstream of the
Yangtze River, a day's journey from his workplace. So, he had to
be content with spending his Sundays in front of this window in
this tiny dormitory room, with four bare white walls, studying
English, sitting before a makeshift tabletop made of a wooden
box containing all his belongings. While he was doing so, Li
slept away in his bed opposite him, shrouded in a mosquito net
that had many holes in it; black and dusty, the net looked as
if it had never been washed. Li, by contrast, never read books.
Straight after work and meals, he would creep into his net and
sleep, with no sound. At first, Jing suspected that Li did not like
him much and perhaps even resented him for learning English,
something that was simply beyond the comprehension of the
whole factory, let alone the team. Gradually, he found that
Li really didn't care one way or another. When he came into
the room, Li would sit on the edge of the bed, staring out the
window, completely occupied with his own thoughts, and then
would quietly lie down, clothes and all, just like that, and gather
the net around him. The next moment, when Jing stole a look at
him, Li had fallen into a blissful sleep.

The workers' dormitory where Jing and Li lived was one

of many three-storey buildings with one staircase leading up to each floor and a corridor in the middle that separated the building into two parts, the Northern and the Southern, each a row of identical rooms, each room the size of two table-tennis tables. Three or four workers shared one room and those who had married with children might be lucky if they got one room all to themselves as a family. It was therefore a mixed community, single males and females sharing their narrow, separate spaces with the families. A newcomer, Jing did not know anyone there except some faces that he would often see on his way downstairs and upstairs. In time he grew familiar with those faces. He would first exchange a nod or a smile, then greet them with a 'Have you eaten?' After what seemed a long time in which these formalities persisted, one of the faces with one eye larger than the other broke into a welcoming smile and said, 'I heard that you were going to sit for the university examination. Is that right?'

In his daily dealings with people, Jing preferred to keep to himself by using his eyes to observe, his ears to listen but rarely his mouth to talk. He was like some proud animal pent up in a cage of self-consciousness that he gathered around him like a cloak, patiently waiting for people to make advances. Until he was convinced he was noticed, wanted, even liked, he wouldn't take the first step in developing an acquaintanceship, to say nothing of friendship, and he would just go about his own business in his own unaffected aloofness, taking his time, happy with this solitary confinement of his own making.

'Yes, but how did you know?' Jing asked, rather pleased with this discovery of his elevated, albeit solitary, endeavor.

'Well, what is there that I do not know?' Xin replied, whose small eye became larger while the larger one became at once smaller, in matching intensity. He said in a mocking voice, 'Ask him if this is not the case.'

For the first time, Jing noticed someone else standing by his side, someone shorter even than Jing himself, with curly hair and a pair of glasses. He remembered that he had met him on numerous occasions, always carrying a book or two under his arm, but had never spoken or wanted to speak to him. The other man did not take the initiative that Jing thought was necessary to make his acquaintance.

'He's Hua, Hua for flower, not China,' Xin said, leering at his friend who nodded with a smile that Jing perceived as embarrassment because Hua lived in a room just across the corridor from his own but never greeted him.

'Would you like to have a read of this?' As he said this, Hua pulled out a magazine from under his arm and thrust it into Jing's hand.

'No, he is too good for that,' Xin said deliberately, knowing it would provoke Jing to say something in his defence. But before Jing could say anything, Xin had already burst into a roguish laughter, unable to contain himself any longer. Jing ended up saying nothing but just shrugging his shoulders, with a helpless smile. In that instant, his mother's mocking words said a long time ago came ringing in his ears, 'Stop shrugging your shoulders like a foreigner!' As she said this, she would pull an ugly face, imitating a Western man, and shrug her shoulders, like she was itching somewhere on her back where she could not reach with her hand beneath the thick cotton padded clothes she wore in winter. A grotesque noise in her throat tapered as it went out of her nostrils.

*

Jing would scarcely pay any attention to what was being said in the morning sessions on safety-related issues or daily assignments as he knew it wouldn't have much to do with him, everyone having their own trucks on their own assignments. Resigned to his standby position, he was happy to take up the opportunity to renew his memory of what he had learnt the previous day, a number of new words he had written down on a piece of paper carefully folded in half. On one side was English and, on the other, Chinese. He glanced at each English word and tried to remember what it meant in Chinese. If his memory failed him for one particular word, he would turn the paper over and take a quick look at its Chinese equivalent. He now got to where 'egg on' was but was not sure what it meant. He knew what egg stood for but what was egg on? In forgetting to put a 'vt' behind the expression to indicate that it was a verb, he could hardly make any sense of it. He was about to turn the paper over when he heard his own name called.

'Jing,' Ba said, holding up his hand with a red form. 'You've got work.'

It was a job assignment form that he was holding. The assignment would involve Jing hauling a truckload of human excrement to a village in an adjacent county. As the session ended and everyone went to their own vehicles, someone patted Jing on his back, saying, 'That is a good job. Believe me!' Jing looked up to see Tann, the tall, round-faced Party member. Jing knew him to be someone who would always try to get the best deal out of each assignment; he would get jobs to travel long distances that took him as far as Shanghai but would always manage to find excuses for not going on short ones such as the trips to the quarry or the counties. Jing soon found out why. It was because he had got one of the best trucks in the team, a brand-new Japanese truck by Feng Tian or Toyota. Jing squeezed a smile at him and turned to Ba.

'Whose truck do I drive?' Jing asked.

'Mine,' Ba said.

It was the Unique again. Jing never liked it but he never openly protested either. In this team, there was a class structure. Some people drove better trucks and got better deals than others. Why this shit business? Why me?

As if reading his mind, Ba said, 'Look, Jing. We've all come from the same shit background and got to where we are. It's a job that you've got to do if you want to stay here. You see, even I do not have a truck of my own.'

'But isn't Unique yours?' Jing asked.

'It's not mine, Jing,' Ba confessed. 'I drive it only because no one wants it. It's a motherless child but it's a lovely baby. The noise is not bad when you get used to it and it's spacious inside. Plus it's powerful and uses cheap diesel oil.'

A motherless child! That was like me in this team, Jing thought. Feeling miserable for himself, Jing could not have known that Ba, of all the people in the team, was the one who consistently declined the offer of new vehicles when they became available on the excuse that his teammates would have a more urgent need than him. This erstwhile *huaqiao*, Overseas Chinese, did this out of his gratitude towards the motherland for having granted him a new home after Malaysia and he didn't mind doing shit jobs that no one else wanted to do. After what had happened in the 1969 race riot in Kuala Lumpur, with his parents murdered and their shop looted, anything in China was bearable by comparison. So, when he used the analogy, there was an underpinning story of his personal history that Jing could not possibly know. Reluctant as he was, Jing took the job, had Xin and Hua, his porter mates, seal his truck with a sheet of tarpaulin, drove the monster to an Excrement Management Station and waited until his truck was filled with a pond of rippling black putty that simply stank.

When the truck was put back in motion, it felt better as it

left the smell trailing behind. Amid the monotonous drone of the engine, Jing found his way out of the city as he picked up two new words related to what he was carrying in his truck: excrement and faeces. He was passing through Hanyang, one of the most beautiful areas in Wuhan, a combination city of three towns, with its densely wooded Turtle Mountain, its Ink Lake of murky waters, its Guiyuan Temple of 500 *luohan,* arhats. While paying more attention to the English words than the local scenery, he was constantly aware of the faeces he was carrying, wondering why the peasants needed this.

By noontime he had reached Grassblades Village at the foot of Fenghuang Hill. It wasn't a bad journey as the wind kept the flies away. Once he stopped his Unique by the side of the village manure pit, the excrement, a word he now had firmly learnt by heart, was fermenting fiercely under the sun, attracting a host of local flies and insects with a lively buzzing noise. Fan, head of the village, welcomed Jing with great enthusiasm, thanking him profusely for having done a great job and inviting him to his house, with a table laden with food. As Jing followed Fan, he saw, out the corner of his eye, that village kids were already clustering around his truck, admiring its enormous size and climbing into his cabinet. One kid had actually got hold of Jing's piece of paper bearing the English words.

'Put it back,' Jing shouted at the kid, smiling.

'What's this?' The kid said, pointing a dirty finger at the English word 'shit'.

'It's "shit",' Jing said.

'"shi"?' '"shi"?' The boy said, trying to get his tongue round this difficult sound, managing to come out with something that sounded surprisingly like 'yes', 'yes' in Chinese.

Jing laughed, grabbing hold of the paper, rolling it into a ball and thrusting it into his trouser pocket. The kid, mystified, laughed, too, his hands hanging onto the side rear mirror, his feet sliding on the mudguard.

'Go home, kids,' Fan yelled in his bare feet stained with mud, his trouser legs rolled up above his knees, as he threatened to put their heads in the shit and make them eat it.

The kids dispersed like birds.

In the spacious hall of Fan's house, Jing was served a big bowl of rice, about the size of a small washing basin, a large plate each of stir-fried shredded pork and stir-fried eggs, together with a vegetable soup. Everyone had gone to the fields. Fan disappeared, too, leaving Jing to tackle the food alone with a crowd of chickens pecking what was dropped off the table, only to reappear shortly afterwards, with a large bamboo basket filled to its brim with eggs. As he carefully placed the basket by Jing's foot, Fan said, 'Just a small gift, not worth a mention.'

'No,' Jing was embarrassed. 'I have done nothing to deserve this.'

'Master Jing,' Fan said. 'You don't know how important this truck of manure is to us. Our fish in our dozen farming ponds need it. The market gardens around this place need manure, too. City people may not know but what they excrete we consume and, in turn, they consume what we grow out of what they have excreted.'

In that instant, Jing was reminded of two lines that he had learnt as a primary school kid, 'Without the stinking faeces, there is no fragrance of five cereals.'

'This is a cycle thing, you know,' Fan said, his hand closing upon Jing's hand, pressing it to hold the basket. 'We have more than enough eggs to eat here but I'm sorry I can't give you better things to take back.'

The cycle, Jing thought on his way home, his Unique having already been unloaded and washed clean by the villagers Fan had called for help while Jing was at lunch. What a wonderful idea not to waste anything in this endless chain of healthy transferences and transcendences between the city and the villages! And this loaded basket of eggs! How could he ever finish them? Already, he was thinking of giving some of them to Xin and Hua.

*

At night, alone in his bed, Jing wrote in his diary:

The earth. The excrement. The night soil. Why are these things all interconnected as if one is part of the other? Why is the Chinese word for shit a pictograph of a body with rice in it? Fan, in another sound and written differently, is cooked rice. He is down to earth but can we say up to sky? Am I someone up to sky as compared with Fan being down to earth? We certainly describe an arrogant person as someone with his tail pointed to the sky. Do they also say that in English? My pocket dictionary tells me nothing. And I have no one to speak English to.

3
—

Summer in White Sand was exceedingly hot. The temperature could reach 40°C or higher and last for days.

During the day, despite the relentless sun that beat down everywhere, on the brown waters of the Yangtze that flowed endlessly towards the bridge miles downstream and beyond, on the enormous tent-like shipyard that invited winds from all directions, on the thick cluster of short willow trees standing on the riverside of the embankment and on the bare top of the three-storey workers' dormitory, it was bearable with a constant wind that instantly dried the sweat on one's back when it hit from nowhere. By night, it got worse as a mass of accumulated heat hung oppressively over and above the Jianghan Plain with no wind to disperse it, the wind having disappeared altogether, driving millions of people in an air-conditioner-less city out onto the streets or onto the open tops of their residential buildings, sleeping in their bamboo beds, on their bamboo mats or in their bamboo chairs or inside their own rooms under a perpetually turning fan. On such red-hot nights, Jing would take a straw mat out with Kuo, a fellow truck driver, to sleep on the flat rooftop of one of the ships moored on the waterfront of the shipyard.

Kuo was considered to be a lucky guy because with the help of his father, head of the Production Section, he got a job in the Truck Team straight after he finished middle school. No sooner had he got into the team than he was given a Fiat to drive whereas Jing, long after he got in, was assigned what he had least expected, the Little Joke, the one-tonner, assembled by Master Tong and Mr Zhu, that ran on diesel but surprisingly had four gears. When there was no replacement work available, Jing would be seen driving this toy truck to transport spare parts or temperature-reducing refreshments from one workshop to another. Because of its poor noise insulation, the noise from the engine was so loud that it almost sounded like a *goupo*, female dog, a common nickname for the thunderous hand-held tractors often seen travelling on the country roads.

Approaching twenty, Kuo had an ambition; he wanted to teach himself to be a trombone player. After dinner, he would regularly play his *laguan* for half an hour in his dormitory building parallel to Jing's. Jing would sit before his makeshift desk, trying to catch up with his day's self-study, memorising a hundred or so new English words, to the accompaniment of the tumultuous musical notes from Kuo. From time to time, he would look up to see Kuo standing in front of his window, holding the cross-stay with his right hand. As he pushed the slide in and out, the trombone bombarded the evening air with monosyllabic notes of a kind that Jing found hard to like, although he said nothing about it; he understood that his English was at a similar stage of development.

On this particular evening, the heat became so unbearable that Jing's loins were nearly drenched in sweat. He had to strip himself bare to his cotton shorts, fanning himself with an exercise book stained with his sweaty fingerprints. Kuo's trombone farted on a faulty note and suddenly went dead.

'Let's go to the dock, shall we?' When he heard Kuo's voice shouting from the opposite building Jing readily agreed. He pushed the list of new words aside and closed the door behind him, carrying a rolled straw mat under his arm.

As they climbed up to the top of the ship and spread their straw mats across the awning over the deck, they found, to their surprise, that there was not a trace of wind from the Yangtze right below them, extending far into the distance, surging among the dim star lights and reflections of the city lights from either bank.

For a while, they lay atop the ship without a word, breathless from the heat. Jing looked up at the sky with its myriads of stars and the moon at its last quarter, lying diagonally near the edge of the city on the other side of the river, his ears full of summer crickets singing. Kuo lay next to him, his eyes closed and his ears still ringing with the last dying notes of his trombone. Neither of them knew what was going on in the other's mind. The only movement was caused by the slow flow of water underneath the ship that gently rocked it, making a sucking hollow noise.

'Were you born in this city?' Jing enquired, after what seemed a long time.

'Yes,' came Kuo's short answer.

'Do you often go swimming in the Yangtze?'

'No. To tell you the truth, I can't even swim.'

'Why not?'

'Because I have a fear of water.'

'Have no fear. If you drop into the river, I'll jump in and save you.'

'That would be nice.'

'You mean dropping into the river?'

'Of course you know what I meant, you!' Kuo chuckled.

'You know this poem by Du Fu?'

'A poem?' drowsily, Kuo said. 'I never read poems.'

'About a river; I thought it might equally apply to the Yangtze.'

'...'

'Are you asleep?'

'I'm half listening.'

'These two lines always come to mind when I am on the

Yangtze.'

'And?'

'*Xing chui pingye kuo, yue yong dajiang liu.*'

'Sounds comfortable but meaning what?'

'The stars are hanging low over an expansive plain and the moon is surging out of a great flowing river.'

'But the moon is not surging out of the river here. It's so low over the roofline of the houses on the other side of the river. Did he, this poet, talk about the heat in his poetry?'

'No. Poetry is not supposed to be about ugly things; it's about beautiful things.'

'But I thought it would be nice if poets wrote about our situation, lying on top of a ship, half naked on a straw mat on a river that does not even have a breath of wind blowing across it.'

Jing did not make a response. One did not know what he was thinking. After that, neither spoke for a long time; indeed, not for the rest of the night, for they soon fell asleep under an enormously poetic sky with unrelenting heat.

*

Rain in the morning. Did over two hundred English words today. Keep forgetting them. Li slept all day. When he finally woke up, he said he had beautiful dreams. I asked like what. He said: beautiful places. But he couldn't tell me what they were like. Just beautiful places. I suggested we go out for a walk. He agreed. We walked along the White Sand embankment, across the railway crossing and came to the bridge over the creek that emptied itself into the Yangtze a few hundred metres away. Night had fallen. Not far off was an intersection where buses and trams were vying with each other for space, crowds of people weaving between them, as busy as ever. I asked where he originally came from.

He said Hanyang. I asked what he did there. He said working in a factory. I said why you didn't go home on Sundays. He said there was no home to go back to. I asked why. He said both his parents were dead. I was struck speechless. For the first time I noticed he looked sallow, a sign of possible malnutrition, and he was wearing a pair of cloth shoes with both his big toes peeping out. He never asked me any questions. He just answered mine. He said he didn't like the previous place working as a welder. He changed to a job in a warehouse but soon grew bored with it, so he got transferred here working as a porter. I got the feeling that he might not stay long in this job, either, but I did not tell him how I felt. I wondered why I always seemed to bump into such people in my life, Li without parents and a home to go to, Pi in Yellow Town whose mother had divorced his father only a few years after his birth and Chiang whose father had divorced his mother and sent him to the army in Inner Mongolia at sixteen, monitoring the Russian planes. I wish I had a broken family like theirs; mine was too normal, too complete, too happy. I wish I could write a story about him. I was a little ashamed of telling him about my learning English. He looked at me in disbelief, as if I was an alien, although, again, he did not ask me why. I have to ask myself why but I don't really know. I suppose I want to rise above this, this dirt, this dirt-carrying river, these sleepy people. I want to show that I have got the ability to do something extraordinary that no one else can even though no one in the team seems to take me seriously.

4

Writing this novel is the hardest thing of all. You thought it would be easy. You have outlined the characters and organised a storyline. You have been awarded a grant for your proposal, so you think you should seriously start the work. A man you met this morning told you the story of being assaulted by his son and of his intention to chase him out of the house. He told you of how much he had spent on his son's education by sending him to a private school, then a university, and by paying his airfare for him to tour Europe and America and parts of Southeast Asia including Hong Kong, Taiwan and China. You remember saying to him that it was not the way, that you yourself would never pay your son's airfare unless he was willing to work to earn it himself.

You don't want to repeat yourself. Still less do you want to repeat others. Which is why you have given up on the option of writing this novel as if it were a dictionary, a method adopted in Le Dictionnaire Khazar by Milorad Pavic and in Maqiao Cidian by Han Shaogong. You also avoid writing in the style of biji xiaoshuo or notes fiction. Years ago you were moved by a Russian novel called Yong Gan, courage or bravery, the narrative of which could provide a model for this novel. Seemingly unrelated characters come from everywhere in the Soviet Union and eventually meet in a Youth League city somewhere in Siberia, similar to this story where a class of thirty-odd people come from all parts of China for a common purpose: learning English for the great motherland. You could even go about the novel the way Gangca Luofu has done, a Russian novelist whose name you can't spell out in either Russian or English. In that novel it took the main protagonist a few hundred pages to even get out of *bed. Someone has done that and so you'll give it a miss.*

There is more than just avoiding the repetition. There is also the reconciliation of the reality with the imagination, memory versus memory loss. It would be facile to say what one cannot remember one can always substitute with imagination. One can't. Take the vehicle called Unique. You know exactly what it looked like, how it drove. Your problem, however, is to find what its real name was and where it originally came from. Conrad's attempt to write to make you feel it, to smell it, to present the whole thing as if you yourself were in it is no longer valid these days. To experience September 11, you didn't need any imagination; all you needed was to switch on the television and watch. Hours spent online in search of all kinds of trucks from Mack to Tanker to Oldies to Dumps yielded nothing. Email messages sent out to China and half the world yielded nothing except for a response from someone in an unidentified country about having never heard of such a truck and his problems with finding information about how to do truck business in contemporary China. You suppose imagination is a good excuse when you can't find the real thing. And you decide to proceed on that basis, partly.

To put it simply, you want to write about something that is part of your life as if it were fiction, as if it was not yours but someone else's, and to do that you randomly chose a name from A Dictionary of Chinese Names *by stopping at the page you opened it at. It showed you Jing, a rare name in today's terms that went back to the Han Dynasty with only two cases of such a name ever recorded in Chinese history and the dictionary. Thus, at one remove, you have done away with the real person and in his place created a character.*

5

Jing killed a buffalo on his way back to Wuchang. He had gone to Huangshi to pick up a truckload of cement. With him was Old Qian, the pockmark-faced man from Production Section, who supervised the entire journey as the task required. This time, it was a dark green Hubei that Jing was assigned to drive to relieve its official driver, Yang Zhu, who had gone on sick leave. Not related to Old Zhu, Young Zhu had a kid with disabilities who needed home care. A short man in his mid-thirties with a flat face of dark complexion, Young Zhu had become resigned to his fate. He would often say, 'I know I'd be a professor now if I had not wasted many years in the countryside but all I am hoping for is to bring this kid up and give him a good education.'

A locally made truck modelled on the omnipresent Jiefang, Hubei ran on petrol, had four gears, carried four tonnes and was regarded as one of the vehicles in the lower order. Jing didn't give a thought to it; he would drive anything, from the fast-running Fiat to the heavy-going Unique, and from Jiefang to the smallest self-assembled nameless car that no one would drive which, running on diesel, would leave a trace of black smoke behind it as it chugged away on the road, leaving people on the roadside covering their ears and their noses. What Jing did not know, though, was the air-operated brake pads fitted on this vehicle had nearly worn out; for some reason, Young Zhu did not tell anyone about it.

It had been a smooth enough journey until mid-afternoon when Jing came to a slope near Knife Spring, an area famous for its cluster of universities. The road here tilted downwards, flanked by tall trees of dense foliage with shadows that made this section of road darker than elsewhere. Jing was driving, his eyes surveying the road before him, his heart giving a leap at the thought that he would soon arrive at the factory, have the cement unloaded and pack up for Yellow Town for a holiday. As the truck filled with a pile of heavy twenty-five-kilo bags of cement hurtled itself down the road, Jing and Old Qian had been exchanging the latest information about what was going on in the team, their talk mainly about accidents, about what had happened to whom. For example, Lu, a fellow driver, recently went on a long-distance trip to Henan when he saw a peasant crossing the road. He immediately braked but did it so suddenly and so hard that his truck swung 180 degrees, pointing its head in the direction where he had come from. Totally unaware of the change, he kept driving on for fifty kilometres or so, before he realised that something had gone terribly wrong as the landscape along the road looked familiar. Feng, another fellow driver known for his super-fast speed, did a return journey in his Jiefang in less than two days to and from Shanghai, covering nearly 2000 kilometres, causing Ba to scold him for risking his life.

As they talked and laughed, Jing noticed something from the corner of his left eye. It looked like a shadow drifting across the road right in front of him. His foot instinctively went to the brake pedal. No response. He braked again, this time putting all his weight on his right foot, pushing the pedal all the way down until he stood up from his seat – all he experienced was the mere sensation of stepping into a heap of cotton. The truck gave no sign of stopping, but rushed ahead without hindrance, under the enormous inertia created by all of its four tonnes of cement, making the truck go faster than ever.

Jing felt as if something had hit him on his right hip. Or, to be more exact, he felt that his right rear wheel had hit something. It was almost like the truck had just rolled over a tiny mound, hitting against a rock or a pothole in the road.

'Stop! Stop! *Tingche*!' Old Qian was yelling, the pockmarks on his face standing out palpably.

Jing turned his head back and saw, through the square window at the back of his cabin, that there was something lying in the middle of the road, a few hundred metres behind him.

'Looks like an animal,' he said.

'*Tingche*!' Old Qian said as he frantically waved his hand towards the right side of the road.

Jing's heart beat so fast that he could hardly hear his own voice, 'Can we simply run away?', as he pulled his truck to a squeaking stop at the right side of the road where the animal was killed. There, he sat still, his heart pounding like a rabbit hidden under his shirt. He threw a look in the rear-view mirror: the road was eerily quiet with no traffic, no one in sight except a lone bicycle coasting down the road. He waited, expecting to see a policeman on a motorcycle charging towards him until he could no longer handle it. He made the decision to go then and there as he said to Old Qian, 'I must go now as no one has seen this. Otherwise, it'll be too late if someone comes.'

For a few seconds, Old Qian did not say anything as he did not know what sort of consequences they were going to face. But, as the truck was put back in motion again, Old Qian, looking at the grim sweaty profile of Jing and realising that it was probably no use trying to stop this reckless young man from moving on, urged him to go quickly, saying, 'Run for your life, Jing, run before anyone sees you and catches you!'

*

The next day Jing was back in Yellow Town, glad that he hadn't been caught. The cow that he had run over, for he was convinced it was a young cow without knowing that it was actually a buffalo, seemed to swim before his eyes whenever he closed them. He had never killed anything in his life. The worst thing he had done in his youth was breaking a young tree. He was honest enough to confess his 'crime' to the principal of the school in which his mother worked, hoping he would be forgiven. On the contrary, the principal saw an opportunity for education and elevated it to the level of class struggle. Apart from imposing a fine of 50 yuan on Jing's mother, which was a hefty amount in those days, Huang, the principal, initiated a political campaign aimed at cleansing the school of any inimical elements bent on the destruction of socialism. He got every student to discuss how to protect the growth of socialist young trees and write down their critical comments. Jing survived that campaign only because he wrote a clever exposé of his own wrongdoing in a lucid and highly archaic style reminiscent of ancient literary masters. To this day, he could still remember what his mother had said to him that night after she was fined. Instead of getting angry with him as she would often do, she said calmly, unusual for her temperament, 'Son, if you ever remember anything, take this from me: you can't trust anyone here. Honesty is not the best policy. Often it is the worst. You know what Field Marshal Lin Biao once said? He said, "You can't achieve anything great without telling lies".'

'But that's nonsense,' Jing retorted. 'You've been telling me to be honest since I was a child. Now you are telling me to tell lies.'

'Jing,' Mother raised her voice. 'You know how much I'm paying for your stupidity? More than a month's salary! Grow up! Don't be silly.'

A smile stole to Jing's lips as he remembered this episode. What happened yesterday seemed bad enough. He had not only killed a live animal but had managed to escape, assuming that no one had witnessed the accident. If no one found out about it, would his soul remain undisturbed by the spirit of the animal? What about the people who lost the animal when they most needed it? On the night of his departure for home, he was so troubled by these thoughts that he was compelled to seek solace from someone. He told Xin over dinner as the latter offered him a piece of homemade dry salted fish, just steamed.

'Don't tell anyone,' he said after he related the story.

'But you have to,' Xin said, his smaller eye now widened to nearly the size of his larger eye. 'What if someone did see you and made a report to the police and then the police tracked you down?'

'I'm sure no one saw it, only Old Qian who was with me at that moment,' Jing said. 'Unless Qian betrayed me.'

'Well, 'betray' is probably not the right word to use. I mean even if he informs against you, he has a right to because he is supposed to have supervised you during your trip to deliver the cement. He is obliged to tell exactly what happened to the factory or else the onus is on him. You see what I mean? On the other hand, he is not even your friend in the first place. How can you start talking about him betraying you? Remember what I said to you about friendship? Even if you two are friends, there's nothing stopping him from giving you away.'

'Your closest friend is often your worst enemy,' the remark came to Jing with an added poignancy as he remembered meeting Xin on the embankment one day on his way to his dormitory after returning from his uncle's house in Glass Street. There was apparently no reason for making such a remark, but Xin made it as if he had guessed Jing's dissatisfaction with himself for not having many friends. It was this throwaway remark that made Jing feel close to Xin at the same time as it bewildered him. Xin declined to substantiate his theory with any personal stories, although he promised to tell Jing some later on.

'The thing is,' Xin continued. 'If you go away like that tomorrow without letting anyone know but they somehow find out about it, which is not unlikely, you'll be in deep shit. Ba would be upset and he is not likely to do anything to bail you out. However, if you prepare him for it in advance, he'll most likely have sympathy for you and throw in a kind word or two for you when they come and pursue you. Leaders are leaders, you know. If you take them seriously, they'll take you seriously and look after you in trouble. Believe me for I know. I've been working in this factory long enough to know how to handle such things.'

So, it was with some trepidation that Jing went to Ba, still not quite sure whether to tell him everything or not. His heart wanted him to tell the truth, his mind wanted him to conceal it, but his tongue said something entirely different that surprised even himself when he arrived. He told Ba that there had been a phone call from someone in his hometown informing him that his mother had fallen ill and he had to hurry back the next day. He was ashamed by his ability to tell this lie and conceal his fear at the same time. Sitting outside his two-room apartment on the ground floor in the twilight, with a fan in his right hand to expel the mosquitoes and create wind, Ba listened and spat on the ground, his brow knit up in a knot.

'How many days do you need to go away for?'

'Maybe just a few days?' Jing suggested.

'You know we are very busy at the moment,' Ba said.

'I know but the Hubei I'm driving isn't working properly,' Jing said. 'I mean the brake doesn't seem to work from time to time.'

'What happened?'

Jing avoided meeting Ba's eyes under his knitting brow and said, 'It's just that …' He paused and resumed, after swallowing a chunk of phlegm. '… when I stepped on it, it seemed to be rushing forward without stopping, sometimes.'

'I keep telling you guys to be careful with these old vehicles,' Ba said, blindly hitting his noisy cat-tail leaf fan at the mosquitoes, imaginary or real, on his hairy legs, which poked out like two thin sticks from the wooden stool he sat on. 'Always be prepared to slow down and stop. You can't trust these dog fuckers.'

By dog fuckers, Jing knew he had meant the crappy trucks used by his team, but Ba's wife, a short fat woman of large round bulging eyes in a flowery blouse heard this as she was just about to finish sweeping the floor near the doorway.

'Stop talking dirty, will you?' She stood there, panting, leaning on her broom as she squeezed her face into a quick smile at Jing. The smile instantly disappeared as her face turned to Ba.

'All right,' Jing rose to go, declining Ba's offer of a drink of iced green bean soup to relieve the discomfort created by the heat.

6

It is a slow process, this novel-writing business. You write chunks of stuff, discard most of it, and write more. You leave spaces to go back to, which will be lost to the reader, as by the time this novel is delivered to them in the bookshop all they will see is pages that have been filled. For this reason, you leave a space for future insertions just to show how it all works or does not work. You realise that this has to go through an editing process and it is very likely that this may have to go, too. How original can you be when a piece of writing goes through so many hands? Writing about the late 1970s you find a lacuna. It is not just a lacuna that exists in the general print media and broadcasting media. It is also a lacuna in your memory and often the hole in your memory is partly attributable to the role of the media that was dominant in those days. For example, why can't you bring back some details of how Jing eats in the factory canteen each day? If you apply your imagination and if it works, will it be true? These things all happened to you once but you have not kept them living in your memory. Imagination without the reality is like clouds, constantly changing without a fixed shape. Don't you want to make novel a history of the extraordinarily ordinary little things that happen in life?

7
—

In Yellow Town, Jing was restless, although he tried hard to put all this behind him, determined to have some fun before he dealt with the big issue: the university entrance examination. When he arrived at the dark-red door of his home, a single office room, now used for accommodation, at the end of a narrow corridor on the second floor of a three-storey building, the door was closed. He knocked on it but there was no response from inside. He knocked on it again. Still no sound. He decided to climb in through the narrow open window over the door. Holding the lintel with both his hands and putting his feet out against the wall on either side, froglike, he inched himself up to reach the opening and crept in, head first. He dipped his head further until his upper body was on the other side of the door and looked as if he was going to fall when he swung his body around, facing outside. Still clinging to the frame of the opening, he put his feet down, one at a time, his whole person now entirely behind the locked door. With a thud, he landed, gathering all the dust from the lintel and from behind the door. He was astonished to see Nei, his brother, sleeping on the bamboo bed in the middle of the room and was even more astonished to see him get up while quickly putting something away. At one glance, he recognised that it was a pair of blue shorts. It suddenly dawned on him that Nei might not have been sleeping. Did he not hear him knocking on the door? Why did he not make any response? What were the shorts that he had in his hand? Why did he wrap his lower parts with a towel on such a hot day? Was he doing something shameful? Without thinking any further Jing came to the natural conclusion that Nei must have been masturbating. He knew this well himself as he would do it from time to time, usually monthly, sometimes weekly, although he was mindful enough of his own secret habit to have never been caught out like that. You should at least be a little more cautious, he said to his brother under his breath, but then, Jing thought to himself, how could he have known that I would come home like this?

Nei, a couple of years Jing's junior, looked nothing like his older brother. He was darker, taller, with big thin ears. His garlic nose resembled his father's and his slit eyes were shaped like his mother's, except a shade narrower. He made a grunting noise, unhappy about being woken up in the middle of his sweet siesta drenched in a wet dream in which he was dating the prettiest girl in his class.

'You should be waiting outside for me to open the door,' Nei said as he made his way out to the communal sink in the balcony at the end of the corridor to wash his shorts, quickly wrapped inside a towel.

'I thought no one was in,' Jing said. 'Where's Father?'

'Why didn't you ask where Mother is?' Nei's words came down the corridor.

Stung by the subtle message in his words, Jing was reminded of his lie that he was coming back to see his sick mother and felt a little ashamed of himself; it was probably on account of him being a filial son that Ba was moved to grant him leave.

'Right. Where is she then?' Jing sounded a little contrite but he was keen to see his father because he wanted to seek some advice on how to improve his English.

'You know where they are, don't you?' came Nei's answer with the noise of tap water running. 'You sound like a total stranger now.'

Jing pretended not to hear the latter part of what Nei said.

If neither of them was home, he knew his mother must be at school, teaching Chinese to her students, and his father must be sorting books in the university library. He frowned and said, to himself, 'Well'.

After he took a bath in the wooden basin, filled with hot water from two thermos bottles mixed with cold tap water, Jing went next door to seek out his childhood friend Pi to play *xiangqi,* Chinese chess, with him. If there was anything to be said about Pi, it was his musicality. He was a self-taught composer with no training in any instruments. The only thing he could play, and play fairly well, was a Chinese *erhu,* a one-stringed violin. Blind Ah Bing's 'Waters of Rivers' and 'Streams' and 'Singing in Sickness' were his favourites. His problem was that in this small town no one recognised his talent. His father would have to occupy a powerful government position to get him into the local cultural troupe. Unfortunately, Old Pi was a travelling salesperson who did not see that anything good could come out of his son becoming a one-stringed violin player, let alone a composer. If Pi was jealous of Jing because he had a most admirable job in a big city, he did not show it. Soon, Pi gained the upper hand by winning one chess game after another until Jing stood up and said, 'I'm a little tired after the trip.' Pi could see that it was not the games but the intense desire to win that had exhausted Jing. What Jing did not know was that in the last few months in which Pi was home *daiye,* a cosmetic term in lieu of unemployment, he had borrowed and read all the how to play chess books he could lay his hands on from the library where Jing's father worked. The victory, though, did not seem to bring much joy to Pi, either, as his forehead remained deeply furrowed and there was no smile on his face.

Avoiding Pi's eyes, Jing said, 'What's up?'

'I wanted to go and visit my mother,' Pi revealed. 'Would

you like to come with me?'

'Where is she now?' Jing knew that he had two mothers but was not sure which one he was talking about.

'You know my new mother has just died?'

'No,' Jing said. 'What happened?'

'Before her death I had a dream. Did I tell you that?' With deep lines surrounding the corners of his mouth, Pi's face looked more like a sculptured Greek image.

'No. What was the dream about?'

'I was walking down the road when an old man stopped me and gave me a piece of paper on which were written these three characters: *si ju shi*.'

'*si ju shi*? You mean four lines of poetry?'

'Yes but there was nothing written on the paper when I had a look at it after the old man left, only his words ringing in my ears, *si ju shi, si ju shi*, like an incantation. It took me a long time to work out what it was but it was too late.'

'What was it then?'

'It is a corpse.'

'So that's what it means?'

'That's what the homonym means, a body, a corpse.'

'Really strange,' Jing wondered about the significance of this, the connection of poetry and death in sound.

He looked outside the window across the black-tiled roofs of a cluster of houses to where the Yangtze bent itself eastwards below the Western Hill, dozens of kilometres away on the other side of the river, against a greyish sky.

'I'll go with you,' Jing said. 'Just tell me when.'

*

At dinner, Jing and Nei were seated side by side facing their parents from across the table, an erstwhile office desk of a deep purple. After hearing Jing's story regarding the cow, Jing senior kept silent but his mother said, 'You shouldn't have run away like that.'

'But I had no choice,' Jing said.

'Then, you should at least have been honest with your Team Leader instead of telling him that I was sick. I am not sick.'

'Who was it who said that honesty is often the worst policy?' Jing said.

'Stop picking on me, will you?' His mother, Zhang *laoshi* or Teacher Zhang, growled. 'It's all for your own good.'

'I know what's good for me and what's not,' Jing said.

'Enough,' Jing senior interjected. 'You may be lucky.'

'It's got nothing to do with lucky,' Zhang *laoshi* barked. 'He should never have used this lame excuse for I am not sick. He is an adult now.'

'So what?' Jing paused and said. 'Yes, I am an adult, which means I can do and say whatever I want.'

'But not without responsibility,' Mother replied.

'Dad,' Jing turned to his father. 'Can I go to your library and borrow some English books?'

This deliberate tactic to cut his mother off upset Zhang *laoshi* immensely. She stood up, pushing her bowl aside, and pulled out her packet of cigarettes.

'Can I say something, Jing?' Nei, who up to this moment had been quietly eating, went to his mother's defence. 'I don't think you should talk to Mother like that. Remember: she is a schoolteacher. Don't you find yourself a little selfish?'

Selfish? What are you talking about? As soon as Jing thought of this he blurted out the English word 'Ridiculous!', which elicited a raucous laughter from his mother. She said, in a smoke-filled voice, 'Oh, it's our Mister Jing now. And he can talk such beautiful Chinglish!'

'What do you mean Chinglish? This is English, not Chinglish!' Jing retorted.

'If you do not even know what Chinglish is, go and ask your father,' Zhang *laoshi* spat out a plume of smoke and laughed what sounded like an ugly laughter to Jing's ears.

'All right. Enough,' Jing senior said, finishing his green bean congee. 'I'll see if I can find some books for you.' In that instant, Zhang *laoshi* caught him winking hard at Jing in a placating manner. She turned away in disgust.

*

The last few days spent in Yellow Town are pleasant. Friends come. We spend the day swimming in the Yangtze. Chiang wonders why I choose to learn English. I tell him it could lead to a great future. He asks why. He always asks questions. I reply that I don't know but my father has said so. I then add that I also think it might be the way. Chiang says he'd like to consider learning English, too. The water on the edge of the densely wooded sandbar is swift, muddy and cold. Not far off, perhaps a kilometre or so away near the opposite bank, I can see a red signal boat. It has been there since I was a young child. At night it flashes, on and off. Soaking yourself in the water or lying belly up on top is nice. Stretching yourself on the sand, listening to the noise of the water flowing endlessly downstream, the sun beating down on your eyelids is the best time. Chiang tells me that he had another girlfriend. They make love all the time. But he doesn't give me any details on how they make love. Pi knew, even though he, like me, did not have a girlfriend. He called making love, 'throw the horn'. I can still remember how impressed I was by his story of how someone threw his horn inside a woman all night without pulling it out.

It is easier with friends than with parents. Mother is a pain. She treats me like one of her students, not a grown-up. Father is special. I don't know why. There is something remote in him, sometimes, something that is hard to fathom. If Mother is like a hot chili, Father is like, well, I don't know. He is like a book. You ask him anything, he knows it, but I don't think his English is that good. I'll catch up and beat him soon.

You are giving it another go. It may be your last attempt since the doctor has given you the final diagnosis: something so terminal that not even literature can save you. As you revise, putting in a 'the' here and taking out a 'the' there, you become keenly aware that your English is not adequate. To put it simply, your English is bad, bad for the purpose of transplanting a life lived in Chinese. On third thoughts, you remove a lot of 'well' as the Chinese did not speak that way. You also deleted an interpolation about your research on White Sand even though the material you found online speaks convincingly of the nonexistence of the place and the worsening situation involving violence and sex, symptoms of a more progressive and more progressively sick age; the 1970s you write about seem infinitely healthy by comparison.

You are now working on this draft in an Asian city, one with its official language being English, spoken like Chinese, with a 'la' to end nearly every sentence and written also like Chinese, e.g., with this phrase 'never-say-die spirit', which reminds you of its Chinese version, in English, 'never-say-lose spirit'. In this city, people speak bad English and make perfect sense. Yesterday, you heard Alan, your Chinese bus captain, inform his English passengers that he would wait for them at the other end of the Immigration to ensure that 'they don't lost'. The English couple, surprisingly, didn't even attempt to correct him. When you ventured across the border into another Englis-speaking country, you'll understand why I say 'Englis' if you bear with me a little, you noticed a more interesting English, with 'bas' for bus, 'restoran' for restaurant, 'tol' for toll and 'sop' for soup, everything perfectly understandable, losing an arm here and a leg there.

The bed in which you are doing the revision can sleep three people and is fitted with four pillows, now secure behind your back. You have five days to go in this country and have made up your mind that, instead of sightseeing, you might as well go draftseeing, seeing this draft through and trying your luck again.

10

A telephone call recalled Jing to White Sand, urging him back without delay. Duan, the old canteen cook, now the janitor, received the call with the only telephone for the whole compound in the janitor's room and passed the message to Jing without giving any more details.

'I don't know,' Duan said, his small peasant eyes sizing Jing up as if suspecting him of some wrongdoing. 'They just wanted you to go back.'

It was impossible to make a return phone call as the phone in Jing's parent's unit was only meant for receiving incoming calls. Jing did not have the factory number, either. He knew instinctively that they must have found out. Steeling his heart against unpleasant consequences, he grabbed his bag, stuffing in a copy of his father's *An English Grammar* by Bo Bing, went to the local bus station, bought an afternoon long-distance bus ticket and hurried back to White Sand.

As the bus pushed itself onto the deck of the ferry and parked, squeezed between other vehicles, small and large, Jing got off and stood against the railing, surveying the river. Born and bred on the Yangtze, Jing nevertheless did not feel that he belonged here. The river at the bend that cut through the two towns was narrow and had a restrictive quality, too. In his review of geographical texts in preparation for the examination, Jing was fascinated by the big rivers in the world, the Mississippi, the Nile, the Euphrates, the Ganges and many more. By comparison, the Yangtze looked like a dirty creek carrying old tired boats and inadequate ships. People in this bus, for example, wore dirty clothes, spoke only Chinese with strong local accents and knew or cared nothing about what was going on outside China. His father, on their way to his library the previous evening, had been encouraging when Jing told him his plan. 'English would be the way out,' Father said. 'It was almost like an "Esperanto".'

'World language?' Jing asked, as he glanced at someone selecting a long and thick sugar cane from a bunch of them at a street stand and getting the street peddler to peel it and slice it with a knife hollow in the middle.

'Yah, something everyone speaks, or almost,' Father said, eyeing a woman wearing a flowery blouse. Jing pretended he did not see it but he hated his father for his tendency to get distracted like that. A father should be man enough to withstand any temptations, even as small as the sight of a pretty woman walking down the street. And it was such a dirty street, strewn with pieces of chewed sugar cane, purple water caltrops with contents eaten, and pigs trotting about, pissing and shitting. Even though the English he had learnt at middle school was little more than slogans like 'Learn from Workers, Peasants and Soldiers' or 'Long live Chairman Mao', Jing found the language provided him with a way out, a 'virtual reality' if you like, although that term would have to wait a couple of decades to arrive on the Chinese horizon.

The endless flow of the yellow waters boring him, Jing went back to his window seat and took out the grammar book to familiarise himself with the concepts of the future perfect tense and practise it by making sentences with live examples surrounding him: 'By this time next year, I shall have successfully passed my examination and entered a university.' As sentences multiplied in his head, they turned into questions: 'What shall I have done in ten years' time? Or in twenty years?' 'What will have become of Mother and Father when I finish my university studies?' 'Will I have married an English person and started a new life?' Jing laughed at the absurdity of the last question. He would never fall in love with a foreign woman and he knew from books that such marriages were not possible, hardly ever successful. Even though he was sometimes nicknamed a *waiguo ren,* foreigner, because of his pale complexion, his relatively deep-set eyes and his naturally curly hair, he was firmly convinced of his unique Chineseness that it was only by coincidence that he looked foreign. After all, it was the Chinese people, not foreigners in disguise, who wanted to learn English. It never occurred to him, though, that learning a foreign language might change the composition of his thinking or the way he felt about things; it might even force change in his physical appearance as he found putting his tongue between his teeth to pronounce the definite article a most difficult act to perform. He tried so hard that he sometimes thought that he might bite off the tip of his tongue.

*

Without any preamble, Ba told Jing what he had already guessed and what he did not know: that he had killed a water buffalo and was now in trouble because someone on the road had taken down his number plate when the accident occurred and reported the matter to the Police and Public Road Administrative Bureau. 'The guy was indignant about the driver's irresponsible behaviour,' Ba said, in a neutral tone devoid of any emotion but there was sufficient enough evidence that he was unhappy with Jing for not previously informing him of the accident. 'When he tracked your number plate down to where you were working in our team, he phoned us and told us that the driver of the truck was a coward and had no regard for public interest and road safety and that you were an irresponsible person. When I tried to appease him, by assuring him that I would do our best to solve the problem, he threatened to pass the story on to the local media.'

'So, what are we going to do?' Jing asked, his face growing paler.

'You have to stop work for a few days because we have to try to resolve this matter first. This is what I am going to do. Tomorrow you will drive the jeep to the local police station in Knife Spring and we shall meet them for a negotiation. Have plenty of cigarettes ready.'

The meeting at the police station in Knife Spring was a quite pleasant one except, that is, for the amount of money asked for. The police officer, Master Zhang, handling the case turned out to be someone who lived in White Sand and had a vested interest, too. As soon as Jing and Ba arrived in their open-top old American military jeep, the officer saw an opportunity. He wanted to borrow it for a funeral as there had been a death in the family a few days ago. Instead of taking cigarettes from Jing, Master Zhang actually offered one each to him and Ba, something rare from a culprit's point of view. While Jing was impressed with the police officer's generosity, Ba, declining his offer, was quick to see through Zhang's trick and managed to suss out his intention.

'No problem, no problem. Just let me know when you need the jeep,' Ba said as he motioned Jing to come into the room.

Unaware of what had been going on inside the office, Jing went up to Master Zhang and offered him a cigarette. This time, the officer took it without an apologetic 'thanks' but directly asked him to tell him what had happened. He listened, with a tolerant smile on his face, as if he had heard the story many times before. He then pointed to someone Jing had not noticed sitting in the corner of the police station and said, 'Brigade

Leader Wang. You go and talk to him about the buffalo.'

With that, the police officer left the room.

With one glance, Ba could tell that this peasant was a hard customer to deal with. From the way Wang deliberately looked at the floor, without greeting back, refusing to take the cigarette Jing offered, Ba knew that there would be a hard bargain to drive. He had dealt with the likes of him before. They looked glum and unhappy only because they wanted to drive a hard bargain. Let's play patience, then, to see who can win over whom in the end.

Jing was less experienced. What he saw was a country bumpkin sitting with his head lowered as if afraid to meet their eyes, too shy to even take a cigarette, wearing a crumpled white cotton shirt that had yellowed from being washed in dirty pond water. He drew back his hand with the cigarette and put it between his own lips, squinting at the guy as he lit up. For some reason, Ba didn't seem to like Jing's presence. He suggested with a glance of his eye that he go and wait outside.

Glad to have this chance to practise his English, Jing went out and sat on the steps, taking out his pocket dictionary to cram his head with his 100 English words of the day. He was at 'I'. It seems strange that in English you always say 'I' do this or 'I' do that but in Chinese you could write a whole story without using a single 'I' as if the word 'I' did not exist. But of course if 'I' write the story, 'I' do not have to assert 'I's presence every time the 'I' appears. The other thing he found about 'I' is that it sounds exactly the same as the Chinese word for love, pronounced *'ai'* or 'eye'. Is there any significance about this similarity? Unable to find his own answer, Jing remembered that he had done some reading on the subjunctive mood in his grammar book but he was quite confused about the need to stick to a past tense for something imagined, like the 'If I were you I would' thing. Can't they just say, 'If I am you I will'? The funny thing is that, in Chinese, the subjunctive mood is called *xuni yuqi*, virtual mood, a fake mood, something like the Chinese word *jiaru* for 'if', containing the word 'fake' in *jia*.

He began wondering what it would be like to study English in a university, where that university could be, what sort of people he would meet and where this could eventually lead. He hadn't read any English literature in the original as there was nothing available. This literature, along with literatures of other Western countries, had been regarded as decadent and banned from the general readership for a long time during the Cultural Revolution. All he had read had been literature in Chinese translation from adjacent countries, Gorky and Gogol from Russia and Tagore from India, whose poetry he loved, as well as an Indian novel about a group of kids playing hockey games. But the novel had its first few pages including the cover torn off by some naughty schoolboys. As a result, Jing never knew what its title was. And there was also this Hungarian poet by the name of Pei Duo Fei, Shandor Petefi, whose one and only poem every Chinese school child learnt by heart. Jing started putting it into English: *Life is precious but love is more so. For the sake of freedom, both can be abandoned.* Should I use 'both' or 'either'? He wondered to himself.

*

Jing was woken from his daydream by Ba who stormed out of the office room and strode to the jeep as he muttered, '800 bucks! Impossible!'

'He wanted 800 bucks, did he?'

'That's what the country bumpkin demanded,' Ba said, red in the face. He motioned for Jing to start the car and back out of the compound. 'He rejected my offer of 150 bucks because he said it was a young water buffalo that would grow into a big strong one in a year or two and could do a lot of work for them. I said what if it got sick and died in its infancy. He said that they would kill it and sell its meat in the market. I said who wanted to eat a dead buffalo's meat? You eat bulls but not water buffalos because their meat is too tough. The peasant said it didn't matter and that as long as it was meat there would be people eating it. I said that they were also to blame because they should have tied their young buffalo properly to a tree instead of letting it run wild.'

'What did he say to that then?' Jing interrupted because he thought that Ba hit the nail on the head and the question would be a hard one to answer.

'Well, he said the buffalo broke free because it was a young one,' Ba said. 'There was not much help. I then put my cards on the table. I said we had sent people to check in his village and found that they had skinned the buffalo, sold its hide and distributed the meat equally among the villagers. For that reason alone, we can't pay him much.'

'That's brilliant!' Jing said, admiring Ba for his thoughtfulness.

'Hang on,' Ba said. 'Not so easy. This peasant guy actually burst into tears, saying that it was such a rare buffalo that could one day grow into a very useful agricultural tool. He got so far as to suggest he did not want any money but he just wanted a live animal back!'

'What shall we do then?' Jing grew concerned, thinking of the trouble he had caused and wondering what to do to fix it.

'We'll come back for more negotiation tomorrow,' Ba said, as he hoisted himself into the open green jeep left from the Civil War in the late 1940s and directed Jing to get on the road. 'I'll get Master Zhang to work on Wang, the bastard.'

Jing had never seen Ba so furiously abusive, though he did witness him lose his temper on more than one occasion. Still, he liked the *huaqiao* from Malaysia for his quaint Wuhan-accented Mandarin, his childlike display of tantrums at any shoddy work done by other mechanics or drivers and his punctilious adherence to punctuality and his clean code of dress, something that he would often boast to Jing that he had inherited from having lived in Penang for many years.

As Jing drove past the place where he had killed the buffalo he said something that surprised himself and Ba.

'Why don't we just say no and give them fifty bucks and leave it at that?'

'What?' Ba almost yelled, in his passenger's seat. 'You don't know what you are talking about!' Jing listened as he raged on. 'A water buffalo is a most treasured animal in a village. It does everything from plouging to turning around the stoneroller to being eaten. Did you ever see people killing a buffalo to get its meat? It is so submissive that it just lets people kill it but it has tears running down its face. Poor thing! No, no, you can't just walk away from it like that. You have to give them something. All we can do is be patient until we make a reasonable deal that both sides are happy with. Understand?'

'As if I did not know,' Jing said in a cold voice. 'I raised cows myself in the country.'

Ba tilted his chin slightly towards Jing on his left, looking as if he was made uncomfortable by this sudden retort but kept his mouth shut.

11

Pi did not know that I had heard things about his mother, things probably never made known to him. But my mother had told me the story. One day when I asked her why some people had such a tragic life. She asked, 'Who?' I replied, 'Pi' and she said, 'Well, it was perhaps not as tragic as you thought it was.' I said, 'What do you mean?' She responded, 'You don't have to know these things.' I kept wondering about them until my curiosity burst out of my mouth: 'But why did his father abandon his mother?' She enquired, 'Who told you so?' I said, 'Pi, because he said his father was not good.' 'Well,' she said, 'that was only because he did not know the real truth.' I asked, 'What was the real truth? Tell me. I won't say a word to Pi.' At first, Mother did not want to tell me but eventually she did. 'All right,' Mother sighed and said, 'But promise you'll never tell anyone this.' 'Promise,' I said. She then revealed, 'Pi's mother used to be a very beautiful woman when she was young and a lot of men fell for her and so she had many affairs. That's why his father had to divorce her; he didn't abandon her. She ended up living with a man on a farm.'

*

Pi came to see Jing. His hair more curly than ever, Pi looked like someone from overseas except for his clothes, which were not as neat and clean as they should have been. He stood outside the factory entrance, watching Jing steer his wheel with all his strength, the enormous head of the grey Unique pointed towards the factory in the driveway leading to the entrance, the noise from the engine deafening. Afterwards, he laughed at the way Jing drove this monster, wondering how much longer he'd have to stay with it.

'Probably not too long,' Jing said. 'When I pass my English exam I'll put all this behind me.'

As he said this he swept his hand in a big circle which, as Pi could see, included the factory premises with its open space in the front, featuring the block of offices on the right and the blackboard bulletins on the left, the keel of a ship under construction high in the dry dock on the waterside, the riverside trees to the left outside the wall of the factory, trailing like a long roll of green smoke alongside the gravel embankment that extended into the far distance, the workers' dormitories in a row behind the embankment and the busy streets of the city to the right beyond the murky Yangtze. Pi grew a little jealous and spat. When Jing looked at him, he looked away, saying, 'It is not a bad place at all,' while what he actually had on his mind was 'What the hell! So what if you did?'

'I know,' Jing agreed. 'But you could be a factory worker or truck driver for the rest of your life, you know? Driving this sort of thing tires me out. You see, the door gone.'

'Yes,' Pi said. 'I did notice it and was wondering to myself if this was the design of the model that made it so.'

'Come on,' Jing knew he was being tongue-in-cheek. 'You don't want to know what happened then?'

'Oh yes, tell me,' Pi said.

'I went to a worksite the other day to carry steel plates. Because it was hot, I left my door open while sitting in it and waiting for the guys to finish loading. Then, when I was ready to go I could not pull the door back because it got caught by a stack of steel plates. I thought I could pull it out if I moved forward but my truck refused to budge. So I put the gear in reverse and released the clutch. The truck vibrated violently, only for a brief second, before the door became unhinged, dislocated and came crashing down. Hence the gaping hole you now see. It's hilarious! Everyone laughed but I got a bad scolding from Ba, our Team Leader. I never saw him so angry in all my life.'

'What about him?'

'Well, he's actually a nice bloke. He's *huaqiao*, you know. In the main, people here are kinda okay. You remember me telling you about Pan the skinny mechanic? He really is a funny fellow. Every time someone goes to him to ask him to fix something he says, 'Come on! I haven't got time. If you've got *lengzi*, I'll definitely do it for you.' As Jing said that, he imitated Pan by making a gesture rubbing his right middle finger with his thumb, his eyes narrowed to one-tenth of their size. 'Nothing seems holy to him. He once told me that even if I eventually get into a university, it only means that I'll get a better job and make more money because that is what life is about: making money and more money and having fun with it.'

'I'd really like to meet this guy.'

'Oh, there are plenty of other interesting people here, too,' Jing said, forgetting the pain of being a stranger, in his eagerness to please his friend.

'Tell me about this storyteller you mentioned the other day, the one who comes in everyday to tell ancient stories to the other fellows in your team. 'Oh yes,' Jing said, his face darkening at the mention of the name. 'He's not that interesting, though. He just tells stories and they are so boring! Everyone else comes to the show and hears him go on and on about the ancient emperors and wars and stuff like that. I hide next door with Shaw. I call him Shaw, like Bernard Shaw, the English guy, with a big moustache, as a way of practising my English. He is a returned soldier from the army, now the team accountant. Shaw is from a country town, like you and me. People from country towns have no place in this big city factory. They are treated like country yokels. You'd know that if you came to work here. So we feel sort of close to each other.'

As he said this, Jing remembered the pale-faced new mechanic, Gu, who had become an instant star in the eyes of everyone in the team, mechanics and drivers alike, since day one, because he could deliver stories off the top of his head. No sooner had he arrived in the morning than he would be warmly greeted with 'Master Gu, come in! Sit here, sit here'. There would be a dozen hands snatching stools for him or grabbing a thermos bottle to fill his tea mug. Cigarettes would offer themselves to him as he randomly chose one for himself and stuck it in the corner of his mouth, complacently waiting for an eager hand to light it. Even Old Canton, who normally had no patience for any nonsense, would relent on such occasions, allowing people to invade his jealously guarded privacy in that public space, though leaving enough room for himself in the middle where he could sit cross-legged on his stool covered with the clean towel, his one knee constantly jerking the other, creating a comfortable vibratory feeling.

Gu took all this for granted. Occupying the centre stage, well, just slightly off-centre from Old Canton, he did not bother saying thank you, not even nodding his head in acknowledgement of the overzealous offerings from his workmates. In a street artist manner, he would begin every story of his in a perfect Wuhan dialect with *huashuo*, something similar, though not quite, to the English, 'I say'. As a result, Gu enjoyed the status of a hero whom everyone treated with utmost respect and admiration. If there was anyone who did not have to do a stick of work, it was Gu because all he had to work on was his tongue. He literally lived by the glibness of that wagging tongue, surrounded by avid listeners who would down their tools in order to hear stories roll off it so effortlessly.

Jing was the only one who refused to follow the herd. The very first time Gu opened his mouth, Jing turned away in disgust. He had read stuff infinitely better than this. He had read foreign stuff in translation. Gu was taking extracts from *All Men Were Brothers* and *An Account of the Three States,* but Jing didn't need to hear a twice-told tale he had read when he was a child. Instead, he joined Shaw in the side office and exchanged his stories with him.

The team noted Jing's thorny absence with disapproval. This at least told them three things about Jing, that he did not conform, that he was being a smart-arse and that he thought he was superior and exclusive because he wanted to go to university. Big Gun, nickname of a fellow driver known for his habit of making frank comments aimed indiscriminately at anyone or anything that happened to displease him, once blurted out at the end of a story about a scholar fallen victim to the tricks played by a prostitute that led to a robbery, saying, 'Believe me, the same thing will happen to that smart guy next door one day, who doesn't even come here to hear your wonderful stories.' Gu, the storyteller, responded by blowing out a long resentful puff of smoke, and said, 'Smart guy? You think people who go to universities are smart? *Goupi*! Dog fart nonsense. The *xiao bailian,* small white face, doesn't even know how to change a tyre properly and he's learning *ying ge la xi,* Englishit!'

Everyone guffawed.

'Shall we go together to see my mother?' Pi offered.

'Of course,' Jing said, waking up from his reverie.

It took them more than two hours by bus to get to a discoloured brick wall with chickens running around in the front yard. Here the sky seemed low and the colour of the place earthen. A wrinkled woman came towards them, whom Pi introduced to Jing as 'Mother'. Jing was disappointed to find her completely different from the image he had held of her in his head: the beautiful woman who had had endless love affairs and caused Pi's father to divorce her. Standing before him was this old hag with a wall-coloured face and an accent that sounded very much like a peasant. He felt ashamed but when he took a look at Pi he saw a face that had transformed, in such a short time, from one of discontent into that of a blessed serenity as if he had finally found his happiness here. But the place and the woman left Jing with such a strong distaste that he was struck speechless, squatting there and watching the chickens scratching the mud, pecking for things to eat.

'My mother is very nice,' Pi said.

'But your mother is not as beautiful as you described to me; you lied to me about her,' Jing thought to himself.

'Her husband is a tractor driver working in the fields,' Pi went on proudly.

'But your own father is a state cadre and she abandoned him,' Jing's thought continued.

'I wish my father had not abandoned her,' Pi said.

'Only because you did not know what she had done to him,' Jing thought.

Jing could see emotions sweep Pi as he kept smoking one cigarette after another, looking pensively at a toddler nearby picking up a straw, putting it in his mouth and beginning to chew it. He remembered something. Reaching his hand into his trouser pocket, he brought up a handful of lollipops wrapped in colourful paper and went over to the toddler. As he squatted, he carefully peeled a lollipop to reveal its amber olive-shaped content, the toddler opened its mouth unconsciously and waited for him to put the olive in. Pi said, 'Call me Uncle!' The boy let out a distorted imitation as Pi removed the straw from his mouth and replaced it with the candy.

'But shouldn't he call you brother if he is your mother's son?' Jing wondered aloud.

'Oh yes, you are right! I got it wrong,' Pi looked around, embarrassed. Seeing no one observing this, he laughed and said, 'It's so *jiba* fucking hard to remember these things as I don't have a lot of relatives in the village. In a village, I know, someone in his fifties may have to call a baby his granddad. That happens.'

12

Diary entry 6. Whooping Yu often says, 'If you have a beautiful wife in the home, it is the root cause of all trouble; if you have an ugly wife in the home, it is a priceless treasure.' Or should I say 'at home'? I'm not sure. I don't know why he always stresses this but probably it is his excuse for having a woman with nothing to recommend her. He has big bulging eyes with sagging bags underneath. He coughs all the time but string-smokes. Or must I say chain-smoke? There's no one to check for accuracy in this place.

Diary entry 7. This morning I went to Shaw's office in the wing, my hideout from the bunch of mechanics and Gu, the storyteller, and the first thing Shaw told me was the love affair that had happened between the head of the Planning Section and his pretty office secretary. The expression he used was funny. He said, 'His dick got so itchy he could not keep it under control.' Is that what Whooping Yu alluded to?

Diary entry 8. They asked why I wanted to learn English but I could not come up with an explanation. I suppose I am not much good for anything else. Because of the Cultural Revolution, I have lost what little I learnt in mathematics and physics when I was a *zhiqing,* educated youth in a village. Learning a new language would probably lead to something new. Already I feel that the language is like a young tree striking roots in my body, nourished and enriched, more unconsciously than consciously, by my blood. I've lost ten years because of all that. And if I win (or should I say succeed?) this time and if someone from the university comes to interview me I'll tell them what I've put down here tonight.

*

In the late 1970s, a workers' dormitory had rooms of identical size, each boxlike and bare of any furniture except beds. Each room accommodated three to four workers free of charge. Each room had a lock fitted onto its door, a square piece of iron with a round knob on it. If you turned the round knob clockwise on the inside, the tongue would slide out of the notch on the side of the door and the door was open. From the outside, all one needed was a key to enter. There were three keys to the door of the room where Jing lived. The other two keys belonged to Li and Yong. Normally, this presented no problem as Jing was there alone, studying or sleeping. However, when Jing's girlfriend, Chenfang, came, problems arose, of which the lock was the biggest one, as it did not have the mechanism reflected in that little metal cap that could be pushed upwards and downwards; so that people could not enter from outside even with a key. It was called the *xiaoshuan,* the small bolt. On several occasions, Li was heard turning the lock and, before Jing and Chenfang could tear themselves apart, Li's face had already appeared behind the door. Li never said a word nor did he even look their way, pretending that he did not see anything. But Jing had the feeling that he must have seen everything. How could he not have seen it all in a room that was slightly larger than four beds?

With downcast eyes, Li would go straight to his own bed by the window and lay down in it, pulling the quilt up to cover himself from head to toe, facing the wall, his back towards them. Soon, Jing would hear him snoring. He was never sure if he was pretending to be snoring. At such times, Jing would wish to have a room entirely to himself, at least a room with a lock that had a *xiaoshuan* in it against any unwanted and unexpected intrusions. Since Chenfang became his girlfriend, he had blindfolded all the windowpanes with local newspapers to give people no peeping-tom satisfaction from the other dormitory building. All this was done in order that he could make love to her without feeling that they were being watched or interrupted. Still, the fear within their hearts was too strong for their sexual desires. On most occasions, he managed to only get as far as her crotch and she didn't seem to mind him groping her there. She was a cook. To be more exact, she was learning to be a chef in a local cooking school. Jing had been stationed on loan as a chauffeur in Knife Spring when he met her.

He was there on an assigned task to work for Commissioner Song and she was there on a training course to exercise her muscles with an iron wok full of sand and gravel. When there was nothing much else to do, Jing would play chess with some of his colleagues working for the Education Commission from the universities around the city, or wash his grass green jeep or just watch the girls play with their woks with their left hands out in the open. For some reason, at one glance, he noticed Chenfang from a dozen of others in a row at the sand pit. And his glance was returned instantly.

As both the Education Commission and the Chef Training School were temporarily located in the same deserted military barracks, everyone seemed to know what everyone did without even asking. Chenfang knew Jing was a chauffeur as she had seen him behind the wheel a number of times. In those days, when few had the means of private transport, being a chauffeur was a great privilege as it meant having a transporting vehicle in one's control and the convenience of manoeuvre.

To Chenfang Jing had a big head that seemed to boast abundant intelligence, particularly with his large black eyes, which looked straight across the grassy lawn towards her from time to time. It was a lovely feeling to be noticed by the chauffeur of a brand-new jeep carrying important people. She took another look at herself in the mirror and the admiring gaze it returned was reassuring: she had good looks, her skin was fair and her eyes were black. She was not an attention seeker – clothing with exotic colours or appeal would be frowned upon as petty bourgeois and decadent – but she could still make herself attractive by wearing slightly tighter trousers that showed the contours of her buttocks. Blouses that were made of *dique liang* or terylene material were also presentable. Sometimes when she had cooking lessons she would become aware of someone standing behind her, smelling her nape and the aroma coming out of the cooking pot; she would turn around expecting to see the chauffeur smiling at her but would be disappointed to see her instructor standing behind them and supervising. In bed she would find herself stroking her own breasts for no other reason than it felt good to be doing so until she put herself to sleep.

For his part, Jing believed in the exchange of these casual glances with women all the time. Most of the women he met did not respond to his wayward signals, known as *yanfeng*. If someone did return the eye wind or amorous glances he blew across, his imagination would be fired up, assuming that the woman who did so might have somehow liked him. He knew he wasn't particularly handsome. There was not much about him that was attractive as a man except his unusually white skin. He was timid and would never dare to make advances to women he liked. In his imagination, though, he was promiscuous. He would bring any pretty women home to his bed and make love with them until he came. Wuhan was a city teeming with beautiful fiery-tempered women and the best place to catch glimpses of them was out on the streets, particularly in the commercial district of Hankou. On one occasion he did not know what he was doing but followed a woman all the way from the Jianghan Wharf to Sanyang Road. It was the strange bird's-nest shape of the woman's permed hair as well as her foreign-looking pants that hooked him. She was wearing greenish skintight trousers that distinctly outlined her bum and the groove between her legs and her leather shoes were of a new style that Cousin Cong was making in his shoe factory.

That night, at his uncle's house in Glass Street, Jing told Cong about what he had seen. Cong laughed. Cong was tall and handsome but was physically as soft as a woman. Jing and Cong would sleep together in one bed whenever Jing stayed at his uncle's place for the night. On such occasions, Cong would throw a leg across Jing's body from time to time and Jing could feel him go hard underneath and would understand. Cong would then get Jing to tell him dirty stories. Jing was a good dirty storyteller, although he had never made any physical contact with a woman. He would start with the girl next door and proceed to women on the streets. He would tell Cong how one of them with curly hair and a big bum fell in love with him instantly and wanted to go to bed with him and because of the shape of her hair, which looked like a widely opened vagina, he would take his penis out and shoot into its dark depths. As he kept expanding on the lurid details, Cong would get Jing to take his penis in hand and pull it out from under his shorts. On the first occasion when Jing did this, he was amazed by how tiny it was, as tiny and short as the cap of a ballpoint pen, compared with his own thing. In no time, as he stroked it hard, he could hear Cong groan and see the stuff coming out like rice gruel. Afterwards, when he cleaned it up, Cong would turn on his side and sleep away like a dead hog. Jing would never allow Cong to masturbate him, although Cong, for some reason, never offered to do so.

Cong was working in a factory making women's leather shoes. Jing would have swapped his position with Cong had he been given the chance. He thought making shoes for women was a great job but Cong dismissed it as something dreary and devoid of pleasure, not to be compared with the position of a driver who could go around the city and from city to city, well dined and wined, meeting different people and having affairs with all sorts of women. Cong never tired of hearing Jing's story about a truck driver who travelled in the mountainous region and would give free rides to peasant women on the condition that they make love with him in his cabin. After the truck driver finished the job, he directed the woman he had made love with to go to the rear of his truck and handed her a screwdriver, telling her to hold it against one of the rear lights and wait for further instructions. The woman waited, not knowing what was going on until the guy got in and started his truck. In the twinkling of an eye, the truck disappeared down the road, leaving the woman behind, holding the screwdriver, totally lost. Eventually, the guy was found out because he had claimed too many screwdrivers from the tools warehouse attached to his team.

After hearing what Jing had done when following the woman with the bird's-nest hair, Cong told him a similar story in which he sat at a dinner table opposite a beautiful – all his women were beautiful – woman and, without knowing it, he ejaculated, his eyes looking deeply into the woman's eyes, like a penetrating penis. It was a summer and, as his semen was slowly running out along the inside of his thigh, his face showed nothing. Jing found the story at once intriguing and unbelievable, although he did not bother disputing the truth with him. He could never imagine himself doing the same sort of thing, no matter how beautiful the woman was. In public all his instincts seemed to have withdrawn into the inner recess of his body and mind and, only in private, and alone with himself, would his flower of evil open, slowly and dangerously, without restraint.

*

There had recently been a national conference on education held at Knife Spring to which people from all over the country came. Jing was busy transporting them back and forth from the barracks to their hotel in Purple Lake, but his jeep was so small that it could only seat four including himself. After the sessions were finished for the day he had twenty-seven people to take back to the hotel. If he allowed five on a trip, he would have to make five return trips. He didn't like the idea. Not a stickler for rules, road ones or otherwise, Jing did some hard thinking. If he managed to squeeze eight into the jeep, he could reduce the total number of five trips to three, thus saving nearly two hours. He could then do some reading in his tiny side office or play chess with his boss. Anything was better than driving these people to and fro endlessly, and, for their part, university administrators, professors and lecturers did not like the idea of waiting in a deserted barracks in the evening either, the comfort of their hotel rooms or the prospect of a fun night in the centre of this new city beckoning.

When Jing casually threw the idea at them, they were thrilled. This young fellow was certainly inventive. Why don't we give him a go? When Jing deliberately suggested that if they didn't like the idea he would certainly not do it, they were even more goaded, vying with one another for a squeezed ride. It was thus agreed among them that, next to Jing at the steering wheel, there would be three seated, one on the gearbox in the middle and two doubled up in the passenger's seat. In the back seat, there would be five, doubled up on each other's laps, their heads propped up against the ceiling of the jeep so that if you looked at the vehicle from the outside, the yellow-coloured canvas looked uneven. Inside the jeep, it was so cramped that everyone was struggling for breath. Jing had to get them to slide the tiny square plastic windows open on the sides in the front and the back to allow some fresh air in. This way he managed to take them all back in three trips, taking extra care to drive the vehicle, groaning under the weight of nine living human bodies. Oblivious to the risk, they were all praising this ingenious young man for his brilliant invention and skill while having the time of their lives. One professor of English even started singing 'Red River Valley' but was immediately silenced by Jing as the distraction resulted in him almost rushing a red light. He skillfully brought the jeep to a standstill, braking quite hard, though not hard enough to cause bruises, black eyes or broken heads; the sudden brake was certainly conducive to the loosening of the big squeeze, only for a moment before their bodies settled uncomfortably in their sweaty spaces again.

When he unloaded the last batch at Hotel Purple Lake and was about to get on his way back to the barracks, Jing saw an old man walking towards him and by his side was none other than Chenfang. His heart gave a leap. Professor Chenfang had met his daughter in the hotel for dinner and had talked with her about her progress at the training school. It was now time for her to get back to her dormitory in the barracks. As someone had just told them to quickly go to the entrance to see if the daring driver's car was still there, they hurried out for a look hoping to make use of this opportunity.

Jing said, 'No problem', assuring Professor Chenfang that

he would take his daughter back. The old, tall gentleman with a long thin face thanked him and said goodbye to his daughter, standing there, watching them leave.

'How are you?' Chenfang asked.

'Pretty good,' Jing said, looking straight ahead.

'I saw you drive the car.'

'I saw you in the training process.'

'Oh, did you? When was that?'

'Well, many times,' he teased.

'Which time? You must tell me.'

'One morning when you were running with them in the barracks.'

'No, that is not true. What was I wearing?'

'Well, you were wearing this red jumper or something but you looked quite nice.'

'You are lying, you are lying,' Chenfang said and pretended to be upset. 'I never wear anything red.'

'No, I'm just joking. I didn't see you running but I did see you, well, I won't say anything.'

'No, you must tell me what you saw me doing.'

'I saw you playing with this wok with other girls.'

'That's right. It was part of the training process. It was very heavy, weighing several kilos.'

'Is that right? What are you training for?'

'Chef.'

'That's interesting.'

'What about yourself? I saw you read a lot. You always hold a book in your hands.'

'Did you?'

'Yes. You didn't look to me like a driver. Rather, you look like a student. What are you studying?'

'I'm studying English.'

'English? Why English?'

'I don't really know but it is something that I like. And …'
Conscious of her intense gaze on him from his right side, Jing
tried not to meet her eyes but looked straight at the street in
front of him as he drove on and said, 'I guess it is the only thing
that I seem to do better than others.'

'How do you mean?'

'I lost my abilities with mathematics and physics and
chemistry and all that through years of labouring in the country,'
he paused to let that sink in, then continued. 'And English was
something I excelled in at middle school anyway. So I thought I
might just pick it up, give it a go and see what happens.'

'You may end somewhere overseas,' she said with foreboding.

'Who knows?' Jing said. 'It's like this road. If you keep
travelling on it, who knows where it might lead?' As he said this,
he thought: since you are here with me, we may travel together
one day. Who knows?

'You are a very interesting person,' Chenfang concluded.

'And you are, too,' Jing echoed.

13

As a member of the Truck Team, Jing was not much valued. In the eyes of the old mechanics and drivers, he was a nobody, a *waidiren*, just a young guy from a country town that few had ever heard of, with no *guanxi* to speak of and to rely on for better job opportunities. His aunt died of cancer shortly after he started with the team. Most of the times he was left lying idle, like a brand-new tyre. When the job of driving a jeep for a commissioner came up, Ba went around checking with everyone to see if they would like to take it but no one wanted it. Who would want to give up their current *feique*, 'fat lack' or lucrative post, for something that was like banishment from one's home and hearth? Even driving the old crappy military jeep for Master Zhang to help with the funeral of his family death was infinitely more interesting: plenty of wine to drink, plates of meat to eat, plus red packets to pocket. On that day, instead of giving the job to people who wanted it, such as Young Zhu, Ba gave Jing the assignment. Perhaps he liked the fellow for his tight-lipped determination and his deliberate aloofness from the rest of the crowd or perhaps Jing's 'away from home status' reminded him of his own lonely days as a youth in Malaysia. Whatever the reasons, he wanted to enliven Jing's days with some fun, knowing that the position would include things like small gifts and free lunches.

It certainly was fun from everyone's point of view except Jing's. From the minute he arrived at Master Zhang's doorstep, he was treated like a lord. Someone seated him on a rarely seen sofa, supposedly to give him comfort, but it was so badly made that its springs jabbed at Jing's bum whenever he moved. Hot tea was served, along with plates of lollipops, watermelon seeds, sunflower seeds, packets of cigarettes, fried peanuts, bottles of soda water and what not. Relatives and invited guests streamed in with gifts, mostly silk quilt covers of various designs and vivid colours. They were stacked conspicuously in the middle of the hall for everyone to gawk at and, then, when guests went past Master Zhang one by one, Jing saw each of them take a red packet out of his pocket and try to press it into Zhang's resistant hand. Someone near Jing told him that the red packets contained money, at least one hundred, but more often than not more than one hundred, to show their respect for the dead, in this case, Zhang's grandmother. In the local speak, this was not a sad event but actually a Bai Xishi, White Happy Event, as compared with Hong Xishi, Red Happy Event, for weddings. If one dies in their eighties, it is certainly an event to celebrate.

However, in Jing's eyes, everything seemed fake: the hand that thrust the money and the hand that took it, pretending it didn't want it; the oily mouths that kept chewing on the meat covering all varieties from pork to chicken to mutton to lamb to beef to bird; the honeyed words exchanged between faces that presented no traces of sadness; and the enormous coffin heavily covered with flowery silk quilt covers, left in the cold in a corner of the house. He could not eat anything. He wondered why no one was crying. He had an idea coming to him out of nowhere. He wanted to see how the dead looked like and if by any chance the dead was not dead, but just pretending to be asleep. So, he did something that he could not even explain himself. He went to the coffin and lifted the lid to have a peek inside. Accidentally, he tugged at one of the quilt covers. They quickly slid to the floor like a slope in a landslide. The atmosphere of the house suddenly changed: mouths stopped eating or chatting or laughing; eyes were all swivelled in his direction; Master Zhang's hand, holding another red packet of money, held up in the air as if frozen; and his grandmother in a wall photo, framed with a black drape, was beaming at this funny scene, seemingly admiring the young driver's audaciousness in attempting to wake her up.

A brief moment that seemed to last.

Then, in a stride that took him more than half the length of the room, Master Zhang rushed to where the coffin was and held out his hands in an attempt to prevent Jing from opening it. It was too late. Jing had already lifted the lid and seen what must have been dressed up as a decent corpse, accompanied with a strong smell of something herbal. Master Zhang's hands snatched the lid from Jing's and put it down with such a force that it banged against the coffin. It was not till then that he realised that in his hurry to safeguard the dead his red packet of money had dropped inside the coffin. This was most embarrassing. He had either to leave it or retrieve it. To retrieve it by reopening the lid would be regarded as most ungracious and unfilial but to leave it would mean the loss of a large sum of money. As he stood there with a face that kept changing colour from pale to red, not knowing what to do, Jing said, 'Let me do it for you' and, with that, Jing opened the lid again and reached inside with his right hand, which came out in a second, holding the red money.

When the lid was closed for the last time and the red packet returned to its owner, everyone sighed with relief, unsure whether to condemn or praise Jing. As they watched him slowly back his open-top jeep towards the main door for the pallbearers to ease the coffin in, their superstitious belief in the power of the driver returned. Perhaps he was only checking if there was anything the matter with the coffin before he allowed them to load it. The day ended without further ado when Jing returned in his old jeep carrying all of Master Zhang's family members, relatives and friends bar the coffin.

The next day, when Jing got back to the team, he did not know that people had been discussing the issue involving the loan of a driver to the Education Commission. 'Let's put it this way,' Young Zhu reminisced. 'Doing anything is better than driving a jeep for the Education Commission because it means that you are stuck with those bureaucrats. If they direct you to go west, you dare not go east. If they have a meeting that lasts all day, you'd have to rot away in your car waiting for them whether it's scorching hot or freezing cold.' Ah Fang, the pretty-faced woman driver, the only one in the team, could not agree with him more. For her, the old adage held an unshakable truth: *laba yixiang, huangjin wanliang*, when a truck honks, it brings in truckloads of gold. Indeed, the truck she drove was one of the best in the team, a seven-tenth new silver Toyota, and she drove it to great advantage. She never came back from her missions empty-handed. You would see her with a big smile on her face, and, depending on the seasons, her hands were alternately laden with baskets of oranges or apples or fish or local produce, all fresh and free, given gratis by her clients. On one occasion, Jing witnessed her demanding a large fat piece of pork from her client in return for the delivery of some goods. In time, Jing would associate her pretty features with nothing more than greed.

Naturally, Jing became the only choice for the job and he was happy to take the offer. He did not belong here in the first place. He had no vehicle of his own to drive and he found the mechanics hard to deal with. They formed a tightly knit clique of their own in which there was little space for Jing to move around. Half the time, he stood there watching them fixing things that he himself had little interest in or listening to them exchanging dirty jokes which, though not particularly repulsive to him, were not meant to include him. On days when there was nothing much to do Jing would hide himself in the tiny side office with Shaw the ex-serviceman, chatting with him or cutting interesting news items from unwanted newspapers. This offer was like a godsend that provided Jing with some diversion; more importantly, it gave him a chance to get away from a close community of people whose only concern seemed to be to get the best out of every deal they could lay their hands on.

With the commissioner, Jing found some respect, if not as an individual, at least as a skilled chauffeur who could say yes or no to people in need of the convenience of transport. Basically, Jing was supposed to be serving his new master Commissioner Song only, but he could use the jeep for his friends now and then. Working for the commissioner also gave him a glimpse into the high life that ordinary people had little access to. To curry favour, people who moved in high society circles would invite Commissioner Song to dinners or treat him with rare foreign films not available for viewing by the general public. On such occasions Jing would invariably be invited along. It was no exaggeration to say that Jing was Song's legs as Song could not go anywhere without him.

With great excitement Jing went with Commissioner Song one night to the Military Commander Yang's private cinema in the compound of the Provincial Military District, taking with him Chenfang. The cinema was the *smallest* Jing had ever seen, compared to the local cinema in Yellow Town. It could seat fifteen people at most and looked like a large bedroom, with thick red curtains fully drawn that did not allow a single ray of light in. Because Jing was Commissioner Song's private chauffeur, he was allowed to sit with Chenfang, next to the commissioner seated in the centre with a tea table laid out in front of him. On the table cups of tea were placed, served by the commander's female *fuwuyuan,* attendants. Jing was hugely impressed. Such awesome decadence he had heard of but had never experienced before. He could not exactly describe his mixed feelings of admiration, disgust, excitement and expectation.

The film had Jing riveted to the screen. Called *River of Blood,* it was the tragic tale of a people living in the jungle of South America. What impressed Jing most was not the bloody fistfights among timber workers on the plantation when they got drunk but the beautiful local woman dancer in the bordello, appearing half naked before dozens of devouring eyes and tucking banknotes underneath a rubber band around her beautiful thigh. That was the bit of the film that lingered in Jing's memory. For some reason, though, no one in the cinema uttered a single word. No laughter. No comments. Nothing except some people smoking, including Commissioner Song, his cigarette smoke ascending in long straight columns, occasionally obscuring the screen.

Back in Yellow Town, films in the local cinema would be shown to hundreds of people chatting in low voices, giggling or chuckling, commenting, with incessant smoking and cracking of melon seeds. Each session was one of great conviviality and camaraderie. But the atmosphere here was too exclusive. Jing found himself growing fearful. He dared not openly, not even secretly, discuss what he liked about the film with anyone, not with Commissioner Song, not with Chenfang. Everyone sat there so quietly, so gravely, that you couldn't even begin to know what was on their minds. Jing was sitting a safe distance from Chenfang, as he pretended they were only casual acquaintances. In the course of the film, he did not dare glance her way, embarrassed by what was shown in the film and at the same time proud of the fact that he had given her the opportunity to enjoy such rare and privileged sights to which no outsiders had access.

To Jing's amazement, Chenfang did not seem to appreciate his effort. When they came out of the commander's private cinema, she looked glum and remained reticent. To make things worse, one of the movable plastic windowpanes inserted in the tarpaulin cover of the jeep, parked outside the cinema, was gone, obviously stolen. In the command headquarters guarded by soldiers, Jing could hardly believe his eyes. This loss, coupled with Chenfang's unhappy face, clouded Jing's heart, joyful a few minutes ago, to the extent that he did not say anything for the rest of the evening. He and Chenfang parted in silence, without saying goodbye.

*

I slept with her tonight for the first time but it didn't feel good. Such a hurry and so unnecessary. It was soon over. Both of us were fearful that people might crash through the door and, like what happened in the story, point their torchlights towards us, ordering us to keep the scene from being tampered with. It was nothing romantic. She was tired and kissed me on the mouth, telling me to go as she was scared of getting pregnant, of being seen, of being heard. I liked her eyes but not her timidity. I told her I would come back again but she said she was not sure. I asked why? She said she did not know. I do not even know if I penetrated. It felt as if I only touched her leg before I came. When I went back to the top of the building, I found everyone asleep on the floor in the open and only my straw mat was vacant because I had disappeared in the interim. It had cooled down towards the second half of the night and many people had blankets wrapped around them. I could not go to sleep for a long time. Listening to someone snoring beside me, I thought of my future with Chenfang and what I had just done with her. I was content, in a way, as if finally I had accomplished something important in life.

14

Jing was upset one evening. He had to drive Commissioner Song to a lakeside resort to meet with an old friend. When they arrived at Cottage No 3, night had fallen. The single-storey Russian-style hotel, brightly lit up at the front, stood by the lake among a cluster of trees and rich flowers rarely seen in the barren city, giving one the impression of uncommon privilege. Knowing Jing was a sensitive young fellow, and, of course, his personal chauffeur, Commissioner Song was considerate enough to bring Jing along with him. Song wanted to show people he was a leader with a human heart and common touch who cared for his subordinates. On one occasion, because he had finished his meeting quite late, he did not telephone Jing to get him to come and pick him up. Instead, he walked the distance back to Knife Spring with the Deputy Commissioner Yun. The next morning, when Jing learnt that they had done so without ringing him for assistance, he was surprised and felt very uncomfortable. Was it because they assumed that he would be reluctant if they asked him? Or did they find him so difficult they would rather walk than sit in his car? He went to apologise to Commissioner Song but Jing sounded as if he was accusing him of not doing the right thing, 'Why didn't you just give me a call? It was true that I was in bed but that did not matter. If you had called, I would have gladly jumped out of bed and gone to meet you straight away.'

The commissioner, a tall man with a large mouth full of nicotine-stained teeth, chuckled and said, 'Don't worry, Master Jing, it was a nice walk, the night air was so fresh.'

Nevertheless, Jing felt very bad about himself. He wondered if this had happened because he had shown signs of recalcitrance to his superiors, or if Song had detected or heard about Jing's tendency to talk back to Mr Jian, their man in charge of logistics. Or perhaps it was their concern for his preoccupation with his English studies? Deep down, Jing knew he could be rebellious, but driving his superiors around had nothing to do with this. It was his duty to drive them where they pleased and he was paid a salary to do that. There was nothing wrong with being a tool used by people. He was treated well by the Education Commission. Everyone, old and young, called him Master Jing, although he was only in his early twenties. Knowing that he was single, Mr Jian, their logistics guy who was also responsible for making vehicle arrangements for Jing, had promised to find someone for him. One day he took Jing aside and whispered in his ear, 'I've found a girl for you.'

'Where?' Jing's heart gave a leap.

'Don't be so loud,' Jian cautioned him. 'She is working in a kindergarten, a quite nice person. I'll arrange for you to meet her if you like.'

'Let me think about it and I will let you know,' Jing said, thinking of Chenfang.

Meanwhile, there was another girl. Her name was Yang. She was an administrator on loan from a university, just as Jing was on loan from the shipyard; everyone working here was on loan, the Education Commission being a temporary set-up to administer and supervise the reintroduction of matriculation examinations after they had been cut short some seven or eight years ago. Yang had big black eyes but her features were a little coarse, the pores of her skin not quite smooth, and her brow seemed too dark and bushy for Jing's liking. Jian also mentioned her as a potential choice. Jing thought about it and quickly put it aside, for the moment. From the way Yang's eyes sparkled whenever she turned his way, Jing instinctively knew that if she did not love him she at least liked him. But he wanted to have a range of choices. He wanted to be able to live with the comfort of the thought that there were a number of girls there, waiting, just waiting for him. It never occurred to him how selfish this thought might be and how potentially destructive it might become. He was Jing who, like his mother once told him, was a young man who 'seemed to value yourself more than anyone else.'

One day Jing went out on an assignment with Yang and another administrative officer. As the conversation centred around a recent accident in which a bus was overturned with its passengers spilled out all over the place, some dead and most of them injured, the officer made a joke about the possibility of Jing losing control of his jeep and ending up somewhere down a gully. Jing suddenly braked, causing all in the car to throw themselves forward, nearly bruising their heads. He pulled the jeep right up to the roadside.

'Get out,' Jing said to the man who made the remark.

'Jing,' Yang pleaded. 'Please don't. He was only joking. And it's raining outside. Please don't.'

Outside, it began drizzling, the grey sky looking dreary. It would be a quite unpleasant half-hour walk to the Provincial Government from where they had stopped.

'I don't care,' Jing said. 'If he thinks it is unsafe to sit in my car, he might as well get out and walk. He can certainly take a taxi or bus if he likes.'

No one said anything. For a moment, the raindrops hitting the top of the jeep became loud until the cadre on loan from a university said, with resignation and reluctance, 'That's fine. I'll just catch a bus from here then.'

On their way back to the Education Commission, something

else happened. At the crossroads, a People's Liberation Army soldier had been hit by a truck and was lying unconscious just as Jing was driving past. Someone flagged Jing down to ask if he could take the man to the nearest hospital. Jing agreed immediately. The problem, however, was where to put the man. If he was to be left lying on the back seat, he would be in danger of slipping down onto the floor whenever Jing braked. Yang was the only person sitting in the back seat. As Jing and another cadre were contemplating what to do, Yang, without a word, picked up the PLA man in her arms, a very young fellow, barely in his twenties, with a pale face. Together, they sat in the back seat, Yang holding him tightly like a baby in a bundle for fear he might slip out of her arms and hurt himself. When they arrived at the hospital and the nurses from the emergency department took the man away on a trolley, Jing saw that Yang's trousers were stained with blood but she didn't say a word. After this incident, Jing's admiration for Yang grew but, conversely, Yang's admiration for Jing diminished, most likely on account of Jing's outburst over a superstitious taboo forbidding people to talk about accidents in relation to the driver himself.

On this particular night, when Song went to meet with his classmate from the old university days, Jing was very happy because he knew the person Song was to visit was the vice chancellor of a university. Potentially, this person might be of some help when the time came for Jing to choose a university after he passed his examination. 'In these things you never know,' as Jing's uncle would often say. 'One thing always leads to another.'

'When the fire comes,' Jing remembered him also often quoting, 'not even the door can stop it from coming in.'

Of course Jing understood what his uncle meant by fire. It was the fortune one was to meet with at least once in a lifetime, and possibly many times. That was how he felt when Song asked him to come along with him. He was proud that he was valued by the commissioner, who sometimes took time to play chess with him, although it was Song the commissioner, not Jing the chauffeur, who always lost the game. At such times, Jing noticed that the commissioner, instead of getting cross, would appear unconcerned and tolerant and generous, patting Jing on his back and saying, 'Well done!' Jing would say nothing, pretending that he didn't care but feeling triumphant within. He would never tell anyone, 'See, I beat the commissioner,' but he would arrogantly tell himself that he was not doing badly, forgetting that he was often beaten by Pi.

Thrusting his nose back into his book, Jing would continue reading his English grammar or an English textbook. In fact, during these chess games, Jing would often have enough time to read his book while waiting for Commissioner Song to make his next move. If the commissioner took four to five minutes to move a *bing* (soldier), or *ma* (horse), Jing would take less than one minute to counter attack with a *ju* (chariot), or *pao* (cannon), before his eyes returned to the pages dealing with the subjunctive mood or the gerund, still managing to win each time. If the commissioner was displeased, he never showed it. He would either say, 'Let's have another game' or 'I've got some work to do but let's come back to it tomorrow.' Jing would sometimes think of the commissioner as 'So slow!' but he kept those thoughts to himself. By playing chess with Song, he didn't have a purpose; he just wanted to win. And it was almost as if Song, seeing his intention, simply let him win. For the commissioner in his late forties and at the height of his power (he had lately been informed that he would be promoted to the head of the provincial Bureau of Education), the game was one of many ways to take his mind off the massive workload put upon him in preparation for his part of the first nationwide matriculation examination. Besides, this strong-willed young man bent on studying endeared himself to him. 'Judging by the way he goes about his work and studies,' Commissioner Song was often heard saying, 'Master Jing will go far.'

When Jing told his uncle about their chess games, Uncle said, 'Don't belittle such trivial things. Playing chess can be an important part of forging an enduring relationship. You don't normally get a chance to play chess with a commissioner. In the old days when I was in Yunnan, I would often play bridge with my company commander. Sometimes he won and sometimes I won but we became very good friends through those games.' Then Uncle would start telling Jing what a wonderful place Yunnan was with its multiethnic mountain people, their colourful lifestyles and a rich variety of mouth-watering foods. Jing would then fall into silence, having lost interest in things of a bygone era in a remote backward border province.

Jing soon found himself in the presence of the vice chancellor in a well-lit up but heavily curtained room. This short and burly man greeted Commissioner Song warmly, shaking hands with him, even hugging him, a gesture that Jing had only read about in foreign novels or seen in foreign films. However, when Jing was introduced to him, he raised his cold eyes at Jing as if insulted by his intrusion, taking the three fingers of the hand that Jing extended and shaking them, only once, before dropping them completely while continuing his talk with the commissioner. Jing's heart went cold as his temper flared up. He was asked to sit down but he did not sit down, standing there by himself, looking as if he was holding his ground or pretending to do so, but against what? Against his own stubbornness despite the painful knowledge that no one here gave a shit about him? He found his eyes avoiding everyone, not even his own clumsy figure in the full-sized mirror, which he caught a glance of anyway, but ranging instead from object to object, the bed covered in snow-white sheets, the extra pair of brand-new leather shoes, the creamy-coloured bedside telephone, the large red peonies on the curtain, until something came out of his mouth that surprised even himself.

'I'm going out to have a smoke,' he said, his eyes fixed on Song, who smiled apologetically and helplessly as if saying there was nothing much he could do about it, and stormed out.

It was a moment of revelation to Jing, one in which he realised that in the eyes of these people he really was a nonentity. Song treated him kindly only because he was his personal chauffeur and, while they joked, he did not want to die or get injured in Jing's hands by incurring his wrath. Jing had heard stories about angry chauffeurs who had driven their superiors and themselves to death. Before Jing got a transfer to the shipyard, he had a driver-mate known for his skillful recklessness. When he was learning his trade, Jing would be paired with Wang Ming out on their assignments. The road they travelled on was often narrow, about two-truck's width. When two trucks passed each other from opposite directions, they had to slow down considerably and pull to the side as much as safety allowed to avoid head-on collisions or hair-width scrapes. At night, it was even more dangerous to drive on such roads, particularly if the truck in the oncoming traffic did not switch its headlights from high to low beam. When that happened, Wang Ming had a way of dealing with them. He would steer his truck slightly to the left, stepping on the button next to the accelerator to put the headlights on high beam so that they shone like a bright broad sword, thrust right into the heart and the eyes of the 'enemy' truck. When it looked as if the two trucks would almost collide with each other, he would steer to the right, suddenly pulling himself out of harm's way. Jing observed Wang Ming doing this a few times successfully and quite admired him for it but he never thought for a moment that this might have put his own life or Wang Ming's in danger. With big trucks like Unique, Jing dared not try such a manoeuvre; they were like clumsy ships floating on the road, barely able to steer let alone attempt such dangerous driving.

With the new Beijing model he was now driving, tiny as a bird by comparison, Jing was prepared to adventure a bit. While a Hubei trembled like a leaf at sixty kilometres per hour, the Beijing had a smooth feel at fifty; indeed, it functioned better when it went faster. One night, when Jing took Song and Yun out to a function, he came to Yuemachang, where the street was at its widest and inclined a bit. As he drove, he saw an oncoming truck taking more than its share of the road with its headlights on high beam. In that instant, Wang Ming returned, prompting as he always did, 'Give the bastard hell! Go for it!' Without a second thought, Jing drove right up against the truck but steered out of the line of danger seconds before the two collided.

'What are you doing?' Song demanded sternly and glared sidewise at Jing.

There was no response from Yun; he had fallen asleep on the way.

'Nothing, I was just going to give that guy a fright. That's all,' Jing was going to say but he thought better and kept on driving, without a word.

The commissioner did not say anything nor did he question Jing again. The matter was left at that.

Now, standing by the lakeside, facing ripples of breeze blowing across the reflections of distant lights, mixed with occasional fallen stars, Jing was completely mortified. For the first time, the humbleness of his status was fully exposed. He was nothing but a chauffeur who had no more merit than the vehicle he drove. He might be privileged to have a car to drive around while millions were only able to commute by bus or bike, but he had less control over himself than someone rowing a boat on the lake. He had to be ordered about like a servant. But he was better than that, infinitely better. He knew this because his instinct told him that he would one day go beyond this little place surrounded by beautiful trees and pretty waters and he would get to a place these people had never heard of. He was not content with being called Master Jing, master of a vehicle; he wanted to be his own master. He wanted to get rid of this jeep and go away, into the distance, the future where he would be highly regarded with respect and admiration, not contempt and dismissiveness. He believed that he was someone capable of doing that and more. His kind of life at present was only temporary. Soon, he would take flight and go.

Jing smoked one cigarette after another, feeling dejected, totally defeated. And, yet, at the same time, he was strangely worked up, to such a degree that a thought suggested itself to him. At first he felt a little uneasy but he grew bolder. Spurred on by his shame and his disgust with the arrogant man, he decided then and there to drive the jeep back to the barracks without the commissioner. As he started his jeep, he gave the horn a pat as a warning for them. Waiting for a few more minutes without seeing any sign of movement inside the cottage, he gave another honk, put the jeep in first gear and released the clutch and the handbrake at the same time. The jeep roared in the quiet night, thunderous in his own ears, accompanied by his heart thumping, with guilt, shame and trepidation. Like a fugitive, he tried to escape from his own fears and shame mixed with an arrogant pride by speeding down the winding path in the exclusive lake garden that concealed the cottage, cursing the man, hating himself, thinking of nothing but his own misery and the wonderful future ahead that he would soon arrive at.

How Commissioner Song eventually came back that night Jing did not know. All he could remember the next morning was Mr Jian's livid face and his trembling hands as he yelled at Jing at the top of his voice in the echoing corridor of the building, accusing him of being disrespectful to his superior, of being undisciplined, of ultimately being *bu xianghua,* a total bastard. Jing took pity on Jian when he saw the old man's face turn the colour of pig's liver, with foam bubbling at the corner of his mouth.

'I'll leave then,' Jing said as he threw the bunch of keys back to Jian, missing his reached-out hand and falling to his feet with a crash, and made to go.

'Come back,' Jian called out behind him. 'I didn't tell you to go; I just wanted you to remember your position as a chauffeur.'

15

Diary entry 11. Spending the New Year with Dad in this small hotel in Hankou. Dad has no friends. Nor do I. It feels strange to be together with him with no one else for company. Next door his colleagues are playing poker games. Dad is not interested in these games. He's only interested in books but there are no books to read. Most of the time, he reads books from his memory. I feel a little bored, having nothing much to do but listen to him talk about this famous literary translator who did not understand a word of English and yet managed to translate 180 foreign literary works like *David Copperfield* by Charles Dickens and *Uncle Tom's Cabin* by an American called Si Tuo something, whose English name I do not know how to spell. When he explained that Lin Shu had to have someone who knew English tell him the story first before he could translate it into Chinese in the *wenyan*, the classical Chinese literary style, I began to lose interest. I am more interested in reading those works in the original, at least in translations done in today's Chinese language. I don't know how he felt. I had a feeling that he was a little let down by my sudden move to go out. He did not come with me. Nor did he show any disapproval.

It was a very cold day but there was sun and people everywhere. Restaurants were open where you could buy *re gan mian* (hot and dry noodle), *fu zi jiu* (rice wine), *you tiao* (fried twisters), *you bin* (fried cake), *mi fen* (rice noodle, – this last one Dad loved – *bao zi* (meat wrappers), *hua juan* (flower rolls) and a variety of other things. There was no festive decoration anywhere, a New

Year without celebration, and we have lived many years like this. I felt a little sad, although it is strange that Dad never seemed to feel the same way. Here he is, out on business with a few colleagues from the same library, finding nothing to do, but he is full of optimism, never tiring of talking about the books he has read and the people he has met in the past. What's the point? I'm sick of this little place, dirty, noisy and cold. Life should not be like this.

The other thing is Dad has some relatives in this city but he did not mention their names. I did not ask him why, although I think I understand. It was like what that ancient wisdom book says: 'When you are rich, you have visitors even if you live in deep mountains. When you are poor, no one asks about you even if you live in a busy city.' To them, he is probably nothing, an ex-Kuomingtang official under a cloud that is being cleared away. Who would want to be associated with him anyway? And he is not even smoking and drinking, surviving purely on the ancient literary anecdotes.

16

On the night when Commissioner Song and Deputy Commissioner Yun decided to walk back to the barracks without giving Jing a call, they chatted all the way. Their conversation centered around the tightening of the rules for matriculation examinations and the expected number of students. It gradually turned to Jing whom Yun commented on as 'a young man who is not there.'

'Professor Ma told me he was very upset about him,' Song said.

'Oh yes, what happened?'

'He was washing his feet one night in cold water as was his habit in Jing's presence, when Jing remarked that he was a *lengxue dongwu*, a cold-blooded animal,' Song said, almost laughing.

'Well, the young man was quite brash. He should learn to control his loose tongue a bit and cultivate some respect for his superiors,' Yun said.

'Not just that,' Song said. 'He is sometimes arrogant. Every time we have a chess game, he'll say "I'll beat you".'

'Did he?'

'He did and …'

'That's an awful thing to say, I must admit.'

'No, not really, but I don't think the guy knows his place. His learning English may have contributed to his arrogance.'

'You think? I would have thought that having the jeep under his control sort of gives him a power over us in ways that he himself is probably not even aware of.'

'Terrible! You remember the other night when he charged

head-on towards the oncoming traffic?'

'He must have been going over the new words he'd learnt for the day. I wonder what good learning English could be for a chauffeur except to make it more difficult and dangerous for all of us.'

*

So busy preparing for the examinations. It is a nightmare. A mess. I come out of the examination room with my left arm, my left palm and the back of my left hand covered with things I wrote on them. It is so hot both inside and outside that I only wear shorts and a singlet, the upper part of my left arm blue with inky words. I spend the evenings on the open top of the workers' dormitory with Pi, getting him to test me on a number of historical and geographical questions. He avoids asking me anything in the preparatory material but tackles me with things like whether Australia is part of England and if Canadians speak French. He also tests me on my English proficiency by giving me a Chinese phrase to translate, such as *lengchao refeng* or *wenhan wennuan*. The first one I readily render as 'cold irony and hot satire' but not to my own satisfaction because I don't know how that would sound in an English ear. The second one I simply cannot handle until I think to myself: why not translate it as it is? So I say, 'Ask cold ask warm.' That sets Pi laughing uncontrollably. He says, 'How can you say English as if it is Chinese? Would they understand it?' That sets me thinking. Even though I am writing English or thinking I am writing English here, others may think it is bad English. Could it be that I am actually writing in Chinese in English disguise? This thought, twisted as it is, needs testing by a genuine English person. 'But then,' I say to Pi. 'If I use English to describe the same thing, I'd have to use more than four words.' I then get him to consult the dictionary he is holding and to tell me what exactly it means. He says something I can hardly understand, the last word sounding very much like the name of one of the Gang of Four, Kang Sheng. I take the dictionary from him and find the definition: 'asking after someone's health with deep concern.' My rendering – 'Ask cold ask warm' – sounds much better than the English because that's exactly what is happening. You ask someone if he's too hot or too cold. We have a big dispute about it in which neither can convince the other.

Because I boasted to Pi that I had read my dictionary from cover to cover, he opens it at a random page and, in his halting English, picks a word out for me to tell him the meaning. The word he reads this time is 'Godfly' and I say 'That's a god fly' but cannot tell him what it means. I ask him to show me what the word looks like. I cannot help but laugh out loud. 'Oh, that is not godfly but gadfly'. It's *Niu Mang*, the novel we have both read, stolen from a library with its first part missing. We both agree that it is a great book but we like different things about it. He likes the clever way in which Gadfly writes articles expressing sharp opinions from two opposing points of view, but I am more impressed with the dusk scenes in which the main protagonist is overcome with a sense of approaching doom or devastating loneliness. That is also how I feel from time to time, sitting by the window as the night approaches. It feels like death is coming, though I can hardly put a name to my feelings. At this time of the day there is a lull that makes you realise that you are all alone in this world. I'm too tired and the mosquitoes are so bad.

17

Towards the latter half of the night, there was a rainstorm. By early morning, the temperature had dropped so considerably that Jing had to put on his shirt and trousers. As usual, the meeting room on the second floor above the mechanics' workshop was alive with early birds: Tann with his big toothy smile and his big round head tilted to one side, saying that his 'Mistress' had prepared a beautiful dinner on his return from a long trip in the provinces; Shaw, the ex-serviceman, wearing his bleached grass coloured uniform, sitting there absorbed in the *Hubei Daily*, oblivious to what was happening around him, offering to smile from time to time as if afraid that if he didn't do so he might appear rude; Old Yu holding his huge mug containing strong tea with steaming water boiled on a makeshift stove, commenting as he went up the iron stairs to the second floor, *jiayou chouqi shi wujia zhibao; jiayou meiqi shi rehuo de genmiao*, If you have an ugly wife in the home, it is a priceless treasure. If you have a beautiful wife in the home, it is the root cause of trouble; and Pan, the tiny-eyed joker, who would question everyone he met with a 'Have you climbed the mountain last night?', followed by an outburst of prurient laughter.

Jing understood the dirty question instinctively, knowing that the 'mountain' was a metaphorical reference to a woman's breasts and 'climbing' the sexual activity a man engaged in. Whenever the weather changed and there was a drop in temperature, this kind of joke surfaced as part of the daily routine and had by now become a set phrase along with greetings like 'Good morning' and 'Have you eaten?'

In this community Jing considered himself only a *guoke,* a passer-by. If there was no work assignment for the day, he would read his dictionary and grammar book, trying to cram more new words into his memory. Or else he would sit there listening to the mechanics and drivers cracking endless dirty jokes, trying not to imagine what the examination results would be or daydreaming of Chenfang. He felt sorry for not doing what she demanded the other day as she lay in bed waiting for him to enter between her legs. He said he was busy that afternoon. His boss, Team Leader Ba, wanted him to prepare an issue of big posters on the blackboard bulletins in the front of the factory to celebrate the upcoming National Day. Holding him tightly in her arms, she looked into his eyes, beseechingly, 'You are so white. You've got such an egglike smooth white skin! Can you please, please, please?' As she said so, she took his penis in hand, soft as a piece of rag, and was trying to stuff it in when Jing broke free and put on his blue overalls. Strangely enough, her mounting passions seemed to have created an adverse effect. All his desires were depleted at the sight of her face contorted with excitement and anticipation.

'I must go,' Jing said determinedly, and closed the door quietly behind him, mindful enough to caution her to put on the *xiaoshuan* just 'in case'. When he reached the factory entrance Jing's heart tugged painfully at the thought of how frustrated Chenfang must have been. 'Perhaps after I finish the job, I'll go and please her,' Jing thought, thinking of her face bitter with tears and what he must do to satisfy her sexual appetite to the utmost. 'But not now, particularly when Li may come back any time.'

Li must have guessed about their sexual encounters. Several times when he opened the door he saw them in different beds, she asleep in his bed and he reading a book in Yong's bed, wearing only shorts. These were embarrassing moments. It was plain to Li that something had been afoot. On a hot summer day like this, why close all the windows, covered with newspapers? Why was Jing wearing so little? He felt sorry that he had interrupted their game but it was not his intention. He had done an exhausting morning's work loading and unloading sheet metal for the team trucks. All he needed was a heavy sleep. Without a word, with clothes and all, he went to his bed, his 'dream source' as he put it, and threw himself in, stretching his hands out and gathering his torn and dusty mosquito net around him, trying not to make a sound. Jing pretended to be occupied with his textbook but his mind kept wondering if Li was watching from inside the net. Meanwhile, Chenfang continued to sleep or pretended to sleep, facing the wall, as if nothing had happened.

Now, when he thought of this again, Jing resented that he did not have a room of his own and began dreaming of new ways of making love to Chengfang in total freedom and abandon. He would be out driving his truck on a country road on an assignment where there was minimal traffic. He would get Chenfang to reach across with her hand to open his fly and pull out his penis. He would get her to massage him, holding his erection up and down while he was driving at sixty kilometres an hour, the fastest he could do with the Jiefang or Hubei. The violent vibrations of the truck would add to his pleasure. Since he rejected her offer that afternoon, however, this seemed unlikely. Chenfang had deliberately avoided him on several occasions, and even when they met, she refused to touch his hand or let him touch her. He knew this was her way of denying him, of retribution, and he took it for granted.

On Chenfang's part, her interest in Jing diminished after her graduation and her new position at the Xuangong Hotel in Hankou. Situated in the CBD of the city, this hotel was a vintage one built in the 1920s, famed since the founding of the People's Republic for its receptions for foreign dignitaries and state leaders, including Kim Il-Song, North Korea's supreme leader, and Field Marshall Bernard Montgomery. It was here that she met someone else. One evening at White Sand, Jing was quick to detect something that was more than a result of her resentment and his denial. It was a coldness that suggested she wasn't interested in him anymore.

'What's the matter with you?' Jing asked.

'Nothing,' Chenfang said, her large, dewy eyes downcast, her fingers twisting the stem of a blade of grass.

'I'm sorry about last time …' Jing began but was cut short by a cursory reply, 'Don't.'

Jing's arm stole around Chenfang from behind and as he tried to pull her into his arms as he would in the past she became stiff and resistant, her voice sounding ugly. 'Don't ever do this to me again.'

As she spoke she stood up from where she was sitting on the grassy slope of the embankment. Before them, a sweep of green river willows, so dense one could hardly see the river flowing beyond the leaves. Behind them, building after building of workers' dormitories, in one of which his semen once trailed her naked body like a snail, luminous in the dark.

'I'm going home now,' Chenfang said, pulling the grass stem apart with her fingers by twisting it until it could no longer hold.

'Can I walk you to the bus stop?' Jing tested.

'No,' Chenfang said and walked away, leaving Jing standing on the slope, a solitary figure without the possibility of pairing, without knowing what this was all about. 'I'll write!' He shouted belatedly to her back.

The sun, now behind the city on the other side of the river, painted the trees in red. Birds, as if in mockery, flew back to their nests in pairs. For some reason, a story that Pi had told him returned to Jing's memory, although it bore no relationship to what had just happened. A friend by the name of Sa, the story went, had a girlfriend, Hui. They met and fell in love. Soon, Hui grew bored because Sa never did anything to her, such as cuddling or hugging or kissing, although she probably forgot she had rejected him when he made his first attempts at loving her physically. Deeply hurt, Sa vowed he would never make the first move again. This also stemmed from a righteous belief that it would only be proper love if it took place after their marriage. Little did he know that Hui had grown tired of him and had secretly fallen in love with someone else whom she had decided to marry. When Sa learnt of their wedding, it was too late. Still, he went and presented Hui with a big gift.

'Guess what that would be?' Pi asked.

'I wouldn't have a clue,' Jing said. 'But I quite admire this guy for his courage.'

'Courage or stupidity?' Pi said. 'But you still haven't answered my question: what gift?'

'Don't know,' Jing said. He thought and gave up. To him, whatever gift the man took to the woman would be useless; it served only as a painful reminder of a past unfulfilled 'unless it's a dagger.'

'How can you possibly entertain such dark thoughts,' Pi said. 'Let me tell you. The gift was a big kiss that he printed on the side of the woman's cheek!'

'What?' Jing said. 'To get back what he has lost with her?'

'Don't know,' Pi imitated Jing's voice and shrugged his shoulders. He'd read enough Russian novels to know how to shrug his shoulders in a manner that he imagined was appropriate.

18

By now you are troubled by the way this novel goes. You feel that you are not doing the conventional thing, not even the right thing. You feel that somehow you have to concentrate on telling a story about the past instead of letting the present come in from time to time. You know that if you tell a straight story it would take you probably only a few months to finish as you did before. You know from Jing that he had an abhorrence of the storyteller as Gu strode into the workshop surrounded by the mechanics and drivers who had set up an altar for him, brought him a bowl of strong tea and waited around sitting on their low stools, making him appear almost as if he were twice as tall as he really was, almost Godlike. To this all Jing was an exception. You wonder why. Even Jing could not explain. Jing could not recall the storyteller's name and he knew that the storyteller disliked him for not worshipping him like the others. He was supposed to be a mechanic but didn't have to do the work as the only thing all the rest of them wanted him to do was tell them stories. You commit a mistake by allowing the story into this soliloquy.

You are a writer writing in the twenty-first century. Do you think that makes any difference? You think it does. For example, you are writing not with a pen or pencil or ballpoint pen, not with a piece of paper or any kind of paper. You are writing on a machine, the smallest machine possible, not much bigger than a dictionary and you are writing this book outside in the open right under the sky in your garden, the light so strong that it obscures your screen, making it murky, even though it is overcast, and the overgrown grass is immediately under your feet; birds are singing somewhere in the distance close to your ears. You can no longer pretend that you are creating a piece of art the creative process of which has nothing to do with your living environment and that you can no longer pretend that as an author you are less important than your work because you are behind everything and yet are inaudible and invisible and all you do is to prolong your life through your work and you are somehow great because you create something out of yourself and in spite of yourself. You want to tell yourself that all that is nonsense, bullshit, hushuobadao, fangpi. *You know you have written much more than you can ever hope to get published in your life. Do you believe that if the rest of it gets published after you are no more you'll be reborn? The clouds floating on high, you know, are the reflections of those dead, the most recent dead bright and the long gone dark, which keep merging into each other and drifting away. Perhaps the only thing you can hope for is to become one of those clouds after death that travel thousands of miles, for free, and freely, to visit different landscapes or windscapes, and, if you choose, turn into rain.*

19

Following his time at the Education Commision, Jing had a short stint as a statistician on loan at the Planning Section to work out figures for them. Although he didn't feel quite up to it, he stumbled through his calculations with an abacus, making many mistakes. He wondered if this had something to do with being involved with vehicles for too long, his mind dulled to a piece of wood only responsive to mechanical noise and vibrations. Section Chief Niu, a short man with a shrivelled face in his early fifties, looked nothing like the licentious fellow that Shaw had described him as. Jing remembered the day when he reported to the office for work. Through his piercing eyes, Niu looked at Jing and said, 'This work may not be very suitable for you.'

'Why?' Jing asked. He did not know that the team, in disposing of him as unnecessary, perversely recommended him to the Section Chief as someone very 'intelligent' who could 'speak good English.'

'Well,' Niu said, sizing up the young man and weighing his words. 'Just give it a go. I'm sure you'll be fine.' He had meant to tell Jing what Ba and the other members of the team had told him but he thought better of it.

Jing noticed the conspicuous absence of Gin, the pretty-faced secretary who liked to wear a white skirt and white leather sandals. No one knew where she had gone. Jing remembered that she had once caught his eye. He had put her name down in his notebook as someone worth taking notice of and struck her off his list when he had learnt of the affair.

'These people are wicked,' he later heard Shaw elaborate.

'They go to other provinces on business and take their secretaries with them. Then, when their affairs are found out, they blame their secretaries, saying that it is they who seduce them in the first place. As Party members, they are incorrigible, you know, and immune from any vice!' 'I know,' Jing agreed, remembering an observation Professor Ma once made about the Party officials. 'These people,' Ma said. 'If they play well, they get the red crown. If they play badly, they get the red neck.' For Jing to understand what he meant, Professor Ma placed his right index finger like a knife and moved it from one end of his neck to the other, creating a vivid image of a severed neck dripping with blood.

In Gin's place now sat Niu's wife, a sharp-eyed forty-something whose duty it seemed more than anything else was to guard her husband from falling into other younger women's traps. While Jing had his head over his abacus, trying to do his sums or subtractions, his thoughts wandered from Niu's affair with Gin to his own affair, if he could put it that way, with Chenfang. Niu complained to Ba. 'The young man we have on loan from your team has a problem,' Niu said, over the phone.

'What problem?' Ba asked, alarmed that Jing had got himself into more trouble.

'His heart never seems set on his work,' Niu said. 'The account book he helped prepare contains so many mistakes that the calculations have to be redone. At the moment we simply do not have enough hands. If we had known that he was so useless, we'd prefer to have gone without him.'

'Well, "useless" may be too strong a description,' Ba said. 'I certainly think he is a smart fellow. The National Day edition of the blackboard bulletin he is working on is going very well. And he's got good English.'

'Good English?' Niu snorted. 'What's good about English? What need do we have for English, for someone who knows

English? Practically nil. You can take him back for all the English he's got. We want someone who knows how to put one and one together, not someone who knows ABC.'

'Of course,' Ba said. 'And you certainly do need someone with a face that lasts.' Without waiting for these words to sink in, Ba hung up on him.

'What did he say?' Niu's wife gave him a hard look, in a commanding voice.

'Oh,' Niu lied. 'He said that he's pleased that you now work by my side and will take good care of me.'

'Better care, I'd say.' His wife's eyes bulged, the way a toad does.

*

Back in the team, Jing now became someone to be reckoned with. Since he was indisposable, thus indispensable, they had to find him something to do, to drive. After all, this was a fellow who had demonstrated his abilities as a chauffeur for senior cadres in a provincial Education Commission. There was no reason why he should go back to his smoky diesel engine. Like everyone else, he should be given a chance to drive a decent vehicle in his name, particularly when he might not be around for much longer if accepted by a university. That was what was going through Ba's mind when he learnt that Jing had sat for the examination. Although he found Jing quite an odd character, at times forbidding and inaccessible, he never doubted that he would one day fly far and high, judging by his writing skills and determination to succeed in a field that alienated him from most of his fellow drivers and mechanics. As a result of Ba's decision, Jing was finally able to get rid of the self-assembled mini truck driven by a diesel engine and inherit an old five-tonne Fiat from Tann, who was assigned one of the latest trucks that had just arrived, a brand-new Jiefang. Content with his lot, Jing did not complain because he could now drive around the city on independent tasks. Indeed, when he first got into the green-coloured cabin with its wide windscreen and heard its nearly inaudible purr, he was exhilarated. What could he not do in his own vehicle now? He was totally in control of himself and his fate. As he drove to a quarry in Lion Hill to haul back gravel for the construction of a new road in the factory premises, the thought even came to him that should he fail to pass his examination he would be happy where he was, alone in this tiny little cabin, driving his truck through a landscape of constantly changing colours and new possibilities.

He quickly became disillusioned, however, when he found that the truck, like nearly all the old ones in the team, was a dud. This Fiat, like the Hubei that had caused him to kill a young buffalo, had a faulty brake system. All the trucks, including the Unique, had the same problem, although no one seemed willing to impart this knowledge to their fellow teammates. Take the Huanghe, the Yellow River, a truck that operated on a pneumatic brake system. Jing drove it as a replacement for a couple of days and it soon came to his notice that the brake's air pump was faulty. Whenever he took his foot off the accelerator, he noticed the hand in the indicator would wipe off a couple of figures downwards, suggesting that air must be leaking somewhere. He was immediately alerted and would pump it up every few minutes by pressing hard on the accelerator. Thus he safely went up and down the Yangtze Bridge without any trouble, secretly congratulating himself on being so sharp-eyed and for having found the solution quickly. When he handed the truck back to the team, he sighed with relief.

A few days later, during the morning safety session upstairs, it was announced that Yong had an accident while driving the Huanghe the previous day. Rushing down the bridge on the Hanyang side, Yong used the brake too many times until the air was all but gone. When he finally realised that he had no brake, it was too late. He had to veer the heavy brown beast towards the side of the hill to avoid either smashing into the rear of the car in front of him or having a head-on collision with the oncoming traffic. As a result, he smashed into an enormous tree that was regarded as one of the Protected National Treasures in the scenic Turtle Mountain Area. Miraculously, he himself escaped the accident unhurt.

Strangely enough, during these morning sessions, when safety, like before, was emphasised to the infinitum, why on earth didn't Cannon tell Jing there was a problem with the air tank? And why, again, when it came to Jing's notice that this was a problem, did he not tell Yong about it? Would Yong tell others about it? There was no need now, as it had caught everyone's attention that the big Yellow River was unstoppable unless you gave it enough attention.

In this little driving community there were things that defied simple human logic. A peach tree, a few thousand years old, had elicited a story from Gu the storyteller. According to him, there was not a single peach tree on this mountain until thousands of years ago when Tao Hua arrived. She was a beautiful girl that the monarch of a tiny country called Xi had fallen in love with, but their happy married life together did not last long as the country fell under the conquest of a bigger country called Chu. The Monarch of Xi was put in a dry well and Tao Hua, because of her stunning beauty, was kept in the new monarch's *hougong*, rear palace, for his pleasure, which she refused to give. By and by, she chanced upon her husband on an outing and saw that he had been reduced to a walking skeleton, hardly recognisable.

When she learnt about his whereabouts from the king who took her captive, she persuaded him to let her visit her ex-husband, saying that she would shame him if he didn't allow it. When they finally met, she pulled out a dagger and thrust it into her own heart, saying on her last breath, 'I'd rather die a devil with my husband than a living doll for you!' No sooner had she finished these words than her husband, the monarch of the tiny country Xi, pulled the dagger out from her heart and plunged it into his own heart, reaching their consummation in their shared death. Where their blood was spilled, like the petals of peach flowers, there grew peach trees that would burst into full bloom in spring.

'Does that mean that I shall never meet with my peach fortune again?' Yong joked.

How could I even begin to explain in English to a foreigner what a peach fortune meant, Jing thought. Perhaps a fortune of sexual encounters? Or plenty of affairs?

'No, it means that you will have to pay a lot for your metaphysical meeting with your peach fortune,' Old Canton said.

Sure enough, the team ended up paying nearly a thousand bucks for the loss of the tree.

*

Jing was driving alone on a dirty country road at high noon in summer with no traffic either way. The sun beat down relentlessly on the bonnet of the Fiat. The country road, bone dry and hard, contained holes, large and small. Watermelon fields all around. Jing drove slowly, at thirty kilometres per hour, to avoid the vibration caused by the unevenness of the road. For some reason, he recalled the tree that Yong had crashed into. Would the brakes be a problem? Might as well check them. As this thought flashed across his mind, Jing's foot went instinctively for the brake pedal, even though there was no vehicle in sight. No response. He braked again but his Fiat hurtled itself forward, pushed by the heavy watermelons behind him weighing over five tonnes. He put the gear in neutral, making the engine roar with a shot of petrol by tapping the accelerator lightly, a trick designed to align the speed of the rear and front gears, not to lubricate the gearbox as some old ignorant drivers believed. He rushed into the third, then second gear by giving the accelerator another hard press. The engine howled and the gearbox sent forth such a roar of clashing steel teeth that Jing was frightened they might break in the meshing. The green Italian truck was brought to a grinding halt. Holy shit! Imagine if he was driving at forty kilometres per hour on the Yangtze Bridge across the river, with cars and trucks streaming by in both directions, and suddenly finding that he had to brake. He would have to head towards the river, break the steel railing and feed the fish with his watermelons. That would be nice. Many a time accidents like that had happened, involving a drunken driver going home at midnight. The bridge railing on either side would be left with gaping holes, living proof of a 'glorious endeavour', as Pan was wont to put it. Jing was not cut out for such heroic achievements. He was more or less a chicken at heart. He wanted safety more than anyone else because, for God's sake, he had a future in English.

With the engine dead, the only sound Jing could hear was the water fizzing in the radiator and some flies gathering around an opened watermelon by the roadside, a mass of black insects moving on a gaudy mess of red. It was midday. The sun was glaring down on the bleached leaves and broken vines of the watermelons in the fields. Gingerly, Jing restarted the engine, got the devil of this vehicle moving in slow motion, and pressed the brake again. This time it worked. But because he overbraked, thinking it wouldn't work, the truck overreacted, sending a number of watermelons careering over the sidewalls. The smashed ones had bloody liquid oozing out of their wounds, staining the dust into balls. He tested the brake a few more times and attributed the sudden loss of function to the overwhelming heat. He pulled out onto the road again and drove at twenty-five kilometres an hour, touching the brake pedal from time to time to test if it worked, braking well in advance and trying to ignore the abusive horns all around him, submissively making way for the reckless ones who dangerously overtook him, muttering all the way, *ge biaozi yangde,* you son of a whore and *ge bi ri de,* you cunt fucker. His face drenched in sweat, Jing braved on, with a heart of iron and stone. When he finally managed to get back to the factory, with a truckload of scorchingly hot watermelons covered in thick dust, who would he see but Ba, inside the entrance with a big smile, waving for him to stop.

'Any problems at all?' Ba enquired, eyeing him to try to search for some clues.

'No, *meishi,*' Jing said, pointing to the back of the truck. 'Take one for yourself, the big one if you like, before it's too late with Niu.'

Ba had been concerned because he knew this truck had a brake problem. He had meant to tell Jing about it but his mind was occupied with millions of other daily tasks. When he heard Jing's response and saw his face half wet with sweat and dust, with a black watermelon seed to the right of his mouth, like a mole, his face relaxed with a smile. 'I'm worried more about you than the watermelons, *huojie,*' Ba said, and advised him to take a break while handing the vehicle back to the mechanics for a check-up.

It was later found out that the problem with this Fiat model was its tendency to lose its brake function in extreme heat, as the brake-oil tubes would become softened, thus losing power, and unable to tighten the brake discs. With his hands spread out, Pan shrugged and said, 'There's not much we can do about it, Jing. Why did you come to this broke team in the first place? I think you should go to the university. You are better suited for English, *huojie*.'

*

Jing went straight to the dormitory. It was dinnertime. Through the open door, Jing could see Hua and Xin sitting side by side at the table, Xin sipping noisily from a bowl of egg soup and Hua reading something while eating, both stripped bare to their waists and both fanning themselves vigorously. Having eaten lots of watermelons on his way back, Jing did not feel like dinner yet. He went into Hua's room, saying as he did so, 'What are you reading?'

'Something you may like,' Hua said, passing a booklet he was holding to Jing, who had a look at the title and saw that it was *Zengguang Xianwen* (roughly, Ancient Wisdoms), something that had been declared forbidden material belonging to the Category I of the three categories of *feng zi xiu* (feudalism, revisionism and capitalism) during the Cultural Revolution. He quickly glanced through the lines arranged in couplets on the yellowing pages, catching something wrongly printed, and he said, putting a finger right below the character, 'This is wrong. See?' Both Hua and Xin followed his index finger with their eyes as they put their heads together and exchanged a glance of amused understanding. What they saw was *'Shui taiqing ze wuyu, ren zhica ze wutu,* If the water is too clean there will be no fish and if a person is too intelligent he will have no friends.'

'What was wrong?' Both of them said at once. They could

not see anything no matter how hard they tried.

'It should not be *taiqing*, it should be *zhiqing*,' Jing said proudly. 'I know this because I remember these lines from a long time ago. *Tai* is a bit vulgar, not as elegant as *zhi*.'

'You really are good,' Hua sighed. What he actually meant to say was 'You really are so choosy, pedantic even!' Instead, he added, 'You should be an editor working with a magazine because you can pick errors like this so easily.'

Jing did not respond. He felt hurt. He knew he would do better than a mere editor correcting grammatical errors. There was something deep within him that he had yet to define, to discover, to form in meaningful words. He pretended not to have heard the remark but kept reading, citing one example here and there for its relevance as he went along.

'Oh, I like this one. Listen: *"Buxin dankan yanzhongjiu, beibei xianquan youqian ren"*, Believe it or not, one look at the dinner parties will assure you that the richest among the diners is always the first to be toasted to. Isn't that true? I wonder how long ago this was written. Must have been hundreds of years ago. And this: *"Pingsheng mozuo zoumeishi, shishang yingwu qiechiren"*, If you do not do anything in your life that causes people to frown upon, there should not be people who gnash their teeth at you. And this …' but he suddenly stopped as if he had thought of something.

'Go on,' they urged him. 'What is it that you have read?'

'No, I can't,' Jing said, his face strained with the pressure. 'I have to go and piss.'

'Just take it with you,' Hua said. 'And have a good read in the toilet.'

The line Jing had come across that stopped him from revealing what he had wanted to say was significant. It was too revealing for him to read out loud in their presence. He repeated it again and again until he could commit it to memory. It went: *Jiejiao xu shengji, siwo buru wu,* If you make friends with people, find someone that is better than you. If you find someone like you, you'd rather go without. If I had said that to them, he thought to himself, they might have been offended, thinking I was snobbish. But aren't I a little like that? Watching the stars overhead, he wondered to himself. I can read and speak some English whereas they only read and speak Chinese. I have an ambition that goes beyond my imagination whereas all they are concerned with is how to get kickbacks like pork or eggs on their sorties into the country. They probably think I am a snob, who is *haogao wuyuan,* reaching for what is beyond one's grasp, or should I directly translate it as it is, seeking high and far, and *zheshan wangzhe nashan gao,* standing on this mountain but admiring another mountain for its greater height? But I never intended to show it. All I have ever wanted to do is to move away from people, from them, from a life bound by materialism into a life of metaphysics. Truck driving is all about moving goods from one place to another. I want to do something like thought driving, moving thoughts from one place to another in a world that seems to lack them.

In time, Jing's thoughts became fuzzy, his eyes weary from watching the stars for too long. His body on the straw mat, hungry for sleep, turned into a world of dreams that he would have loved to record if he was to know twenty years down the track how important they would be.

20

When Jing got his results in the mail, his heart went cold. He thought he had failed. Immediately, the future was a rotten corpse prostrate before him with all its bleak skeletal features: he was standing in his overalls, stained salt white with sweat before his Fiat, his workmates doing their usual thing, being abusive, telling dirty jokes, listening with eyes and mouths agape to the story-man telling his ancient tales – endless watermelon fields, endless quarry stones, endless bamboo beds and bamboo chairs, the tiny room in the dormitory he shared with two other men and no Chenfang, replaced probably by a country girl that he'd had to content himself with, like Ba. He could hardly bear the thought and decided then and there not to tell anyone of his failure. He folded the hard white piece of paper revealing the scores for each subject he had studied into the size of a pack of cigarettes, and was about to thrust it into his trouser pocket when he noticed something seemingly irrelevant, his mathematics score. He suddenly realised that as he had never intended to study anything along the lines of natural sciences – he had only intended to study social sciences – his mathematics result bore no relationship to his outcome even if he had managed to get a score of 10. The rest of the five subjects scored far more than 300, the threshold score, in total. His eyes brightened, hope returning; it meant he had gained his passport to a key university, indeed, to any university. He could have jumped for joy but he didn't. He could have made the announcement to his workmates who were smoking and drinking tea but he didn't. He could have sneaked into the side office in which he had shared many a story with Shaw but he didn't. He wanted to keep the news entirely to himself until he was absolutely sure, that is, until he was accepted by a university or, as they say, until the nail has been hammered into the plank.

But his mouth was too fast for his mind. Hardly able to conceal the fact of his winning, he told Shaw straight away as he arrived at the team office. In no time the news spread about the factory, even to the porters such as Xin and Hua, who came wearing their overalls to look for him, calling out to him that he should buy them candies. A perceptible change came over Jing's fellow drivers and mechanics. Some of them seemed embarrassed at such an achievement. No one had expected one of them to succeed in passing a university entrance examination, least of all an outsider who had absolutely no support, moral or otherwise, no acquaintances or connections that were prerequisites for career advancements in this little place. Old Canton, reputedly the most skilled mechanic who had never had much respect for anyone but himself and had taken little notice of Jing before, suddenly became friendly. He went so far as to invite Jing to his home for tea. No one in his team had ever asked Jing home for tea before. This was unprecedented. Jing went and wondered what was on Old Canton's mind. He found that Old Canton's apartment was spacious and neat, compared with Team Leader Ba's, although a bookcase against the wall stood almost empty, containing very few books. This was a common domestic sight in those days, when possessing books was not considered a virtue. When Cousin Cong got married, he had a beautiful bookcase made but, instead of laying it out with books, he used it to display vases filled with artificial flowers. When Jing heard Cong talking about his plan to turn the bookcase into a spare kitchen cabinet should the need arise, he felt sorry for him and he was moved to tell his own dad that if he were to get married one day, the first thing he would do was have a big wall-to-wall bookcase made so that he could line his walls with books.

'Was it true that you passed your examination with flying colours?' This question took Jing by surprise and he quickly withdrew his glance from the half-empty bookshelf and looked into the smiling face of Old Canton. This was unusual, for he was a stern person by temperament who did not usually smile at anyone. Sometimes he would carry his fastidiousness so far that anyone misplacing his tools or wrongly sitting on his stool covered with the clean towel would elicit a harsh rebuke from him. Finding him a difficult person to deal with, Jing hardly ever spoke to him, save for a nod or two that he felt he somehow had to do as part of a daily courtesy routine.

'No,' Jing said, modestly, though in his heart of his hearts he was overjoyed that this guy, the erstwhile professor, now the best mechanic in the team, should come to seek his friendship. 'Slightly better than normal, just enough to get me into a major university. That's all.'

On this very hot Autumn Tiger evening, Old Canton got his wife to bring out his newly bought pedestal electric fan into the courtyard-like entrance to his apartment. The fan was as enthusiastic as Old Canton, turning itself around in a 180-degree sweep in its overzealous attempt to spread the cool, his attitude also having turned 180 degrees. On a red-wood tea table, which Old Canton personally placed before Jing, he laid out two white porcelain cups on even more delicate saucers. As the kettle was boiling he insisted his wife make tea with the Dragon Well. While Jing answered Old Canton's questions absent-mindedly, his attention was caught by something else. He became aware of a third entity hovering somewhere nearby, more imminent than the man and his wife. It soon became clear that this third entity was a much younger female that Old Canton addressed as his 'daughter', who would very much like to learn English in the future. From the way Old Canton spoke about this, with averted eyes and sucking noises coming from his nose while his habitual knee-jerking movements momentarily stopped, it dawned on Jing why Old Canton had suddenly become so enthusiastic, even more so than the electric fan, though not as transparent or efficient. At his beck and call, his daughter, Lan, came out of the depths of their apartment room and, with a big smile, called him *Shifu*, Master. She was quite pretty, young, with large eyes, of the same size as her father's but with little of the latter's austerity. Jing was reminded of Chenfang whom he sorely missed. Besides, Jing could see that Lan did not take much interest in him, either. She did not take a seat on the stool her father pointed out for her but excused herself and disappeared. Perhaps, Jing thought, I am *zizuo duoqing,* imagining things that were never even there in the first place? Perhaps Old Canton likes me because my success has rekindled his desire for learning and scholarship and by having me here for tea he is showing his appreciation of my talents, with absolutely no intention for me to marry his daughter? What a preposterous thought!?

*

Jing wrote a letter to Chenfang

Dear Chenfang,

I think you misunderstood me the other day, for some reason. I didn't mean that English is all that matters. Sometimes I think you matter more than English, if you know what I mean. For a long time, I have had a feeling that I am an outsider in this place, as I'm sure that's how you feel at your school. Not only that, I find people here are also outsiders even though they may have been born and brought up here. They are outsiders to themselves, their life is only temporary. They do not know how they came here, why they are here and why they do what they do. Same with me. Why English? I mean there's certainly many other choices that are probably better. You remarked on my whiteness as if that was a virtue but I sometimes regard it as a stigma because being too white in my hometown was considered to be bourgeois, petty bourgeois even. I systematically and regularly burn myself black with the summer sun and I used to take a huge pride in it. Pi once joked that I may have been born of mixed blood, but as far as I know, there's nothing foreign in my family, except my father who used to fight with the American army and has good enough English.

You didn't seem happy when you learnt about my success. Was it because you think I may discontinue our relationship once I get into the university because of what you described as the change of personality that is bound to come with a change in social status? I don't think it is likely with me. You know I like you, no, love you, and would like to be with you for always.

I'll have to stop here as I'm having an interview soon and have to work hard in preparation.

See you soon,

Jing

*

The interview took place when a representative from East Lake University came to the factory one afternoon in August. Jing was working on the *heiban bao*, blackboard bulletin, for the Truck Team. It was a task Ba had assigned Jing as he thought he was the most learned of all the Truck Team members. Ba wanted

Jing to write something to celebrate National Day as part of the general October issue for the team. This was something Jing accepted readily. He did not find it hard to do. In fact, it didn't take Jing long to design the whole thing in his head. He would write a short story about how Ba had organised the whole team in a neat and efficient manner using the organisational and managerial skills he had learnt overseas. He would write a poem or two to sing of the Party's victory over the Gang of Four, which ended the disastrous Cultural Revolution. He would write a few essays about various aspects of the team life, namely, how the team members were bonded in their common effort to eliminate accidents and ensure safety, throwing in his own story about the buffalo to enliven the atmosphere. He would then use a pen name for each piece he wrote, giving people the impression that it was done by more than one person. As he was going through this in the side office he shared with Shaw for private conversations and his paper clippings, a telephone call brought him to the Production Section at the front of the factory. Their answer to his question was 'Something important!'

It was a young man who held out his hand to him and said in English, 'How do you do?'

'What's your name?' Jing asked. Before he realised that he had asked the complex question on a rising tone, it was too late.

'My name is Fu.'

'Oh, Teacher Fu, how are you?' Jing blurted out, again on a rising tone, perhaps a little too excitedly.

'Call me Mr Fu if you like.' In a perfect English accent, Mr Fu corrected Jing without meaning to, keeping a sharp eye on this younger man wearing oily blue overalls with his right hand dripping chalk dust. 'And please be seated.'

'Be seated?' The question baffled Jing but only for a brief moment for he saw Mr Fu's hand indicating a chair next to him and immediately took the hint.

Mr Fu then briefly introduced him to East Lake University, one of the newly established universities that had sprung up around the city. Located at the foot of the Mill Hill by the East Lake, it was flanked by the famous Wuhan University on one side and the well-known Wuhan Steel Works on the other. Jointly funded by a private organisation and the government, the university had a bright future as it planned to expand into a major multidiscipline one with international connections.

'Did I make myself understood?' Mr Fu asked, pausing to observe Jing's reaction.

Jing knew Fu was playing the passive voice game with the word 'understood' and, not to be outdone, he immediately responded, 'Of course, you made yourself understood.' After which he felt the need to add something further and said, 'by me.'

Mr Fu smiled a knowing smile but did not comment. Jing was quite pleased with his own cleverness when Mr Fu asked, 'What's your surname?'

'Jing,' he said.

'Which Jing?' Mr Fu enquired. 'Jing for scenery or Jing for respect?'

'Neither,' Jing said. 'Jing for capital or Beijing.'

'And your first name?'

'Ying,' Jing answered. 'Ying for hero.'

'Ah, a great name,' Jing noticed that Mr Fu avoided his eyes as he said this. 'Can you tell me something about yourself, please?'

'Oh, my name is Jing Ying,' Jing said, trying to be as fast as possible, thinking that speaking English quickly would impress, but only managing to stumble along. 'I am a truck driver. I like this job but I more like English. I want to do my bit for my motherland to study English hard. If I am accepted by East

Lake University, I'll study more harder. Thank you for coming to see me today.' Jing finished his speech as if he was reciting from memory. Indeed he had been turning this over in his mind for the last few days but he had only managed to condense his thoughts into a few sentences, forgetting the best part of it and, in his overenthusiasm, omitting the niceties of grammar.

It was all over in less than twenty minutes. Mr Fu stood up and thanked Jing for giving him the opportunity to visit him in this 'fantastic factory'. As if he had remembered something, Jing asked if he could add something to what he had just said. Mr Fu stopped, looking through his glasses at him, and said, 'Yes?'

'I wanted to show you something I'd written when preparing the *heiban bao*,' Jing said. 'I don't know how to translate that into English, I am sorry. But it's a short poem I've written in English. It's called "The River". It's like this: "The river is long, it longs to go away; the more it longs to go away, the longer it becomes.""

'Ah, the poet,' Mr Fu was truly delighted. 'You'll have plenty to read and write about when you go to the university, I am sure.'

Red in the face, Jing watched Mr Fu walk back out of the entrance of the factory and disappear into the bus on the embankment. Jing's heart was already flying to the lakeside.

21

Is it true that one can see the future in a dream? If so, I have seen it. I see the backyard of a house in an unspecified country, very quiet, so quiet one can hear the sound of a bird picking up a seed from the soil, rain drenched soil mixed with the sunlight. I see a tree twice as tall as me, getting taller with each wind. I notice I am writing in a strange way but I don't seem to have any control. This grey-feathered bird, also unnamed, is thrashing something that it takes in its beak until it breaks the thing in half and eats it. The white clouds are receding, carrying the sun on their backs, giving way to the blue sky, a blue that one has never seen before. Flowers are everywhere, even on the nose of a passer-by and the tip of a cloud. I hear something speak a language that sounds slightly familiar to what I have learnt although try as I can I cannot decipher what it is. It sounds as if someone is giving me a difficult test and I am going to fail. I hear the word 'death'. I struggle to say 'si' and wake up, horrified at the scene and then delighted with the discovery that the reverse could be true as it could be a *fanmeng*, a reverse dream. The reality surrounding me is the same as it has been for the last two years. The mosquito net has become grimy with dust and blood from my own body. The wooden box that I am using for my desk is now bursting with books and exercise books and my diaries. The calendar on the wall has many dates ticked or crossed. Only I know what they stand for. When Pi sees them he asks what they are. I say they mean I have important appointments or some such things. From the way he looks at me, I know he does not believe a word of what I say. I am ashamed of myself for being so profusely masturbatory. I must stop doing it when I go to the university. It will be a different life there. What shall I do to make myself a great man?

PART II

Living Under English

1

'My name is Ma Tian. I come from Taiyuan. Let me explain my name first. You may think I am a horse in a field, Ma for horse and Tian for field, but my middle-school classmates used to call me Horse Sweet because Tian sounds exactly like Tian for sweet. When I turned it the other way round like a foreign word, to make me Tian Ma, they started calling me Sweet Horse until one day someone mispronounced it Swift Horse. I grabbed the opportunity and started calling myself Swift Marr. Now that's how I got this name and please call me Swift Marr or more simply Tian Ma, a heavenly horse whichever way you prefer it. In any event, I would like to thank you all for giving me this opportunity to be with you and, in particular, I'd like to thank Mr Fu for thinking of such an ingenious way of practising oral English.'

'I come from Harbin in Heilongjiang Province. I'm Zhenya. Have you been to Harbin? If not, come to my place one day. It's really beautiful. Very Russian I must say. In winter, ice everywhere and there is an annual winter ice festival. In summer, the Pine Flower River is a pretty sight to see. I don't know what else I can say because my limited English but I want to learn from all of you.'

'I'm Jing. I'm from White Sand but I'm not a local. As a matter of fact, I come from a small town not far from this city. I drove my truck a few days ago to this university with all my belongings, a box of clothes, a bag of books and a friend from the same team. He drove my truck back to the factory. I think my aim in learning English is simple. I want to catch up. I have lost so many years mucking around, altogether ten years, some in the countryside and some in the factory that I just mentioned. In the meantime, I feel I have grown doubly old. I envy some of you who come fresh from the middle school, having lost no time in your learning process, straight from middle school to university. I've said what I wanted to say. Thank you. Before I go, can I say something about my friend's name Tian Ma? With your permission, I remember a poem by the Persian poet Omar something, whose surname I've forgotten.

How time is slipping underneath our Feet:
Unborn Tomorrow and dead Yesterday
Why fret about Them if Today be sweet![1]

For this reason I think being sweet is actually very good. I am finished with my presentation now.'

Designed to improve the students' spoken English, the morning presentation continued as Mr Fu had planned. In this classroom with newly whitewashed walls was a smiling Mao on the front wall, a poster bearing Lenin's 'Study, Study and More Study' on a side wall and, opposite it, Mao's famous slogan, 'Keep a daily upward learning curve!', a remark that Mr Fu himself had translated from Mao's virtually untranslatable, *haohao xuexi, tiantian xiangshang*. Fu was in his element. One student after another went to the podium in front of the blackboard. He was pleased with their performance, and made comments at the end of each presentation. After a number of presentations throughout the week, he had a pretty clear idea of who was good at what

1 From *The Rubaiyat of Omar Khayyam*, quoted from Chek Ling, *Plantings in a New Land: Stories of Survival, Endurance and Emancipation*. Brisbane, Qld: Society of Chinese Australian Academics of Queensland, 2001.

and the level of English each of them had reached. This seemed consistent with the examination results he had gone through before he handpicked them. Experience told him it was hard to predict what each of the students would become careerwise in the future, as the potential of each individual could vary greatly. 'The only thing you know is that you don't know anything,' he reminded himself. He had already forgotten where he had come across this remark and who had made it.

Fu liked the looks of some of the girls in his class, Zhenya, for example. Her full name was actually Alexander Sergeyevich Zhenya, possibly born of mixed white Russian and Chinese parentage, although she appeared more Chinese than Russian, with a large round moon face and small round eyes, extremely white skin, a little tired perhaps because of her long train journey, over forty-eight hours. He remembered after her presentation making a comment to the effect that she should try to improve her English by eliminating her Northern accent. Her face blushed a deep red, which made him feel a little sorry for having been so forthright.

He was most impressed with Tian Ma, the heavenly horse, who excelled in his spoken English and, of course, in his examination results, having gained more than ninety per cent in English. From Ma's file, he knew that his father was a Professor of English at a university in Shanxi. The connection was unmistakable. You couldn't expect someone from a working-class background to achieve that score, could you? Take Jing. He wasn't sure about Jing, although he had interviewed him and after a long deliberation decided to accept him. He didn't know why but he had made his decision by instinct. Something told him that this was no ordinary person. Jing's results in English and everything else, except poetry, were average. Was it sympathy that moved him to make that decision? Fu dismissed the suggestion. Or did

Jing remind him of his own humble background as a peasant boy? Well, that Fu couldn't disprove. He trusted his instincts, his gut feelings. It was the whole person, the way he talked, the things he talked about, and the poetry he managed to recite, that somehow impressed him.

If there was anything else, it was Jing's eyes. They had a penetrating effect on him that lasted a long time after he was gone. Otherwise, Jing was no different from any other factory worker in his overalls, even in his manner of speech. A couple of days ago, a student had reported hearing Jing use dirty language on campus; she wondered if it was because he had come from a factory background. Fu didn't tell Jing about this, but he kept a close eye on him. He wanted to wait and see how he developed.

Fu felt a little hot. He pushed open the window in his room. A breeze came wafting in from the lake, carrying frog croakings, insect chirpings, and a whole raft of fragrances of lotus and mountain flowers, mixed with some wild grasses he could not name. The lake was shivering in semi-darkness, occasionally sending forth a faint lapping noise. The hill stood black and still to the side, concealing half the sky from view. At its foot a big pond overgrown with lotus leaves reflected the bunch of feeble stars scattered across its surface, wrinkling from time to time when there was a fish coming up for air. What a beautiful autumn, Fu sighed with relish. To familiarise himself with the English class he was to teach tomorrow, Fu took out a piece of paper carrying all the names of his students and took a final look at it before he went to bed:

Bao Hongjun
Cen Zhengyi
Dang Jie
Hu Chenggeng

Jing Ying
Liu Ya
Ma Tian
Wei Hua
Xin Shen
Yang Guizi
Yu Hu
Zhao Feiyan
Zou Ganmei
Alexandra Sergeyevich Zhenya

By now, he was able to tell who was who by looking at the names alone, some of which caused him to wonder about their family backgrounds. Did Hongjun (Red Army) come from a family of old revolutionaries and did Zhengyi (Justice) come from a family with a legal background? You could sometimes tell the age of a person from their name. Take Ganmei (Expelling the Americans), who must have been named in the early 1950s during the Korean War. Others had an artistic twist, such as Yu Hu (Jade Kettle), which, by the sound of it, reminded him of a line from an ancient poem that thus ran, *yipian bingxin zai yuhu*, a piece of icy heart is in the jade kettle. Fu was trying to match the faces specifically with the names but found it hard, except for a few he had already taken note of. His memory was failing him as he was dog-tired after four classes in the morning and had spent a long time preparing for the next day. He turned off the light and fell asleep with a sense of expectation.

2

You are now faced with a most serious problem. You have not been able to write a single word for the last few days. You know that this whole English thing is for real as it did happen some twenty years ago. You knew everyone of them. Yet, unless you could outlive them all, you have to reinvent it all over again, different things, different people, different places. It is not hard to imagine a situation where real people come to you at the launch of the book and make claims about misrepresentation. Even if you change the whole thing, will they not pick up clues that may reveal something of themselves? Besides, student life at a university is not particularly interesting. It is being repeated on a grand scale year in and year out not only nationally but also internationally. Perhaps the only difference is that this university no longer exists and that the characters only live in this book and have no connections whatsoever with the real people and real things? As the rest of the world is having a holiday, you are sitting on the couch near the window, your iBook on your lap, your fingers on the keys, hitting them from time to time, trying to make connections to the past, a recent past that exists in your memory or imagination or both.

How are you going to structure the middle part of this novel around twenty or so people of an English class that takes four years to finish? You could approach it the way Jing once did in a novel about his final year before he finished his university degree in English. It was titled On the Eve of Graduation *and it was never published. Perhaps this novel writing is about the moment, the moment lived that will pass, the moment retrieved from memory or simply imagined.*

3

Jing was assigned a room with six others, Yang, Bao, Ma, Wei, Xin and Hu. When he arrived, panting, carrying his blue quilt tied into a fat tofu-shaped square, and a yellow and red mosquito net containing a brand-new washing basin, a gift from Ba, he found he was too late. All the best places were taken. Of the four bunk beds sandwiching two desks, joined end to end in the centre of the room, he had to be content with the upper bunk near the door. It was the last remaining bed. There was nothing he could do. He was to spend the next few semesters living near a door that constantly opened and closed onto a corridor ringing with the footsteps of the students from other classes, the noise they made calling out to each other or when singing to amuse themselves. When people living beside the window wanted to get in and out of their little spaces, Jing had to stand up from his seat or double up to let them pass, flattening himself against the desk. It was not something he was used to, after the usually deserted dormitory room in White Sand. But this new environment, consisting of books, school bags, classrooms, a school canteen, a library and so many new faces, promised a better world than the one he had just left behind. At least there are people to keep me company, Jing thought. He had finally managed to get into university and now, all Jing wanted to do was excel in academic studies. As it turned out, his roommates came from all over the country, Ma Tian from Taiyuan, Bao from Beijing, Yang from Guizhou, Wei from Shanghai and Xin Shen from Jiangsu.

At night, after the bell sounded three times to signal the

switching off of lights and they had washed, the students would all creep into their own separate beds and exchange information about themselves: who had achieved what scores in the entrance examination, what the long train journey was like and what some of them had learnt in middle school. Jing did not participate in these conversations but listened, eyes wide open in the dark, and would often think about his years spent in the driver's cabin. Out of sync with their concerns, he found it hard to even begin to tell them about his life. Suddenly, they all laughed. He sensed that their laughter was somehow directed at him. Bewildered, he asked, 'What's so funny?'

Through the window, he could see the lights shining from the windows of another building and he could smell this newly occupied building with its cement floor trodden by shoes from many provinces.

'Ah,' one voice said. 'Our truck driver has fallen asleep and thus missed the fun.'

'Don't call me "Truck Driver". Call me Jing,' he said. 'Or I'll have no truck with you.'

'Hey, what's that supposed to mean?' Wei asked, his Shanghai accent unmistakable.

'That means he'll have nothing to do with you,' Ma said. 'It's a good phrase to use.'

'All right then, we'll call you Jean,' a voice said. It sounded like Bao's, but Jing could not be sure as he was still not completely familiar with the locations of their bunks.

'Is that an English name or a French name?' someone asked.

'You mean Jean?' It was the know-all Ma. 'In English it is a woman's name but in French it is a man's name. However, in French, it sounds like Rang, not Jean. The English Jean sounds closest to the Chinese Jing.'

'How did you know all this?' someone from the lower bunk

near the window enquired.

'Well, I just did,' was Ma's proud voice.

All this conversation was conducted in Chinese with a smattering of English words, such as Jing and Jean. 'But you still did not tell me why you all laughed?' Jing insisted.

'Well,' someone explained. 'They laughed at my name Guizi because it sounds like another word for devils and then Yang Guizi sounds exactly like the English equivalent of "Foreign Devil". You know what I can do to you guys if you change my name like that?' Yang said.

'What can you do? Tell us,' they cried out in unison.

'I could turn all your names inside out with completely different meanings,' Yang threatened, followed by a loud chorus of challenge for him to do so. 'Well, I'll skip Ma, as he has already given us ample examples of how his name varies. From now on we can call Bao "the Red Army Man", Wei "the Chinaman" because Hua refers to China, and Xin "the Saint" because Shen sounds like Saint. As for Jing, let's stop calling him "Truck Driver" because his very reason for coming to university to study is to get rid of the truck. If we continue to call him a truck driver it will only succeed in getting him upset with memories of something he doesn't wish to remember. So, let's call him "Jean" or "Rang", as Ma suggested, shall we?'

Everyone agreed except Wei. He said, 'I don't think I like your Chinaman for a name. I remember my father telling me that it was a derogatory term used overseas to refer to the Chinese.'

'How come?' Bao asked.

'Yes, Wei is right,' a shrill voice from a lower bunk near the door confirmed. This was quite unexpected for up to that moment Xin, like Jing, had remained silent, more silent than Jing, not even making a response when Yang mentioned his name, but he could no longer stay quiet. 'It was a term very objectionable to the Overseas Chinese, particularly in Australia.'

Now it was their turn to be silent for no one could find anything to say about Australia; in fact, none of the students knew anything about that country. In the middle-school text on world history, Jing remembered, Australia was described as part of the British colonial empire. That was all. If he could go abroad, he would want to go to the United States of America, the top country in the world. His train of thought was interrupted by the offer of some additional information by Xin who said, 'I know because I have a relative in Australia.'

Xin's face grew more distinct in Jing's mind as he tried to remember what he looked like. To say he behaved like a girl was no exaggeration. He wore red pants! And he spoke in a soft or shrill voice depending on his mood swings. The way he looked at you, it was almost as if he could fall in love with you or something, making Jing uncomfortable when establishing eye contact with him. He even brought some wild Cape jasmine flowers back to the dormitory and put them in an empty ink bottle filled with tap water. Instantly, the room was full of a particular kind of fragrance that almost brought on Jing's asthma, which was why everyone except him praised Xin for making their room so comfortable with the flowers.

Jing also remembered that he had corrected Guizi when the latter mispronounced Shen as Xin. The character looks like Xin, a word meaning bitterness, but has a radical indicating grass over the bitterness, pronounced Shen, not Xin. After that, they all regarded Jing in a new light, not a vulgar driver but someone with a good knowledge of the Chinese language. Xin was particularly grateful. For the first time, there was a classmate who could pronounce his name correctly. When he threw a thankful look Jing's way, he saw Jing literally wince, for some reason. He felt warm towards him, this rough guy who used to be driving trucks around the country. It must have been a very exciting life for him. Why would he want to choose English if he had a truck to drive and go places? When he asked Jing that question on their way back from the canteen, Jing simply shrugged his shoulders.

'Why did *you* choose English then?' Jing asked.

'Well,' Xin said, looking a little coy and perhaps a little cute, too. 'I want to learn English for our motherland.'

'Come on.' Jing frowned and with his chopsticks quickly put a mouthful of rice to his lips to conceal his contempt.

Xin did not notice but continued, more seriously, 'I am learning it because I want to go abroad. I know this is not a very good thing to say but, well, never mind. When we know each other better I'll tell you more.'

It seemed that Xin had this habit of only speaking half of what was on his mind and he would always stop short of revealing what was below the tip of his thought iceberg. Why would he do that? Jing shook his head at the prospect of having to share a room with him for the next four years. On Xin's part, he also found Jing somewhat unfathomable, one who revealed little about his past and seemed to present a haughty façade towards people despite his obviously humble background. Yet the budding love in him for men and his innermost desire to ultimately become a woman attracted him to Jing, with his ugly but manly features and a mind that seemed to soar above his. On several occasions, Xin had suppressed his intense desire to call Jing 'Brother' as he suspected that this might displease him. Instead of using any endearments, he followed Jing everywhere, finding chances to talk to him, sitting next to him and asking to see Jing's composition piece, an amazing one that both excited and shamed him. How I wish I could write like *that*, he thought to himself.

It was a poem Jing had written in Chinese, titled, 'Who Am

I?' with six stanzas, the second of which went, 'sometimes I wake up to suddenly find my body covered in gaping bullet holes'.

Jing hardly ever noticed Xin. He had a feeling that this girl-like boy seemed to prefer his company because he enjoyed listening to him talking about his past experience as a truck driver but that's where his patience ended. He found him too lightweight, and his insistent questions about English grammar in class annoyed him. 'Teacher Fu, you said we could say "I'm going to do this or that", but what about "I'm going to go", can I say that? Does it sound strange to say that?' or 'What about a doctor who is called Mr not Dr someone? Is that a deliberate mistake or did that signify something?' or 'We can say "we have been doing something" but can we say "we have been being someone" if we want to say that because didn't you say "I am being funny"? And so "I have been being funny" would make a good instance of present perfect continuous?' until Mr Fu cut him short and said, perhaps a little too sternly, 'Classmate Xin, will you just forget about the grammar for the moment? We'll get there when we do. Right now all you need to grasp is the idea of "going to" as an indication of what you intend to do. Okay?'

This sort of obsession with English grammar sickened Jing to the point of nausea. In learning Chinese, he remembered, he never read any grammar books. He had never encountered any grammatical problems. He could say anything he liked. He could say, '*Ni chuqu ma?*' You are going out? or '*Chuqu ma ni?*' Going out, you? Only yesterday, while strolling by the lakeside, he overheard a woman saying to her man, *'Zenmehuishiya, ni?'* What's the matter, you? With a 'with' inserted in the sentence, it would be a perfect example of English spoken in Chinese. Perhaps languages could express the same things in the same way? He was interested in finding out more through literature, although he was aware that grammar held the key to the mastery of the language itself. To get ahead academically, he wanted to find someone who was not only his match but was better than him. *Jiejiao xu shengji, siwo buru wu*. His eyes fell on Ma who seemed to excel in both written and spoken English and had no difficulty understanding the English he heard on radio stations such as the BBC and Voice of America (VOA). While Jing could only understand thirty per cent of what was broadcast in English on Radio Beijing, Ma did not even tune in to that. For this, Jing envied him. He wanted to catch up fast and the only way he could do that was to follow in the footsteps of this guy who stood over 1.85 metres but, surprisingly, wasn't good at any sports, or even interested.

At first, Jing found it hard to draw him out. Ma wouldn't say much, his eyes fixed on a book he was holding in his hand, its pages heavily thumbed. Jing thought he might still be resentful of his comment in class on the word 'sweet', for already there were classmates who called him 'Sweety' behind his back. When he explained that he didn't really mean it, Ma said he had forgotten all about it. Then he said he remembered something and made a comment that Jing liked. He said, 'The lines you quoted were quite nice.'

'You think?' Jing asked.

But Ma's thoughts had gone back to his book, his face sunken into nonrecognition, untouched by the outside happenings, not even by this eager classmate. Jing resented this and decided not to tell him how he came upon the poem and what it was all about. Obviously, Ma had no interest in it. He said it only because he couldn't find anything better to say or perhaps he said it to stop him from bothering him with any more questions. How unlike the factory this university situation was! In the factory, Jing remembered fondly, people were infinitely more direct, more forthright, although they were sometimes a little uncouth.

Jing got a trifle agitated with the thought. He got up, took his school bag and, without saying goodbye, shut the door behind him with a loud thump.

Over the next few days, he tried to avoid speaking to Ma; he did not even look his way. Meanwhile, he tolerated Xin's attempts to ask him out for an after-dinner stroll by the lake, where he enjoyed the scenery more than his chat. Xin told him that he was from a remote mountain village in Zhejiang. As his parents died early, he was adopted by an aunt in Nanjing and was brought up like a girl. After graduating from middle school, the only thing he ever wanted to do was become a woman. Xin said all this in confidence, warning Jing against telling anyone, but talking in a brisk manner as if he didn't take it too seriously; he spoke like he was telling him a joke. Jing listened in silence, without making a comment.

Then he said, 'I don't really think it's a bad idea, to be honest. I have a cousin who is more like a woman than a man.'

He stopped short of telling him about the masturbating adventures he had had with Cong; it was too early for him to share that secret with him. His understanding was so encouraging that Xin suggested they come out every afternoon to practise their spoken English. Despite the misgivings he had about Xin's oral English skills, Jing agreed, still not having got over the imaginary hurt inflicted on him by Ma.

However, what happened subsequently drew the unlikely two together. Not long after they were enrolled at the university, students were issued with a student card bearing their names, gender and class numbers, which they could use to borrow books from the library and prove their identity when requested. On the back of the cards were ten rules that the university stipulated for the students, what Liu Ya, a girl from Sichuan, called the Ten Chinese Commandments. When Jing had a glance at them, walking back from the class with a group including Ma and Xin, he could not help but laugh out loud.

'What's so funny?' Ma asked.

'Well,' Jing began. 'Didn't you notice the irrelevance of some of these rules?'

'But political instructor said that we were required to recite them because we would be tested in one of those political examinations,' Ma said.

'I can't possibly recite them, so boring. Maybe you can?' Jing said this provocatively but Ma ignored it, saying, 'If we must, we must. There's nothing you can do about it; it's just a rule.'

Jing thought for a while. An idea came to him. 'How about we try something more interesting?' he proposed. 'Since it's so hard to remember any of these rules, can I suggest we go about it in a different way?'

'What do you mean?' Ma said.

'I mean we can translate the whole thing into English and by so doing we may remember some of them or possibly even all of them.'

'Oh, you can't do that,' Xin said. 'That sounds silly.'

'No, that's not a bad idea, actually, not bad at all,' Ma said, nodding his head approvingly, the first time Jing had seen him impressed with a suggestion by anyone. The proud bastard, he cursed inwardly.

'How would you translate this?' At *wanzixi*, evening time for self-studies, Jing asked Ma, pointing his finger at one of the commandments, which says in Chinese, *buxu tan lian'ai*.

'That's a hard one, I agree,' Ma nodded his head and said. 'It does not make sense in English. I mean *tan lian'ai*, what's this?' He thought for a moment, rolled his eyes, threw up his hands and said, 'Just a minute. Let me check my dictionary. Well, they do have an entry here that says *tan lian'ai* means "be in love" or "have a love affair".'

'But that's not right because *tan* in Chinese means "talk" and *lian'ai* in Chinese means "love". So the three characters actually mean "talk love" and the sentence, if directly translated, means "don't talk love".'

'I know, I know,' Ma conceded. 'But that's how language works because it works by not making sense, I mean by not making logical sense, by not making book sense. I mean we Chinese greet each other with *"ni chile ma"*? Can we greet in English the same way with "have you eaten?" Can they, I mean?'

'Perhaps eating is not so important to the English or English-speaking people, what do you think?'

'According to my father, that seems to be the case. When he studied in the USA, he found their way of eating austere.'

'Austere? You mean boring?'

'More along the line of suffering or torturing. Let me check my dictionary again.'

'But why is it that whatever works in English is acceptable in Chinese, not the other way round? Why can't they greet each other our way? I mean what's wrong with our saying "Have you eaten?"'

'Well, that beats me,' Ma said, putting his index finger on the definition of the word "austere", as if afraid that it might escape. 'I suppose it's only wrong when you say it in the wrong places, like in a toilet. If you come out of a toilet, someone greets you with a "have you eaten?", that of course is embarrassing. Otherwise, I don't really see any problems with our way of greeting, no.'

'To come back to this talking love business. The commandment obviously asks us not to talk love, which by your definition …'

'Not by my definition,' Ma corrected Jing. 'But by the

dictionary's, or to be more exact, by the publisher's, in this instance, Beijing Foreign Languages Institute.'

'Never mind by whom. What I meant was that if we render a direct translation, it would then become something like "Don't talk love". Would that be wrong?'

'Well, I guess, if someone says *"ni chile ma?"* to you in Chinese, you would translate it into English as "how are you?" And that's not even funny because it makes sense. Similarly, in this instance, when you say in Chinese "don't talk love", you actually mean in English "don't have girlfriends" or boyfriends if you are a girl.'

'Are you saying direct translations will never work?'

'Or, perhaps more appropriately, you could render it as "Thou shalt not talk love!" or "Thou shalt not maintain a loving relationship with anyone while studying in the university!" How's that sound?'

'What do you mean by this "Zhao Xiao"? I don't understand,' puzzled, Jing looked across the table at Ma who, true to his name, snorted sonorously, sending forth a hot bad breath mixed with garlic, nearly choking him.

'It's from the Bible where the Ten Commandments come from, don't you even know that?' Ma was surprised, quietly pleased with himself for possessing more biblical knowledge.

'But why "Zhao Xiao"?'

'It's not Zhao Xiao but Thou Shalt, an ancient way of saying "You shall".'

'I see.' Mortified, Jing said no more. He would have to go to the library the next day to check it out. He would not let Ma know. There was an urgent sense of competition building, even though he was only vaguely aware of it. As for Ma, he knew nothing about what was going on behind Jing's unattractive white face, save for a pair of intensely penetrating eyes.

4
—

One night at the Mid-Autumn Festival, the girls were having a party of their own on the dormitory rooftop. It was not exactly a party as no one organised it. As the moon rose in the east, people came out of their tiny dormitory rooms to have a look. Zhenya came out first. As soon as she saw the scarlet moon, she cried out, 'Wow, what a red moon!' It was red except for some dark spots and it looked not round but like the flattened dough for dumplings she used to make at home. With its rise, the atmosphere seemed to become quieter and cooler. When other girls came up in twos and threes, they saw Zhenya's silhouette against the brightening moon, totally dark now except for the edges, which were bathed in silver.

'You look so beautiful,' Liu Ya said, the Sichuan girl who had just finished middle school and for the first time in her life was living away from home.

'Come here, Liu Ya,' Zhenya held out her hand and pulled her to her side. The two stood there together, like two sisters, watching the moon, forming two dark lovely figures against its brightness. Liu Ya was shorter and more slender than Zhenya, but Zhenya already had more of a womanly figure; both were about the same age.

'Do you miss your home?' Zhenya asked.

'Very much,' Liu said.

There was a remote look in her eyes as they moved from the moon back to Zhenya's face, a face that was distinctly Chinese but bore subtle traces of Russian lineage. 'If I were home now, I would be eating moon cakes and drinking jasmine tea and eating hot food as well.'

'Are you from Hunan?' Zhenya enquired.

'No, Sichuan,' Liu said.

'Ah, Tianfu Zhiguo (Country of Heavens)! Is the food really hot there?'

'Depending on how you mean by "hot",' Liu said. She looked away to the moon again, which had now climbed a little higher in the sky, becoming smaller in size but brighter. In a little while, it would be cleansed of the various colours that clothed it, becoming a piece of pure jade bathing the world in its clean silvery light.

'Where in Sichuan?'

'I like the moon,' Liu did not seem to hear the question.

'How do you find the school here?' Zhenya changed the subject skillfully.

'Not too bad,' Liu said. 'But I don't like the way the classes are conducted.'

'Too strict, you mean?'

'No, it's not that. I think it's too simplistic.'

'You mean the textbook?'

'Yah,' Liu said, reciting in a mocking tone a passage they had learnt that week. 'How time flies! This is my seventh week in college and life is very interesting. There are so many things to learn …'

'Such as "the history of Chinese communism",' Zhenya followed on in her thick Northern-accented English, making Liu Ya laugh despite herself. She made a comment that surprised even herself. 'Interesting, I suppose, for the suffocating heat, the blood-sucking mosquitoes, the lack of variety of food in the canteen and anything to do with the West.'

'I think we need to have our teachers replaced by foreign teachers,' Liu said.

'We agree.' Some other female students who were also enjoying the moonlight overheard this and came over. They were Yu Hu, Zhao Feiyan and Zou Ganmei, aged between eighteen and twenty-six. Their formidable presence would make any shy male classmates uncomfortable. Ma and Jing usually did not even greet their female counterparts, to say nothing of speaking to them, a feudalistic legacy that men their age found hard to dispose of. After their initial difficulties settling in, these girls were now more in their element than ever, with no parents keeping a watch over them and in a space entirely their own where men were not allowed. On this night some of them even wore just their shorts and bras, each holding a fan to expel the deadly mosquitoes hidden in the grass by the lakeside and in the hills. Zou Ganmei, who had changed her actual name from Ganmei (Expelling the Americans) to Ganmei (Dare to be beautiful), was the oldest and for this reason was accorded the title Dajie (Big Sister). Her command of English was not among the best, but she had practical sense and experience in dealing with people as she had worked as a school administrator in a Tianjin primary school. In her own words she had escaped 'the stifling environment' by gaining admission to a university. Basically content with her lot, she tried to act the pacifist.

'I think these things will come to us eventually if we are patient enough,' she began. 'Besides, I can't see anything wrong with the Xu Guozhang textbook, which is intended to give us a solid foundation in the language. Don't you think?' She directed her question to Zhao Feiyan, the pretty one who had her hair partly permed, an act that few girl students even dared to think of in their freshmen days. She didn't seem to be interested in this sort of conversation, though. In fact, her thoughts were far away, and, affected by the moonlight, she was lost in an amorous mood, remembering snatches of her past experience with her man who had recently gone overseas to the USA.

'See?' Ganmei whispered to Yu Hu, who was a girl of few words from Gansu. 'She is missing *ta*!'

The girls burst into hilarious laughter, except Qi who didn't quite understand whether this *ta* stood for 'him' or 'her'. Not to be outdone, she laughed the loudest until Zhao said, 'What are you laughing about?'

Qi stopped as soon as her eye caught the glaring stare from Zhao, but Ganmei intervened, saying, 'Please don't, Feiyan! Our little sister only laughed with us, not at you. And you look gorgeous tonight with your long silk dress and black leather sandals. The shape of the heel is perfect. Isn't that right?' She kept the forum open with this deliberate question, expecting everyone to agree, but what came next was quite unexpected from Liu Ya. She said, 'I'd better go back to my room to do some more study.'

With that, the rest of the crowd followed suit, leaving Feiyan alone under the smaller but brighter moon, trembling slightly with a sense of humiliation, gradually replaced by a deepening sense of gloom that stayed with her for the rest of the night. She did not like the place. She liked it even less now. What was there for her to look forward to except a long, arduous road paved with hard labour that they called English? These bookworms treated the language as if it were their God, poring over their textbook like it was the Bible. What was the point? It was a language that people overseas used daily for a living. As long as she could speak it and write it like any normal person, she would be fine. There was no need to work so hard that she become a scholar or something. Philip, her lover, went to San Francisco with minimal language skills and managed to live there. He told her over the phone that there were people in their eighties who had lived there all their lives without speaking a word of English.

For Feiyan, life should be fun, pleasure and love with as little work as possible. Her attitude set her apart from the rest of the class, though this was not because of anything special in her family background or her upbringing, of which she never spoke. She did not like books. A woman ages faster if she reads them, she believed. What attracted her was not the cultivation of the mind but that of the body, much like a bodybuilder's view, but coming from a different motivation. She was convinced that her purpose in this life was not to live it like a working animal but to love it like a bee, a beautiful flying bee, sucking the nectar wherever it was available, loving herself, loving people who would in turn love her. And again the nursery rhyme returned to her memory: 'Row, row, row your boat, gently down the stream, merrily, merrily, merrily, merrily, life is but a dream.' Without realising it, she hummed the tune, searching for her own image in the moon, which she regarded as a mirror. Instead of her own face, she saw someone else's and, as if suddenly remembering herself, she turned her head around, in time to catch a glimpse of a figure disappearing downstairs outside the building. It looked like one of the students from her own class but she could not remember his name.

Already she noticed her male admirers on campus stealing furtive glances at her on her way to the school canteen or walking down the stairs or in the library, just about anywhere, their eyes on her flowery blouse, her black skirt and her several pairs of leather shoes, heeled or otherwise, all bought from Shanghai. It was like being in a cartoon where a girl's skirt was decorated with men's eyes, drilling the skirt with many eye-shaped holes. As long as these were eyes, it didn't bother her. They wouldn't hurt but could only add to her pride and sense of self-satisfaction. Although she would never openly show it, you could see her hold her head higher and walk even more confidently than someone who had just got a grade of 100 per cent in a term examination. If there was anything that made her proud of herself, it was not her academic results, sixty-five per cent on average, but the number of admiring glances thrown her way and head turns that she never failed to draw. From that alone, she could easily get a rating of ninety-five per cent. It wasn't long before she was known among her male admirers, in and outside her class, as 'the One'.

5

After a few weeks on campus, Jing began to know his classmates a little better, particularly those he shared his dormitory room with, such as Ma, Bao, Xin and Dang. He had thought of Dang as someone unapproachable because of the connotation of his surname, which literally meant 'the Party', and also because of his unsmiling, sometimes even sad, face until one day when Dang revealed that all he wanted to do was become a 'useless person'. Jing found this remark drawing him irresistibly closer to Dang in a way that he couldn't explain. He would chat with Dang over lunch and would sometimes ask him out for a walk by the lake. Dang rarely seemed keen on going out with him, as he was always busy reading and as soon as he finished his classes he would go to the library and spend many hours there.

'What are you reading?' Jing asked.

'Anything and everything,' Dang responded.

'Such as?' Curious, Jing persisted.

'Well, if I tell you, you'd lose interest,' Dang said.

'Come on,' Jing got impatient and said. 'Tell me what it is that you read?'

'Some herbal stuff. Some *fengshui* stuff,' Dang said.

'Why is that?' Jing was mystified.

'As I said,' Dang said. 'You wouldn't be interested.'

'I thought you said you would one day become a scholar or something.' Jing reminded him of a study session in which classmates were encouraged to reveal what plans they had for the future.

'Well, that's not exactly what I said. I said I did not want to be anything. And I said that, if possible, I would rather spend my life in a library sorting out books and reading books than anything else. As a matter of fact, I said I would prefer to be a useless person.'

'It's very bold of you to say so,' Jing admired.

'No,' Dang said. 'You probably thought I said that to attract attention. I mean why would I do that? Did you know I spent some years with my *shifu* collecting and gathering herbs in the big mountains in Southwest China?'

'No, actually,' Jing opened his eyes. The short, thin man walking beside him suddenly revealed something unexpected, but he looked directly ahead, so lost in the memory of some past events, long gone, that he seemed remote and his words directed more towards someone in his reverie than the person beside him asking him the question.

'It's all *yincha yangcuo*,' Dang began, 'that I got into this area learning English whereas I could well have entered into a medical college to practise traditional Chinese medicine or some such thing, you know.'

'Maybe it's God's will that you learn English so that in some not so distant future when you go overseas you will be able to cure the sick and the diseased in the West with the skills you master here, don't you think?'

'A good guess. Many years ago before the Liberation my father saved a missionary from America with a kind of herb when the man nearly died of a snake bite,' Dang recalled, 'although I have never even dared to think as you suggested. I mean what about yourself? We didn't get to hear what you had to say last time.'

'I don't really know,' Jing said. 'Call me the One Who Does Not Know. That's really what I am. I want to do all sorts of things but I find I am not able to do anything. Once I am stuck in something I am doing, I tend to turn my attention elsewhere.

Like this English we are currently studying. For some reason, I find the more I learn it the less attractive it becomes. In fact, it sort of drives me back to Chinese. I mean I haven't even mastered my own language and literature, and here I am, going for a degree in English and American literature. That's weird, isn't it?'

'What's wrong? What are you scared of? Why do you have to be so greedy that you have to master two languages and two literatures? Don't you think life is already too complicated and that it should be made simpler instead? Why, isn't this the whole point of using the simplest thing, the herb, to cure the most complicated diseases such as cancer and diabetes?'

Dang's volley of questions delivered at such a rapid pace did not please Jing. On the contrary, he fell into a silence that lasted the whole evening, at the end of which he remembered what Dang had said in Chinese – *yincha yangcuo* – and wondered to himself if he could express the meaning in English. He took out his dictionary and found the answer on page 826, where he realised that the correct expression should actually be *yincuo yangcha,* meaning 'a mistake or error made due to a strange combination of circumstances'. This was hardly the definition Jing expected to find. 'Yin' and 'yang', he knew, were a pair of concepts that formed the Chinese world view but did not make much sense in English. 'Cuo' and 'cha' mean mistakes and errors and, in a direct translation, this expression could be rendered as 'yin mistakes and yang errors'. He smiled at his own silliness for coming up with this scarcely understandable expression but was thrilled with its originality. What would a foreigner think of this, he wondered. Ma, sitting across the desk from him, asked what he was smiling at. He told him. Ma said that for this sort of expression direct translations would never work as there was a rule governing it, which, again in Chinese, was *yueding sucheng,* like the transliteration of Paris in Chinese as 'Bali'. It did not sound like Paris, although it had long been accepted as part of the Chinese language. You simply can't redo it or undo it.

Unconvinced, Jing went to bed, going through all the words to do with 'yin', *yin feng, yin ying, yin leng, yin an, yin si, yin mou, yin xian, yin hun, yin mai, yin zai, yin jian*, all related to women, the yin, and all considered bad. Hence *yin* wind, *yin* shadows, *yin* cold, *yin* darkness, *yin* privacy, *yin* conspiracy, *yin* danger, *yin* soul, *yin* clouds, *yin* thief, *yin* world. Is the Chinese culture also *yin* because it has a long history? If not, why did the ancient Chinese poets write about the moon all the time instead of the sun, the *yang*? Why did they only write about the rivers and lakes but never about the ocean? Jing remembered coming across an English poet's reference to 'heaven, earth and sea'[2], whereas sea was a word never seen in classical Chinese poetry. Are there cultures out there that are only concerned with the yang as opposed to the yin? Is English as bad? Jing could only remember an English word, history, which seemed to suggest that it was a man's story, not a woman's. His memory became blurred as sleep pervaded his senses. He thought he fell off a cliff into the pond behind the hill.

The next morning it was time to make another oral presentation. A well-prepared Jing strode to the platform in front of the blackboard, his heavy footsteps knocking on the wooden floor, making a clumsy and rude noise that caused the girls to giggle. This pleased him because in a curious kind of way he enjoyed being found funny by the girls. He whipped out the paper on which he had written his translation of the Ten

---

2 *Sir Walter Raleigh, the Poems, with other Verse from the Court of Elizabeth I*, selected and edited by Martin Dodsworth, Everyman Paperbacks, J.M. Dent, 1999, p. 59.

Commandments and began to read:

'First, we should passionately love the Party, passionately love the people, passionately love the socialist motherland and obey the order of assignment.'

Amid rising laughter, he continued.

'Secondly, we must seriously study Marxism-Leninism and Mao Zedong Thought, gradually acquire the proletarian viewpoints of class, of labour, of mass and of dialectical materialism.'

More laughter followed as the class became increasingly hysterical listening to the unfamiliarity of something that was so familiar. Mr Fu watched and frowned. When Jing got to Rule Five and said, 'We must pay attention to hygiene, do not smoke, do not drink heavily, do not spit everywhere, do not litter with melon skin and scraps of paper, and do not throw rubbish around', Mr Fu cut him short and said, 'Well, I am afraid your time is up.'

'No, I have not covered the whole thing yet,' Jing protested. Excited beyond control, he continued headlong, 'Pay respects to the teachers and the elderly; be united with classmates; be civil; be polite; treat people amicably; do not wax abusive; do not fight and …'

'Sorry,' Mr Fu said resolutely. 'But we must stop here for other students to have a chance to make their own presentations.'

At the end of the session, Mr Fu summed up the presentations briefly, then shifting his focus to Jing's translation, spoke critically, 'There are a number of things I would like to point out in regard to Classmate Jing Ying's presentation, which was generally good, although the way it was presented did not seem serious enough under the circumstances. Grammatically, I must say that there is much room for improvement. For example, in Chinese we tend to repeat certain words and expressions whereas in English this could be made simpler, like in Rule One where the words "passionately love" need to be used only once. Also, "pay respects to" should be "pay our respects to" because the phrase is "pay one's respects to". There are certain Chinese expressions that can hardly be translated into English such as *'fucong fenpei'*, which, rendered by Jing as "obey the order of assignment", could be improved upon as "be willing to accept whatever jobs the organisation assigns one to do". As for "do not wax abusive", the word "wax" is not properly used. You could say "wax lyrical" but not "wax abusive".'

But for Rule Six, Jing would have got up to face the teacher and openly protest. There did not seem to be any appreciation of his efforts, which he thought would be considered a good way to learn English. And he took particular exception to Mr Fu's suggestion that his intention was not serious enough to warrant any praise. People did laugh, but it was only because they were having so much fun learning the language. What if there was a foreign teacher, someone from the USA or Canada? How would they react to this? Would they understand and appreciate what he did? Forty-five minutes went past without Jing learning anything, as his mind was preoccupied with these thoughts, staring blankly at Chairman Mao's motto on the wall: *haohao xuexi, tiantian xiangshang*! He was to find out years later that someone had done a grotesque literal translation of it as 'good good study, day day up'! On that day, in that class, he did not do anything; he had always wondered what it meant in English but he had never attempted a translation.

6

You found this article that criticised China for following the West and it attacked many Chinese writers for going West to seek a better life. All it was really saying was that the writer of the article had not achieved the sucesss he deserved but you remembered what a jazz musician said when you watched a television program many months ago. He said that there was nothing that he enjoyed doing better than to please the white man. You think that was Louis Armstrong, although you can't be sure but the remark made a deep impression on you. If the writer of the article complained that those Chinese writers, poets and novelists, gone overseas, did not write for their own fellow countrymen but catered to a foreign market as if it were a crime, it was only because he knew nothing about what it felt like living in a foreign country as a writer of a different ethnicity. You begin to form the view of this world in which everything is perfectly arranged, the East and the West, the yin and the yang, the night and the day, the real and its shadow. Then you read about this novel winning a prize, whose author has never been to China and will never go there, although the book is set entirely there. Inwardly, you laughed. That is the West. You just can't help it. That is what they want to see of China: the imaginary China, the China in their imagination, the imagination that they value over everything else. Fine. They imagine China and the Chinese realise them. You don't think your description gets there. What you want to mean is that they take an imaginary approach to China whereas the Chinese take a realistic approach to the West. Something that has remained mysterious to you thus far seems to have been resolved.

7

For many months, Jing did not masturbate. He was too busy learning English to do that. The girls in his class were not attractive enough for him to fantasise about. Besides, they were too close for masturbatory comfort. Some of his classmates also shared the view that all the attractive ones seemed to be in the other classes or even from other universities, such as Wuhan University, which was not far away. During his after-dinner strolls, Jing would often walk there and back. It took him about an hour but it was always pleasant as there were many things to see. On one side of the road was the lake and on the other side was the continuous undulation of the Mill Hill mountain range, covered in thick wood, where, towards the evening, he could hear wild doves cooing from the invisible depths of the hillside trees. The falling sun would set the lake waters ablaze with fire, throwing down a long wide shaft of myriad colours and hues. The air was scented with wild flowers mixed with the smell of the lake, a kind of raw fish, and memories of the recently dead. It was said that the lake would customarily claim a couple of lives per year. In the distance was the university hidden among dense foliage with the roofs of its buildings half visible, most conspicuously a column of black smoke twisting every other way above the old library at the top of Luojia Hill. It took Jing quite some time to work out that the smoke was formed by millions of mosquitoes flying together towards the sky.

Sometimes Jing would go out with Xin or Ma but mostly he preferred to be alone, walking with a book in his hand, a Shelley or Keats in Chinese translation, sitting on the concrete in one of the abandoned water-side swimming pools or picking his way through the grassy path along the edge of the water. University life had helped him think, more than ever before, about the meaning of life, why he was here and where he wanted to go from here. As his confidence grew, the fear that his intellect had somehow been dulled by years spent on the road, stuck in a driver's seat and confined to a tiny cabin, had finally gone. The beautiful environment in which he lived, by the lake at the foot of a hill, was conducive to the blossoming of creative energy long buried within him. At the same time it drew him more into himself with each passing day, so that by the first winter since his enrolment he found himself alone, again, without any friends to speak of. It was not that he didn't have anything to communicate with the others; it was more a problem with himself. He saw that his classmates were working hard, in fact, so hard that no one could spare time for afternoon activities. They all preferred to stay in their overcrowded bedroom-study poring over their textbooks, himself included.

Unlike Ma, who always forged ahead before everyone else, Jing was working hard, and hating it at the same time. He didn't understand why one should work so hard to catch up. Ultimately, what was the point in learning a language that would eventually land you overseas, or get you a job in your own country that connected you with a foreign world for the rest of your life? Jing was not entirely sure what he was going to do. One thing was certain, though, he would never entertain the idea of going overseas. For some reason, he found the idea completely objectionable, even traitorous. Learning English, then becoming English? That was ridiculous. He hadn't even mastered Chinese, his own language. Learning English made him even more aware of his own cultural and literary heritage and, consequently, more determined to claim it back. There were Chinese writers born many thousands of years earlier than Shakespeare that demanded his attention. He wanted to understand both literatures, not just one. Right now he was keen on Chinese literature, particularly that of the early 1900s, which was easily accessed from the library and offered him an escape from his dreary English study.

Despite his congenial surroundings on and off campus, Jing found many things not so congenial, such as politics, a compulsory subject for everyone. He found his memory fading against page after page of written material about the history of the Chinese Communist Party and its political struggle with all of its enemies. As the end-of-term examinations drew near, politics was the one examination that worried him most. His entrance examination in this subject had gained him a mere score of sixty something. Ever since he had developed an abhorrence of political jargon, whose only function seemed designed to defeat his memory and make him impotent. This he knew from experience. At the approach of a political examination, Jing would become restless. He would eat little and became constipated as a result of over-worrying about his poor memory. Even when cramming, he could never remember the political significance, say, of the Zunyi Conference. The most notable result of this push for political excellence was his loss of sexual drive. One night, after many hours reviewing the political material for his examination, Jing was dismayed to find that he couldn't get erect, however hard he tried. It wasn't till the next morning when he found the overnight reservoiring of his urine had brought him to full attention that his doubts about his masculine abilities were temporarily dispelled.

No one else in his class seemed to mind politics in the least. They simply took it for granted, each one of them reciting the texts parrot-like from cover to cover. With his exceptional memory, Ma could recite his English textbook from beginning to end and he applied the same ability to the Party's history, at which Jing gasped with admiration, envy and a secret sense of disgust. Jing found it hard to remember even the new English words they had learnt, to say nothing of the words and expressions as well as the concepts that repulsed him in the first place. Questions such as: 'What is the difference between metaphysical idealism and dialectical idealism?' 'What is the core of the Party's ideological line, everything starting from reality, theory combined with reality, seeking truth from facts or verifying and developing truth in the practice?' Usually, after a night's sleep, Jing would forget everything he had memorised the previous day, proving it to be a complete waste of his time, while Ma and the others progressed steadily, ready for any twisted examination questioning. Amazed by Ma's ability to deal with such absurdities and by the others' nonchalant willingness to accept something he found so questionable, Jing said to Mr Miao, the political instructor one day:

'Can we do the exam a little differently?'

'How do you mean?' Mr Miao's eyes were so small that there were only two slits where the upper and lower eyelids met.

'I mean can we do it like, like poetry?'

'I don't understand you,' Mr Miao said. His army uniform, though bleached by too much washing, was neat.

'I mean can I write my answers in the form of poetical lines?'

'No, you can't,' Miao said, the smile fading from his tiny-eyed face. 'It's meant to be serious. If you approach it with poetry, it's intention is to be funny and, as a result, will be treated as inconsequential and deemed unacceptable.'

Jing told Ma of his displeasure and Ma said Mr Miao was right, albeit admitting that using poetry was an interesting concept. Jing also knew that Ma was sensible enough not to antagonise the instructor. Jing then told Xin and Dang of his idea but both of them laughed at his absurd request, dismissing it as a joke. When everyone was getting ready for the final political examination Jing was still seen walking around the campus with books by Byron and Wordsworth; he simply could not cram anything political into a head, designed, it seemed, exclusively for the entertainment of poetry. He did not prepare until the eve of the examination, when he spent the whole night pressing every single detail into his head until he felt like an idiot, a tape recorder, wooden with lack of sleep, mechanical because of the drilling and totally exhausted. He managed to get another score of sixty.

On the love front, there wasn't any progress, either. Since his last letter, he hadn't heard back from Chenfang. She disappeared like a deleted text. More and more, he turned his attention to the girls in his own class, in particular Zhao and Zhenya. It was strange that their names shared Z as if there was some sort of connection. Zhao came from Shanghai, as Jing had learnt from her oral presentation, whereas Zhenya came from a Russian background, which he'd overheard from the boys' bedtime gossip. One of them, Yang Guizi, or the Foreign Devil as his nickname went, was good at gathering private information from the grapevine. He seemed to know everything about everyone, boy or girl, although he would never reveal the source of his information, giving the impression that part of it may have been a product of his imagination, for example, Zhao's affair with a foreigner. How did he know about that? It was whispered that Yang came from a military background and his father had worked in the Intelligence Department, although he presented no evidence of this. He dressed informally and dealt with people in a casual way. In fact, his attitude towards politics was the most casual that Jing had ever known. He simply did not bother. While everyone else was up to their ears in heavy-going exam questions, he was out on the field playing basketball or volleyball with friends he'd made from the Physics and International Relations Study departments.

It was a mystery how Yang ever managed to pass his politics exam. Jing failed to notice that Yang had secretly made a deal with Ma to sit next to him so that he could copy his answers by throwing secretive sidelong glances Ma's way. As Yang boasted, if he could get sixty percent in every subject, he would be happy and he would most often get what he wanted, sometimes sixty and at other times sixty-one or two but most of the times just sixty. As Mr Fu read out the results, Yang sat back, reclining on his chair, rocking back and forth as if it was an easy chair. Its legs making a creaking, scratching noise, causing the heads of some girls to turn his way, with him basking in the sunshine of the surprise he had elicited from them. When sixty was read out along with his name, he just shrugged his shoulders and whispered to his neighbour, usually Ma but sometimes Jing, 'See, I've passed again.' As he said this, he chuckled quietly to himself.

Jing was not so much interested in Zhao as in Zhenya, for he saw in Zhenya something he liked, a kind of balance, medium height, fair skin but not so fair; she could be compared with a Westerner, plump but not fat. Actually, it was not just that. There was something else, something so fleeting that it caught his attention and left a lingering impression. It was, he remembered, at one of the numerous school meetings about fighting against bourgeois spiritual pollution that he happened to meet her as she came out of the toilet. The second their eyes locked, she looked down at her feet, her face flushed a deep red. This and the smell of sweat and something strangely exciting that emanated from her body aroused him. He could not resist a second look, but she had gone, leaving him looking at the outline of her bra straps and his penis flying up in spite of himself. He shut himself in the toilet and masturbated furiously. The pungent lingering smell from her flesh commingled with the stacks of shit in the toilet so intoxicating he instantly came, shooting spasms of semen five or six times into the piles of human excrement saturated in the yellow urine. He had missed much of the talk on spiritual pollution but what he had gained in the toilet made him feel wild with elation.

8

As soon as you lay down on the grass in the afternoon sun you realised that you were not an Australian. When your body first hit the ground, you felt kind of nice as your vision was level with the top of the short crowned grass that stood brownish in wave after wave rolling from side to side until the edge of the park. You lay on your right side, with your eyes closed, feeling the heat of the sun on the left side of your face, only for a fleeting second, for a sensation soon crept up on you that someone was stealing from behind you with a club in hand. You raised yourself up with one elbow and turned round to see acres of the yellowish grass spreading out with not a single person in it and trees standing mostly alone, wind soughing through the leaves, fallen gum leaves everywhere. You lay down again, this time on your back, remembering a common sight you had seen: a total stranger sleeping in the grass face down or face up, eyes closed, acting as if no one else existed even if there were a dozen people around the place, some having a quiet lunch and others sitting together, chatting. But you felt unsafe again and involuntarily opened your eyes to check that there was not someone stalking you. Finally, you had to get up and walk home, the only safe way you knew how. You wondered why. Was it an inbuilt distrust in you that made you fearful of strangers once outside your own home? But why in a park in the open with no one in sight? Was it the Chineseness in you that made you so doubtful, so suspecting, and thus so un-Australian? It was kind of intriguing, really, that you could be so lacking in confidence in a situation that most Australians would have no qualms about, like the guy you saw this morning. He was lying half naked on the grass, exposing his chest and chest hair to the *unrelenting summer sun that tinted his skin the colour of a cooked lobster. There were people around him everywhere but he went on lying there as if it were his bed, his eyes closed against everything, the sun, the pedestrians, the grass-sitters.*

9

Zhenya saw little that was attractive in Jing, except perhaps his funny and awkward way of answering the teacher's questions in class, sometimes by simply posing a question in response to a question. This had the unsurprising effect of upsetting the instructing lecturer, Associate Professor Luan, more than once. Having taught English grammar all his life except when he was removed to the country for re-education during the Cultural Revolution, Professor Luan was meticulous in his approach to the subject. His personal Bible was *Zhang Daozhen's English Grammar,* which he would bring to each of his teaching sessions and consult at each recess, his eyes peering over his glasses, looking quite impressive despite his slight build and a limp that accompanied his walk, reputedly inflicted on him when he was beaten up by the Red Guards about a decade ago.

As soon as Professor Luan walked into the classroom, Ma, the class monitor, would call out, 'Stand up!' followed by the noise of feet shuffling, chairs scraping the floor and the uniformity of the whole class moving from a sitting position to a standing one, shouting in unison, 'Good morning, Professor Luan!' while Professor Luan, looking pleasantly surprised, would respond with a 'Good morning to you, too! Please sit down!' Unlike Mr Fu, who would always allow his students a chance to practise their spoken English, Professor Luan would start the day with 'Word Study', proceeding to the main body of the text and then lingering at the grammatical structure, his favorite topic. Zhenya dreaded his questions about the tenses as she would sometimes mix them up, not knowing whether to use a 'has been' or 'had been' in relation to an incident that happened in the past. In Chinese there was not such a clear-cut sense of the tenses between the past and the present. This question and answer time would normally last twenty minutes, swinging between the male students and the female students like a pendulum, one boy, then one girl, until everyone was asked a question or did a grammatical exercise. The girls showed more patience and tolerance as they would concentrate on every question, take copious notes and try to analyse the mistakes others made, fearful of their own tendency to make errors.

Boys were a different story. Apart from a few who listened, most would just make do, finding the lessons boring but staying on, not wanting to rock the boat. Ma, Xin and Jing sat at the back, the furthest away from the blackboard, heads bent over their books, Ma reading Noam Chomsky's *Studies on Semantics in Generative Grammar*, Xin staring blankly at a piece of paper, his pen at the ready, and Jing reading a copy of George Gissing's *Four Seasons*, a book that he happened to see at the library among a raft of other books donated by a Dr Someone from Canada. His interest was immediately aroused by the opening two sentences: 'For more than a week my pen has lain untouched. I have written nothing for seven whole days, not even a letter.' He had never read anything like that. So simple and yet so deeply moving. There was something that connected him to the author. Was this literature? Before his doubt was dissipated he had already taken hold of the old-looking, thin book, with a very simple drawing of a cluster of flowers on a creamy background, and had it processed at the front counter with his library card. It was while he was reading the first part of 'Autumn', where it goes 'How the mood for a book sometimes rushes upon one, either one knows not why, or in consequence, perhaps, of some most trifling suggestion' that he heard his own name mentioned, in a mild voice that was unmistakably Professor Luan's, which said, 'Classmate Jing, did you hear my question?'

He raised his head and saw half the class turning their heads back to gaze at him. Quickly, he shoved his book underneath the yellow textbook, opened to a page that did not match Professor Luan's question, and said, 'Oh yes, Professor Luan, I did. You mean to say what happened in the History of the Chinese Communist Party? Well …'

'Excuse me,' Professor Luan said. 'Which text are you looking at?'

Before Jing could find out what was the matter the class had burst into a boisterous laughter as they realised that Jing had read the wrong text.

'Can I bring your attention to this exercise at Lesson 18,' Professor Luan frowned and said, 'and my question about the modal verbs?'

'Model verbs?' Jing was bewildered. 'You mean like model workers? I don't understand.'

By now Zhenya could no longer contain her mirth. She was shaking with a laughter that rippled through her whole person like a big wave but stopped when she became aware of the others staring at her, particularly her female counterparts. She had to bite her lower lip to stop it, feeling tortured by the need, her face compressed into redness by the inner tension, her eyes downcast, looking at her shoes, a pair of black cloth slippers that looked quite convenient and comfortable.

'You would understand if you listened,' Professor Luan taunted. 'I mean verbs like "may, must, can" and so on. Now if you can translate this Chinese sentence into English for me, please? *Buneng zai tushuguan chouyan.*'

'You can't smoke in the library.'

'Zhenya,' Mr Luan's authoritative voice demanded. 'Can you

please do something to improve that sentence?'

'Yes, sir,' Zhenya stood up, her face still red, her eyes still looking down, having shifted from her shoes to the table top where there was only the yellow textbook and a pencil case. Beside the book lay a pocketsize English-Chinese Dictionary and a red pencil that she used to underline important words and expressions. On that day, she had underlined the word 'litter' and written next to it in Chinese that it also meant a number of young things at birth. 'I think he should say "You mustn't smoke in the library" instead of "you can't".'

Jing was quick to defend himself for he said immediately, 'Why should you say "I should"? I think you should say "I could say", don't you think?'

'Now, no more argument here, okay?' Professor Luan said. Knowing that Jing and the other students were having a quiet read at the back, he did not try to forcibly remove their books the way teaching staff in the old days would have certainly done but simply gave them questions to direct their attention back to their textbook. 'It is important that you pay attention to these exercises. They may seem simple at first, but, as time goes by, you will realise their importance in building a solid foundation in your mastery of the language. Now you both may sit down.' Seeing that Jing and Zhenya were still standing there, he patted the air with one hand as the bell rang for the end of the session and said, 'Class dismissed.'

You asked yourself is there not a racial way of seeing? Is the way an African used to the savanna sees something the same as a Chinese confined to the life of a small town? Does second-language writing, if there is such a thing, reduce its importance by placing it on the same level as that of second-language teaching? Does it make it second-rate, secondary? How do you use the English language to write the local accent of Yellow Town, for example? Like Zhang Guruo translating Thomas Hardy into a Northern-Chinese accent? Making Hardy's characters like Tess speak a heavy Chinese accent? Thus making them Chinese? Is this fleeting feeling of yours true: that no matter how much writers from non-English speaking backgrounds write their writing will only be regarded as informative and food for thought? What about yourself? How are you going to act to draw laughter from your audience in order to be applauded? This guy advises in his rejection letter you received today to 'show don't tell.' What if you don't feel like it and you tell but do not show? And what if you do not even want to know this so-called 'scripting/film rule'? Do you follow rules all your life? You never follow rules and that's why you are you.

11

One might think that there would be no interest in someone like Mr Miao, whose line of business was to supervise politics. Wrong. His tiny little room in the compounds of the Teacher's Zone occupying part of the university had frequent visitors, mainly from the English class, the key class under the Party's surveillance. Well, surveillance might be too strong a word but it was certainly a class that was much cause for concern. It was stressed time and again in the political meetings chaired by the Departmental Party Secretary, Mrs Mao, that this class was part of what was classified as Foreign Affairs and, to quote the late Premier Zhou Enlai, *waishi wu xiaoshi,* nothing in foreign affairs is a small affair, therefore the English class was the first line against bad influences from the West. The task of putting everyone on guard against those influences naturally fell on Mr Miao's shoulders. A retired army soldier, Mr Miao had fought the Americans in the Vietnam War as an intelligence officer and had worked his way up to platoon leader when the war ended. He was lucky enough to get a job in the university where, lean, neat and grave looking, he was having the time of his life. Why, pretty girls twenty years his junior would flock to his room to worship him – at least so he imagined, and boys would look up to him as a kind of war hero and would sometimes confide in him what they would never tell their own roommates.

One girl who would often go to see Mr Miao was Ganmei. He knew this girl was motivated because she wanted to become a Party member and he was still considering her application for membership. In the application, he remembered, she described herself as a passionate supporter of the Chinese Communist Party cause with a strong wish to sacrifice her life for her motherland if need be. He was touched and wanted to see her very much but was disappointed by their first meeting. He found her to be what could only be categorised as 'an old sister' with nothing much to recommend in her looks. Nevertheless, what she said was interesting, as she told stories of her classmates with 'thought problems'. Once their meetings became more regular, she told more stories. One person she never ceased to talk about was Zhao Feiyan. From his visits to the class, Mr Miao knew she was a very pretty girl and had always half expected to recruit her into his stable of informants. For Feiyan, politics was the last thing she wanted to be involved in. Her grandfather, a shop owner, had been executed in the early days of the New Republic. To Miao, stories about Feiyan provided necessary diversion and stimulation, even though she never came to visit him. So it was in one of those conversations or, more appropriately, confessions to the Party, that Zhao's name was mentioned again.

'What happened this time?' Mr Miao asked.

'She's very aggressive in her ways,' Ganmei complained.

'Tell me more.'

'By aggressive I mean she is very outgoing. She puts on a lot of make-up, even when she goes to the classes, and she does not do much homework but spends her time poring over fashion magazines and making phone calls to who knows whom.'

'You mean she uses lipstick?'

'Oh yes,' Ganmei said with disgust, and envy. 'Not only that but she also wears highheels and short skirts. But her English is deteriorating!'

'Well, *you suode biyou suoshi,* although I don't know how you can say that in English, I mean do they have the same concept in English? Just say it for me. Say it.'

'Well,' Ganmei was embarrassed. Her English wasn't great, although she was sure that she was better than Feiyan. 'It's like, it's like "have gains must have losses", something like that.'

'All right then. Go on, what else?'

'Oh yes, there's also Liu Ya. You remember her, the short one from Sichuan?'

'I think so. Didn't they say she was hot-tempered?'

'It's not really that; it's rather hot-tasted because she loves hot chilies,' Ganmei said, remembering the small bowls of chilies that Liu would eat during lunch or dinner every once in a while.

'What about her?'

'Well, I think she was organising the class to sign a petition to get the school authorities to consent to their request that an English teacher be recruited directly from overseas.'

'How dare she!'

'I agree,' Ganmei sighed. 'But the problem is that they are generally not very happy with the way the class is conducted.'

'Do you think that's the real problem?'

'I'm not quite sure,' Ganmei knit her brow, looking puzzled and pretending that she didn't really know.

'There must be an ulterior motive to this, I know it.'

'Like what?'

'There are people who use English to pave their way to go overseas and advance their career prospects for all kinds of purposes but the good ones. We must remain vigilant against such people.'

Mr Miao's wife came in with two thermos bottles full of hot water from the communal kitchen and said 'nihao' to Ganmei as she put the bottles down on the dining table. She picked up a bar of soap from there and went out to the corridor to do some laundry on her *cuoban*, a piece of wooden board with deeply carved wavy troughs. Used to people coming and going, she did not stand on ceremony.

As if she was suddenly reminded of something, Ganmei said, 'I must go now as I have left my homework incomplete for tomorrow. Have to catch up.'

If it wasn't for his wife, Mr Miao would have liked to have kept Ganmei longer as he wanted to find out more about Feiyan and the others, particularly the boys. He would need to 'develop' someone, as they said, among the boy students as his eye and ear to keep watch over them. It didn't take him long to find the one, and this happened to be Hu from Hunan, whom nobody seemed to take much notice of, his diminutive size and quiet manner avoiding attention. Behind a thick pair of glasses his eyes didn't miss anything, though. They shot out glances that were searching and cold.

While most students were keen on making progress in English and believed in the superiority of the language over Chinese, their command of Chinese not that good in the first place, there was someone who thought otherwise. This was Wei, a pale-faced handsome boy from Shanghai. If he was not very good at English, he didn't care, as long as he could get a passing mark of sixty per cent. In this he had something in common with Yang, but Wei was better at both politics and Chinese. Wei spent most of his time reading ancient Chinese novels and poetry, perhaps writing some himself. One day he baffled the whole class by posing a question to Mr Fu, who said that English was to become the international language and it would be of great benefit if one could master it as soon as possible.

'Mr Fu,' Wei said, his pale face appearing very serious, so serious that one or two girls looking at him became pale faced themselves. 'Can I say something?'

'By all means.'

'I don't think English as a language is all that important or fantastic. There are many things that can be expressed perfectly in Chinese that cannot even be expressed in English.'

'Like what?' Mr Fu's voice sounded a little shaky. Zhenya could see that he was displeased; no one had so openly challenged him this way before.

'I think our language is infinitely better than English. For example, we can say "as soon as I hear that sort of thing, my head bigs" by using the word "big" as a verb in Chinese. Can you do that in English? We can also use a noun as a verb. Why, I mean, you can describe someone as very China …'

'Well, I am afraid,' Mr Fu cut him short. 'That is you. *You* are very China, both in your name and in your approach to the study of the English language.' Secretly, however, Mr Fu had to admit to himself that this pale face had caught him unprepared with something he had only a slippery grasp of himself, despite having a degree in linguistics from Malta, of all the English-speaking countries, a fact that he was reluctant to boast to his students, save that he had been abroad and received training in an English-speaking country. Still, he was quick to rise to his own defense, or, to be more exact, to the defense of a language for which he had been awarded a degree of livelihood, if nothing much else. His mind turned to the undifferentiated gender and the lack of a sense of time in Chinese, but he thought better of it by deciding he'd rather state the facts of life clearly once and for all.

'Unfortunately, with all its advantages of expression, Chinese is not a language you came to this university to major in. You have to face the hard reality whether you like it or not that once you enrolled in this English class you made a decision that is too important to ignore or retract from. As they often say in Malta, I mean in the UK, take it or leave it. If you think Chinese is preferable to English, why don't you think twice about the degree you are taking? Why waste all our time arguing about the benefit of something that is so plainly clear to everyone?'

Far from convinced, Wei said to Jing after the class that he was often troubled by this intense conflict between the two languages. It was almost as if his mind was being torn apart by them. Casually, Jing said, 'Don't take it too seriously, Wei. It's just a language, a tool. If you learn how to use it skillfully, you may find it comes in handy one of these days. In a way, I share your view. There are many things that can be expressed in Chinese that cannot be expressed in English. For example, *houpa*, which may roughly translate as "hindfear" in English, although they only have "hindsight".'

'Well, that's exactly what I meant,' Wei said, excitedly. 'You should have said that in class in my defense!'

'I'm not sure,' Jing said. 'Perhaps you could teach the *laowai*, old foreigners, and give this to them one day.'

12

If Wei was sad and confused because he had to learn the English language against his better judgement, Jing felt the same about poetry. As a truck driver, he had led a pretty simple existence. University life presented a different pattern, which seemed to progress in a linear, upward line, with everyone struggling to get to the top, much the same way monkeys do, climbing up, always climbing up. But poetry seemed to be dragging him down. Something that kept niggling him, saying: Relax, why bother? Life is to be enjoyed and we'll all die one day. Why work yourself to an early death when you could be having fun and doing something more interesting than reciting boring passages from textbooks just so you can get higher marks?

Then something happened that was so unexpected it threw Jing completely off balance. A few days after he and Wei had their conversation about *houpa*, Wei committed suicide by jumping from the library buiding. On that cold morning when Jing learnt of the news, he went to the place to see him, lying in a fetal position in his yellow military overcoat. Quiet and peaceful, his nineteen-year-old face pale, paler than ever. There was a pool of blackened blood where his brain had hit the concrete. Why why why? Jing was obsessed with this question and would never be satisfied with the answers to why Wei never did well in his English tests or examinations and why he'd got a mark well below sixty for his latest exam. According to Yang, Wei had gone to Mr Fu to ask him to have his result marked up, but he met with Mr Fu's refusal. Hence the open confrontation in class. Could there have been something deeper going on than that?

While most of Jing's roommates remained unperturbed by this incident, some even dismissing it as silly and unthinkable, Jing was deeply troubled. He thought a lot about the death of the boy and the lack of consequences: the news of his death was blocked by the university authorities so that few outside knew what had happened and what was the real cause behind it. Nothing was reported in the school bulletin. The memory of Wei dwindled with each passing day until it died on its own. A few days afterwards no one even talked about it, except for noticing his empty bed, now unoccupied. It was such a constant reminder of something so unpleasant that no one put anything there.

It seemed that Jing was the only person who persistently dwelt on the subject for the next couple of semesters, through poetry that only occurred in his head, catching him unawares like a sudden shower, a mosquito bite or a fragmentary daydream. Wei's death saddened him to a degree that he was not aware of, falling into blank reveries even in class, making it impossible to compete with the sportsmanship of his male classmates. Too much thinking reduced him to half man, half automaton, woodenly daydreaming his time away. While his classmates were busy preparing for their end-of-term examinations, Jing was busy reading Gissing, finding him engrossing, at times bewildered by his frustrations as a writer and his advice against anyone becoming a writer. If there was anything that he could do one day, Jing thought, he would probably become a writer. There was no actual reason why. It was as simple as the water that wanted to empty itself or the cloud that wanted to go somewhere by presenting itself in various forms until it disappeared. Jing could not possibly have understood what sort of situation in which George Gissing found himself in the late 1800s and early 1900s. Although he had never met a writer in his life, authors in Jing's time were worshipped in official terms as people's 'soul engineers', and in popular terms as people who would be *qiangu liufang*, fragrant for thousands of years. Writing to be known and to be liked so that one's name was mentioned and remembered. That was the thing.

So far, Jing was too busy to take up his pen. The English language often overtook his entire life. He did not hate this language as Wei had, because he believed it would provide him with a way out, perhaps a better way out than the trucks. Since he decided this was his future, he might as well take up the challenge and 'face the music', a saying he had recently encountered. His exercise book was full of such phrases culled from various dictionaries, textbooks and his desultory readings. One word could lead to many. Indeed, that was what he was going on some of the time in class. When he learnt a new word in a text, he would check the dictionary for its other meanings, which would often lead him to other quite strange things. Take the word enemy. He found that it could mean time if you asked: 'How goes the enemy?' So, immediately after he learnt it, he put it to use when he went to the school canteen for lunch with Ma.

'How goes the enemy?' he asked.

'What?' Ma responded, mystified.

'How goes the enemy, I mean?' he said again.

'What do you mean? I don't understand?' Ma said as he unconsciously knocked his big white enamel mug with his spoon in a rhythmical pattern.

'I mean what time is it?' Jing asked proudly, having beaten Ma again or thinking he had.

'Oh, is that what it means?' Ma said. 'I thought you were asking about the friendly fire.'

It was Jing's turn to be bewildered. 'Friendly fire? Fire between friends? Fire started by a friend? Fire that was friendly?

How do you mean?'

'Ha, ha, ha,' having got the upper hand, Ma was pleased with his own cleverness. 'Go back and check your dictionary after dinner.' As he said this they arrived at the overcrowded canteen, with long queues formed before each ticket box, five of them in total. It was a place that Jing was to display his greatest talent in writing about when Dr Wagner arrived but, at that moment, he, as usual, took no notice of anything except what was written in chalk on the blackboard menu hanging on the wall and decided to have spinach and a salted egg with rice. Once again he was only able to keep down half of what he had ordered. The spinach chewed like stringy weeds and was only half washed, leaving the bottom of his white enamel bowl literally covered in a thick layer of mud. And the egg had obviously been salted for too long as its yolk had turned red. There was no way to get around the school canteen as there was not a single restaurant nearby, the nearest one being kilometres away, and he could not afford it anyway.

Over lunch, Ma put the expression in context. He said that he had heard this on Voice of America but it didn't make much sense to him until he consulted his dictionary.

'I see,' Jing exclaimed. 'We would call it *wushang*, wounding by mistake. How different we are in describing the same situation! Friendly fire. It almost sounds as if you lit up a fire for your friends.'

As he shook his head at this absurdity, Ma had plunged into his lexicographic search for something else before getting ready to hit the pillow for his daily afternoon nap. He shed all his clothes, including his warm shoes and socks. He didn't seem to mind in the least, firmly believing in his own motto, 'A good sleeper will do a good job.' Who knows where he got this idea, but in this tiny dormitory room there was a tacit understanding that everyone could do what they wanted to. Once again, Jing picked up his beloved Gissing for a quiet read, with his lunch indigestibly grassy in his stomach and the bad taste of egg lingering in his mouth.

At night, after the lights were put out by the central control room in the university, with the third ring of the bell, everyone put down their books reluctantly. Some cursed the bastard that had switched off the lights too early, although no one could specify exactly who the bastard was. Some sighed, relieved that their day had finally come to an end. Others simply picked up their toothbrushes, basins and towels to go to the wash room with its multiple taps and pipes positioned over communal multipurpose sinks, which they used to brush their teeth, wash their faces or do their dishes or laundry. There was no hot-water service. You needed to take a thermos bottle with you. To strengthen his willpower, Jing had recently adopted the practice of taking cold showers. He continued with this into the depths of winter. While everyone was crying cold, he stood there in the darkness, clenching his teeth, scooping handfuls of cold tap water on his chest, arms and thighs, to prepare himself for the onslaught of pouring the whole basin of water onto himself, from head to toe, until he was totally drenched. At first he was shivering, his skin tingling like tree bark in a rainstorm, but soon he fought off the fear of cold and stood triumphantly in his nakedness, repeatedly telling himself that there was nothing to be afraid of and that it was good for his body. This way, he even felt slightly warm when he dried himself. As he groped his way back to the room, he found that the others were talking about him.

'What were you guys talking about, huh?' Jing said to the darkness, not to anyone in particular, as he fumbled for the place that he normally put his washing basin and hung his towel.

'Ma was saying that he admired you.' Without guessing, Jing knew this was Xin.

'No,' Ma denied. 'I didn't say that. I was only saying that I wished I could be so bold as you to take the plunge.'

'But did your thing get frozen up?' Bao asked.

'Not mine,' Jing knew he was pulling his leg and retorted. 'I'm sure if you take a cold shower, your staff wouldn't be able to get erect.'

'Come on,' said Dang, who was sleeping on an upper bunk bed. 'Keep quiet you guys. Let's continue with this "Words and Their Stories", okay?' As usual, he had his ear glued to his portable wireless radio listening to Voice of America.

'I wonder when we shall get someone truly American to teach us,' Yang sighed. He had been complaining about the poor quality of teaching and the lack of a native speaker.

'Perhaps never,' Ma said. He didn't worry too much about having a truly foreign person to teach him as he had always taught himself in a way that he thought worked. The advantage of being at university was that it afforded him plenty of time and space to strengthen what he had already learnt.

'Well, if that is the case, we are finished,' Xin said. 'What is the future for us in this field? If we go out for a job, people will ask if we have been taught by foreign experts. If we say we have not, they will not take us on. As far as I know, all the universities around us have recruited foreign teachers for their English majors. Even students majoring in Russian or French get their Russian or French counterparts. Why not us?'

'Well, ours cannot compare with theirs, you know,' Yang said, 'because it's a *minying* sort of thing, although I am not quite sure what *minying* translates into English. Hey, Ma, how would you render that?'

'I don't really know but it seems that it's a nongovernmental or semigovernmental thing, with funds collected from the local, reportedly, big company.'

'What big company?'

'No idea.'

'Let me give you some food for thought tonight,' Jing said, as soon as he got into his bed, covering himself with his mosquito net for extra protection against the coming chill. 'What sort of person do you envisage that we are going to get, can anyone make a guess?'

'Well,' Xin said. 'Possibly someone like Charlie Chaplin in *Modern Times*, with a funny gait, maybe?'

'Then our university will go bankrupt,' Bao said. 'I'm sure if they do get someone, they'll get a teacher from a primary school in a remote county in America because that would cost them a lot less than hiring someone from a big university like Harvard.'

'I don't agree,' Yang said. 'It doesn't work that way. The foreign teachers are all recruited by a central agency at the ministerial level through the Ministry of Education, I think, and are distributed to various universities as required. And they are paid quite good salaries, somewhere between 1000 and 2000 kuai a month or thereabouts.'

'My gosh! That's a lot!' Dang exclaimed.

'Our Voice of America lover was more interested in something else,' Bao said. 'Namely, money.'

'No, that is not true,' Dang said. 'I had actually dozed off until you said that.'

'That just goes to prove my point,' Bao said. 'Because you woke up at exactly the right time.'

'To tell you the truth,' Dang said. 'I'd rather we have someone coming here not just to teach us language and grammar but more …'

'I don't know about that,' Yang said. 'In my opinion, we'd be lucky if we could get a middle-school graduate like the one we got the other day.'

'But she was so simple,' Jing said. 'I couldn't stand her saying such nice things about everything.'

'But that's what these foreigners do all the time, haven't you noticed?' Bao said. He had met some foreign teachers at his father's university and observed them at work and play.

'What if they couldn't get anyone from America?' Jing asked.

The question threw everyone into confusion as none of them had considered this.

'Then they could get someone from Wuhan,' Bao said, getting everyone laughing.

'I would have thought they could grab someone from any of a dozen English-speaking countries, like Canada or Australia,' Jing said.

'Or Malta, like Fu,' Bao said.

'That may well be the case,' Ma agreed. 'If so, we would be worse off.'

'You think?' Jing said.

'In terms of purity of English, I don't think those two stand a chance,' Ma said. 'You either get someone from the USA or the UK. Otherwise, you don't want anyone else. I mean, our English could even be better than theirs.'

'Well,' Yang said. 'My knowledge of those two other countries is not sufficient for me to draw such a conclusion, but since Ma is our heavenly horse, I guess I'll have to follow him.'

'All I know is,' Dang said, 'Australia is a convict country and Xin has a relative there. What's he doing there?'

'Oh, it's a she,' Xin said. 'She is running a restaurant and has married someone there.'

'An Australian?' Hu enquired.

Everyone was taken aback for ever since the lights were turned off, Hu seemed to have disappeared, whereas in fact he was lying in his corner bed, as quiet as a frozen fish.

'Who knows?' The nonchalant tone of Xin's voice was unmistakable.

'I think we can go without those foreigners,' Hu said.

'Why?' Jing was curious.

'We've got everything we need. We've got fantastic teaching staff here and good textbooks. We've got Voice of America and BBC on radio that we can tune into any time we want to. We've got Ma, our best horse. What more do we need? I mean you'll only have trouble if you get anyone else. As far as I know, incidents have occured when foreign-teaching staff come to Chinese universities.'

'But that does not mean the same thing will happen to us,' Jing said. 'It's getting boring around here. If you think what is being taught is fantastic, I may have to agree to disagree. I don't care where we get a teacher as long as the guy is a white native speaker.'

No one responded. Silence fell in the room, a brooding silence, broken by the sudden noise of a howling wind somewhere in the trees and the breaking of an occasional wave nearby on the lake. Soon sleep overtook everyone except Jing, who was thinking, wide eyed, about nothing for a long time.

13

Have you reached the end of fiction? It's raining after a day of long hot hours. At the end of the day you were so tired you threw yourself onto the sofa amid a disorganised house, everything in disarray after the guy went through it hot-vacuuming the carpet. She opened all the windows to let in the heat and let out the dampness created by the vacuuming. There were even two flies buzzing around. Now the rain is pouring, hitting the roof of your makeshift garage with a crisp sound, much like sand being scattered. When you go into your own room, closed lest the smoke might disturb her, you hear the unmistakeable noise of hailstones. The sky flashes as if someone is taking a photograph of you with an enormous camera. You are brought back to yourself. It is this thought, long contemplated, that now begins to attack you. A sense of weariness seeps into your mind, making you aware of another machine beside you, and actually, inside you. Soon, you are overcome with the feeling that the way you go about things you are no more than a machine that can speak and make love. The minute you go out into the garden after dinner, with a bag of rubbish to put in the bin, you remember you had meant to bring a chair out on the grass and sit there for a smoko while doing some quiet reading. Then you realise what you are missing. In your mind's eye, there is a group of people sitting around a table in the garden, drinking tea, playing poker, chatting about nothing or everything, joking until it is totally dark. They look up at the sky for stars unknown to them, not to search for anything but to convince themselves that another day has gone by without much happening. You realise that this is what you are missing, years ago in China, seconds ago in your imagination. Life that way was good.

14

When Jing went home at the end of term, he did so alone; all of his roommates were either local or from other parts of the country. Even though they returned home, too, probably alone, like himself, for Jing the loneliness was acute, as his girlfriend, Chenfang, had left him for good. For a time, he felt as if his heart had been wrenched out of his body and trampled upon. Dusty and bloody, it was thrown back to him with the words: Go back where you came from, you are no longer required. As a result, he did very poorly at school. He didn't fail but he barely got above seventy per cent in each of his subjects. When some of his classmates received excellent reports, Jing looked glum and didn't offer any compliments. So what, he thought to himself. I don't care. Most of the time, he kept to himself, preferring instead to read Gissing and books like *Jean Christopher* and *David Copperfield*, both in Chinese translation. He carried these home in his old school bag, together with his yellow-covered textbook to brush up on over the school holiday. He returned home feeling as though he hadn't made any friends or achieved anything. People around him were only temporary tenants whose purpose was to acquire the language and go, each on their separate way, each on their own. Perhaps more than others, he had incurred a loss and there was nothing he could do to dispel the sense of sad helplessness that accompanied it.

As he sat by the bus window, endless thoughts came to him like the changing scenery rushing past. It was a hilly region that he was travelling through, a place he used to visit to pick up blasted quarry stones in his Unique. The hills were geometrical blocks, round, square or triangular, bare of grass, of trees, of any human figures. There was an occasional cemetery on the slope of a hill, the white gravestones its signposts, exposed in the withered grass from last summer. A village appeared from nowhere at the edge of the range of hills, with its black-tiled roofs and white walls, chickens pecking on the ground in front of the doors and pigs either lying around or biting the dust with their snouts, searching for food. Outside the village there was field after field of green wheat. Between the green fields and the village one could see stacks of rice that had grown greyish after the rain and wind of the past few months. A caked mud-grey buffalo was taking a bite of the stocks and pulling it away sideways with a downward shake of its head. Another pond flitted past, reflecting a quick sky, with some rusty lotus leaves in it. There would be much to fish in summer, Jing thought. Fishing reminded him of Chiang, his old friend from middle school. He would often go fishing with him during summer holidays. Although there wasn't much to do in winter, visiting him and chatting about the old days would be nice. Jing was cheered up by the thought.

He was now going through one of the most fertile regions in Hubei Province, lying between the City of Wuhan and the ancient town of West Hill. With thousands of ponds dotting the landscape like sparkling stars, and the mighty Yangtze River flowing east within sight, the place abounded in rice and cotton in summer and wheat in winter. For Jing, this was only ever a place he went through, in a bus, a truck, or occasionally in a jeep if his father's work unit happened to have one going to Wuhan or back. His father hadn't written to him for a long time. Nor had his mother. In fact, since he had gone to university, neither of them had written; it was as if they had forgotten they still had a son. Upon leaving home last time he and his father had quarrelled, about what he couldn't remember. Both Jing's father and mother were what were known as state cadres, his father working in a university-attached library, having been affected during the Cultural Revolution because of his past history as a Kuomingtang officer, and his mother teaching Chinese in a middle school

'Where's Dad's books?' Jing asked, putting down his bag. 'Jing, you are back.' Mother was sitting on a stool in the middle of the room. A bed took up half of the room, leaving one corner occupied by a table, with an electric cord with a bare globe hanging over it, and three leather suitcases of the old style squeezed between the table and the bed; the rest of the room was vacant, large enough for three adults to sit around. On the wall against which the table was placed was Chairman Mao's smiling picture, exactly the same as the one hanging in Jing's classroom. Part of the school staff living quarters, this room was one of ten in a row on the ground level, punctuated at intervals with unpainted wooden pillars. The space between the pillars and the doors formed a half-open corridor.

'Have you eaten yet?' Mother looked up at him. Straight away he noticed a strange look in her eyes.

'What happened?' Jing demanded, refusing to take the other stool that this mother had pulled out from the table.

'Don't you talk to me like that,' Mother said sharply, pulling out a cigarette from her packet and lighting up.

'Can I have one?' Jing asked, his hand shooting out, grabbing hold of the pack.

'Here,' Mother offered the burning fire on the tip of the matchstick with one hand, the other hand cupping it to protect it from being blown out.

'Ah,' Jing took a deep drag and breathed out a long shoot of blue smoke, directly into his mother's eyes.

'Stop it,' Mother almost yelled. 'What are you doing?'

Jing tipped his chin, blowing the residual smoke sidewise, which hit the globe, raising the dust that had settled on it over time.

'I'll kick you out of this room if you do that again,' Mother said. There was something fierce in her tone. Knowing that she was such a clean person, Jing was surprised to find how unkempt the room was. The quilt lay unfolded and there were cigarette butts everywhere on the pitted uncemented ground. Mother smoked as she freely spat, clearing her throat from time to time.

'Dad is not coming back tonight?' Jing changed his way of asking, getting straight to the heart of the matter.

'I'm going to the toilet,' Mother said as she got up and went out.

Jing suddenly remembered that whenever things became unbearable, his mother would say that she wanted to go to the toilet. What was there in the toilet that so appealed to her? Was there a solution there? He took another look around the room. His father's quilt was not there. Normally there were two side by side, folded up neatly in one corner of the bed. On the back of the door where face towels were hung, there was only a flowery one, for his mother. He quickly glanced to where the washing basin sat on a stand and noticed that the yellow glass that his father used for rinsing his mouth in the mornings was missing.

When Jing's mother came back from the toilet, she seemed to look neater and there was a faint smile on her face. After she dried her hands on the single towel hanging on the back of the door, she said to Jing, 'I'll get something to eat for us from the school canteen. What would you like? There isn't much, though. Rice, *woju* fried with pork and perhaps *red caitai*.'

'Not if you don't tell me where Father has gone,' Jing insisted.

'All I can tell you is that he won't be back for a few days,' Mother said, with a sigh.

'You mean you both parted hands?' Jing asked, dreading the consequence of his question.

'What nonsense!' Mother put the two iron bowls together with a clank and went out without another word.

Jing lit up another cigarette and waited, watching the gathering dusk outside, brooding.

It seemed a long time since she had left for the canteen and when she returned it was already dark. Jing had expected something delicious, something meaty, but all she came back with was two bowls of rice covered with greens dotted with minute pieces of meat. The situation was made even more desolate. All of a sudden Jing felt an urge to go, to leave this shitty place and go right back to the university but he was stopped in midthought when he realised that the last bus would have left by now. Helplessly, he grabbed hold of the bowl and was about to eat when his mother said, after she carefully closed the door behind her, 'Just a minute. I'm going to fry an egg for you.'

She produced an electric stove and plugged it in, Jing watching the coil turn dark red, then bright red, sending forth a burning smell, while his mother took out two eggs from a whitish cloth bag, also hanging from a nail on the back of the door, cracked them one by one and scrambled them in an empty bowl, putting a plate over the stove, pouring some oil on the plate, and, with an iron *guochan*, started frying them. The room was soon filled with an enticing egg smell that made Jing hungry. When both sides of the eggs turned golden, his mother added a pinch of salt to each of them and said, 'Take them both.'

Jing did not decline the offer but ate them as he should, together with the greens and the rice. In no time, the meal was finished.

After he washed the dishes outside in the cold in the common sink shared by the other households, Jing said, 'I'm going out.'

His mother did not ask where he was going but simply said, 'Don't be too late. I'll make your bed for you in the middle of the room.'

This visit is even worse than the last, Jing thought. What had caused them to make this change? He must find out from Pi. After Nei went to the army, they were supposed to have a bit more space but this went beyond his expectation. And Father wasn't even coming home for the night. Jing belched and heard his mother say, 'Disgusting! You should never belch so openly in my presence or anyone's for that matter. Didn't university teach you any manners?'

Paying no attention to what she said, Jing went out, pulling the door behind him with a bang and was soon swallowed in the darkness.

15

This is trying on your memory. You found, as you said to her, that you are beginning to doubt your ability to write. Not only that. You are more doubtful about your memory. As you write you keep forgetting what you have written before. You can do a key-word search for missing links but in such a long-drawn out battle, it is inevitable that certain threads are lost somewhere. This would not happen if it is a two-hour film. Even when you read a novel, you forget quite a lot of things by the time you reach the end. In a year or two, you'd forget most of the things. In the previous section, for example, you have forgotten if Jing has one parent or both his parents are still alive when he goes home for the winter holiday. You then have to go to the first part of this story to search for the missing link while vaguely remembering that his parents were still alive in the first part but you were not sure what work they were doing. You nearly replaced them with your own parents when you decided not to identify with your characters too closely.

If you have his parents intact, it would become unavoidable that they may become shadows of your own parents. And that's the last thing you want to happen in fiction. Even while you were having a shower a few minutes ago, the thought came to you that you might simply have his parents split up because of marital discord. Your own parents never had much problem during their life. May they rest in peace in their graves side by side near a small pond by the side of which you once saw a peasant ploughing the field with a yellow ox.

Jing could go to visit his father in the library at night and not return home. It felt better than at home because at least it was larger, less crowded with things and was brighter with the fluorescent light.

Besides, it was warmer, too, as he could sleep next to his dad who didn't mind him in the least. You don't want to go on describing that. Let your readers imagine what's going to happen between the son and the father. The reason, if there is any reason and if any reason should be given, is that his mother and his father had separated for some time. But neither of them told Jing anything about the separation and he did not particularly want to know. In fact, he enjoyed this newly found freedom of moving between the two opposites. He stayed at his dad's office for a few days, enjoying the books that he had borrowed for him from the library, among them two big volumes of Cervantes' Don Quixote in Chinese translation that he found so engrossing he read until very late, until his dad had to say, 'Come to bed or else I'll have to switch off the lights for I can't go to sleep with the lights on.' What he did was not surprising. He stood up, turned off the lights, and went out, pulling a chair behind him to the corridor where he sat down and read on, sullen and brooding, it seemed, to his dad, the librarian most people did not take notice of.

16

Lying perfectly still, Jing senior was not asleep. He was aware of what his son was doing. Several times, words came to his lips but he kept them back. He had reached a stage where he couldn't care less. Or was that true? Perhaps not, although he admitted feeling indifferent about a life that hadn't produced anything fruitful for himself. He had little to expect from it after what he had gone through; once there had been a land far away that used to lure his dreams, but now it was no longer there. He felt like the *wutong* tree outside growing cold in winter, shedding all the leaves it had had throughout such seasons, the fallen leaves symbolic of the things that were going away: his wife who no longer loved him, perhaps never in her life; his son who was growing away from him each day; a past that belonged decades ago in the depths of the mountains in Yunnan; and a woman whom he had passionately fallen in love with but who had disappeared forever … The only things he had were the thousands of books in the library that he was paid to look after, and even they were not his. Through one of the holes in the back of his shorts, he stuck in a middle finger and scratched there until the itch was gone. He felt better now. Then he put the finger under his nose and smelt it. It stank, with a familiar and endearing smell. He wiped it against the inside of his quilt, forehand and backhand, and smelt it again. It now smelt of a quilt that was long unwashed but it didn't matter to him in the least.

What did matter was what his son was doing. Instead of pursuing a career that would reap huge benefits in the future or at least lead to a stable life, he seemed bent on something ephemeral, something so transient that not even fame could sustain it. The occasional noise of a page turning seemed to merge with the silence of the night. His mind began to wander, trying to gather together the features of a woman lost to him for so long. Again, he failed. In all those years in this small town of slightly more than 10,000 people he had never met anyone like her. The only person who looked like her was his son, whose high forehead and direct eyes nearly matched hers. There was also something matching in his character: a quick temper and a readiness to tell the truth, very dissimilar to his own personality. He would have died a thousand times if he were ready to tell the truth. It was the wrong country for that. Perhaps any country would be wrong for that. The story he could reveal about Zhang Zhixin was horrific; she had her tongue cut off as a result of refusing to tell lies. He would often admonish Jing when he saw him begin reading another translated novel: Jingjing, reading too much fiction, particularly Western fiction, will not do you much good. Jing would normally ignore him, continuing on with the book. Or if he was engrossed in something and felt that he was being interrupted, he would say, 'I don't care what good it would do to me as long as I feel good about it and no one interrupts me in the middle of it!'

That is the whole problem with this generation, Jing senior sighed an inaudible sigh. They want to do things as they please, not caring about the consequences. Does he want to be a writer? That thought came as a shock. It would be unthinkable. No one in Jing senior's family was a writer. His father ran a clothes shop and wanted him to follow the trade but he joined the army after graduating from university. A couple of short stories was all he managed to produce, when the blood in his veins was running at a high tide with vain aspirations and when glittering things represented by words in print meant more than dull things of solid substance. Since then he had seen generations of talented writers rise and fall, their books burnt and confiscated, shovelled in truckloads for paper-recycling stations, or gathering dust and mildew in forgotten corners of the library. He congratulated himself for having unwittingly ceased to write a long time ago. Now, taking up his residence at the library, on his own, he felt strangely relieved. It was not like a library but more like a graveyard where he kept watch over the dead in their transmuted form, book form, transformed and muted. Jingjing must not pursue this path so diligently or it could lead nowhere; worse, it might find him in the same trouble that he had gone through. Stung by the thought in all its cold cruelty, he raised himself from the bed, with difficulty, and called out: 'Jingjing, come to bed. It's getting too late for your health.'

Meanwhile, Jing had not done much reading. To anyone who happened to walk by and, at this time of the night, not even a rat walked by, it would seem that he was hard at work. Only he knew he was not. His thoughts were miles away and the flow of his reading was interrupted from time to time by his wonderings about life in general. He felt sad; he did not know why, but he felt sad. Not about anything in particular, his sadness was something that seemed to move him to a state akin to writing or rather a desire to write, even in English. With some regret, he remembered that he had not practised writing in English as much as Mr Fu suggested they should.

'Writing in English will take your English to another level,' said Tiger, which was Hu's nickname, as his given name 'Hu' means 'tiger' in Chinese. 'Learning English, you know, is about two ins and two outs, at this stage at least. That is to say: if you have words coming in at your ears, you should be able to bring them out of your mouth by speaking them, and if you take the words in by your eyes, you should be able to let them out through your hands. Make sense?'

It certainly made sense to Jing but what interested him was not these two cycles; rather, it was the oddness of the language that set him wondering. Make sense? What a weird way of expressing things! They make love; they make believe; they make haste; they probably even make hate or do they? They can make everything but they wouldn't make sense in Chinese sense, Jing thought. You'd have to turn it into something like *mingbai*, bright and white or brightly white. That is, instead of saying 'make sense' you'd say 'brightly white'? That would make little sense in English! Linguistic entanglements like this easily tired him out as he muttered and chewed them until his tongue got tied, tired, tarnished by the Englishness of his thinking. Then he heard his father call him to come to bed, again. He didn't respond immediately but sighed, a deep sigh that did not escape his father's ears.

'A young man like you should never sigh like that,' Father said. 'Come to bed quick!'

'Father, can you say "make person" in English?'

'How do you mean?'

'I mean in Chinese we always talk about "make person" *(zuoren)*, as if it were the most important thing in life, more important than make money or even love. I wonder if "make person" is not an ideal that the English or the English-speaking people aspire to or if it is an idea that exists in their language, that even makes sense to them.'

'All I can remember is that I read many years ago someone commenting that he could admire a poet as a great poet but not as a man. In that sense, I guess you could say those foreigners do regard being a man as important, although I doubt if they treat it as importantly as we do. I've spent all my life trying to *zuoren* or to "make person" as you put it, and behave myself but – well, just jump in. I'm getting sleepy now.'

It was a night fraught with no meaning, and quietness. Occasionally, Jing could smell the silkworm chrysalis in the air from the local silk factory, making his mouth water for the lusty taste of the dark-brown insects when dried and fried with vegetable oil. Otherwise, the night was perfectly still, dead. His father was lying at one end of the bed and he at the other end. He didn't like the touch of his father's hairy legs and instinctively drew away from him. His father made a low noise through his nose and Jing's face touched the fluffy towel that was stitched around the edge of the quilt, a lazy way of protecting the quilt longer against the dirt. He smelt his father on it and he smelt his father's hair on another towel covering the pillow. This made him uncomfortable but he didn't say anything. Soon, sleep overcame him.

17

If this was a scene in a movie, they would have to at least shed some light into the room to illuminate their half-concealed faces; unfortunately, that will have to wait. All you can hear are the rhythms of their uneven breathing, his heavier than his father's, keeping the latter awake nearly the whole night at the other end of the bed, where Jing senior was lost in thought over a long-forgotten past that Jingjing was never to know, at least not during his sojourn in China.

Does a character's mood change with his creator's? I mean is it true that when you feel sad your character also feels sad? Regardless of what others do, this seems what is happening now. Depending on what time you write tomorrow, similar patterns may also happen. Perhaps you could apply the same principles to a story that happens 2000 years ago? Still, writing the novel on a laptop in bed gives you infinite pleasure better than any love or holiday making. Fiction? This is fiction, this very act of you writing, accompanied by your sole companion, time. What a strange thing to do! While your composer friend has to have a whole orchestra play his composition to a whole auditorium packed with audience, music filling their ears, yours has to be done in silence and read in silence, years afterwards, in places far apart, in languages far apart, by people far apart. And that makes you sad.

18

It was soon Spring Festival, but it was to be different from all the previous ones in that there was not going to be a New Year's Eve dinner as Jing's father and mother had irrevocably separated. Jing had to shuttle between them, staying with each for a few nights and trying hard to ease into this unromantic situation at odds with what he had read in Keats and Shelley at school. Initially, he did make an effort to bring them together, sort of, but nothing worked. Only yesterday he mentioned to his mother that she should consider inviting Jing senior back, at least for the dinner if not anything else.

'Are you afraid of something?' This was his mother's defiant voice.

'What do you mean?' Jing raised his own voice. 'It was well meant for both of you!'

'It's none of your business,' Mother said sharply. 'Children don't meddle in adults' business.'

'Business or affairs?' Jing said the latter word in English, amused by his own cleverness.

'Don't you be rude by using English against your mother. You think now that you can speak some rotten English words you can play jokes on your mother? How dare you!'

Jing laughed uncontrollably. Whenever he saw his mother get angry, which she did so often these days, he would burst into loud laughter in spite of himself, nevertheless hating every second of it. He didn't like to be put down like that.

'You'd better go back to your father for the dinner, but you may have lunch with me on the day before the festival,' Mother suggested but it sounded more like an order.

'Is it true that Nei is not coming back for this occasion?'

'Well, that's what he told me over the phone,' Mother said. 'He said he was going to stay in Kunming as it was more fun and warmer. I may go and visit him myself.'

'But it's so far away!' Jing protested, knowing that he was being jealous; his mother had never even written a letter to him and Nei never called him.

'I know,' Mother said calmly. 'It's four days and three nights by train.'

'Then why bother?'

'On New Year's Eve, we will have something good for the occasion from the school canteen,' Mother did not respond to his question but went on about the food. 'There will be a grand annual lunch with dumplings, *roubaozi*, *hongshaorou*, *hongshaoyu*, at least eight dishes and one soup.'

'I'm not interested,' Jing said.

'What *are* you interested in then?'

'Nothing.'

With that, he picked up his yellow textbook, read a few sentences and put it away in disgust. There was a splattering of firecrackers nearby, set off by some local children, reminding Jing of the old days when he would do the same. Not any more, he sighed inwardly, as he had grown up into an unable-to-enjoy-himself adult. What a bleak future was waiting for him!

He went to Pi's place but he was not there. He went to Chiang's place but he was not at home either. Both seemed to be trying to avoid him somehow. On his way home, he bumped into Gao, who was much taller than him with a wan face that suggested lack of sleep. They had not seen each other for quite some time since they both went to university, Gao to another one in Wuhan to major in Chinese literature.

'How interesting!' Jing said. 'If only we could swap places, you majoring in my English and I majoring in your Chinese!'

'Why don't we do that?' Gao said, eying a girl going past who was wearing the very tight trousers that had become popular lately.

They were standing by a street corner near the Nonstaple Food Shop, a shop that had been there since their childhood. It wasn't like anything you would see in a Western film where friends meet in a café or a restaurant. It was perfectly normal in this late 1970s small town, where people would meet on the streets and talk to each other by the street corners, on the steps of a bookshop, in the middle of a bookshop or near the gate of the post office, in fact, anywhere. People were everywhere in this town, peasants standing on either side of the street, behind their bamboo baskets, held at either end of a shoulder pole, containing vegetables or white turnips, narrowing the street to a lane, primary school pupils going home, carrying their colourful school bags, people riding their bicycles and occasional trucks and jeeps rushing by, honking constantly at the pedestrians who paid no attention.

'Tell me why you want to learn Chinese?' Gao was a guy who always wanted to get to the bottom of things.

'I don't know yet,' Jing said, 'although I do feel that without commanding one language you can hardly command the other. There is something common that exists between languages, I think.'

'I would have thought it was the other way round,' Gao said, his eyes following the contours of another young woman passing by. 'I would have thought you could only learn a language well by forgetting your own mother tongue. It's almost like quitting your mother for the attraction of a new girl, I think.'

'Right,' Jing agreed, ignoring his analogy. 'That's exactly

what our teachers kept telling us, but then I found it hard to actually achieve that. I ...'

Before he could finish his words, in which he wanted to say that in learning a new language, it was more like keeping both, Gao interrupted with, 'You know what? You grow more and more like a foreigner.'

Bewildered, Jing asked, 'How do you mean?'

'I mean look at your nose. You've got such a high nose and your eyes seem deeper-set than ever.'

'That's just me. I am always like that,' Jing said and, turning his full attention on Gao, lunged for a counter-attack. 'You yourself look more like a foreign devil than me. You know few Chinese are as tall as 1.75 metres but you are nearly 1.8.' He might have added that Gao's constant attempts to make eye contact with nice-looking women on the streets was also a Western trait but he kept this one to himself and continued, 'That's some sign of foreignness, no? As a matter of fact, I have a theory about this.'

'What theory?' Gao became intrigued for he was always curious about new theories.

'I've got a feeling that there is something foreign in us all, in you and me and all the other people we know or do not know that are walking on this street. Look at that woman that seems to interest you. She is wearing high-heeled shoes, an imported style. That is the foreignness that she is keen on wearing, or perhaps it is her very own foreignness coming out of her.'

'Come on,' Gao laughed. 'Stop attacking others because I pointed out your own foreignness. On second thoughts, you're probably right. There is no pure Chinese because many hundreds of years ago there was a chaos created by the Five Hu in China, commonly known as *wuhu luanhua*. A mixture of bloods must have carried on since.'

'Well,' Jing said nonchalantly. 'I don't know because I am

not into history like you. All I care for is the words, the Chinese words and the English words.'

*

At night, in Jing's mother's tiny room, by the deep-purple table against the wall, under the single yellow dusty globe, Jing was washing his feet in a white basin, looking into a hand mirror, pretending to examine his nonexistent moustache, but the way in which he did this did not escape his mother's eye. She had guessed what was probably the matter but she didn't make a single comment until Jing seemed to be obsessed with fastidiously examining his looks, when she said, 'Won't you put that mirror of mine away? You are like a woman. Looking too long into a mirror for a man is no good. Mirrors are for use by women only.' She said this in her bed behind the unfurled mosquito net to prevent herself from being seen, a natural barrier between herself and her son when he stayed the night with her, his bed inches away from hers, crowding the room.

Jing did not respond but continued to look into the mirror at his own eyes. For the first time, he realised that his love affair with Chenfang might have never happened. It was all part of a fantasy. He was only dreaming that he had once invited her to have an afternoon stroll along the lake, stayed there until after dark, stripped her bare, laid her on a flight of steps leading to the water near a deserted swimming pool, penetrated her until he came; that, despite his six room-mates, they had managed to sleep together in his tiny little bed of two-bodies' width for the entire night without being discovered by anyone before she slipped away; and that they were actually embracing and kissing in a park before the entire public, his tongue shooting into her mouth, his saliva wetting her lips. It was all so true that he could hardly disbelieve it. Why didn't it bother her that they hadn't contacted each other for such a long time? While he was missing her, did she also miss him? If not, what did that mean? There was one thing that he was sure about: she had never commented on his 'foreign features' because they had never been together even once in the first place!

This realisation took him completely by surprise, so much so that he began to look at his surroundings and past life with a renewed vision. Perhaps the circumstances in which he had lived were only temporary, like the clothes that he could one day grow out of. There was something else that kept him company, invisible but tangible, like a shadow but more insubstantial, forming a parallel world beside him, in which he had been living for as long as he had lived in the physical world. All these women that he had made love to: were they real? He could not even begin to call them either by phone or mail or even name. They were simply not there. And yet he could accurately point them out one by one on the street and say: I made love to her, and her, and her in this way, this way and this way! What was the matter? He caught the deep shadows underneath his large black eyes and wondered if that was what had made Gao comment on his foreignness when the whole room was plunged into total darkness with the small click of something near the bed, followed by his mother's stern rebuke: 'I've told you to stop for at least three times but you completely ignored me. Do you want to continue or come to bed straight away?'

'Continue,' came his defiant response.

'Then you won't have any light,' Mother said.

Instinctively, he reached out to grab the switch but suddenly remembered he did not even know where it was located. Then he recalled a little incident that until now he'd completely forgotten: one day a moustached electrician by the name of Lao Zu came into their room and fitted a gadget at Jing's mother's bedside, which was attached to a red electrical wire 'for', in his words, 'her convenience in winter.' Looking at Lao Zu's masculine face, Jing had a fleeting thought: did they have an affair? As quickly, he quashed the thought, feeling a little shamefaced about implicating his own mother in such imagined scandals.

'So you used that *man*'s thing against me!' Jing said.

'What? What are you talking about?' Mother flared up. 'Be specific, you *bu dongshi de dongxi*! How can you be so cruel, so heartless, while I have been labouring all these years to enable you to go to university and perhaps become a professor who won't even treat his own mother with any respect? If I had known this earlier, I would have gladly had an abortion and killed you, you bastard!'

Jing went silent. Once again, he felt the futility of arguing with a woman, even if this woman was his mother. It seemed that whatever a woman said was right, particularly if she was your mother. Why did those writers keep harping their sweet nothings about the great mother in the world, dedicating their masterpieces to their mothers? These writers were so fake. If he became a writer in the future, he would never write about his own mother. He was determined about that. He groped for his shoes and put them on in the darkness. He groped for the edge of the table and put the mirror on it in the darkness. By now he had decided that he would spend the Spring Festival with his father without even telling his mother about it.

'If you do so, I'll go to Kunming,' Mother said.

'Well,' Jing said, hotly, 'If you do that, I'll never come back again!'

'What? What did you say I'll do what?'

Silence.

Perhaps she never said anything. It was all in his imagination.

'What did you say I'll do?'

'Go back to sleep, okay?' Jing said. 'I'm not going to talk to you again. I want to sleep, okay?'

'Who gives you the right to speak to your mother like that, ha? Was it your father who taught you so? Was it your university teacher who told you so? Now university educated, you are more rude than ever. What's the point of us financially supporting you to go to university then? You know in the West children go to college entirely on their own without their families' support.'

By now Jing had slipped into his quilt and wrapped his head up in it to stop her words from coming in. Determined not to say a word back, he was trying to remember the words from *Auld Lang Syne*, 'Should old acquaintance be forgotten and never brought to mind', that they sang so often together in class. Oddly enough, he felt at peace with the world, and with himself.

19

This character has now turned into a real character in that he no longer resembles you. He is your intimate stranger. The world is becoming infinitely unrecognisable. Friends yesterday, strangers or enemies today. Alive last minute, gone this second, mourned only by the closest related but watched by billions with nonchalance or amazement containing no ingredients of sympathy.

20

At his father's place, on New Year's Eve, there was nothing much for dinner except a large bowl of steaming dumplings, perhaps the simplest dinner they had ever had in their life as father and son, together or separate. This was the quietest time of the year on campus as the students had all left for home, Jing's father being the only one using his office room in the library for temporary accommodation, surrounded by the deserted classroom buildings, like abandoned unread books standing in the twilight, far away from the concentration of the staff living quarters. No one had invited him to their houses for dinner, but a colleague did offer this bowl of dumplings, together with two small white china bowls, into which Jing senior was pouring a dark black soy sauce. Jing had many questions to ask but in the end he did not ask a single one. Instead, he picked up the chopsticks, took up one dumpling, dipped it in the sauce and savoured it, wrapping it up in his mouth before he chewed it and swallowed it. It wasn't bad. He threw a look at his father, whose eyes met his and a smile stole to his lips. Or were they his lips, too? In that instant, he saw something in his father's eyes that was not quite his. He had never looked his father in the eye like that and it always felt a bit awkward, even womanly, to look into one's own father's eyes. But, if he remembered clearly from last night, his own eyes had a quality that his father's lacked because his eyes were so Chinese whereas Jing's had something exotic. Yes, that would be the word, his thought temporarily hovered around this word, transliterating it as *yi ge zuo di ke*, just as the word 'romantic' had been incorporated into the Chinese language as *luo man di ke*, and wondering why they did not do the same to 'exotic'.

Instinctively, he raised his eyes to look again but this time his father's head was bent over his bowl, sucking the dumplings in with a noise that made him wince. It was the kind of noise his mother had inculcated in him as bad table manners from an early age, although it could also suggest a deep pleasure the eater was experiencing. Still, Jing could not let this go by lightly.

'Father,' he started. 'I think your slurping is a little too loud.'

'Is it?' Father looked up from his bowl containing the dark sauce and a half-eaten dumpling wholly soaked in it, with an apologetic smile on his face. 'It doesn't matter, does it? There are only the two of us. No one can hear it.'

'But it's the kind of bad table manners that Mother would hate to hear, you know.'

'I know, I know,' Father said, biting into another dumpling with energy, his mouth smeared with the sauce.

'But you're still making noise,' Jing said sternly.

'Why, you are like your mother now, so fastidious!'

'No, I'm not like her,' Jing said, with vehemence.

Secretly amused by his successful little tactic of diverting his son's attention, Jing senior managed to keep down another big dumpling while adding, with a mouth full of minced pork and bok choy, 'you are like a Westerner then.'

'Was it true that I was born of a Westerner'?

'Where did you get *that*?' Father's eyes nearly popped out of his glasses.

'I mean was it true or not?'

'It was true that when you were young you had a habit of fantasising about things. You still haven't grown out of it.'

'You are not answering my question. I want to know whether I am a genuine Chinese or not.'

'You are as Chinese as I and anyone else. There is no doubt about it. What made you question your identity all of a sudden?'

'I don't know,' Jing said, shamefacedly. 'It's just that lately I've been obsessed with the idea that I was somehow born of different parents than you and Mother. That's all.'

'Come on,' Father urged. 'Let's finish this bowl and have a good night's sleep before it gets too cold.'

Outside, a cold wind was blowing. One could hear the blasting of firecrackers. At first, it was sporadic and intermittent. Then it became intense, almost as if people were getting impatient to set fire to their feelings, trying to get rid of the old year as soon as possible with all the noise in the world that they could manage to ignite. Neither Jing nor Jing senior liked it much, which was probably why they, including Jing's mother, never celebrated New Year with any firecrackers. This haughtiness separated the family from the rest of the crowd. There was probably a suggestion about their foreignness without anyone being aware of it. As midnight drew closer, signalling the approach of New Year's Day, the noise of firecrackers became even louder and denser until the night was drowned in it, deafening the two of them, numbing the country and its people. Jing cursed it a few times for keeping him awake but Jing senior did not say a thing, glad that once again he had kept the secret intact and determined that it was still not yet time to reveal anything.

That night was especially cold, despite both their attempts to throw all their cotton clothes and trousers on top of their quilt and to lie as close to each other as possible. The next day, they woke up to a morning changed beyond recognition with a snow that had turned things white and fat. An eerie quietness was reigning supreme. Not a single whiff of wind. It was actually warmer than the previous night. Still, the office where they slept was a freezing hole. After his father went to the school canteen to buy breakfast, Jing found some broken table legs outside the library and put them in the middle of the office, away from the folded-up bed, the desk and a large wooden bookcase containing works by Karl Marx, Frederick Engels, Joseph Stalin and Mao Zedong, mixed with a number of Russian authors such as Gorky, Gogol, Pushkin and obscure Russian novels like *Cement* and *Courage*, all in Chinese translation. He put all the stuff together, the sticks and pieces of wood stained with snow, one on top of the other. Then he set fire to them. By the time his father came back with steamed bread and congee, there was a brisk fire, half of the room shrouded in heavy smoke, looking as if the office was covered in flames.

'Quick, quick,' Father said. 'Put the fire out!'

'It's nothing,' Jing said, as he opened the only window ajar to let the smoke out. In no time, the little office room was filled with warmth.

As they ate in silence, Jing senior observed his son out of the corner of his eye. He sat there, gazing into the fire, thinking; he always seemed to be thinking. In his eyes, Jing was still a kid, although he was nearly twenty-seven by his *xusui* (nominal age) now, alone, like him. Stung by this thought, he looked at Jing more closely and saw the change: there was a circle of air around him that strongly reminded him of his mother, his other mother. It was like a shadow at high noon that almost totally withdrew into itself under the direct noon sun but in a little while would come out either way as one walked, gradually lengthening. He was the only one, he believed, who could see the edge of that shadow as if it was plain day. He could not help but hold out his hand and touch Jing's hair, ever so lightly.

Jing quickly looked up, surprised, a question standing in his eyes.

'I was just going to pick that ash from your hair,' Father said.

'That's all.'

'Don't you worry about me,' Jing was vexed about his thread of thoughts being broken for he had been composing something in his head as part of his winter holiday writing assignment. It went like this:

I believe I was born into an aristocratic family and that there is quality blood running through my veins. Although there is no evidence of my belief, I find I'm naturally different from people around me. I am poor but I despise people whose behaviour is poor. When I hear what people say and see what they do, I am filled with a scorn for them as if they were infinitely inferior. There is nothing I like better than to be left alone, alone with trees, with a lake, for instance, or with the winter itself with snow or even with myself, which I think is another person living in me, sharing my life. My father must have been a king, not this old man sitting in front of me with no ambitions other than a pig's desire for his three daily meals; he doesn't even read books any more, reasoning that books should never have been written to make people miserable. I hate my surroundings and people, always wishing I were somewhere else; anywhere …

When he raised his head, it all left his memory. He was no king's son; he was only this unambitious half-century man's dreary son who traded thoughts for fun to while away a winter's day. Before long he would go back to that lake-side college for his English classes, taught by Chinese teachers with colourful accents smelling of unauthenticity. How he wished there was someone from abroad to teach them, especially him, the real stuff! Mr Fu once let out that this might happen sometime in the future. At the thought he brightened up, an image swimming before him, of someone tall and handsome, a bit Karl Marx–like, with ponds of knowledge, speaking impeccable BBC or Voice of America English, coaching them in a way no other people did or were able to. Once again he fell into a reverie that lasted a few minutes when he heard his father utter a cry of surprise. He looked up to see Jing senior grabbing hold of the basin of water he had used to wash his face, ready to pour it onto the fire. Then he realised what had happened: the pages of the book he had been holding in his hands but hardly reading had caught fire. Through his father's rush of action, first with the water in his tea mug, then with this basin, the fire was immediately extinguished but the book, *Courage*, a Russian novel, was drenched through, one page burnt black to more than half its original size.

'How I wish that this fire had burnt the whole building down and destroyed all the books!' Jing said.

'Why?' Father said, alarmed.

Without answering his question, which didn't need to be answered anyway, Jing strode outside and took a handful of snow and buried his burning face in it.

21

You saw snow earlier today in a television program where a man was putting cloth protection on this dog so that he could run around without being snow stained. If there is a coincidence, it is not intended. It has become unpredictable. Are you Jing? Are you becoming your character? Could we change our life's course like we can do in fiction? What if Jing knew that it all might go wrong because he had picked English as a career? Would he decide then and there to shift his course? How would he ever know? How would we? How would his father know, who only assumed that English might provide access to an outside world where one could find things to be different? Different? You laugh, in silence.

22

When he left to return to the university, Jing felt as if he was pulling out fresh roots that had struck in the soil of his hometown during his short stay. It caused his heart pain, thinking in particular of the warmth he had felt sleeping next to his father, his long creamy underpants smelling nicely of soap, and the times he had spent with Pi and Gao chatting about the old days while cracking melon or sunflower seeds over a cup of *yingshan* tea. It was soon over. The bus that took him back to Wuhan was filled to bursting with people returning home after the Spring Festival. The top of the bus was piled with bulging luggage pulled together with a large tightly stretched rope net and the narrow aisle inside was left with no standing room. People were talking loudly, smoking heavily and spitting freely. Jing hated it but he did the same; once again the feeling of being trapped returned, his eyes dimmed, his heart darkened and he sat dully in the bus without noticing anything, lost in his own thoughts, as was his habit. Many years later, he was to replace this crowded world with a sparsely populated one and would keenly miss this lost world with bitter irony.

The new teacher who was recruited for this term was a man with little hair but a large head and a strange dint immediately under his lower lip. He appeared almost as short as Mr Fu when he followed the latter into the room. The class became visibly disappointed upon seeing what some of them would later call a 'Little Foreigner'. Several boys started exchanging comments in an audible whisper. A girl could hardly suppress her embarrassed giggle at the sight of his deep eyes set in a bald face sitting on top of his yellow leather coat.

'Dr Wagner,' Mr Fu said, 'is from Melbourne, Australia. He is here to stay, to teach us oral English and writing from this term onwards. Let's give a big hand to welcome him.'

Applause arose, but it was not loud enough to be called enthusiastic. Was this a German? Why was he a doctor? If he was a German doctor, how could he be teaching them English? Why did they not find a genuine English person to teach English? Would that cost too much money? And why would they find someone from Melbourne, Australia, not New York or London? The class was full of unasked questions, eyes probing, brows knit, lips pouted, fingers uneasily fiddling with the edges of textbooks, shoes scraping the floor meaninglessly, all except Jing, who was looking at the man intently from the moment he entered the room and wondering why Dr Wagner looked nearly exactly the same as the man who appeared in one of his dreams. In that recent dream a doctor was trying to give him an injection to help him to sleep but he did not understand why. 'Sleep is good,' the bald-faced doctor said. 'It'll help you learn the language better.'

'What language?' He asked and woke himself up.

'Call me Bill, not Dr Wagner,' the short man said, removing some books from under his arm.

'Beer,' Bao imitated the word in a low voice, causing instant laughter among the girls, which was soon suppressed with a quick warning glance from Mr Fu.

'And,' as if to address the unanswered question, Dr Wagner said, 'I am not German. I'm an Australian. What that means is that I eat beef, drink beer,' he paused on the word 'beer' and pointed at Bao with his index finger, for a brief moment, before he continued amid a fresh chorus of laughter, this time more directed to Bao than Bill, 'and get bored, most of the time.'

'B-B-B,' someone said, and this time the class was surprised to find that it was issued from no other than Jing, who was known to be a quiet personality unless provoked. The monotony of these three Bs did much to fuel everyone's mirth, aptly capturing the essence, at least for the ignorant class, of what Australia from the example of this foreigner temporarily stood for.

'And did you know,' Dr Wagner said after Mr Fu left, 'what I enjoyed doing most in this city? Or do you want to have a guess?'

No one responded. Glances were exchanged but no one said a word.

'Perhaps we should introduce ourselves to each other, as a way of practising spoken English? Or oral English as Mr Fu put it? How about we start from the first student in the first seat of the first row on the left? If you could tell me, not about yourself, but about your neighbour sitting next to you, what her name is, how old she is – I mean you don't really have to if you don't want to or she doesn't want you to – what she likes and doesn't like, why she learns English, what she wants to do with English in the future and all those sorts of things. It doesn't have to take long. A few minutes each will do.'

This quaint way of introduction put the class in a more lively mood than before as it got the students moving, trying frantically to think a way of describing their neighbour, groping for words that had grown rusty during the winter holiday. The first victim sitting at the far left was Liu Ya, whose task was to say something about Qi Lili sitting on her right. She stood up, her face flushed a deep red, but Dr Wagner waved for her to sit down, not to bother with the formality. It was with some difficulty that she began, 'His name is Qi Lili and he comes from Tianjin.' Immediately she realised what she had done but it was too late to correct herself. Not only did the other girls scoff at this glaring mistake but Dr Wagner seemed amused, too.

Without making any comments, he picked up his pen and wrote something down in his notebook.

'But as far as I know,' stubborn enough to persist, Liu Ya went on, '*she* is quite nice and *she* is always ready to help people and *she* once said that *she* wanted to go to Australia one day.'

'Is that true?' Dr Wagner said, the tip of one of his eyebrows raised.

'That's only because,' Qi said, in her gentle voice, 'she, and a lot of the others, said that the only place they wanted to go to is America. So I said, I don't know out of what, Australia.'

'Perhaps antagonism?' Bill suggested.

'Jealousy would be a better word,' someone insinuated.

Dr Wagner turned to see this someone sitting by the window, his face half concealed by his khaki-coloured army cap, supported by his left hand, with a look that seemed to suggest that he didn't care one way or another.

'Let's say "out of an attempt to subvert the status quo", how's that sound?' Dr Wagner was trying to placate both of them. Then he realised he might have gone a bit too far. 'All right. Let's get back to the introduction. Perhaps you could tell me something about your friend?' he said to Ma Tian.

'He is Dang, Dang for Party, also for Codonopsis pilosula. From this you may have already guessed what he is up to for he is a medicine man. I'm sure he may come handy one day when you fall ill in China, although he can't help you with spiritual problems because he is really not a Party member. Or are you?'

'Nah, nah,' the narrow-eyed Dang Jie patted the air with one hand and gave the Horse a push with the other.

Introductions went round from the left rows to the right and from the front rows to the back until they reached Jing, sitting away from the rest of the class. There was no one for him to introduce and no one to introduce him, either. One could see that he was getting quite tense, although he tried not to show it, his eyes gazing outside the window at the leafless plane trees and his posture showing that he was not listening. When it was his turn to speak, however, he promptly stood up and, realising what he was doing, he sat down again, causing Bao to say, 'BBB' and Zhao Feiyan to giggle. Then he began, 'As I am learning French at the moment, I think my name should be Jean because it sounds like my Chinese name "Jing", although it is certainly not the English equivalent for Jean. Am I making any sense here? Without further ado, I must say I learn English for the English sake or for the sake of English because I seem to just like the language and I don't know what I can do with it in the future, maybe teaching it like you or something. Future is most unpredictable.' With that he withdrew much the same way a clamshell would, but he was secretly pleased with himself, particularly with the way in which the fashionable Zhao seemed to be looking his way.

'But,' Dr Wagner said, 'you will have to introduce someone other than yourself as I said before because this is the rule of the game, even though I do appreciate that you have introduced yourself for the whole class in such an efficient manner. Can you nominate someone or do you want me to choose someone for you?'

As Jing made no indication whom he wanted to talk about, Dr Wagner scanned the class, his eyes falling on a girl sitting in the middle row, also alone, and pointed her out. 'Tell me about her.'

Without looking, Jing knew that it was Zhao. This was impossible! Of all the people, why did he choose her for him to introduce? Was this some sort of conspiracy? He always had mixed feelings about Zhao. While enjoying her looks and fashionable dress in a detached way, he had little admiration for her poor academic progress and lack of focus on her studies. He did not know much about her except that she was from Shanghai and that she spoke good English but had a tendency to mix her 'l's for 'r's, pronouncing 'rice' as 'lice' or 'light' as 'right'.

'All I can say is this,' he began, thinking as he went along, 'that I don't have much communications with girl students in this class in general nor with her in particular. What can I say? I don't think I have even spoken to her for the whole length of last semester, not because I have anything against her or anyone else but simply because we did not speak to each other. Is that odd? I think so. Is there anything you can do about it? I don't think so. That is all.' With this Jing or Jean sat down abruptly but got up at once, adding, 'I haven't observed the rule, have I? I mean if we have medical doctors, architects, writers and what not in our class, we may also have fashion designers or even models and I have got a feeling that Ms Zhao may fit into one of these last two categories in the future but who knows?'

As Jing sat down, his glance met with Zhao's and he was convinced that she seemed grateful. That made him feel good about himself.

23

In reality, we cannot rush ahead to live. For example, we cannot live tomorrow from today even if we want to or choose to. In writing, however, we can. You, that is Jean or Jing, have covered half the distance in calendar time but in psychological time you seem to have reached the end of the tunnel where you wonder at all the absurdities of life, one of which is the so-called poetry that once thrilled you. If you had persisted in it, you would be no more, dying quicker than the rest of them put together. Indeed, it seems the best way for a genius to leave this world. Living anywhere after forty is a daily reminder of approaching old age and death. You can't bear to see the old faces associated with honour printed all over the pages of a newspaper or a book. And these people have the cheek to boast! But the poet in you has died, quietly, without a declaration again.

24

The first spring on campus was unforgettable for Jing, not only because of the arrival of Dr Wagner, but also because of Zhao, who seemed to have affected him in a way that could only be said to be a detrimental influence on his ability to study. Encouraged by Bill, who wanted to see a more healthy pairing of students in terms of the male-female ratio in his class, Jing now went out nearly every evening for a walk along the lake, ostensibly to practise speaking English with Zhao, but secretly to just enjoy being with her regardless of whether she felt the same. On this particular night he set out near dusk with a sense of expectation, a copy of *The Golden Treasury* under his arm, full of stories to tell Zhao, like 'The Western sky was smeared with blood-like cloud paint, throwing long expanses of sunset waves on the lake, to where the lotus pond was'. Last time he had told her of a story he had read about the life of a Chinese poet. It was based around the turn of the century and the poet's parents had arranged a marriage for him. The woman he was to marry was from the country, but she had a pair of beautifully bound feet, something that all rich families regarded as a prerequisite for their daughters-in-law. The poet, however, did not like this. On their first night after the wedding, he did not even go to bed with her, insisting that they sleep in two separate beds. And the next day he left for Japan, never to come back to her, although she turned out to be a dutiful daughter-in-law, looking after his parents well into their old age. But the story left Zhao cold. She did not say anything except that such things were common in those days. Her response didn't surprise Jing. He was actually practising telling this story for a purpose: he wanted to test it on Dr Wagner to see how he reacted to it, being an outsider to their culture. On their last couple of short lakeside walks, there was a sense of uneasiness between Zhao and Jing, mainly on Jing's part. He had struggled to find things to say and noticed that Zhao was not responsive. In fact, she always listened but seldom said anything. Only on one occasion when Jing commented on how lovely it would be to fish in the lake like the occasional fishermen they spotted during their stroll did Zhao say something. She responded harshly, 'What is there to fish for in this dirty lake?' It was not until then that Jing noticed the grey foam on the water's edge, the broken chopsticks, plastic rice boxes and unwanted scraps of paper. It was quite embarrassing, too, particularly when he was constantly made aware that he was walking beside a fashionably dressed girl who drew attention from all around. After that neither he nor she could concentrate much on anything.

Darkness was fast approaching as he walked in the lake grass, watching the faint stars on the water becoming brighter and listening to the croaking of the frogs growing louder. It was at such moments that Jing began to wonder why he bothered about studying to become something and why, instead, he wouldn't rather be a peasant or a gardener – at least then he could have all the quietness in the world and work in beautiful surroundings with the stars, the frogs, the wavelets receding and surging, with the fading hues of the setting sun, and the cool descending directly from the sky and the depths of the hills. Again, he went over his story in his head in preparation for his evening walk with Zhao. It would go something like this: I went to the adjacent university this morning to have a look in their departmental library. The old librarian was very nice, no, I mean he was very kind. When he saw that I was keen on getting hold of any English books to read, he allowed me to go into the back room to have a peek. The back room was really a storeroom that didn't seem to have been touched by anyone for years. It was cluttered with old and broken student desks covered in thick dust. You could hardly move between them, I mean you could hardly find room to swing a cat in or is that the phrase we've learnt lately? I am trying to put that into practise if you know what I mean? I squeezed myself in, leaving my other friends behind as they were quite reluctant to follow, seeing that it was such a dark hole full of dust. I managed to get in and I saw heaps of books in the furthest corner of the room, again holding loads of dust. I picked up one and had to blow the dust away like this: *puchi*! Or should I say *pootsi*? Anyway, when the title revealed itself, I got quite a shock because guess what? It was a book by William Thackeray, called *Vanity Fair*. It was a masterpiece, did you know? Then there was Charles Dickens' *Great Expectations* and *Oliver Twist*, Thomas Hardy's *Jude the Obscure* and *Tess of the d'Urbervilles*, poems by Shelley, Byron and Wordsworth, and this *Golden Treasury*. Did you know how much I loved this poetry book? Oh, you only have to read it to appreciate its beauty. You could read it ahead of me if you like.

Jing got more excited as he rehearsed this in his head, tasting the words on his tongue, as if he was speaking to Zhao directly. In a wild moment, all he could see was her face and he dared to hold out his hand in an attempt to touch it, much the same way the ancient English poets would do to the ones they loved as they described in their poems. But the hand he held out hit something hard and it hurt. It was a willow tree standing by the pond that he'd reached for in his attempt to feel for Zhao's hand, thinking it was hers. This was absurd. He looked again towards the path where she would normally turn up and was disappointed to see no sign of her approaching. What happened?

He got impatient as he wanted to see her and recite this poem that he had learnt by heart from the *Treasury*, which, he repeated to himself for the tenth time, went:

Gather ye rosebuds while ye may,
Old Time is still a-flying,
And this same flower that smiles today
Tomorrow will be dying …

He wasn't quite sure how he would pronounce 'ye' properly as his English textbooks contained nothing about this, so he would have to check it with Dr Wagner. Until then, he would have more interesting things to discuss with Zhao for he had discovered something in Tang Dynasty Chinese poetry that was so strikingly similar to this English poem that it caused him to wonder how people centuries, continents and languages apart could entertain such similar sentiments. On the lakeside avenue, he could see shadows in twos and threes moving back towards the campus and he realised that it must be getting late. Upset by her absence, which he thought was deliberate, he decided to turn back. There was a short cut he could use to get back to his dormitory. which meant taking a path by the foreign-experts building. When he reached there, his footsteps slowed down with the thought that he might drop in on Bill, who had often urged his students to visit him in their spare time. Jing was hesitant as he was not sure if this was proper etiquette for a foreigner, and what if he was to see improper things such as nude pin-ups in his teacher's room. With no direct experience with Westerners, Jing had nevertheless learnt from the books and newspaper stories that he had read that Western men were particularly fond of sex. It would be embarrassing if he surprised Dr Wagner in the act. Jing had almost gone past the building when he found himself turning around the corner, going straight inside and aiming for the door that was open through which a yellow globe was shining. It was not hard for him to pinpoint Bill's room as each door had a nametag on it inviting entry, with a welcome message. Dr Wagner's door had a piece of paper pinned to it with a hand-drawn kangaroo above his name 'Bill' and the words: Please leave your message here. Dangling alongside this was a pencil nearly worn to its butt. Jing hesitated again as he heard laughter inside but his hand was quicker than his mind; it had already reached the door and was knocking on it. It would be too late now to retreat. Where the door opened, he heard his own name being called, 'Oh, it is Jean, our quiet man!' and 'Come on in and take a seat!'

The first thing that struck Jing was the smell. Nowhere had he smelled such a pungent foreign scent. It was so exotic that it made him heady. The tiny room was packed with people, and, in one glance, he knew he had come to the wrong place at the wrong time, for the room was full of his female classmates, including, most unpleasant of all, Zhao Feiyan, who was sitting in a corner sofa below the floor lamp, pretending to be engrossed in her book, not even raising her eyes to see who had come in. Bill, who was wearing a checkered red flannel shirt and grass-coloured corduroy trousers, came over and said, 'Welcome! See, your mates are all here.'

Not true, Jing mentally retorted and reluctantly sat down in a high-backed chair that Bill had pulled over amid a fresh bout of laughter from the girls, who seemed to find everything Bill said funny. But all Jing could think of was why Zhao had failed to show up for their appointment and why she was now doing what she was doing. He found it hard to suppress an urge to rush to the corner seat where Zhao was sitting and shout in her face why didn't she come to practise oral English as she said she would. Was it because he was too ugly for her? Or was it because he spoke worse English than her? Was it because he had revealed something to her about his family background that she felt uncomfortable with? Or was it because she had already shifted her attention to this foreign devil thinking he might one day take her to Australia or something? He did not know what he was doing but he stood up and went straight to the door, to the amazement of everyone, including Bill, whose question into Jing's ear 'How's your day today?' was completely ignored.

In a second, he had gone. No goodbye said, not even a short one. Just a whiff of wind that the shutting of the door had brought into the room.

Back in his dormitory, after he had washed his feet, Jing began reading his book again, desultorily, listlessly, drained by his outburst, when his eyes lit up at the opening lines of a poem, 'Love a woman? You're an ass!/'Tis a most insipid passion/ To choose out for your happiness/The silliest part of God's creation.' It suited his mood at this particular moment so much that he went on to finish reading the whole poem in one sitting, then read it again. He did not agree with 'the silliest' but he was happy that someone dead a long time ago could have reflected his sentiments so accurately. He told Dang, who was lying in bed reading, what he had just read. Facing the wall, with his back towards him, part of his body wrapped in his flowery cotton quilt, Dang said nonchalantly, 'That could have been written by an old man, you know? Someone my age would never write like that. I mean would you?'

'Unless you were jilted or something,' came a comment from Hongjun, who was at his desk doing some exercises to be handed in the next day.

'What are you talking about?' Jing was deeply hurt. 'I'm not jilted.'

'What's the matter with you, Jean,' Bao said. 'I didn't mean "you", you know? I mean "you" as anyone, a generic term, you know that.'

Jing fell silent, knowing he should not have responded like that. Reading anything was out of the question now. So he crept into bed and decided to go to sleep as quickly as possible but he was not able to. His ears picked up every little sound from outside and inside the room, the shuffling of someone walking in the corridor, the throaty voice of several people next door singing a theme song from a television drama recently broadcast throughout the country, someone farting not far away from his bed, the turning of pages by Dang, the occasional sucking noise Bao made inside his nostrils, the clinking and clanging of the mouth-washing mugs hitting against the bottom of the basins when his other roommates came back from the library, and the creaking of the wooden boards below him each time he turned from one side to the other in his bed. And, long after the lights went out when the only light that came through the window pane was from a distant road lamp, Jing was still wide awake. It was only when he half dreamed that he had somehow taken Zhao in his arms and made her make love with him until he was totally exhausted that he finally fell into a deep sleep. When he woke up the next morning, it was well past nine; he had missed the first class, for the first time in the whole school term.

25

You wonder if reality ever matches what is traditionally worded in terms of love, friendship, fame, fortune, and if evil plays a far greater role in driving these than virtue; and in which your daily realisation gravitates to the zero level where you neither feel hot or cold; and in which the changing of a continent and a country for another seems to have constituted the worst mistake you have ever made, irrevocably, and the learning of English has finally resulted in your tragedy, one that not even Shakespeare could have imagined; and in which you can laugh at Jing for not having the slightest idea where he was going in the course of his life and what he was going to achieve in the scheme of things, very much predetermined like the rain.

Dr Wagner's arrival had little, if any, effect on Jing, except that he was made aware daily of a foreign presence on campus. His life, like everyone else's, took its own course in spite of or because of or even 'under' English, a preposition Jing liked to use. Indeed, from time to time, he felt as if this sky over him was being replaced by a different sky, called English, with words like heaven and firmament, and he was literally living under English, willingly, masochistically, uncritically and perversely poetically. English now filled him with romance, romantic poetry and melancholy, with which he saw his local lake through the eyes of Wordsworth and Coleridge; it helped him feel sadder for no reason at all by empathising with Keats, Shelley and Byron; it reduced him to a walking heap of pessimism who hated life with the kind of vehemence of *Jude the Obscure,* imagining that the place where he was currently living was as desolate and forlorn as the Eden wilderness. He was determined to forget his mother tongue, Chinese, urged by the advice of Mr Fu, who said, 'The best way to master English is to forget Chinese! Do not just speak English; think in English.' And that was exactly what he was doing, thinking through English, and under English, of course. If there was no woman he could bring himself to love or even like, or, in other words, no woman who could love or even like him, there was at least English as a language that could hold his attention for weeks on end, a linguistic woman if you like, that could bear his love or like for as long as he loved or liked. His daily schedule demonstrated this obsession:

7am: Get up and jog along Lake Avenue while reciting the previous three lessons;

8am: Read the new lesson loudly and repeatedly until you can read from the first word to the last without any interruptions or mistakes;

8.30am: Breakfast over *Vanity Fair*;

9-11.30am: Class;

Noon: Read some English poetry;

Afternoon: More classes;

6-7pm: Oral English on campus or along the lake;

7-8pm: Copy *The Golden Treasury* in longhand;

9pm: Review lessons learnt or do exercises;

10-11pm: Listen to Voice of America or BBC.

English, English, English. It's all EEE, not BBB as Bao mocked, secretly giving it to Dr Wagner as a pet name, but Jing loved it all the same and for this he also earned the nickname 'E Jing' from Bao, based on the sound of the *Book of Change* (Yi Jing in Chinese and I Ching in English). E Jing would read his dictionary from cover to cover, one of the daily activities that he hadn't marked on his list as it had already become a habit. A few pages a day and by the end of the year, hopefully, he would acquire thousands of words and would become the most learned person in the class with the largest vocabulary. What could he not do with *that*? On the other hand, there were some things he could not achieve – getting top marks, for example, like Sweet Horse. In every exam Ma would always score over ninety-five per cent, whether it be on grammar, or word study or a quiz on the text they had just learnt. All those Ma managed to do with apparently no difficulty, sleeping much of the day away in his neatly organised bed or just sitting by the window drinking tea from a large white iron mug bearing the Chinese characters 'Ministry of Coal' with a five-cornered star in striking red, in deep meditation or just enjoying the lovely aftertaste of his surfeit of sleep.

In the evenings, Ma, E Jing and Dang would often wander along the lake, ostensibly to practise their spoken English. After a while, though, their talk would gravitate into Chinese conversations about other things, mainly bits and pieces that had happened during the day concerning other classmates or discussions about the quality of the meals or that of the teaching staff, a topic that Ma and Dang never tired of but that was not particularly interesting to Jing. For him, his sole purpose in coming to the university was to learn, to acquire as much knowledge as was humanly possible in the shortest time as the pain of having lost many years, first in a village farming the field, then in the factory driving the trucks, was too real. Politely, he listened to them arguing about the benefits of having more frequent examinations while he was thinking what was the best way to learn by heart all of those good poems in *The Golden Treasury*. While they were talking about Dr Wagner speaking English without a standard accent, sounding quite vulgar as he did, Jing felt thankful to him for lending him a range of books including *China: Alive in a Bitter Sea*. Perhaps because of Jing's reticence, they shifted their attention to him. It was Ma who first spoke, 'A penny for your thoughts, E Jing, you are in a brown study again!'

'No,' Jing said. 'I'm actually in a green study.' He said this as his hand swept the air in an arc that included the tree-lined bank encircling the lake and the greenish hills beyond.

'Study? What are you guys talking about?' Dang asked.

'When he said "study", he didn't mean study,' Jing said, pointing a finger at Ma. 'But when I said "study", I did mean study, the green study we are in. Don't you see? Better than anything we have got.'

'Come on, you are playing with words again,' Dang said, feigning disgust.

'I don't know if I am,' Jing said. 'Fact is, I often feel that words are playing with me.'

'Interesting,' Ma said. 'Go on.'

Whenever Ma assumed a half-serious tone in his conversations, Jing could not help but suppress a chuckle, but this time he felt that he did have something to say. 'You see. I don't know how to say this but the other day when I found my name changed from Jing to Jean, I felt as if the words themselves had a power of changing one's, one's … er, what was the word Dr Wagner once used to describe that sort of status in which one lost one's, er, er …?'

'Virginity, you mean?' Dang said and burst out into a prurient laughter.

'I know what you meant,' Sweet Horse said. 'It's more than that. It's also something that ends in "ty". Oh yes, let me see. Was it something to do with one's being or character or personality or …'

'Identity!' Jing exclaimed. 'That's what it was. Bill used that word so frequently that I ended up checking it in my English-Chinese dictionary but was no wiser. All it told me was something in Chinese that meant *shenfen* (the status of the body). Pretty meaningless, for that purpose.'

'I suggest you use an English-English dictionary now,' Ma offered.

'That would make you a real EEE,' Dang joked.

With his fist raised up in the air, Jing made as if he was going to strike at Dang, who evaded the fake blow by quickly hiding behind a roadside tree. It was such a big tree that he lost himself entirely behind it, so dark against the shining lake that spread itself in an expanse of water for miles around. One could smell a mixture of fallen and rotten leaves, fish, dead or alive, and the water, which was prevalent in the air. After a while, when he didn't show up, Jing was afraid that he might have dropped into the water even though there was no noise of splashing; he might have slipped into it like a silent block of roadside soil. Just as Jing was about to go around and have a look, with a loud shriek, Dang came out from behind the tree, holding something in his hand that looked like a snake, which so frightened Jing that he stepped back instantly.

What he was holding was actually an abandoned woman's black nylon stocking, which he dangled before their eyes for fun when both Ma and Jing caught something white on its tip and stopped him by calling out together, 'What's that?' but were disappointed to see that it was only a used condom.

'How could these things have found their way here?' Jing was curious, while Ma fell into a silence from which he didn't come out for the rest of the evening.

'I think some people must have done that sort of thing here, you know,' Dang said.

'Could it have been that they were only playing with the stocking?' Jing was shocked by his own speculation because it was very revealing about his thoughts.

'Nope,' Dang dismissed the idea as unthinkable. 'You would have to wear this to do that. You mean you never did it before?'

'What nonsense!' Jing was about to say when he changed his mind; he would have sounded too naïve or innocent. 'Did you?'

'What have I not done?' Dang said, his eyes showing that remoteness again. 'Despite my younger age.'

'What did you do then?' Jing was reminded of his medicinal adventures in the depths of the mountains.

'I don't know,' Dang said, without much interest. 'I think

it's time I go back to the library to get some reading done. What about you guys?'

'You mean it's time you went back?' Jing said.

'Oh, you picky grammarian!' Dang said.

'Well, I might just go to bed, I think,' Ma said.

'I'm not sure,' Jing said, thinking of his poetry for the day.

27

Dr Wagner's approach to teaching was simple, even simplistic, because he was told so by the stern-faced Madam Mao, who summoned him one day into her office and told him in her broken English that he was not allowed to teach his students more than what the Party had regulated.

'Just plain oral, you know,' she said. 'Oral, you know, with your tang, saying, spoking, right? Right. US and UK. No other cunt trees. Andersdand?'

It took Bill some time to understand what she actually meant. And when he did he felt insulted, not of course by the 'cunt trees' for he knew she would not be *that* literate but by her willful interference. He did not come to China with a hidden agenda, as they assumed he had, but he had come to see it for himself, to experience Asia or what was quintessentially Asian. Perhaps there had been an exotic attraction but that was only part of a larger excitement whose significance he had only begun to grasp and was yet to find the words to express. Already, he was faced with a class of young people whose aspirations travelled far beyond the borders of China, whose motivation was like nothing he had ever seen in a comparatively dreary Australian suburb, and whose learning skills were amazingly intuitive, coupled with a respect for their teacher that few of his peers could experience in Australia. Call it slavish but he liked it for its own sake. He was never called Bill, it was always Dr Wagner this or Dr Wagner that that his students called him. After many years' teaching English in a private school, this was a great change, almost a catharsis, purging him of years of accumulated inaction, indifference and institutionalised boredom. He had come to show the light; instead, he had seen the light, the light shown by these transparent human beings. Secretly, he would hate to teach them anything Western, even less Australian. Why, such young hearts need not be laden with Western cynicism, conceit and contradictions, driven unilaterally towards a monetary god.

Still, business was business. He was recruited to teach English and he needed to show the best examples of the language to these aspiring students. But, as he argued forcibly, he did not have any intention of inculcating his students with bourgeois ideas; he himself did not even know what these ideas were. Nor would the kind of English that he taught corrupt them so that they became monsters instead of more refined human beings. Apart from the designated teaching syllabus emphasising the importance of the great proletarian nineteenth-century American and English authors, stopping at the turn of the century, he had also brought what he thought might be beneficial to his students, Australian fiction consisting of Christina Stead, Xavier Herbert, David Malouf and Patrick White, to name but a few, with an emphasis on their more recent work. This was the early 80s and why did they want him to teach something nearly a hundred years old, supposedly revolutionary and proletarian, such as *Uncle Tom's Cabin*, *Middlemarch* and *Torrents of Spring*? That was absurd. He nearly screamed but, curiously, remembered what his wife, Deirdre, said years ago when their relationship was relatively good, 'Keep your cool, Bill, and never lose your head.'

Dr Wagner had come alone, determined to do it his own way. The kind of life he had been living so far was too much for him to bear, a wife whom nothing he did seemed to satisfy and the lack of children that made their life even more empty. It did not mean that their relationship had completely broken down. What it meant was that the belief that they would somehow be part of each other's life forever, a belief as much a societal one as a familial one, had been severed. In an intense moment he had said, coolly and strangely, 'I think you and I will die early because of our togetherness. Don't you see your eyes and mine are black, brimming with poison?' What he did not say was that perhaps each time he ejaculated into her, it was pitch dark poison that he shot out instead of a life force containing semen. With all that behind him, he was now enjoying the new status of being Dr Wagner from a respected developed country, even with the pain of having to deal with the politics of teaching an English class.

There was another inconvenience. One of the terms and conditions in his contract when his application was accepted for the job was that he must be a married man and he filled out the insulting form as though he was one. The contract seemed to blatantly imply that if he came to China as a virile male he would open a Chinese Pandora's box and create endless trouble womanwise or otherwise. His solo arrival was thus eyed with suspicion and mistrust. He had to present the faculty with a letter together with a medical certificate explaining that his wife would soon be joining him when she recovered from her imaginary illness. In fact, she had long been suffering from insomnia, an incurable ailment that could only be treated with patience and perhaps an improved marriage, which was never going to be, an oxymoron in itself. As one's life invariably draws to a close, one's marriage invariably dis-improves. That's at least what Dr Wagner thought.

While waiting for Deidre to arrive, Bill was having a ball, a bachelor again, surrounded mostly by his female students who were keen on learning more about Australia and seemed to admire him immensely. Occasionally, he was also visited by his younger male students such as Bao, Hu and Wei. He was expecting to see more visitors but some of them seemed quite resistant to the idea of paying homage, a mere visit really, like Ma, for example, who spoke effortlessly fluent English, and Jing, who never showed up again after that weird incident in which he stopped for less than a few minutes before flying off in a storm; no one could work out why he did what he did. However, from what he had read of Jing's written exercises, Bill perceived a sharp and sensitive mind at work, more so than the man's face revealed, which at times alternated between remoteness and woodenness, a cold façade and an impenetrable, or what he would sometimes call inscrutable, mask. He would love to know more about Jing and of course all the other students but he was limited in his capacity as a language instructor. Unless they came to him of their own accord, he would not offer to visit them in their dormitories as it might cause disturbances or breach the discipline the school authorities were so uptight about.

Still, he had a plan, unformulated at first but gradually more focused, in which he wanted to introduce more of the West to them in an attempt to make them more knowledgeable about the larger world. If they did not show much interest in Australia, it didn't present a serious problem. As their interest widened, they would gradually notice things and make their own decision about their own future wherever they wanted to anchor it. He was there to lead, to give guidance, to inspire. Yes, inspire. 'To colonise, to civilise', words by the author of *Westward Ho* wafted into his mind, matching his conquering mood.

So he said to Madam Mao, in a very gentle voice, almost soft, supple, subtle, 'You are right. I won't touch other "cunt trees", only two, as you said, Madam. And you know what we say in Australia? It's a bloody good idea, mate! And she'll be right.'

28

You are Jing. Yes, that's what you are and who you are. You are who you think you are. You think you are whoever you are, therefore you are.

29

Overnight, the days had turned so hot that eight out of the nine suns that Hou Yi had shot down from the sky in ancient times seemed to have all returned to their original places, vying to outshine each other. Jing and his classmates were left wearing nothing but their shorts and using whatever they could find, a piece of school newspaper, a borrowed magazine or an exercise book, as a fan to expel the never-drying sweat. Outside, cicadas were sonorous, bringing in a summer in full swing without announcement, the trees all on fire, burning day and night, in total green. Girls were so exposed that you could see the shape of their underpants through their skirts in a distinct 'V' and the inverted 'P' of their bras through their half-transparent blouses and you could get a hard-on straight away if you were standing in such close proximity. If this was not true of other people, it was true of Jing, as that was what he saw and how he felt at the sudden approach of that summer. The old, odd feeling that he had somehow grown wooden from years of working in a factory had gone, replaced by a new understanding that he could gradually create a different, though elusive, reality for himself with his newly acquired language.

Powered by the imagery from *The Golden Treasury* and a range of other books that were not included in the school syllabus, not even suggested by Dr Wagner, but all obtained through his own efforts, Jing picked up his old habit of keeping a diary again, writing fragments of poetry or prose, all in English, and tried to sharpen his powers of observation by taking notes on people around him, from those nearest him, Xin, Bao, Ma, Dang, and those furthest away from him, Zhao, Liu Ya and Zhenya. Soon he found that he had cultivated a taste that deviated from the current literary trends favoured by the mass print media, a taste that favoured the pessimistic, the sad, the unsuccessful, the disadvantaged, in a word, the outsiders and the social misfits. In a mixed group discussion about what favourite colours people had, he had nominated 'dark' as the one he loved best. 'Dark, deep night; a dark forest; a dark river on a dark night through a dark wood; a heart dark in its pumpings; a mind as dark as my eyes …'

'I'm sorry,' Zou Ganmei could no longer contain her anger. 'If you love darkness so much, why, for God's sake, do you not go to Africa or choose a black fellow as your friend?'

She might not have been as aggressive as he had imagined her to be but his response was, 'To tell you the truth, one of my best friends was an African man called Kwame who is a student here. Why, darkness is not a crime nor is a belief in it, I don't think.'

'I guess,' Dr Wagner, who had been watching the students practising their oral English, cut in, 'what Jing meant by darkness is more a philosophical or poetic concept than a real fact. I guess he likes to probe beyond the surfaces, to reach, as it were, the root of things. Is that right?'

Jing did not say anything but his eyes showed that he was appreciative of what Dr Wagner had said.

'Oh yes,' Bao agreed. 'I've worked out why this is philosophical because Hegel's Chinese name has a "hei" in it, *hei ge er*, meaning black, which sounds like Black Girl when backtranslated, weirdly. German author Hesse also has something dark in his Chinese name, *hei sai*. See what I mean?' He winked at Xin and Jing, both of whom smiled knowingly.

'*Heiye gei wo yishuang heise de yanjing, wo yong ta lai xunzhao guangming,*' Xin said.

'What was that?' Dr Wagner was bewildered.

'Darkness gives me a pair of dark eyes with which I search for light,' Jing translated and said, 'It's by Gu Cheng, a poet, although I don't think highly of him.'

'Why not?' Xin Shen asked. 'Because you are jealous of him? He's quite famous.'

'Being famous does not mean everything he writes is necessarily praiseworthy and we don't read someone because he or she is famous.'

'Can you give us an example of what you mean by this?' Bill encouraged him as he glanced at a few knit brows and one glare from Xin.

'Well, the other day I read a novel titled *The Old Wives' Tale* by an Arnold Bennett. I can bet my bottom dollar if anyone of you has ever heard of the title or the author but of course I don't mean you, Dr Wagner, and I'd like to thank you for teaching me the "bottom dollar" phrase. I mean it's not a novel that you would compare with works by the "famous" people such as Flaubert, Stendhal, Dostoyevsky, Tolstoy, but it is something so ordinary, or engrossing, so how can I describe it …?'

'You mean so true-to-life, so vivid, so resilient, so earthy?' Bill prompted.

'Yes and more,' Jing said. 'I mean you almost felt as if you became part of the character herself and it was truly touching to the core. I nearly cried myself on several occasions. And yet there's nothing so special about the whole thing, just two old women.'

'Well,' Zou Ganmei blurted out. 'I think there's a problem with your attitude towards women. What do you mean "just two old women"? You sound as if you were saying "just two old cats" or "just two old dogs" or something. Don't you think, Dr

Wagner? According to our Chairman Mao, women can hold up half the sky, right?'

'Oh, yes, you certainly are and certainly can,' Dr Wagner said. 'I really think you should go and find a copy of *The Female Eunuch* to read, Gun May. It will be fantastic for you guys if you know how to handle it and not go over the top. As for Jing, he should be given some credit for saying that he was full of tears several times and that he felt as if he had become part of the character himself. That to me doesn't show that he is callous towards women, what do you guys think?' He turned towards Liu Ya who was watching him.

'I would have thought he was a man of kind heart if he cried from reading fiction.'

'On the contrary,' Zou counteracted. 'People who cry, say, in a cinema, do not necessarily do so in reality. That is to say they may be moved by what is described in a movie or a story but when they encounter similar kinds of situation in real life they often make no response.'

'Do you take me for such a person?' Jing exclaimed. 'How dare you?' He could have said that he was a man of feeling, that he cried when Chenfang broke his heart and that he would have a sense of *bisuan* whenever he left his dad and his friends like Pi and Chiang for the university by the lake, but he was struck speechless by his own sudden anger while at the same time bemused by the translation of *bisuan* as 'nose sour', a kind of sour sensation in the nose when one feels sad or moved.

'How goes the enemy?' Bao said to cut the tension, repeating the familiar phrase that he had heard Jing use from time to time, causing everyone to laugh except Jing, who sat there brooding, and Bill, who was perplexed by the intensity of the conflict.

That night, Jing made a diary entry with these words:

I don't like real people. I prefer them fictional. Jude, for example, or Tess, or Jean Valjean, or Gatsby. Real people are intolerable, Bao with his stinking runners never washed; Ma chewing noisily like a horse while having meals; Xin with his faulty pronunciation of 'sub tell' for 'subtle', 'hand some' for 'handsome' and 'wore' for 'whore'; Zou with her literary aspirations and pretensions, reducing everything to her level of a schoolmarm; Zhao with her heavier make-up that ceased to win a glance from me; even Dr Wagner with his eyes set so closely below the brow that they sometimes threaten to disappear in the dark cloud that the black brow throws down and his tiny cornlike teeth that seldom show themselves, even in a laughter, except perhaps Dang, who was always clean and organised. There was something about him that I found, hmmm, quite hard to describe. It was something, well, perhaps something that belongs to another world. I don't know. Sometimes, I prefer to be a fictional character myself, not living in this world, but in a book, like a piece of text that can be shifted from one book to another, copied, translated, discussed, inserted etc. I don't know. I have yet to find myself.

You think you'll allow this bit in considering the fact that you've deleted such a large portion of it, just for you to glimpse a bit of the process. In those days, 'finding oneself' was a catch-cry. You could pick up a handful of them from any number of published stories or poems or essays. It became an instant cliché. Everyone loved it. You were not Jing, although he is threatening to enter your life and story with increasing magnitude. There are other places you want him to be involved in, such as Kunming, and other people to be involved with, such as his younger brother and his mother and other times as when his father fought in the war. You are prepared to let these regular interruptions go as they may be considered to be irrelevancies, or experimental, or an excuse for your inability to weave an interesting yarn?

In fact, the story of Jing's mother can be told in a few sentences. Over the Spring Festival, she went to Kunming to see Jing's brother Nei and had fun in the City of Spring. For some reason, or for obvious reasons, she left by herself without telling either Jing or his father. She stayed there until after the Lantern Festival. She thought by so doing she could forget Yellow Town but the more she stayed in Kunming, the more she thought about Jing and the connection of Jing with Kunming, Jing's birthplace, not to her, but to someone else, a foreigner who had long since gone back to her country of origins. Now, you don't even know if this is true but you spin up the fictional lie as if it were nonfictionally true.

Her old parents were there, too, for it was the place where she was born and bred until Jing senior came along and took her away, to a backdrop town in Hubei, thousands of kilometres away from the pearl-like Dianchi Lake and streets with cloth shoes and fragrance of tea leaves and all the deliciously eatable insects. When he met her, he already had a baby, renting at a place called Sangshu, after he got discharged from the army. Their meeting was quite accidental, he holding the baby in his arms sitting in the sun out at the gate and she passing by. It so happened that the baby wanted to piss and he held him, face out, legs spread open, his little hard dick up and out, of the bottom-less baby trousers, while whistling a tune that quickened the pace of pissing. Up went a shaft of glittering urine that landed right on the flowery trouser leg the owner of which was no other than Xiang, Wang Xiang, the fragrant king. Xiang was on her way to a nearby market to buy watermelons. She had black hair, black eyes and wore black cloth shoes but her light-coloured blouse had tiny pink and blue flowers near her breast and her shoulders as if she had just walked through a wood with rain of flowers. She was nice-looking and held her head high in the sun.

The baby boy's naughty act and his father's cry of surprise gave her a shock as she felt hot then wet then hot wet on one of her feet. It was too late when she realised what had happened. Jing Fang, father of the baby, stood up with the crying baby as he pinched him hard on the bottom, and apologised. His accent gave him away at once as someone from a different place but Xiang took more notice of the baby than his father as she could see it was a lovely boy with a beautiful white skin, much whiter than any Chinese babies she had ever seen. She was invited into the darkened room while Fang got a stool for her and, with his disengaged hand, was trying to wipe her bottom trouser leg clean. It only made things worse, leaving smudges on it as his towel was not clean. What a pretty mess! Xiang did not know whether she should cry or laugh but the sight of the baby calmed her down. She would much love to caress him, fondle him and even kiss him on his red lips.

You realise that the story is getting too long now and you'd have to stop here for Dr Wagner's wife to come to the scene and some other things to happen before that happens. Anyway, that's how Xiang and Fang met for the first time.

31

The summer was so hot, sometimes getting to more than 40°C, that male classmates only wore their shorts in their open rooms or corridors except for Dang who insisted on proper dress with his white short-sleeved shirt and creamy colored western-style short trousers while girl students on the top floor had a sign put up before the staircase that said: NO MALES BEYOND THIS POINT. On several occasions, Jing suggested that they should go out and spend a night on the hill but no one listened, thinking he was only joking, until one night, on the spur of the moment, he said, head over homework under a single lamp that seemed to be burning fiercely, 'Sorry, guys, I have to go. If you don't want to come, you can stay here burning like hell while I'll enjoy the cool up there.' With his chin pointed towards the hill, he started rolling his straw mat with a pillow inside.

'You'll probably need to take your quilt with you as I'm sure it will be quite cold up there, even though it's so bloody hot here,' Xin said, fanning himself with a large exercise book in which he had been doing his homework.

'I think I'll go to sleep now,' Ma said, picking up his towel and toothbrush and toothpaste. Jing was amazed and at the same time dismayed by his ability to sleep under whatever circumstances, hot or cold.

For Jing, however, heat was only one of many reasons he was having trouble sleeping. Lately, he had grown weary of a career geared towards success. Why bother getting a straight 100 per cent in every subject just to please your parents and your classmates so that they could look up to you as a model student?

Why bother studying even further in English or American literature so that you could eventually become a professor of that literature? Why bury yourself in books for the rest of your life? What's the ultimate purpose in all that? The more he thought of these things, the more weary he grew and the more poetry he read, particularly by Wordsworth, the less he liked his surroundings and his daily realities. 'What's the point?' he wrote in a short story never intended for publication, in the words of the main character called 'He' who questions the meaning of everything in life until he is on the point of committing suicide by jumping from the top level of a building.

'Just as he throws one leg over the short wall, looking down at the ant-like people crawling underneath along the campus path, a thought comes to him: "what's the point of doing this?" and he instinctively withdraws his leg, instead of throwing another leg over it in the final preparation for the big jump.' Xin could hardly contain his mirth when he read this. Dang took a different view. 'He is not dark enough,' he said. 'If you keep questioning everything, you end up doing nothing, like Hamlet. I think I prefer to be a man of action.'

Tonight, Jing thought he was a man of action because he wanted to do what he had long desired to: go out and spend a night on top of the Mill Hill and do it for no other reason than the sheer pleasure of it. As he took his rolled-up straw mat with his pillow inside, he heard Dang say, 'I'll come with you' and then Xin say, 'I'll come also.' He stopped, relieved to know that he had somehow touched a soft spot in them; somewhere deep within each of them there was a desire to transcend the language, for things beyond the merely successful. On their way, they passed Liu Ya and Zhenya from their class, who were just coming back from a sweaty after-dinner stroll by the lakeside and kept complaining about how hot and sultry it was.

'Where are you going?' Zhenya asked, not particularly to anyone.

'Oh,' Jing said. 'We are going to the Temple.'

'Where is that?' Liu Ya said.

'On the hill,' Dang said. 'Where there are monks.' But his words belied his facetiousness: he chuckled before he could go into further details.

'Look,' Jing said, assuming a serious tone. 'We are going to spend a night on the hill over there where they say it is very cool. If you guys are not frightened, you are welcome to come along with us.'

'Who says we are frightened?' Zhenya said. 'I'm even taller than you.'

'And I am not afraid of anyone,' Liu Ya said. 'I had a lot of fights with boys when I was young, did you know that?'

'But you are barely eighteen,' Jing was about to say but he bit his tongue.

'Then why don't you go back to your dormitory and bring your things with you?' Xin reminded them.

In no time, the five of them formed a motley crowd and went on their way up the hill overlooking the lake. At first, no one said anything. Partly awed by the beauty of the night with a lake darkly lit up by the distant city lights and even more distant starlight, and partly embarrassed by the thought of the possible consequences that might result in spending the night together on the hill, they listened to their own heart murmurings and footsteps beside a melodious hill of singing night insects as they went past a bridge flanked on either side by the *jiazutao*, sweet scented oleander, trees in full bloom, through a deserted wood by the lake, past a still pond, until they came to the foot of the hill, wrapped up in dense foliage where it suddenly fell dark. With the shrieking of a strange nameless bird, Liu Ya 'ah-ed'.

'You see,' Jing said. 'Since we are not too far from campus, if someone gives up, they can still turn back.'

'There's no turning back at the gate of hell,' Liu Ya recited Karl Marx's famed remark.

'To go or not to go, that is the question,' Dang said.

'To go is not the question and not to go is out of the question,' Jing said.

'Stop playing words, will you?' Zhenya said, her thick-strapped sandals stamping along the road, splashing dust as she went ahead.

'All right,' Jing said. 'We'll elect Zhenya as our team leader tonight, okay?'

'You think I want to usurp your power?' Zhenya said. 'All I want to do tonight is shed the burden of the class.'

'Good,' Jing said. He began nightdreaming, a word he coined based on the word 'daydreaming' as it was now night, first in a low voice, then getting louder and louder, as if in a play, his interior monologue unashamedly thinking out loud, streaming out as they were getting higher and higher up the hill step by leaf-covered step. 'I wonder why people never cease in their pursuit of material gains as if that is the only thing they ever care about. Even this ceaseless effort made by other students is similar to that in the sense that they know with higher marks they earn at school they will get a better job in the future but I am so tired of this capitalist progress and I would love to do nothing for days on end but just enjoy mother nature itself, to return to her arms and become part of her.'

Oblivious of what was going on in Jing's mind, the others followed but engaged in their own small talk, Zhenya perversely talking about the ice sculptures in Harbin in winter, Liu Ya about the very hot chilies from Sichuan that she liked, Dang about the tall mountains he had scaled in search of herbs, and Xin, having nothing much else to say, kept trying to frighten the two girls with imagined snakes and insects, until they reached the pagoda on top of the hill. From here, they could feel a rippling breeze touching their faces. In Jing's mind, this would be an ideal place for contemplation, surrounded by waves of smaller wooded hills rolling out on three sides in deep dark blue under a sparse starry sky, with one side dominated by the lake that shimmered and twinkled with a myriad of lights, some from the reflections of the ambient city, some from those of higher up and others from within the bowels of the waters. An embankment cut through the lake like a dormant snake, with green plumes of dense trees. What would he not give for a life lived alone here! For the others, however, it was an occasion for celebration as they were convinced that they had made the right decision: it was much cooler than anywhere else down below and on the campus. Zhenya even grew fearful that it might get colder during the night as they hadn't brought warm clothes.

'We can sleep closer together,' Xin ventured but was struck speechless by a stare from Liu Ya who disliked the prurient tone in his voice.

'Why not?' Jing said. 'You two can sleep in the middle and then we can sleep around you on three sides, like a wall, a male wall. That way we can keep you warm and out of harm's way.'

'He's at it again,' Dang said. 'You always play with words.'

'What do you mean by that?' Liu Ya asked.

'There's *nüqiang* or "female wall" in ancient Chinese language, which is why Jing used the "male wall", although the latter doesn't exist in our language,' Dang explained.

'It doesn't matter as long as it exists in our mind,' Jing said.

'Stop playing with words again, I say,' Zhenya said. 'But I like your male wall idea. That's more like a team leader.' She felt better with this than a few moments ago when she had felt resentful towards Jing for his total silence all the way up the hill and for his arrogance in not joining them in their conversation.

'Still, what does a female wall mean?' Liu Ya wondered aloud.

'Oh, it's the low wall on the city wall,' Jing said.

As they laid out their bedclothes, in the way Jing suggested, they found, belatedly, that they could have brought along more things with them if they had not come in a great hurry, for example, a few bottles of soda water, something to eat like melon seeds, which Zhenya and Liu Ya enjoyed, and, most obviously, a watermelon itself. However, it was not until Jing said that he would like to go down the hill for a swim that they realised the essential thing missing: swimming trunks. None of them had come with any. Which meant, Jing immediately realised, they had to either swim naked or with their clothes on. Without thinking, Jing opted for the former and whispered into Dang's ears. Dang smiled but said nothing. The others didn't even realise what was going on until Jing announced, matter-of-factly, 'We'll swim without our clothes. Those who want to come are welcome. Those who don't can stay on the hill.' The mere mention of the idea amused the two girls, who nevertheless found it unacceptable and decided to stay. To keep them company and dispel their fears, Xin offered to stay with them. Besides, he had his own reasons; he liked Liu Ya and desired her company. Meanwhile, he could tell them plenty of ghost stories to entertain them.

Down below, at the edge of water, Jing began to take off his clothes, his artificial skin, layer by layer. Here, apart from his friends, the only living things that were watching were the two pine trees on the cliff face, standing at such an angle from the cliff that they threatened to fall down at any moment. Other trees stood far and high, asleep or indifferent, a few glowworms flitting from blade to blade of rampant lake grass, giving out greenish tantalising lights. If you put one on your palm, it feels cold.

'Can you swim, Dang?' Jing asked, half jokingly.

'Oh yes,' Dang said. 'Don't you worry.'

'Where did you learn?'

'By the pool,' Dang said.

It was Jing's turn to say 'Oh, yes' as he quickly stripped himself bare and slipped into the water, the skin of which felt warm to the touch. As he pushed himself forward, skin to skin, his skin wrapped up by the water skin, and, stroke after stroke, suddenly he could feel the coolness rising to the surface, momentarily making him fear that he might be dragged down by the leg of that life-destroying force in disguise, but he soon forgot this and turned himself over, resting on his back, pedalling with his feet, looking up directly into the sky, something he never ceased to tire of. People who die lie floating on the surface of the water face down, different from fish that die floating belly up, but what a wonderful feeling to lie alive, face up, face to face with the sky! Nowhere else was it better to gaze into the clouds or the crowds of stars or a completely blank sky than resting on your back on the skin of the water, in fact, any waters, whether it was on the hometown Yangtze or on this part of the Donghu. Jing was in full contact with something that normal people hardly ever had any time for. What if he could stay afloat like this and continue to gaze unthinkingly at things so many million light years away and then become part of them in a transient moment, doing nothing, thinking nothing, feeling nothing. From somewhere he heard the splashing of a big fish and he could smell pine cones, perhaps deep from the mud on the lake bottom. And for some reason or for no reason at all, his dick became erect, pointing to the sky, reminding him of the expression *luochaotian,* dick skyward, as his hometown lingo went. Assured that there was no one watching except perhaps the stars, he indulged in this new sensation of having intercourse with his natural environment without any human interference.

Just as Jing was lying on his back on the surface of the water, enjoying his communion or intercourse with the sky, he gradually became aware of an eerie quietness. A while ago, he had heard some plunking but had not since heard anything except his own breathing and water movements stirred by his naked limbs. As if waking from a trance, he realised that he had not seen Dang for some time. Where was he? Where could he be? He became frantic and, treading the water, he craned to see a shimmering of lights on the tip of the ripples, expecting to see a black head or hear Dang's familiar voice. There was nothing on the lake, not even a fish, just himself. He crept up to the sand in a great hurry, almost panicking and forgetting in his haste to put on his clothes. He began to call out at the top of his voice, 'Dang, Dang Jie, where are you? Come out quickly! Don't play games. This is serious!' A series of thoughts flashed through his mind, too fast for him to get a grip on: Dang committed suicide; he could not swim but Jing caused him to swim and to drown, 'to go under', that horrible phrase he had learnt; he would have to go back to the university without him and report to the authority and explain why; he was to face disciplinary action by being expelled from the school; he was never going to enjoy the benefits of learning English again; and all this because of Dang who committed suicide without telling him beforehand!

The more he thought of this the more he grew frightened until he burst into tears. He had never cried like this before, not even when Chenfang left him. Facing the deserted lake, he cried and cried until he heard a noise from behind. When he turned to look, he saw the quick withdrawal of Zhenya and Liu's heads and realised that he was standing in full nakedness. Jing was so ashamed of himself that he ran as fast as his legs could allow him, hands cupping his balls and their root, to where he had left his shorts and singlet, putting them on wind wind fire fire. The three heads, no, there were four of them, belonging to Zhenya, Liu, Xin and Dang, emerged from behind a cluster of undergrowth with an outburst of laughter. Jing was so angry that he shouted abuse at Dang, putting the girls to great shame.

'Why did you *ta ma de* play games with me?' He yelled at the top of his voice. 'I was nearly frightened to death.'

'I wasn't playing games with anyone,' Dang said calmly. 'I was only having a look deep down there.' He pointed at the expansive lake with his long chin, which seemed longer when wet.

No one knew what he meant by that and it would have made much more sense if they had known where he was coming from, being someone whose interests went beyond merely learning English, beyond a future career in that language. While Jing was looking up at a sky that would never help him anywhere, Dang was probably turning the other way, poking into the depths of the lake for something outside the normal comprehension of regular human beings, having learnt early the skill of holding his breath for as long as possible under water. But he wasn't one to reveal his secret, if there was any. He stood his ground, putting up with the rude Jing with a smile that seemed mysterious to the other three but was only natural to him, as he had been wearing that smile all along, ever since his master told him so as a young boy: 'Always present a smiling face to the world. No one strikes at a smiling face.'

While this was going on, there was a sixth person at the scene, invisible to them all, hiding in a thick growth of chrysanthemums, and he was to report the whole incident to the school shortly afterwards.

There was no sixth person. That sixth person is you as you are invisible to them all, hiding behind a great wall of many solid years, treating them as actors in a film. Actors? Extras or nonprofessionals is probably a better description. These people of yours are no professional actors or players; they live their lives with no pretensions, no intentions for anyone to watch or read, not even for themselves to record. Among them, Jing was probably the only one who consistently kept a diary. Perhaps in a more perfect age than yours, people will be born as natural actors who live with a sense of performance throughout their lives, watched through webcams and staging their live performance as it is. However, in those days, these extras were lucky that they did not have to play act for anyone's benefits, as previous generations of many thousand years had been doing before their death. And so, you can tolerate people's shortcomings with intolerable thoughts: Zhenya and Liu horrified by the big hairy member they saw and could not forget about; Xin disliking Zhenya's repulsive presence of bigness while preferring to be alone with Liu; and Dang's tendency to look down upon them as imperfect things that needed to be fixed up one way or another. In his eyes, Dr Wagner probably needed that most urgently as he was so temperamental, so unbalanced, so monolingual and monocultural. Secretly, Dang had hoped, he could become his teacher, perhaps along with Wei, the passionate believer in the superiority of the Chinese language; together, they could give Bill a clean bill of health.

3 3

The letter that Jing received from his mother ran thus:

Son,

I'm sorry I did not catch up with you sooner after you left me for your father as I went to Kunming myself. I think your father knew this and he probably told you about it. Your *didi* is making good progress in the army there, soon to be stationed near the Laoshan Frontline, although I'm sure he'll be fine. I'm glad that I did the right thing because the weather there was warm and flowers were everywhere even in winter.

How's your study coming along? Did you still find English as hard as before? I'm sure you'll have a bright future with that language if you work hard enough. And you know what? You probably belong to that language as your father often says.

It's getting late. I'm a bit tired and so will just lay down my pen for now.

Mother

P.S. Write to me if you like.

Jing read this letter while he was on the toilet. He read it again, his eyes stopping on 'belong to that language' momentarily before moving on, but, again, he misinterpreted the comment, like when Gao mentioned he had a foreign face. Gao was actually observing his white skin, which, while temporarily tanned in summer, returned to its creaminess in winter, but he missed the point and, instead, started searching his own deep-set eyes for a clue. However, there was no time to dwell long on this as he had to go and meet with Mr Miao, the political instructor, who wanted to have a word with him. It was an unpleasantly loud summer day with loud colours and a loud campus alive with loud students doing their exercises and playing ball games. By contrast, the political instructor's office was bare of anything except a clear desk and Mao's portrait on the wall. It didn't look like a place much used by anyone. There was thick dust on the desk, no sign of books, not even a piece of paper. The instructor with his hammer face was already there, waiting, when Jing arrived.

'*Ni hao ma?*' Mr Miao asked, taking a sharp look at Jing who was wearing a singlet and shorts, very tanned, with a few books under his arm.

'Not bad,' Jing answered.

'What are you reading?' Mr Miao enquired, indicating to the books with his index finger.

'Nothing,' Jing was reluctant. 'Just a few textbooks.'

'Was it true that you took some classmates out last night?' Miao asked.

'Who said that?' Jing was alarmed.

'Now, you see, it is stated in the Students' Manual that students should be in bed in their dormitories after 10pm and this rule is not to be breached under any circumstances. You know that, don't you?'

'Yes.'

'Despite that, you took several other students from your class and went to spend a night out together in the hills. Were there any females?'

'I don't know.'

'So you took several students including some females out to spend a night together in the hills last night and did you also swim together?'

'I don't know.'

'So you took several students including some females out to spend a night together in the hills last night and swam together, with clothes on or off?'

'We swam, no, I mean, I swam but not together with them.'

'Who did you swim together with then?'

'Dang,' Jing said.

'I heard that he nearly got drowned. Is that right?'

'No. He's still alive and jumping.'

'You didn't deliberately do anything to cause that to happen, I gather?' There was a hard edge to Miao's voice.

'No,' Jing was furious. Where did he get all this information? And he was now trying to force words into his own mouth. 'He swam by himself and I didn't even know if he ...' He stopped, breathless, before he could blurt out 'meant to commit suicide'.

'Quite apart from this, Classmate Jing,' Mr Miao said, 'I must caution you against any bad influences of bourgeois liberalisation. This going out at night, men and women together, swimming naked, and perhaps sleeping together ...'

'No, we did none of that,' Jing interrupted Miao impatiently, eager to explain.

'Please don't interrupt me before I finish.' Miao's hammer face became hard and cold, ready to strike. 'What I was stressing is the fact that those are symptoms of your being under a bad influence. Life on campus is boring and so you want to have some romance outside, doing whatever you like, enjoying yourself. And this we believe is inevitable as China is opening its doors to the outside world. If you open the window, a fresh breeze will come in but flies, mosquitoes, insects, rotten smells and other bad things will also come in, such as the books you are reading. Now, can you show me those books you are carrying?

Oh, no, I can't read English but look at those pictures of half-naked women. They are a corruption on our young minds. You should concentrate more on your professional studies, learning to be a good future diplomat or university lecturer to serve the country well. And these books, the less you read them the better. By the way, did you read a book titled something like *China Alive in a Bitter Sea?*'

'No, I didn't,' Jing lied; he had already finished reading it.

'It's a big poisonous grass that Dr Wagner has brought in and it is spreading a bad influence among our students. We are now investigating the matter.'

'But what have I got to do with that?'

'Nothing except that you are advised to observe the school rules and regulations more closely than before. As for last night, we'll find out more about it later.'

This conversation left Jing with little consolation. He thought about it, wanted to speak to Xin about it, gave up on the idea and decided to keep it all to himself. Strangely, none of them, Xin, Dang or either girl, ever mentioned the matter again, as if it had never happened, making him suspicious about some conspiracy afoot, while wondering once again if it was not something imaginary, something that only happened in his mind but never in reality.

*

During the afternoon class that day, possibly because of the blazing heat, something else unpleasant happened. It was all on account of Dr Wagner, who now arrived later and later to the class, although it used to be the other way round. Usually at the beginning of class he had to call the roll and wait for late students to arrive before the lesson could begin. On one occasion, Bao was late and crept in by the back door, when he heard his name called in a sonorous voice, 'Good morning, Mr Bao!' It was in fact so loud that the greeting sounded almost like a yell, causing everyone to turn their heads to focus their attention on him, putting Bao to great shame. Now Bao could have done the same to Dr Wagner by shouting at the top of his voice, 'Welcome, Dr Wagner, you are very early!' if he had dared. On this searing afternoon everyone was struck down by a lethargic sense of inaction, aware of only an irresistible pull towards either one's bed in their dormitory rooms or lying under deep shade at the lakeside or, better still, immersed in the water of the lake. Few were enticed by the prospect of a dragging oral class with a weary Bill who, when he finally emerged from the corridor, yawned audibly with heavy eyelids and an expression of infinite boredom. He began, 'Guys, I'm sorry I was late 'cause this *wushui*, siesta I have lately become accustomed to is soooo sweet. Thank God I'm in Wuchang! And how about you guys?' Curiously, he was greeted with silence, a silence that seemed to suggest more than just lethargy. He immediately noticed a girl gesture as if she had something to say. Trying to shake the sleepiness that was stuck on him like a piece of chewed gum, he struggled to look in her direction and motioned for her to speak. It was Zou, who said, 'I find your expression "Guys" quite discomforting, no, I mean disconcerting, because we are here not just guys but also girls, don't you think? Whenever you address us, you always say "Guys" and, to borrow something you like saying, it's not fair. Even when they speak to a formal audience, they begin with "Ladies and Gentlemen" but here it's just "Guys", "Guys", as if we were all *gaisi*.'

Wide awake now, traces of pillow still visible on one side of his right face, Bill found himself taken aback by this outburst. Was this the so-called Chinese 'half-sky' speak? What correctness!

Bloody hell! He recalled how the Party secretary had told him to pay more respect to the female students in his class and not to tell obscene jokes because some of the girls had complained. No names were revealed but he had a fairly clear idea who these ones might be, Zou certainly among them.

Still, he was confused by her use of the expression, *gaisi*.

In response to his question, Zou said, 'That's the Chinese expression that phonetically sounds exactly the same as "Guys" but means "should die".'

'You mean deserving to die?' Bill said but his joke fell flat on the girlish ears and the boyish ears as well. Then, remembering something, he turned to Bao and said, 'You once seemed to suggest that Chinese language is infinitely superior to the English language. Now, will you be able to give us some examples to illustrate your point?'

Caught unprepared, Bao became red in the face and stammered, 'This was most uncomfortable, most uncomfortable, because I did not prepare, did not prepare. It was Wei said it, not me. But if insist, I can find something that I wrote in here.' He groped in his school bag, got out an exercise book, took a look at one of his scribbles and said, 'I see. You see. English is morotona, no, I mean is monotone, no, monotona, no, no, mono, torturous, monotonous, yes, of course, you are light, because, for example, you use one word for many things, make friends, make money, make enemy, it's all one word, make. In Chinese, in the same situation, we use three different words for these three things, *jiao* (friends), *zuan* (money) and *shu* (enemy). Our language certainly is better than yours in this regard.'

'I'm sorry?' Bill said. 'But wouldn't it be better if you could explain what these Chinese words meant that you just used as I don't understand them?'

'I really don't have the English equivalents for them, sir, and

I'm sorry,' Bao said. He had meant to say 'But you should at least have learnt some words and expressions by now, mate.'

'Could you do us a favour, please?' Bill turned to Ma, whose head was circled in his arms on the desk, ducklike, sound asleep.

One would expect Ma to take a few minutes to wake up and a few more to respond but that was obviously not necessary. He sat up bolt upright and said, 'Yes, Dr Wagner, *jiao* as in communicating and *shu* as in tree used as a verb as if you put up an enemy like a tree, although I'm not sure whether it makes any sense to you in English. As for *zuan*, that's a hard one. It sounds like *zhuan*, turning around in circles, I guess, because the coins are round and to make money you have to turn around them all the time. Hence turning about the money or *zuan qian*, sir.' This explanation was so unexpected, coupled with Ma's apparent ease of transition from the world of slumber to the world of wakefulness, that the class rippled with laughter until Dr Wagner's voice cut in, 'What are you reading?'

The class looked at Ma, then at Dr Wagner, and realised that the question was actually directed at Jing sitting at the back, furthest away from the crowd.

'Something Chinese,' Jing said.

'Why something Chinese? Is this supposed to be an oral Chinese class or what?' Dr Wagner raised his voice.

'Who cares?' Jing said, his defiance surprising even Ma, who winked at Jing for him to stop arguing, but Jing ignored him. 'What's the big deal? English is a pain in the arse or in the neck? Is that how the expression goes? I mean since we get stuck in English we might as well move along its line. Who knows what's going to happen in the future? Some of us might even end up in English, don't you guys, I mean girls think? I mean ending up in England, right? I sometimes get the feeling though that the place where the language originated may not be all that wonderful as the language makes it appear, lacking the vividness and power of our language.'

'I'm sorry? What are you talking about?'

'I'm going through the notes left by our suicide victim, taking particular notice of his use of Chinese characters as verbs. For example, "bad" as in "He bads my good thing". Meaning? He ruins my good thing. He also notices the deception of the English language in the word "believe" because it's formed of the word "belie". He is an inventor who changes the English word "bird's-eye view" to "rat's-eye view". And if you were lucky enough to arrive before he left, you would have heard him pronouncing "receipt" as "re cee pt" and "bombing" as "bom bing", evidence of English absurdities …'

'What's so funny about them?' Dr Wagner asked. 'But it's all so incorrect. You have to get it right the first time or else you end up speaking broken English.' As he said this, Jing's word "pigmatic" came to mind but he bit his lip and did not mention it.

'I know what you are going to say. You are going to say that my inventions like "pigmatic" to replace your illogical "dogmatic" are baseless and bad English but I think they work much better than any English you can think of. If I like, I can even use "catmatic" or "fishmatic".'

'Then why don't you use "Jingmatic" or "Weimatic", eh?' Dr Wagner almost yelled, beads of perspiration seeping out and running down where the pillow traces were. 'I think you've probably read too much proletarian communist literature in bad English or Chinese translation that your so-called professors have compiled for you. Why don't you try some Shakespeare or *Paradise Lost* or *Sound and Fury* or *Farewell to Arms* or *Voss* or *Catcher in the Rye* or *Catch 22* in the original? There's plenty of interesting stuff around. How's your Chinese going, by the way?'

That hit Jing in a tender spot as he had recently barely passed a Chinese examination, getting only sixty per cent. He hit back relentlessly. 'My Chinese is none of your business and it's certainly better than yours.' Despite Bill's 'haw, haw, haw', he continued, 'And I don't think your English is that great, either. It sounds like a cross between American and English. And it's more pidgin than anything else. This is not just my opinion. You ask my classmates and I'm sure most of them share my view, too.'

'What! Are you nuts or something, Jean or EEE? You can hardly tell the difference between lend and borrow or sin and sink or thin and think or smile and mile and you are telling me my English is what? Our English has produced a Nobel Prize in Literature. You know that?'

'And our language has produced millions of more brilliant writers than yours and lasts thousands of years longer than yours apart from having produced expressions like *bugong daitian*, "not wearing the same sky", better than your "not sharing the same ground", you know that?' Jing duplicated him in mock tone. 'Besides, why would I want to know all the Englishit? There are so many better things to do; even watching the sun set on the lake is infinitely better than this. Why do you have to act as if you were superior or something, thinking that you knew more? You don't even know what "see dogshit better days" is.'

'What the fuck do I care whatever it means in broken English? What do you think they are paying me for? To teach you bloody English! But you can go if you don't like me or my class,' Dr Wagner growled.

'I certainly will,' Jing said, as he rose from his seat and left, to the amazement of everyone.

'Cheers,' Bill said, pretending to sound lighthearted, adding, under his breath, 'Let's get on with our class, and good riddance.'

'What a fluck!' Jing was heard murmuring as he slammed the

door behind him.

'Fluck or fluke or luck or fuck?' Bill roared at Jing's back with the door in between. 'Get your English right, mate!'

Hu giggled but, as he saw no one share the joke with him, he stopped his laughter as suddenly as he had begun, while Ganmei frantically thumbed the pages of her *A New English-Chinese Dictionary* to where the 'fluke' was and started to search in vain for any traces of the word 'fluck'.

34

For the first time Jing lost his way on his lonely after-dinner walk. He had thought he was coming back to the campus; instead, he found himself going deeper into the woods until there was not a house to be seen. He kept walking, believing he was on the right track and that if he continued he would find his way back, but the winding path led him from one wooded hill with occasional birds calling to another, like a cloud, apparently with no destination. He wondered if he was retracing his steps to his previous life, a concept that would be most alien to Dr Wagner who was too scientifically born and bred to understand it. He wondered and wandered. He thought he heard movements and people talking. Before he realised where he was he found himself in the middle of a town that he had never been to before. Its houses were entirely built of green bamboo, facing each other across a narrow cobblestoned street, along which people were walking with large bamboo baskets on their backs or their heads as if they were women. At every turn he saw a mountain creek running briskly alongside the street. If it was not too wide, there would be a piece of stone placed there for you to walk across, but if it was too wide, there would be a bridge, one of which he had just come to.

On the head of the bridge, he saw a man and a woman sitting together, seemingly quite tired. In fact, the man's head was hanging so low it thrust down between his legs, like a capital M with its middle part collapsed. The woman looked foreign. The man never raised his head from between his legs. He might have been dead or a sculpture purposely put there for show.

Further on, he saw a Buddhist temple, a monk in brown *jiasha* selling incense sticks at the entrance where a row of shoes were laid out. A few English visitors entered without taking their shoes off. Jing asked the monk why. The monk said, 'They can do whatever they like.' 'What about me?' Jing asked. 'You and the locals have to take your shoes off upon entering the temple to show your respect to the gods here because the temple is a clean place, not to be dirtied by everyone's shoes.' 'But why did the English visitors go in without taking off their shoes?' The question asked itself one more time before Jing felt thirsty. He asked where he could get something to drink. The monk said, 'You can drink anywhere. See the creek, its water is clean enough to drink.' Sure enough, the water was clean but also tasted sweet as Jing found out when he put his mouth to it and sipped. He felt rejuvenated after drinking like a fish, or as the Chinese put it, like a cow. Raising his head and wondering who the foreign woman might be, he turned around but no one was sitting there as he had thought. Jing kept wandering, watching the brisk creek as he walked, until he saw an old man sitting in front of a door, looking at him. His eyes held him so he stopped.

The old man said, 'To write is but to act out a court jester's life.'

Jing asked, 'What has this got to do with me?'

The old man said, 'One came from one knew not where and ends up one knows not where. Everything in between is grey. Borderland here it is.'

Jing said, 'I know that. Needless to say.'

The old man said, 'I've got to go. The sun is falling behind the hill now.'

35

The summer holiday passed easily. There was nothing much else to do but go fishing with Chiang in the numerous lotus ponds on the outskirts of the town where the factories were located. In one of these factories Chiang worked as a machine operator, an operator with an ambition because he was learning English! Possessing the smallest eyes in the world, Chiang had a very slow temper and complied easily with Jing's wishes. Although he never seemed to aspire to anything much, operating a machine, seemingly with little ambition to become more important, he was very good at catching fish. Which was what Jing liked about him. He admired Chiang for his consummate skill in knowing precisely where to put down his hook with the red and white float among the dense lotus leaves and when it was time to pull up to get the fish, not when it bobbed up and down violently but when it suddenly shot up and lay prostrate on the water. Jing could be standing at his own spot for hours without catching even a shrimp, his neck growing sore from craning too much to watch out for the never-moving bobber, his hand painful from holding the bamboo rod. He had a heart bigger than any fish he could catch because he would always go for the longer and heavier rod and large fat red earthworms, thinking that these would get him the big one. Chiang just let him have his way while he himself humbly picked up a short rod with a few grains of rice wrapped in a dirty piece of paper together with some dead flies or, better still, maggots from the shithole that Jing would never touch, dismissing them as too stinking and unthinkable.

'But they help you catch the fish best,' Chiang said.

'Well, that may be the case,' Jing said. 'But they'd be too small for my hook.' Jing didn't mention the dirty bit as he did not want to be considered weak. Besides, he didn't have the skill to pierce the rice and keep it on the hook, let alone catch a fish with it; wrapping the hook in a big worm was easier.

'You see carp like rice,' Chiang said as he carefully placed one grain of cooked rice on the tip of the hook and, gently swaying the rod, accurately placed the hook, line and bobber in an opening among several big fat lotus leaves.

The midmorning sun had half-dried the dewy grass on the slope where both of them were sitting. With a big lotus leaf each underneath their buttocks, Jing could feel the soft morning soil squash a little. The paddy immediately behind them contained rice stocks that were turning yellow, nearly ripe, giving forth an earthy smell of abundance. Occasionally, there were rice birds calling in small shrill voices from the depths of the paddy fields close to the water. Up above, in the blue sky, where uplifted eyes would be blinded by the dazzling sun, there were skylarks chirruping. One could never see them but they made you aware of their omnipresence. Right in front of them was this pond densely covered in lotus leaves, some as big as a small dining table, standing at different heights, with shafts of light playing inbetween. Occasionally, one could see the dark edge of the back of a fish emerge from nowhere and instantly disappear, leaving circles of water behind. In the distance, across an expanse of black-tiled roofs and behind the Baota, the Tower of Treasure, was the Western Hill standing bluish on the other side of the Yangtze River. From time to time, one could hear a ferry sounding its siren signifying its departure or arrival, adding to the peacefulness of the surroundings. It was there that Jing preferred to go as he had more experience fishing in the river.

'When I was young,' Jing said. 'I fished a lot in the river.'

'I know but it was not for me,' Chiang said. He was more comfortable with ponds where he could find a place to *daweizi* or scatter fish baits by strategically spreading his bait to lure the fish so that he could continuously fish without disturbance, whereas the constantly running river water would allow no such thing to happen.

'And it was much easier in the river,' Jing said. 'You just throw your hook as far away from the bank as possible and leave it there with a big fat black earthworm and then you do your own thing, reading or playing. Then, when you go back to your rod, the float is no longer there on the water. So you jerk your rod up and there it is, the big catfish with whiskers!'

'Well, catfish is a stupid fish and its flesh not very tasty,' Chiang said.

'But they say it's good for cooking with noodles,' Jing retorted.

'Here I can get the best fish, carp or *ji* fish, sometimes even grass fish,' Chiang said, dreamily. 'You know, *ji* fish is a stimulant for the breasts of women with babies.'

At this, Jing went silent, his eyes wandering to where his float was and, seeing that it looked as if it was frozen in the water, he glanced at Chiang who happened to raise his rod with another shining specimen of his patience: he never even cried in excitement as Jing would most likely do. The strange thing was that even when Jing moved closer to Chiang, thinking that he might get some luck by staying near, his luck did not improve. The fish somehow recognised who was who and kept taking Chiang's bait instead of his.

'Did they know you were a woman?' Jing asked, jokingly.

'Maybe,' Chiang said. 'Maybe they think I'm a pretty woman and so they follow me, stupid fish, and then they are eaten by me.'

'But they may eat you one day,' Jing warned.

'Which is why I never fish in the rivers or the ocean,' Chiang said.

'You can't fish in the ocean anyway; it's too far from here,' Jing said.

'You probably will be able to do that one day as your study seems to point in that direction,' Chiang said, wistfully.

'You will, too, because you also study English,' Jing said.

'Don't laugh at me,' Chiang said. 'It will not get me anywhere. I'll remain an ordinary worker.'

'Come on,' Jing said. 'Life is not like that. No one will remain the same.'

'Not true,' Chiang said. 'A fish will remain a fish. I'm a fish. That's why fish like me.'

'You are joking. You are better than that. You are a human being,' Jing heard himself asserting loudly, almost shouting.

'Hey,' came Chiang's soft but firm voice. 'Don't yell. The fish will hear you and will go away. With quiet beings, you have to be quiet, too.'

That was the most sensible thing that Jing had ever heard Chiang say and he began wishing he had Chiang's patience. And he told Chiang so.

'It's nothing,' Chiang said. 'It's better your way because you are much faster, say, with the language. You get more fish that way and bigger ones. As for this one …' he said as he pulled up his rod, its tip suddenly going taut, together with the line, forming a huge arc over the water and the dark green lotus leaves. In no time, a live silvery fish was out of water, flapping with noise like a living bird. 'It's good for nothing but the stomach.' He finished his words as he went to take it off the hook and put it in the plastic bag sitting in the water, held with a string on a piece of branch stuck in the muddy slope.

36

You remember Jing said years ago that there was nothing more he wished for than being written about by others. He thought that would be an achievement, although he could not possibly have known the implications it would involve. The classmates who had heard him say that admired him for it. The author of this book, you know, has sort of achieved that but he is not particularly happy and you know that he has gone beyond that to hanker for an anonymous state at a higher level. From him you also know that Jing's summer was soured by one incident in which he had a row with his mum and dad over some trifle and left home at night in pouring rain and did not return till he was completely drenched. And this happened after his mum and dad had got back together at the end of an uncertain period of separation for reasons that escaped Jing, but that the author told you he did not intend to write about because he had got hold of a short story written by Jing at the time, ostensibly about a young university student spending a night out alone and accidentally catching himself in a big rain.

37

Deirdre Wagner's appearance in the class was brief but took Jing, more than anyone else, by storm. It was on an autumn morning when the soft sunshine played on the leaves of the French *wutong* trees, turning them golden. Jing was reading a red hardcover copy of the selected writings of Thomas Addison and underlining words or phrases or remarks that he found interesting. The class was waiting for Dr Wagner to turn up. Just as Jing was about to underline a remark where Addison said that to describe a woman's breast as beautiful or plump was nothing but if you say it was also as cold as ice it would produce greater effect, Dr Wagner came in, followed by someone dressed in black. The whole class saw at one glance that it was a woman and heard Dr Wagner's announcement that it was his wife, except for Jing who was absorbed by what he had just read. It was only when Xin nudged him in the ribs that he quickly put his book aside and raised his head to assume an air of nonchalance. Then he noticed her. She was slightly taller than Dr Wagner, perhaps because she was wearing those shoes, but the black woollen *tao zhuang*, two-piece suit, she had on so accentuated her figure that Jing's eyes could not help but try to circle around her, up and down and behind her.

She had a small, white face, with eyes faintly lined that made her immediately attractive, and there was something about her that was Asian or even Chinese as her eyes were so soft and expressive. Jing knew instinctively that this was a woman that he liked. But, of course, it was absurd. She was Mrs Wagner, not any woman on the street that he happened to see and desire.

Then he heard, 'Don't call me Mrs Wagner. Call me Deirdre. I'm here to observe today.' And without any preamble, she came directly towards him and found a seat next to Jing, of all the seats! Jing's heart missed a beat and his face flushed red, his head lowered, until he heard his name called as he heard his own heart beating wildly.

'E Jing,' Bill said. 'It's your turn to give us a presentation.'

*

Jing and Bill had made up after they accidentally bumped into each other during one of Jing's after-dinner strolls early in the new term. The first thing Bill said to Jing was, 'I think I know what you meant by "fluck"?'

'What?' Jing asked, surprised by how easy it was to make up with a Westerner; if the same sort of thing that happened between him and another Chinese, he doubted if anyone would give in first.

'You mixed the two words together, "fluke" and "luck", because you want to mean that one has an element of the other, right?' Bill said.

'Not exactly,' Jing said. 'I found it hard to remember the word, fluke, but, with luck put in, I found it easier to remember.'

'Oh, is that what it is?' Bill laughed and, immediately, both of them became relaxed, in fact, so relaxed that Bill actually came over and put his hand on Jing's back. 'So, Jing, you are such an inventive man! Give me some more examples of your invention. Come on, don't be shy.'

'Well, English is such a monster that the only way I can tame it is through my own inventions,' Jing said, lowering his eyes to his hand when Bill noticed that he held some scraps of paper there. 'I've found some differences, that's all. For example, you say "call a spade a spade" but we say *youyi shuoyi*, which literally means "call one one" or "if it is one call it one". Also when Shakespeare says "green-eyed jealousy", it reminds me of our description of jealousy as *hongyanbing*, literally, "red-eyed disease", or "red-eyed jealousy" if you like, even "blue-eyed" and "black-eyed" jealousies depending on what nationality you are. Hang on, one more thing, when someone says, I forgot where, that "more sinned against than sinning", I immediately recall an ancient king by the name of Cao Cao who says, *ningke wo fu tianxia ren, buke tianxia ren fu wo*, which is exactly the opposite of that: "more sinning than sinned against", his preferred way of living!'

'Tell me what you meant the other day by "see dogshit better days",' Bill said.

'It's my way of playing with your expression "see better days". When you describe someone as lucky, you call him or her "a lucky dog" but we would describe that person as having a piece of "dogshit luck". See?'

'Ah, the Jinglish! Listen, this is what I'm going to do,' Bill said, still impressed with Jing for his linguistic flair and 'fluck' and more so because of this 'dogshit luck'. 'I'm going to lend you some more books to get you right into English, the best of it, because, as I can see, you are ...' he paused and changed his mind about what he had wanted to say; he had wanted to say 'because you seem to be stuck between the two languages and that would not be an ideal situation for you.' Instead, he said, simply, 'I'm sure you'll make greater progress if you get acquainted with the best of our literatures.'

'There's something I'd like to ask you,' Jing said. 'You have never told us what you were most impressed with in China, and also when Liu kept using "he" to refer to Qi what you noted down in your notebook.'

'Oh, that!' Bill laughed, his neat row of tiny teeth bared. 'I told the girls in my room but you did not stay long enough, remember? I told them that I was most impressed with the number of smiling faces in China. The other thing was I've only just realised that in your language you don't differentiate between him, her and it in sound, quite similar to us in using "them", a generative pronoun that denotes men, women and things.'

'You are learning,' Jing said, the harmlessly joking tone of his voice unmistakable.

*

At Dr Wagner's beckoning, Jing got something out from his pocket, a crumpled paper ball. Slowly spreading it open, crease by crease, he began scanning it in silence, as if to deliberately try the patience of the whole class. There was a giggle or two at the paper-ball expansion. There was a throat being cleared, as if on his behalf. A wristwatch beeped twice for the half-hour. And Jing had found it; he began:

'August evening. He was strolling on the Yangtze bank. The evening glow painted the edge of the river trees in the sandbar red. The light receded inch by inch so that darkness first appeared on the back of the buffalos soaking in the water of the branch river cut away from its artery by the sandbar. A bat fell tumbling from the sky and he held out his hand as if to receive it. As he walked further away from the city, there were fewer and fewer passers-by until all around he was the only person walking, under the darkening sky with the evening glow gone, the river on his left hand, the fields on his right and the dusty road with deep ruts in the middle under his foot. He was entirely alone. And he felt tired, his legs weary from walking, his heart perhaps also weary, though with what he was not sure.

He found a spot on the grassy slope, not far from the edge of the water where he could smell the cow dung. He touched the blades of the grass and felt the dew. As well as something else, which was tiny and round to the touch. He picked up one and peered at it, recognising at once that it was the sheep's shit. Even so, he thought, it was cleaner than the city where people lived in such close proximity that they breathed in each other's poisonous gasses. Closing his eyes, he tried to sleep but could not. A mosquito was buzzing in his ear. He waved it away but it came back. He pulled off his shirt and covered his head up. It felt better but his mind went blank. He needed to open his eyes and see the stars there, right above him, and to be aware of them when he closed them. When he did open his eyes, though, with his shirt pulled off his head, he felt the first blow of wind on his face and saw at one glance that the stars were gone. In their place were dark clouds rolling ferociously.'

'How much longer have you got?' Dr Wagner said, impatiently.

'Actually, I am finished,' Jing said as he sat down. 'That's it.'

Bill rolled his eyes and shook his head, amused and amazed by Jing's obsessiveness. Meanwhile, Jing heard Deirdre whisper her appreciative comment in his ear, 'very nice little piece' and he was pleased.

It was not long before they met again and this time in a quite unexpected place, a group session of criticism and self-criticism held in the dormitory room Jing shared with his other male classmates. It was a session to which some female students came and to which the political instructor also attended. It soon became clear that the focus was on the state-initiated campaign against bourgeois liberalisation and spiritual pollution, a topic that Mr Miao introduced with much feverish foreboding.

'Dear Comrades,' he began, as if addressing a 100-strong audience, whereas in fact there were not more than ten students including himself. 'It is a critical moment in the history of our Party and our nation when the reactionary forces in the West and bourgeoisie are all aiming at changing the colour of our third and fourth generations as our Chairman Mao has said. As we open our doors wider to the outside world, they come in with more poisonous things, both spiritual and materialistic. I won't mention names but there are some foreign teachers who do not teach serious stuff according to the school syllabus but introduce our students to the so-called modernist writers. I can tell you this that modernism is harmful to our minds as it emphasises a world view of pessimism and destruction with things like *huangyuan* (wasteland) by an English man called something like – I can't remember such long names – and a French man, yes, his name is Sa Te with his theory about destroying other people.'

'It's not destroying other people,' Jing interrupted and said, 'I think his most famous saying is "the Other is hell", is that right?' Jing turned to Ma, who was again half asleep.

'I'm not asking you,' Miao said sharply. 'Although you may be right, which only goes to show that you are probably more poisoned than others by their writings. As students of literature, you should try to avoid following the Western trends and steer clear of all sorts of bourgeois ideologies but keep an optimistic view that our socialist system is definitely superior to their capitalist system and will eventually prevail over them. Now, I want to know what problem areas you can find existing in your behaviour or in your studies that you think are a result of the bad bourgeois influences and how you can improve on them. We'll start with a male student, shall we?'

All eyes fell on Ma as he was sitting at the head of the table and seemed quite inattentive. But he came alive instantly as the political instructor's voice died down. He said that he realised that his drive for excellence in English and other academic courses might have been a result of spiritual pollution as it proved that he had not paid enough attention to politics. He cited an example that while he quite enjoyed some of the classes Dr Wagner gave, it might not be right as Dr Wagner was from a capitalist country and one should be always on guard against what he was teaching. He then remembered an incident in which Dr Wagner read them a short story preaching the moral of guilt and wanted everyone to write a story about their own guilt but 'I do not feel guilty for something I have not done and I can't pretend that I am guilty because we happened to have a story read to us. And I think this is where the problem lies: they want us to believe that we, like them, are born with a dirty conscience, I mean, with guilt but that is wrong because they are the Westerners and we are Chinese. We are different people. In teaching us to be like them, we, we …' Ma felt tongue-tied as he hit upon something that seemed larger than he could express. 'But never mind,' he said and left it at that. If Bill was present, he would most likely have urged Ma to explore the subject a bit more but it was Miao, not Bill, and so it had to be left at that.

Other students followed in echoing his views but the drift of the conversations began to turn, from food to fashion even to mood, and seemed to go nowhere.

'I found the stuff he taught was a bit boring,' Liu Ya offered. 'Things like "The drover's wife"'and "abcdefghijklmnopqrstuvwxyz". What has that got to do with us, I mean, with our current reality?'

'That's right,' Bao echoed. 'Or Patrick White, the Nobel Prize winner but his characters fart so much!'

'It's not funny,' the political instructor said, with a stern face, and the laughter instantly died down. 'It only goes to show how corrupt these Westerners are, even in fiction.'

'And I think there is bad influence, too,' Zou Ganmei said. 'More and more of our girl students now have perms and lipstick as they spend more time on their looks than on their books, which I think is dangerous.'

The silence that followed was almost unbearable until Hu chimed in, 'I couldn't agree more. Some male students also start doing this, wearing Western suits, for example, and ties.'

'That's right,' Bao said. 'Dr Wagner is doing that on a daily basis.'

Seeing that this was again threatening to throw the whole group into another fit of laughter, Mr Miao intervened again, 'Be serious, boys! Everyone must say something about his or her thoughts no matter what. Now, what about you, Jing?'

All eyes were turned in his direction, where he sat with a lowered head, examining his own fingers.

'I mean what do you think of this?' Miao urged.

'Not much,' Jing said and he was about to launch into a lecture of what he had been thinking when there came a knock on the door, followed by an 'Excuse me?' Obviously a woman's voice.

Mr Miao sat bolt upright, a bewildered look on his face. He never liked the idea of a political session being interrupted by a foreigner and he motioned for Hu to open the door. Where the door opened, Deirdre's face showed, with her golden hair and red lips, something that Mr Miao disliked intensely. He frowned.

Deirdre did not notice the frown. She came to find Jing because she had read his short story, the beginning of which he had read aloud in the class the other day. She was so impressed with it that she came straight to his dormitory, after asking several students the way. However, confronted with a roomful of faces, some of which she was still not very familiar with, she paused and presented a smile to Hu, who said, 'Mrs Dei De, we are, sorry, we are having a meeting here.'

'I'm terribly sorry,' Deirdre said. 'I am, but can you pass this on to Mr Jing please? Is he here?'

'Just give it to me,' Hu said, taking the roll of paper that was Jing's story together with Deirdre's comments in red, as Jing watched without moving. Xin was watching him, too, taking note of the fact that Hu did not seem to have any intention to pass it on after Deirdre left. In fact, as soon as Hu returned to the table, by the side of Mr Miao, he gave it to Miao, not Jing, who was only sitting opposite them. Xin noticed that Jing did not even protest but seemed to take it for granted. But he was wrong.

'Give it to me,' Jing said, not particularly to anyone.

No response, either from Hu or Miao.

'Give it to me,' Jing raised his voice. 'It's mine.'

'Are you talking to me?' Miao said, in an equally loud voice.

Already, Xin was pulling at Jing's elbow and Ma, wide awake, was making eyes to Jing to stop.

'Yes and I want you to give my paper back to me. It's mine, I said,' Jing demanded.

'What if I do not give it back to you?' Miao asked.

'Then you are, you are …' Jing was so angry that he did not know what to say and finally he managed with, 'You have no right to do that.'

'Yes, I have all the right in the world to do that,' Miao said. 'I'm the political instructor here. My work is to ensure that you do not get corrupted by the pernicious Western ideologies and to guard against potential harm posed by hostile forces from overseas. You will have it back when we have a look at it, I can assure you.'

At the words 'session dismissed', everyone left except Jing, who was livid with anger but his eyes could not help but follow the graceful shape of a woman pacing outside downstairs. He immediately recognised that it was Deirdre and she was waiting for him!

38

Your thoughts kept wandering back to this episode with its impossible ending. Again, Jing must have got it wrong or have only imagined it. In fact, what was happening was that the instructor actually offered to give back his article along with the comments with a remark 'I can't understand it anyway. Just take it back and continue with your story.' Jing accepted it graciously, his heart warmed by the instructor's humane understanding and his respect doubled for him instantly. The Berlin Wall has gone for ever but this invisible wall that divides the East and the West still exists, so much so that if you stand on this side of the wall the focus of the story shifts. You would love to be able to sit on the wall but then the wall keeps changing its position, too.

39

'I want you to help me,' Jing whispered into her right ear as he held Deirdre close to his heart, half squatting in the dense undergrowth on the Luojia Hill. As if to echo this, a wild dove cuckooed somewhere and went silent.

The noon sun struck down, through the branches, on her hair, making it hot.

'To do what?' she murmured.

He did not answer but struck, one side of his buttocks hollowing with his forward movement. She 'ahhh-ed' with pain and pleasure. Meanwhile, her tongue, like a penis, shot into his mouth, for him to hold and suck. As he drained underneath, his mouth was suddenly flooded with a mixture of his body fluid and hers, ejaculated, as it were, from the tip of her tongue. He kept sucking on it, sipping its cool tasteless liquid as if to quench his thirst caused by the sudden sluice below.

It was soon over. Afterwards, Deirdre looked into Jing's eyes and asked again, 'To do what?'

'To get out of this country, to go anywhere, to get to the corner of the earth, anywhere but China!' Jing said with resolution.

'Shush,' Deirdre said. 'Don't be so loud. They might hear you. Now, speak to me like this.' She pulled his head towards her and literally kissed the words into his left ear.

'No,' Jing tossed his head off and declared. 'I hate China. I'll die early if I continue to stay here.'

'No, you won't,' Deirdre said. 'I'll make sure you come with me.'

'What about Dr Wagner then?'

'What about him?'

'Aren't you,' Jing hesitated.

'Married to him? Is that what you mean?'

'…'

'We can divorce and then …'

'Marry with me?'

'Oh you are so shameless,' Deirdre said. But from her sudden powerful embrace, Jing knew instinctively that she liked the idea.

'And we'll go to Australia?'

'Oh yes.'

'Where in Australia then?'

'Melbourne.'

At that, Jing felt silent. He had heard of Melbourne but knew nothing about it. 'What do we do there?'

'Live.'

'Just live? Like D.H. Lawrence? To the hilt?'

'No, like ourselves.'

But Jing's own mention of Lawrence made him wonder if he was not daydreaming again. How could he have done this with a foreign woman, a white woman from Australia, a white woman married with a white man but having an affair with her Chinese student? Crime of crimes!

40

Fiction rushes ahead of life. You have already thought of what you are going to write. In fact, the story is already finished even before you actually put it down on paper. Part of that dream you had last night relates to Canada and you remember hearing yourself admire how wonderful that country is, from Vancouver to the northernmost part of the country. At that moment, your heart aches for what you have lost. Then, again, when you manicured your fingernails after you felt that there was nothing else to do before the end of the night, you had this thought visiting you that your life literally stopped here where you remember people but people no longer care and in a little while you are gone and nothing of you shall remain, like an email message deleted and trashed.

41

It did not require a detailed investigation to expel a student from the university, although that decision-making process might involve a lengthy period of obtaining evidence and rationalisation. In private, Mr Miao interviewed everyone in the English class except Jing and, from what information he had gathered, he was able to draw the following conclusions: the student in question was a man of haughty character who ruthlessly pursued academic excellence, a legacy of the old *baizhuan daolu,* the road of a white expert, without cultivating a good relationship with his classmates and without showing the least bit of interest in the current issues that the Party demanded its youth to be involved with. Some male students found him secretive, reading suspicious books such as Oscar Wilde's *The Portrait of Dorian Gray* and Thomas Hardy's *Jude the Obscure* and sometimes spreading pessimistic views about life, making people who shared the same accommodation with him uncomfortable. According to one student, he was unapproachable, preferring to be all by himself, and, so gradually, his classmates ignored him by leaving him alone. Female students did not have much to say except that they found him an oddball who never seemed to even look their way, much less enter into an interesting conversation with them. They also found him expressing strange thoughts about the current socialist system and exhibiting a fascination with the West. Apart from this, there was also evidential documentation: his diaries, stolen by a student who handed them over to him, and the stories and poems he had written that were also in his possession, although the originals were still with

Jing, who was perhaps not even aware that there had been copies in circulation at higher levels. As Miao was going through them again, his eyes fell on a passage highlighted in red:

The whole of China is like a prison, he said, and I could not agree with him more, although just to say it would require as much courage as insight. You don't need to go far to find the evidence. Some of us may feel blissful because they tend to shut a blind eye on reality and that is fine but I can't. There are so many things that upset you these days. Only last week, the instructor behaved as if he had the power to decide one's future, threatening that I could face endless trouble if I did not confess my crime. What crime did I commit? Writing a couple of poems that directly expressed my 'dark' feelings? And because ours is a great system, everyone should present a smiling face or else he or she is a criminal? How does that current popular saying go? Laughter is better than crying? What nonsense! Things are deeper than laughter. And ours is not such a great system anyway.

As he shook his head, his eyes moved onto another page with another highlighted passage:

I know what happened between D and I is not proper but I can't help it. The other day he told me that he had recently made a few acquaintances with the local guys and had great fun with them. What they told him was astonishing. They said that they did not want to get married too early but wanted to have multiple girlfriends and multiple sex with them, the more the better. One boasted that he would be happy if he could make love to fifty women all his life. Another said he'd like to make love to 100. They all competed with each other to try to increase the figure. It sounded incredible. I can't imagine how they can manage that and in a time when such things could easily lead to jail unless, of course, they were the children of *gao gan,* high-level cadres or high-positioned leaders in the government. He laughed at my ignorance and said that they were young workers and what was happening outside the campus was much freer than inside it. I would much love to have that kind of adventure, although the only woman I have ever made love to is D, apart from C who has long gone and I can't even remember her features now except a tiny little mole on the thin edge of her upper lip towards the right side. As a rule, I am above seeking help from anyone but this time I went to D as I think she may be my only chance to get out of this big prison.

Finding this boring, Mr Miao thumbed through the pages until he got to his favourite part, where a man and a woman are engaged in a most explicit sex scene, described in graphic detail. He could not help but feel a little aroused himself, although he would not admit it to anyone, least of all to himself. If caught in the act, he would vigorously defend his action by saying that he was on a fact-finding mission to prove Jing wrong:

In a hurry, I could not find the place but she helped me find it, guiding my missile into it. It was hot beyond description, both outside and inside. As I went deeper, my eyes tightly closed, there appeared a hole in my mind, dark and deep, that kept dragging me down, until I did not know what was happening but I felt like collapsing with mounting sensations of pleasure. When I opened my eyes again, I saw that she took my root in both her hands, like a bamboo flute, flooded with my egg-white semen.

The political instructor had a hard on. He would have loved to have read more of this stuff but that was it. Some of the political sentiments were wild but boring, which, if he wanted this guy to be expelled, could easily be used against him but he wanted to bide his time. He wanted to find more solid evidence to prove their illicit love affair, such as photographs or witnesses.

42

You are now fragmenting. In fact, you have been fragmenting ever since the day you got infected with English. You are now watching the author reclining against the head of his bed, with the computer on his left lap, the quilt between his computer and his lap, his fingers hitting the keys, slowly or quickly, depending on the speed of his thoughts. You know that he has got things to say and write but for the last week or so he has not been creative. Already, his thoughts have left him for some remote places in Yunnan, Cloud Beyond the South; for Lijiang, the Beautiful River; Yulongxueshan, the Jade Dragon Snow Mountain, and, for a brief moment, you realise that he has already vacated this novel and is there. The person who is doing the hard work here is actually you, no one else. Perhaps, this is better for you can now stop this stupid pursuit. Already, the bookshop is bursting with unsold copies of published books.

PART III

The Price of Freedom

1

Sometime between the end of winter and the beginning of spring around the beginning of the new millenium, on a sunny afternoon when the flowers of the neighbourhood trees around Cheong Park brought back images of Wuhan cherry flowers in Gene's eyes, Deirdre and Gene were sitting in the back garden of a small house in Cheong St, at the foot of the Dandenongs. As Gene sat there, he maintained a total unsmiling silence, not looking at anything in particular, as if he was upset about something, but gazing at the lemon tree with its few thin and discoloured lemons, which he found, to his amusement, looked a little like himself. The cheap plastic chair that he sat in had one of its legs thrust into the soft soil, rain-soaked and grass-webbed, so that he was only half leaning. One could see that both of his hands were trembling slightly, as if they were in perpetual motion. Deirdre, meanwhile, was trying to force a tiny pink pill into his mouth. After he resisted it for a few seconds, Gene gave up but raised one of his jerky hands to make as if to strike at Deirdre, who brushed it aside and, magically, that hand dropped by itself, like a piece of dead wood. Afterwards, Deirdre sat down in front of Gene, face to face, a strip of green lawn between them. She was a little tired, her face worn with fatigue and there was a hint of resentment in her eyes. And you could see the lines of grey in her hair, too. Carefully, she brought out a letter from the pile of letters and newspapers on the table and, slitting it open with the side of her long index finger, she drew out the contents and remarked, 'Another one pager.'

'Read,' Gene ordered, morosely.

'Don't you speak to me like that,' Deirdre said, acting as if she was going to put the letter back into the envelope.

'Please don't,' Gene whispered, not looking at her.

Deirdre pulled out the letter again and ran her eyes over it, from beginning to the end. Then she began:

Dear Jing and Deirdre, to respond to your query last time, I'm sorry that it has taken me ten years to respond. I have now, through practise, reached a stage where I can see things that ordinary people cannot see. Black air, for example. It's called yeli. You wouldn't understand it anyway. To put it simply, what we strive for all our life is to get rid of this by building up the level of the white air, the more the better.

Always your friend,

Ma from San Francisco

'I black or white?' Gene interrupted her impatiently.

'Hang on, Gene, let me finish,' Deirdre said. 'You've got to be patient'.

'No,' Gene said.

'All right then,' Deirdre put the contents back into the envelope and went inside the house.

'Big mountains,' Gene murmured to himself.

'What are you talking about?' Deirdre said as she came out of the house again, this time with a tray and two teacups.

'I'm writing,' Gene said, not looking at her.

'Oh yes,' Deirdre said. 'You are. You always have wanted to be a writer, haven't you?'

'Only in my head.'

The clanging of the teacups on the tray caused a bird nearby to fly away.

'Us,' Gene said.

'What, us?'

'The cups.'

'The cups are us?'

'They're wrong.'

Silence.

'Mountains and rivers I saw.'

Her silence continued, water being poured, turning tea coloured.

'Music,' Gene said, loudly. 'I want music.'

Deirdre looked up from her sun-drenched hair, into his motionless eyes for a moment, and said, 'Gene, you can't do this all the time. You really tire me out.'

Tears came to Gene's eyes, which suddenly became alive with fire. He shot his foot out at the leg of the table and upset it; the teacups with tea and the tray as well as the metal thermos all came crashing onto the lawn.

'You fucking idiot, how dare you!' Deirdre muttered audibly. She came over and slapped Gene on the face. At once, Gene became quiet, as docile as a baby, holding his shoulders together, like a school kid who had done something wrong. 'I'll take you back to the hospital if you do this again.'

'Sorry,' Gene said. 'I'm sorry. Please don't take me back.'

'Then you have to listen to what I say,' Deirdre said. 'I'm so sick of all this.'

'Can I listen to music, Madam Deirdre, Mister Deirdre, can I?'

When Kiri Te Kanawa's voice came from the CD player, Gene, intoxicated, drifted into a dreamy state in which he stayed for the rest of the afternoon.

2

⸺

At night, they went to bed early. There was not much else to do except sleep. If they did not listen to music or watch some television, the house would remain totally silent. Empty. Side by side with each other, in the darkness, he was listening to Deirdre breathing evenly. No words were spoken, although he thought he was speaking, his heart louder than his tongue. Again, writing formed itself in his head:

Dear Deirdre,

After these many years, when you ask me why we are still together, I think the only answer I have got is I don't care any more. I am alone, even when I am with you, side by side here. For so long I have been doubtful about my genesis: was I born of a Chinese father and a foreign mother? Why has no mother ever turned up to claim me? Why do I still look as Chinese as ever, even more so than before? What is it that makes it impossible for me to return to my origins and where are they? In Yunnan where my Chinese dad supposedly met my English mum decades ago? If so, why did I come to Melbourne instead of go to Yunnan or London? Will you accompany me in my journey there? I'm not searching for anything but I need some peace ... Father sent me some material about his past before his death but I can't read it. It splits my head. Perhaps when we go out on the journey together to that small town where he stayed after the Burma Road, we will know more because his spirit will visit me. In fact, he is urging me to go, my dead dad. Perhaps even you are not real, as unreal as myself, two halves of an incomplete world, complementing while splitting each other, incompletely. I don't think I'll go with you for I don't think you have acquired my ability to hear voices yet. You have to reach that level of uncomfortableness. This will be a walkabout with live spirits of the dead to whom you are denied access. Dear Dree, years ago I imagined my home lay elsewhere, born to someone else of another language, until I came to you and realised that I was no match. I now go back into the shadow, cast over my ancestral land by your language, my semi-language. Perhaps your ancestral land, too? Why, the minute you opened yourself up fully to, my metaphysical morphing, there was not a single shred of doubt that you were as ancient as me, like a written character, any written characters. Deep inside our organs, there was no race.

I'll go on the walkabout alone. I can already feel the core of the mountains, yes, the call of the mangteng, Python Leap. Don't take me for a fool, thinking that I can be cured with medications, manufactured by the correct Caucasian mind. As Dang our medicine man said, the Western medicine could only treat the symptoms but not deal with the root cause.

Gene yawned and the writing stopped instantly. An idea took form in his mind, which kept him so excited that he couldn't sleep until early morning when he felt exhausted and finally collapsed in a dream, his bed pal. By now, Deirdre had got out of bed to do her morning exercises in the garden, fresh with dew. Before she got up, she had touched his genitals and had found him warm, hard. She stroked him slowly and gently, taking it in her hand like a huge chalk with which she taught students, until he grew harder and, then, came without warning, like a sudden flood, wetting her fingers. The semen felt like the dew, heavier and whiter than the dew, carrying a smell of pity in it. He uttered a small cry and turned on his side, sinking deeper into his sleep. She plucked a tissue and wiped her fingers clean. She felt a little guilty but forgave herself as she put the kettle on in preparation for breakfast. As usual, it was a simple affair of toasted bread with butter and jam, plus a glass of microwaved milk, something that she never tired of but that easily bored him. There was nothing much else she could do about it; he had to marry a Chinese woman who could pamper his tastebuds. He would read the morning newspapers that she bought for him from the local milk bar, run by a Chinese couple who never took holidays. He would sometimes go himself and read the newspaper there. Then the locals would see this short man opening his newspaper solemnly, absorbed in the news of people dying of famine in Africa, someone in the USA receiving an envelope of anthrax, a rape in Sydney, all bad. People never asked him what he did and he never felt compelled to tell them, either.

But Gene was never as relaxed as he was now after his illness, although he wouldn't ever admit it. There was no call on his time. When he finished reading his newspaper, he would go out to the garden and sit there in the sun, as quiet as an unloaded gun. Or if there was rain, he would lie down on a sofa, listening to music. The upshot of this was he would be found lying on his back, sound asleep. He was like that, day in and day out. Whereas he used to joke with his classmates, 'How goes the enemy?', he no longer said that as it would suggest that his employer, Time, was his enemy. It was not, because he had greatly benefited from this employment: having absolutely nothing to do but just living, eating, drinking and opening his bowels, leaving his mind at rest, writing in his head as he was wont to do before he went to meet his bed pals. Indeed, he would have to update this joke to something like, 'How goes the friend?' Of course Deirdre did not know what was going on in his mind, though his doctor had suggested that his patient's mind might be like a machine turned on working itself inside out.

This morning, as Deirdre put the breakfast on the table, Gene came over and kissed her neck, smelling the single mole there, as dark as a blood plum. She had once told him that having a mole on the back of one's neck, according to a blind Chinese fortune-teller, was bad luck but he wouldn't believe it. He would say, in his happier moments, that she was so lucky to have him cook her two Chinese meals a day, whereas other people had to pay through their noses for such luxury. She would retaliate by saying that he had a lot to thank her for bringing him to Australia in the first place, but their banterings, exchanged mostly as a pastime, would never last more than three sentences as she would always do something to stop him, like picking up his hand and rubbing it against her cheek or, if she was in a bad mood, giving him a gentle slap on the wrist, which would send him immediately into a silence that lasted throughout the day until she pulled him into her arms, with an endearing 'Gene Dee', Dee being the sound of a Chinese word for younger brother and for a man's penis if doubled, as in Dee Dee. She turned round and looked into his black eyes, their eyes, blue and black, locking together for a brief moment and coming apart. She thought of the morning ejaculation and grinned. As if getting the hint, he said, 'Did you know what? I think I *paoma*[3] last night.' Her command of Chinese was such that she knew all those dirty words and she said, 'I know. You must have *zhaoji*[4] last night in your dream.' With that, she gave him a big hug, her firm breasts pressing against him, making him go slightly hard but not as hard as he wanted to, his steam having been let out without his knowledge.

After breakfast, he said to her, 'I want to go away. There's something wrong.'

'What's wrong?' she asked. 'There's nothing wrong except perhaps yourself.'

---

3 Literally, run the horse; figuratively, night emission.
4 Literally, find chick or look for a chick; figuratively, going to a prostitute.

'Perhaps I'm too wrong from your point of view, you know what I mean?'

'That's when you were a student in Wuhan but I think you should do something, write, for example.'

'Right, I don't tink anything these days. Headwriting suffices for me.'

'You need to find a way to make your existence visible, palpable.'

'You tink?'

'Gene Dee, I tink you should take your morning medications now.'

'No, I won't.'

'Listen. If you don't take them, I'll call the CAT Team and they will come here to make sure you do.'

'Even if you call the police, I won't.'

'You will or you won't?' Deirdre suddenly swung around, scowling at Gene, her heavy rotundity bearing down on him as if to crush him.

'But I must go.'

'Go? Go where?'

'Go ho me,' came Gene's tearful reply.

'You don't have a home to go back to, Gene. This is your home, our home. You said you'd never go back to China again. Your parents are no more. Your brother is no more. You hate the Chinese. What is there for you to see? Who is there for you to meet?' She stopped as she saw Gene pick up the bottle, uncapping it.

Without a word, Gene tipped his head back and swallowed the capsules with a gulp of water. 'As long as you let me go,' Gene said. 'I shall be fine.'

'Fine, fine, you always say fine, but fine with what? You are fine as long as you are here, with me, at ho me, as you say,'

Deirdre sighed, her eyes brimming with sudden tears. 'Perhaps, I might as well let you go and, and, get lost in your mountains that you even rave about in your dreams!'

3

—

Deirdre was not a Wagner. She was Deirdre Sandringham. That remained unknown to her students in East Lake as she was then only a partner to Dr Wagner. She was now Deirdre S Gene or D.S. Gene, an acronym that she hadn't decided to use but that Gene was happy about. 'DS,' Gene called out one day when both of them went shopping. Gene suddenly found Deirdre missing and panicked. He started yelling, 'DS! Deee-Yeeessss!' All heads were turned in his direction. Frowns followed. One old lady in red stopped and said, with concern, 'Are you all right, young man?'

Gene ignored her and continued yelling until a security man took him aside and asked what was the matter.

'My wife is missing,' Gene said.

'Where is your wife?' the fat man asked.

'She said she wanted to leave me,' Gene said.

'What's her name?' 'D.S.,' Gene said and added, 'D.S. Gene.'

Deirdre heard the name in the toilet when the loudspeaker was paging someone, repeatedly: 'D.S. Gene, please go to the information desk. Your husband is looking for you.' It took her a few seconds before she realised that she was being paged. I told him that I wouldn't be a moment, she thought to herself. Remembering what had happened in the past, she came out and went to the desk hurriedly, only to find that Gene was engaged in a lively conversation with the security guy.

'What happened, Gene?' Deirdre asked.

'Don't interrupt,' Gene said, not looking at her. 'Andrew is telling me a story. Go on, Andrew, what happened next?'

'Sorry, but I've got to go. There you are,' Andrew the security man said to Deirdre. 'I'm handing back your husband, intact.'

On their way Deirdre said, 'I know this is crazy but I wouldn't stop you if you wanted to go.'

Gene said nothing.

'The only thing is as long as you promise to me that you take your medications with you and keep in touch whenever and wherever you can, I'd be happy for you to go. Just make sure you stay safe.'

'I'm sorry but they are calling me. I hear Dad's voice all the time.'

'There's another thing I want you to promise to me, Gene,' Deirdre said.

'You are such a control,' Gene said, holding the last word on the bow of his lips before he shot out, 'freak', arrow like.

'Come on, Gene,' Deirdre said; there was a hard edge to her voice. 'You want me to let you go or not?'

'I do.'

'Then you must promise me one thing. You'll record your daily happenings on your trip to the Burma Road for me. Okay?'

Instead of answering her question, Gene reached out with his hand to touch her crotch, a familiar enough act for Deirdre. She knew he was checking and would be disappointed. He was. 'But I thought I'd come back to see you big with our baby!'

'Not yet. You and I have a long way to go,' Deirdre said, her hand groping responsively for his private parts and remembered with a smile how Jing once described himself as 'a man of many private parts'. It was for this that she liked him, intensely.

'But keep them buttoned up,' Deirdre said, grinning, showing her neat white teeth.

'Oh, don't you worry,' Gene said. 'I'll have plenty on tap.'

4
—

You had such a busy week that you did not write anything in this novel. From time to time, though, you would see the story fragment into a multitude of people and events, and you would see Gene leave things behind in his wanderings away from Deirdre, both of them in their forties now and she slightly older than him. You now have gained some distance from Gene so that you do not easily allow him to live your life or him yours. Once a proud student of English, Gene is incoherently monosyllabic. It is only by going away that he becomes coherent again.

5

Monday is today. I have never liked Hong Kong, but I have to go through it in order to reach my destination, the Burma Road. Years ago when I went through the old airport at Kai Tak on my way to Melbourne to meet with you, I was frightened by the sight of Hong Kong policemen in dark blue, wearing berets and carrying shining carbines, and I was ashamed that one of the new runners I was wearing was split open on its side. That was how badly shoes were made in those days in China, the material used inside being cardboard paper!

James is trying to get me an itinerary for a trip to Dali, Lijiang and Ruili, where the old Burma Road, also called the Stillwell Road, is located. I want to find my Dad there or his ghost. I hear voices all the time, his voices, other voices, too. Only just now, I heard him saying: *It's a dawn alert. Dive-bombing.* I don't know what that's all about but he sounded like he was fighting.

The further north I move, the more tranquil I become. The Chineseness, long lost in me, or half lost, vigorously resisted like a cancer and trashed like a piece of garbage, returns, bit by bit, to me, as I am amused to find absurdities here, such as the 'Don't Disturb' sign on my hotel door, translated in corrupt Hong Kongnese Chinese characters as *Qingwu Saorao,* 'Don't Harass'. It brought me to the realisation that the Chinese language has now also entered into a process of creolisation.

The physical features of Kunming, by contrast with Hong Kong, were quite plain except for the moments before touching down as the land below looked like a palette of raw new paints splashed all over the fast approaching earth, red, ochre, dark brown, even black, wonderfully mixed. But you know what, Dear Dre, people here don't say thank you. They never do. At the customs counter, I hand in my passport and travel documents with a smile, a 'thank you', but meet with absolute aplomb. No, I think this is a wrong word. I meant meeting with absolute nonchalance or unconcern. When my stuff is handed back to me, my habit prompts me to say, 'thank you', again, and a 'bye' but once again there is no response. When I look as I go past I can see the man in the dark blue uniform looking absolutely unsmiling, his hand held out above the counter, like a moveable object, waiting for me to place my document. I can't understand why this people, my former people, never say thank you or goodbye. I think if you were with me, it would be different for they had probably mistaken me for one of them, instantly departurable.

In my hotel room, I took a look at myself in the mirror and saw someone else. It was my character from the past, a past that was more past than ever before, a past anchored in a war that had destroyed so many lives and yet managed to create me. My character, whose name is not yet given and known, had just arrived in Dali by bus. It was in fact my dead father Jing senior whom I found inside me, struggling to get out.

Back in China, even though in a place I had never been to, I felt as if something lost had been returned to me. It was like a story I had read many years ago in my childhood. The hero was pinned down to the ground, on the point of being killed, when he gathered all his strength from his contact with the earth in a last-ditch effort and threw his opponent off him and killed him instead. I don't have to speak English now; no one speaks it here except the hotel receptionists who give themselves names like Sarah, Dave and Julie, English names on badges under Chinese faces. The girl I met emerged as if out of a dream. I can't tell you this but our lovemaking sessions so exhausted us that we fell into a dead sleep at the end of each session, drenched in sweat. I am no longer monosyllabic. I am less correct than Australia. Finally, I am able to stand firmly on my own soil, vulgar and primitive, but full of energy, better, in a way, than a sanitised, deodorised and sterilised recent past.

Only yesterday I chucked out the whole package of the medications containing Prozac, Zoloft and Celexa into the Curled Dragon River or the Curling Dragon River; the air here was medication itself. If I have another relapse, I'll breathe, the air.

6
—

To fill you in, Dear Dre, I've now begun my thousand-kilometre-long journey across two big rivers, the Lancang River, which becomes the Thanlwin in Myanmar, and the Nujiang River, which becomes the Mekong in Vietnam, through three tall mountains, the Gaoligong Mountain, which is over 5000 metres above sea level, the Nu Mountain and the Yunling Mountain, right to the China–Myanmar border. The rivers are long, the mountains are tall and, needless to say, my desires are deep for exploring them. I know my last few days sound like a mess. That's only because I was too tired to put down everything. Realities and imaginings copulate on such a massive, medication-free scale that I find it hard to handle. I've now spent a whole day in Dali, somewhere in the middle section of the Road.

The only gain I had yesterday on the Erhai, the lake in Dali, was the Cangshan under the setting sun. It was so beautiful, it turned into an enormous black stone of night before darkness had time to swallow its miles-long range. I wonder why no one painted it like that. As I sat, alone, watching the sun bathing the mountain in constantly changing colours, mainly purple, mixed with burning smoke that came up from the surrounding fields, I daydreamed again, seeing a man in his early twenties coming to me and saying in a heavy Hubei accent, 'About sixty years ago it was here that I first came to.'

It was 1944, the year of the Burma Road, when I had just graduated from university. I had left my girlfriend in Kunming and had just arrived in Dali on my way to the Burma Road. The troop, part of the Y-Force that I belonged to, had stationed at Dragon Tail Street, near the two wells. This was late April. In the evening, after dinner, I went out alone, hoping to see something different. My ears were getting used to the local dialect, which was curiously similar to the one I spoke, the Hankou accent, except that it was softer, like the weather here, crisply clear, sweetly refreshing. People walking by wore colourful costumes with tall headgear and strange footwear. I could recognise the Hui people from the white tea-mug-like caps they wore. Otherwise, the ethnicity of other people was entirely lost on me. I saw street vendors selling things I had never seen before: bamboo smoking pipes as long as an arm, longer than an arm, and as thick as a big bowl; eggs held vertically with straws and people eating fried grasshoppers while downing their locally made liquor! At first, I thought I had got it wrong but when I went over, a man wearing a white *duijin* and loose blue trousers asked if I would like to have a taste. I grinned but shook my head, inwardly shaken by what I had seen.

'It is very tasty,' the man said, as he demonstrated it by picking up a cooked grasshopper, golden and crisp, from the fried lot and began chewing it noisily. 'This is *zhuque*.'

A moment or two went past before it dawned on me that what he had meant was 'bamboo birds' and I could not resist another chuckle.

Back in the barracks, late in the evening, I told Lieutenant Kilpatrick what I had seen, taking particular delight in revealing the name of the insects eaten. Ash, for that was his first name, was flabbergasted and asked, 'Did they also eat dogs and rats and cats?'

'Unless you are talking about the Cantonese but this is Cloud Beyond the South; we are further south now. About 600 kilometres from here southwest beyond Wanding, it is Burma that the Japanese have taken.'

'I know. But let's talk about something else, shall we? Otherwise, we'll have another sleepless night,' Ash said.

I noticed his mood swing and sensibly stopped, to allow my own mind to absorb what had happened in the last few weeks, thinking my own thoughts while Ash was thinking his. I think I could work out what he was thinking because I know.

'I've come here to die, fighting Japanese or no Japanese. I don't know why; maybe I'm sick of the mad chase for materialistic gains back at home or maybe, like they said, there is a better place than America out there. Who knows that one of these days I might not disappear behind those purple mountains with snow-capped peaks that overlook the deep-blue lake without a speck of dust and become a monk in a Taoist temple? I know I am an oddball but I am no more odd than any other fellow Americans, who never allow themselves a single day of rest from their mercenary pursuits. I wish I could be simpler, like the locals here. Perhaps the war will soon teach me how to achieve that.'

Ash did not have the habit of keeping a diary but the thoughts that went through his mind would make most interesting reading for posterity. He didn't tell me what he was thinking either, although I said that I already knew.

'Are you missing your home?' I asked.

'How do you know?' Ash lied.

'Because I miss my home and so I assume you do, too, as you come from even further away,' I said.

'Thank you,' Ash said, 'for reminding me of a world of which I am no longer a part.'

'Same here,' I said.

'And you have a girlfriend, too, I guess?'

'Right,' I said.

'What does she look like?'

'Quite pretty, I must say, lovely eyes, lovely face, in fact, lovely everything,' I replied.

'Avoid being repetitive in describing someone.'

'I'm sorry but my English is not up to a scratch,' I said. 'Or was it up to scratch, not a scratch?'

Ash ignored that and said, 'Say, for example, she has almond eyes, an olive-shaped face, cherry lips etc.'

'Why all trees and grasses? Her eyes are as black as, well, the bottom of the wok. How's that? And she is, well, quite nice whatever that means,' I said, groping in my linguistic darkness for the right words.

'I'm only joking. Your description is as good as mine, perhaps better.'

'Death is a big mountain,' I said.

'How do you mean?'

'No. Did I say anything?' I said.

'Yes. You said death is a big mountain.'

'No, I didn't. Someone else must have said it in his dream In fifty years, would we, if we are still alive, regret what we are doing today?'

'What, you mean fighting the Japanese?' I asked.

'That and dying for the sake of dying?'

'Don't really know but what a strange question you asked,' I said.

'Why did the Japanese want to conquer China?'

'Because they want the land mass,' I said.

'Is land more precious than human bodies?'

'Apparently so, I think,' I said. 'Sometimes, land is the body. Landscape, in a way, is also bodyscape, on a national level or, perhaps, international level when people of different nationalities die together.'

'Sorry but you sound like a profound philosopher. I feel

quite sleepy now. Cheers.'

'See you tomorrow.'

'Time to disembark,' the boat manager announced, waking me from my daydream, no, my dusk dream of heard voices and headwritten deliriums. I opened my medicine box, my eyes, again, and saw the man had already gone, leaving me with a lake of evening showers of colour, like fresh blood newly spilled. The mountain facing me totally dark against a pale evening sky that looks like granite, for which the place is known, the afterglow so sharp it penetrated my eyeballs which, upon closing, can still see the tiny white sun half dropping behind a white mountain as if on a negative.

I thought of the woman again, who had promised to keep me company today but had failed to turn up. I wondered what she was up to tonight for, tomorrow, I would set out on the real Burma Road.

7

I woke up to a gusty wind in the morning, rattling the windows of my hotel room. It's plain day outside, the moon still in the sky, streets dry as dead bones.

Last night, whenever I thought of the journey I was frightened. I actually dreamt that my coach overturned a few times and I tried to ring you in vain to tell you that if I do not ring you tonight it means something bad has happened. However, when I arrived at the bus station this morning, I was reassured because of two things. One that there was plenty of room on-board the bus and the other was that the passengers looked surprisingly clean and educated, unlike the images I had of them in my brainwashed and medication-eroded head. There were also children. A teenage girl was making use of her time to catch up on her homework, reading a textbook loudly in Chinese by the window. Next to me was a boy of twelve or thirteen, who also had a book in his hands. The bus was a very new Iveco, with a television and air-conditioning. On one side of the television, there was a sign bearing the names of the two drivers and their photographs, one called Ma Zaicong and the other, Ma Li, the former with cropped hair and thick, black brows, and the latter, a short man with long slit eyes that seemed swollen for lack of sleep. There was another young man with them whose hair was slightly dishevelled and who was picking his nose in public, his fingers playing with what was obviously the snotty stuff that came out of his nostrils. My seat was No 1 by the window and I could see all this as if I was watching a scene on the television in front of me. Under the names of those two drivers, their driving record was spelt out in large print in Chinese: 'A safety driving record of 480,000 kilometres without any accidents'. As my mind was put at rest, the Hubei-accented Chinese voice tinged with my father came rushing back:

We had arrived at a small town called Shunning in the Angry Mountain (Nushan Mountain). We were in high spirits, singing loud anti-Japanese songs, I taking the lead as I was known to have a good voice, much to the amazement of our American liaison officers who did not understand a word of what we were singing. I myself had difficulty explaining some of the words as my English was not quite up to scratch. So I simply said, 'These were songs for us to fight Japanese with. Don't you have your own songs for that?'

Ash replied, 'Oh yes, we certainly do, but can you tell me what was the first line of the song that you sang so aggressively a moment ago?'

'Aggressively? How do you mean?'

'I mean, so forcefully,' and, with that, he made a gesture with his hand that looked like pulling the trigger and that made me laugh.

'It was something like swinging a big knife at the devil's head,' I said.

'Sabre or sword?' someone said behind me. I turned my head back and saw his face, the full-moon face of a Chinese but one who had never so far spoken a single Chinese word to us during the whole journey. This was Cheong, the Chinese-American soldier, also a liaison officer. We all resented him for not speaking Chinese to us. Zhang, a friend of mine from Sichuan, told me in private that he was a fake foreign devil. In fact, in one of the training sessions in Kunming, several of us audibly made negative comments in his presence, although he remained affable all the time, perhaps because he was American or he didn't know what was being said.

I turned my face back and said to Ash, 'It was something like that,' while thinking: so if this guy did understand Chinese, how could he then pretend that he did not wish to speak our language as if, as if he was too good for us?

'Devil? Did you say devil?' Ash asked.

'Yes. Why?'

'I heard people calling us that,' Ash said, 'when we were in Kunming.'

'Yes, but that was only for fun. This, however, is serious because it is these Japanese devils that invaded our land and wanted to conquer us. They are worse than devils.'

Everyone remained silent after that. The truck thundered into the town, jumping on the pitted road, raising a cloud of dust behind its buttocks, through which I could catch an occasional glimpse of a black-tiled roof against the pale background of a green mountain slope or of a meandering creek just cross the road, half hidden by nameless trees.

'The landscape here looks so untitled,' I said.

'What?' Ash was startled. 'What did you mean, untitled?' He looked dazed for a moment and murmured to himself, 'This guy is weird. He is so poetic.' Then he said loudly, 'Get ready for camping, guys. See if we can grab some accommodation from the locals.'

Following them, I climbed off the truck, swinging the big American-made pack on my back, which contained, among other daily necessities, a mouth organ and a notebook that had a photo of my girlfriend between its first pages. At the thought of her, an intoxicated rush overcame me but I resisted the temptation and merged into the marching line of dark green, all wearing berets.

It soon became apparent that our problem was not to find accommodation but to find people, as no one turned up when we went in search of them. Each house looked dark and deserted, doors thrown wide open or tightly closed. A cold wind was moaning in the trees, making the one-street village town even more desolate and empty. One could almost smell death, and death it was when we finally found him on the face of an old man sitting alone by the doorstep at the end of the deserted street. Ash motioned for me to go over and ask him what had happened.

The only thing the old man kept saying was, 'Dead. All dead.'

'What happened,' I asked, looking into his tree-bark face with two holes for eyes. I thought I had seen a ghost.

'Changchi,' he replied. 'Miasma. They all died of it. All.' He burst into tears, uncontrollably. I had never seen a man cry like that, let alone an old man, but I could understand his feelings.

A giggle from the boy sitting next to me pushed the voice back into recess. When I turned to look at him, all I could see was his smiling profile over an open book to a page bearing two large characters for a title, *Xiang Pi,* Fragrant Fart. That must be the source of his delight. I tried to invite the voice back but the pond was too deep for fishing. The bus, meanwhile, was set in motion, beginning its meandering journey.

8

If you are busy with making money, you stop writing.

That's right, doing something and not doing something at will, like smoking and quitting smoking at will. Writing and quitting it at will, too. Wu ke wu bu ke, *Nothing possible but nothing impossible. Or, more likely, nothing can do and nothing cannot do. As you said to him, there's a long way to go. Friends are few but days are many. Books are too many. And he says: what you write is always more important than how you write. The film you went to based on a novel was so predictable that you started foretelling the story one or two steps ahead of the time: the son is carrying his father up a mountain to a temple as the father is dying. His estranged wife is chasing them in a hurry, hoping to catch up with them without being aware of her husband's approaching death. You know he will die a few minutes before she arrives. That is the price you pay for making stories. Why would you make stories deeper than necessary? After a day's work, who can stand that sort of thing? As she said, sometimes all she wanted to see or watch was a bit of shallow fun. And you said: fifteen years ago when you first met I introduced him to you as a* yansu zuojia, *serious writer. No one uses that term any more. You can't afford to be too serious. If you are serious, you end up with no one buying. Scary, isn't it? But you still have to carry on regardless.*

9

A thought, Dear Dre. As I go deeper into the mountains on the winding road, my senses become gradually tuned with the surroundings, such immense beauty of open-legged valleys, ejaculatory rivers as thin as bullets hundreds of metres downhill and clouds that sometimes drift straight onto our windshields. I keep wondering why I would be bothered about what happened in the 1940s to someone who's long dead, even if he was my dad. What is happening now seems more interesting.

I did not see a single foreigner in Ruili, but at lunchtime I saw one backpacker. He was the same guy who got into another bus next to mine in Dali that went to Baoshan. After lunch I went to the toilet. When I came back I saw him standing among the passengers in a line, waiting to board their long-distance bus. Because his eyes met mine, I said 'hi' as I went past him but he made no response. I had the impression that this guy was overcautious about meeting strangers. He was obviously a Westerner but I didn't know whether he spoke English or German or Danish. I saw someone I thought I could identify with but he saw a completely Chinese in me. Stupid.

At one stage, I think my old fear came back, of people, indeed, of any people of any nationality, particularly of my own people, my previous people. I want to keep my journey in life as lonely as possible, so lonely that only I know what it is like to be living totally alone, like this foreigner, to whom I must have seemed also a total foreigner. My isolation is my strength, like these mountain strangers or stranger mountains. They are massive, powerful and silent in their each and individual isolation. Deep down, there are communicating underground rivers. It is unbearable to think that I am sitting with forty or so strangers in the same bus that may overturn anytime and roll down the hill so that we all die unknown to each other! What's the difference between now and then, when people killed each other like they had never done before, strangers killing strangers but dying together, their bones mingled with their blood, enriching the soil below, when only the maggots, the flies, the mosquitoes, the wild dogs, the wolves, the vultures, the meat-eating ants would intimately know them, so intimately that their fleshes become one?

*

I do not know what the place is called, although I would name it Mutton Valley as I saw this afternoon with my own eyes a dead sheep lying peacefully in a clearing where we stayed for the night. When I approached him, I could not find any injury on him but he stank so much that I stepped back in horror. At that moment, I think I saw the flitting smile of death high in the sky and felt an instant desire to throw up despite the beautiful river of yellowish waters running below in the steep crotch of the valley.

Ash and I agreed that we should exchange stories to while away our dreary, sometimes frightening nights. I don't know why but it is perhaps because I sort of wanted to elicit a kind of jealousy in him that I told him my father had three concubines. That certainly got him, excited him even. He responded by boasting that his parents possessed an expansive plantation in Texas that was as big as half of Yunnan Province. I then said that was nothing because we had troupes of servants waiting upon us at meal times, at bedtimes and, when we went out, we travelled on *jiaozi*. Although he did not know what I was talking about, he scoffed at the idea, saying that they did not need any servants because America was a free and democratic country where people were their own masters. He went on to say that they had mechanised their agriculture by planting and harvesting wheat with machines for miles around, hinting that I'd probably never seen those in my entire life. I was quick to defend myself by saying that the Chinese were an ingenious people who had invented gunpowder and fireworks, which formed the basis of all the modern-day inventions, but he said that the recent mattered more than the past. I got myself so worked up that I challenged him to a session of arm-wrestling and found that he was more than my match. Eventually, when both of us were exhausted, I said to him, jokingly, 'I'm sure you'll enjoy your stay here because of the prospect of taking a crowd of concubines,' and he said, also jokingly, 'But I'm certain that you'll come to America one day and become a capitalist 'cause that's what all of you Chinese are.' We laughed until Cheong shushed us by cautioning us that we might be heard by enemies hiding in the surrounding mountain forests.

Oh, those mountains! I had never seen such tall mountains before in my life. One stood thrusting into the sky like a sword, its edge shining with almost green ice. Another spread before me like a massive wall of rugged surface, bare of grass or trees, its rain-scoured rock face like a tremendous ink painting. Hundreds of metres down there was a river of brown waters hurtling itself against any rocks blocking its way, polishing their faces and skins, with white flowers of water opening every once in a while, dying and reliving, dying again, their tireless roars heard miles away, day and night. By comparison, Turtle Hill in my hometown was truly a turtle, a crouching dwarf by the Yangtze.

That night I set up my tent in a square at the top, thinking

I was clever as I found the way the Americans pitched their tents gave them little space. When it began raining at midnight, however, my tent soon received enough water to flatten it. I woke up from my sleep, drenched through inside my sleeping bag. It was Ash, woken up by the terrible noise, who pulled me inside his inverted V-shaped tent, warm and snug, and got me to change into some dry clothes while he was holding a flashlight in his hand, only for a brief second before he remembered something and turned it off. Everything was plunged into darkness again, with rain coming down in sheets outside, thrashing the tent and the surrounding trees and other tents in a continuous spread of concert-like rain noise. My sleeping bag full of water, I was now lying side by side with Ash in his bag, feeling the squeeze. I think I smelt him as I never had of any other Chinese. Otherwise, everything else seemed fine. Our bodily warmth generated an atmosphere in which I felt as if I had entered a foreign land. He did not say a word but just listened to the sound of the rain. I listened, too, but it was a different kind of sound that I heard: an insistent voice I had heard in the past, telling me to give up on life as it was not worth living and that the best way to achieve that was to fight in the war and die heroically. Then the voice changed to my girlfriend's parting words in Kunming: 'You should never leave me like this to go to war because you don't have to if you don't want to. It is like taking away my life from me and it makes me feel like dying in peace ahead of you in war. War is not worth fighting for; no war is.'

My father's voice was ringing in my ears, 'One day you'll know.' He said that when I read an ancient Chinese story at the age of eight and did not quite know what it meant. It was about two brothers fighting for the throne. One of them didn't reveal his intention to take the throne till he got ready and raised an army.

Then he took the kingdom that his brother had been occupying and killed him. I found it to be a very uninteresting story and it didn't make much sense. Now, I think I know. I don't know why I mention this to you, Deirdre, perhaps one day you'll also know?

10

In creating this character in He, you, the author, have thought of something that you put down on one of those scrap papers. The first is a fragment of a conversation that takes place between He and Ash, as follows:

'Don't call me Hee,' He said. 'Or I'll call you Sash.'

'Sorry? But how do I pronounce your name?' Ash said. 'Ho?'

'No, He,' He said.

'Her?' Ash said.

Both of them laughed and He said, 'No, damn it, Sash, I'm not her but He!'

'I see, Ho, ho, ho, ho!'

You know that the whole fragment consists only of the first question asked by He, the rest you composed as you typed along.

The other is an ability you found that He has got for he can create new English words, although his command of English is yet to improve; he did not even know how to say 'piss' when he felt the need and, so, he pointed to his private parts and said, 'I must go' and, after a pause, he said, 'How do you say if you want to do this?' He pointed to it again.

'What?' Ash said, his eyes full of mischief. 'You mean make love?'

'No, no, of course not,' He said, grinning, showing his small teeth. 'I mean ...' He got stuck on the word and so had to be content with making a gesture indicating a curve from between his legs to the ground in front of him with the index finger of his right hand.

'Piss,' Ash said. 'p, i, double s.'

'I wonder why we were never taught such things in our training courses in Kunming,' he wondered aloud as he went to the temporary toilet behind a gum tree. On his way back, he thought of something and was eager to tell Ash.

'You know, Ash, I've found something new,' He announced.

'What? In the toilet? Behind the tree?'

'Yes. It's piss change,' He said proudly.

Wide-eyed, Ash could not believe his ears. 'How do you mean, piss change?'

In his awkward English, He told Ash what it meant. In his hometown, people referred to the tendency to change one's mind quickly and unpredictably as 'piss change'. That is as soon as they finish pissing they change their mind.

'Hey, how did you say it in Chinese?' Ash was intrigued.

'E niao bian,' He said.

Again, you found it irresistible to move on along those lines as your fingers keyed away.

You can hear the rain outside and now it is 10.35 pm.

11

The meandering mountain road is lined with watermelon fields. Every once in a while, you'll see rows of huge oblong watermelons on the roadside minded by ethnic Dai people, supposedly the ancestors of the Thais. At one such row, I asked my ethnic Bai taxi driver to stop and I bought an armful of watermelon, half of which I shared with him, getting him to keep the other half. The sellers were all ethnic Dai women, wearing white clothes and white headwraps. When I raised my camera they ducked for cover, uttering small cries, as if I aimed a gun at them.

Among other things, my driver told me a number of gruesome stories, all related to the Japanese. I'll only tell you two, Deirdre. The Japanese had many ways of killing the local people and the Chinese soldiers. One of these was to cook them in big woks. They put water in them and firewood underneath them, heating the water till it was boiling. Then they put the soldiers, one at a time, into the huge wok, soaking in the boiling water, laughing as they listened to them shrieking in pain and seeing them gradually turn into soup, gravy. To tell you the truth, Dear Dree, I should never have told you this. It is beyond human endurance. The other story is a little more romantic. In a mountain village occupied by the Japanese, a Japanese officer had an affair with a local woman in the valley. One night when he went down to meet with his woman, the locals surrounded them in a surprise attack and killed them both. He added that every inch of Songshan, Pine Hill, was covered with human flesh, of both the Japanese and the Chinese.

*

Cheong, who looked every bit Chinese except for his mud-stained combat boots, his green army pants and his American rank insignia, which I believed to be colonel, called me to his office and said, in a Mandarin-heavy-with-Cantonese accent, 'Do you know why I want to see you today?'

A series of incidents flashed across my mind: the noise I made last night in the heavy rain, which might have woken up quite a few of my fellow soldiers; the casual manner in which I dealt with other American liaison officers; and, in particular, my habit of wandering around our camping ground admiring the beauty of the surrounding mountains and rivers as if the approaching battleground was not a major concern.

'You have not answered my question,' Cheong said.

'I'm sorry but,' I said, tongue-tied.

'I want you to help us to interpret the language as the situation is getting more serious on a daily basis.'

He explained to me that as we were advancing towards the Nujiang River (Angry River), there was more need than ever to relay military information, oral or written, between the American liaison officers and Chinese student interpreters, or Fan-I-Kuan as they called us. He had observed that I was more fluent in English than others, and he decided that I should act as team leader. Surprised, I was about to say no when he cut me short and said, 'But I must warn you not to be too loose with the discipline for we are in a war zone and death may happen any time.'

Seeing that my face darkened, he sought to lighten the atmosphere by saying, 'Are they still calling me a "fake foreign devil"?'

Surprised again, I mumbled, 'No, I suppose not.'

'To tell you the truth,' Cheong said, without prompting, 'I am a true foreign devil because I was born in San Francisco, of Chinese parentage. Afraid that I might totally lose their language and culture, my parents sent me back to China to attend school, which is why I can speak such good Mandarin, *ni jue de ne?*' He looked at me challengingly, his eyes so foreignly Chinese, a completely different landscape from us.

'Oh yes, even better than mine,' I said, tongue-in-cheek.

'Come on,' Cheong said. 'You are not serious, are you? But you see I can't speak to you guys in Chinese as I'm an American officer and I am not allowed to behave like one of you in their presence. You guys probably resent me for that, don't you?'

As he spoke, I could hear the staccato noise of ack-ack in the distance and realised that my kind of beauty was now in danger.

When I told Ash that one day I would write a story about our life there, his interest was only temporarily aroused. 'There is no point,' he said, dismissively. 'Writing drives me crazy. I'd rather die and let someone else tell my story. Besides, after the war, there will be a lot more ways, more interesting ways, to make money than being a mere writer.'

'Really?' I asked.

'Being a door-to-door postman,' he said.

'Is that all?' I was amused. All my Chinese classmates at Southwest United University were ambitious people. Some wanted to be generals. Some wanted to go to the United States of America because, to them, it was the best country in the world, as Yiming, the class monitor, once said, 'It's got to be the best because it starts with an A and ends with an A.' I challenged that by saying, 'Come on, you've got to be joking, for by your logic, Australia could also be considered the best because it also starts and ends with an A, right?' No one except myself had entertained the idea of becoming a writer, it seemed, of becoming famous if not rich. But this guy from America — all he ever wanted to be was a door-to-door postman! I could not imagine how one could be content with such an ordinary life, like a bird or a tree or just a slow snail or a running creek or a mountain peak that stands there or a piece of sky over it or a blade of grass that turns yellow and green as seasons change or … but then I couldn't imagine what an ordinary life would be like in America, supposedly the best place in the world. More ordinary than here, perhaps?

'Things are pretty much the same there,' Ash said, with sophistication, with nonchalance, with a world-weariness more world-weary than mine. I am supposed to be more weary of the world since I came from a much older civilisation but here I am, full of optimism and hope, whereas he seemed to be frightened and content with little.

News came that in Pine Hill, only a few hundred kilometres from us on the other side of the Angry River, we had heavy casualties, so much so that the soil there was reportedly soaked with blood and flesh from bodies of both Chinese and Japanese soldiers bombed into pieces or hacked into pieces by bayonets or torn into pieces with human claws entangled in a death struggle. When rain came, all the creeks and rivers in the surrounding area became awash with the red waters of blood carrying limbs, fingernails and messy hair. Then the sun shone and the whole place stunk worse than excrement, with millions of swarming flies and vultures seeking to feed on the bodies.

'I hate wars,' Ash said one day as we both stood outside our tents, watching a path floating half visibly in and out of the dense trees on the mountain. 'You know what I would like to do?'

'No, what?' I said, thinking of what I would like to do myself.

'I'd like to go places, just like that guy over there, with a pile of firewood on his back, a black turban around his head, climbing up the path. I'd like to keep going, from mountain to mountain, from river to river, stopping at villages for a rest and a bowl of rice, and if need be, I could do some work for the locals picking up firewood and fetching water; I would do anything.'

'How would you communicate with them then?'

'No problem,' Ash said firmly. 'I'd bring you along as my Fan-I-Kuan.'

'What if I don't want to go?' I said, tersely, testingly, teasingly, looking directly into his eyes, so blue that you'd think they were made of a cloudless sky.

'Then I'd go alone,' Ash said, avoiding my eyes.

I could tell that he wasn't particularly happy but I didn't want to pretend that I agreed with his proposition. I had my own ideas about what I would like to do, have fun, for example, like my father whose life was spent mainly doing three things: smoking opium with his concubines, playing sessions of mah-jongg and talking about ancient poetry; at least that was the version of the story I told him. I could not predict what life was going to be like after the war but I'd certainly pursue some studies, like mathematics or physics. But the main thing was, again, enjoy life and have fun.

'How would you describe a narrow path like that?' I asked Ash, pointing to the distant thread of a path for him.

'Winding or serpentine maybe?'

'We would call it a *yangchang xiaodao*,' I said.

'What is that?'

'A tiny path like a sheep's intestine,' I replied.

'An intestinal path,' Ash said. 'That sounds quite odd, I mean oddly interesting.'

'And the other night I got wet through. How would you describe that in English?' I asked.

'Maybe a water rat? I'm not sure,' Ash said.

'We'd call it a *luo tang ji*.'

'Meaning?'

'A chicken dropped in a soup!'

'You mean a dressed chicken?' Seeing the puzzled look on my face, he burst into hysterical laughter.

12

Before it was time for 60 Minutes, *you found the urge irresistible to grab a beer from the fridge. It had never been like that before. You'd normally be content with the third or the fourth cup of your daily tea. Now, you found your mouth getting unreasonably thirsty. The house was too quiet for anything. The late setting sun on the other side of your carport made the opaque plastic enclosure almost transparent. Then came the sound of the first raindrops on the corrugated roof, which was actually the beak of a bird searching for food. The minute you drank your first gulp you felt better. You did not care any more about the fact that you lived entirely with yourself. The East and the West will always remain as separate as life from death. Here you live death. There death lives.*

As you went out for a walk a character came to you of his own accord. For some reason, he had never contacted you before. As you walked briskly, with beer in your blood, making your head slightly dizzy, he followed you closely at your heels and seemed to suggest a grave. What grave, you asked?

Book grave, he said.

Book grave?

Dead books by dead authors.

What about them?

Keeping them alive is my duty.

How?

Writing about them has been my interest as I'm never interested in the living authors.

Who are you?

You have such a bad memory. I'm from Jing's class years ago.

You turned your head back but there was no one behind you. Across the road, a tree cast a sidelong glance at you with its own shadow. Somewhere down the road, a figure flashed behind a tree, with the bouncing of a ball. The sky was there, pale and infinitely speechless. You heard your own footsteps. God, my God, were you destined to be living like this forever?

13

The variety of foods available at the breakfast table in Luoping was incredible, in both Western (cakes, biscuits, various kinds of breads, croissants, eggs, tomatoes, milk, coffee, fruit etc) and Chinese styles (*youtiao, xifan, doujiang, zacai, luobugan, furu* etc). In the end, I chose the Chinese, as I always do.

After breakfast, I went back to my hotel room and stood at the window, looking out at miles of canola flowers rolling ahead in wave after wave of pure gold. My heart felt as if it was washed clean by this unearthly music. Years ago, I had heard that this place was hell on earth, a destination equivalent to an early convict Australia for the unruly and the unorthodox and the unlovely. I should have come here instead of going to Australia; at least I would have the flowers for company every year. And the Chinese faces.

'No, you wouldn't.' As if by magic, I found my thoughts answered by a loud voice at the open door. When I turned my head I saw a man with a fat face smiling at me but I could not recognise him.

'How goes the enemy?' The man said. 'I can still hear you crying tears for me.'

'Oh, my Goodness! Dang, my dear Dang,' I said, quoting, in a mocking tone, the first line of a popular song dedicated to the Chinese Communist Party. 'I've finally found you.'

'No, it's not my "Dear Dang",' Dang replied. 'You have been residing overseas far too long. It's "Dear Dang, my Dear Mother!"[5]'

---

5 Title and first line of a pop song that translates as 'Dear Party, my dear Mother.' Dang, meaning Party, is also a common surname.

'How's everybody?' I asked when we walked off the steps outside the hotel entrance, across a briskly running creek, its water so clean that it took our eyes right to the bottom where the shadow of a fish paused before it disappeared. 'You mean my family or …?' Dang enquired.

'Of course you know what I meant?' I interrupted him impatiently.

'Oh yes,' Dang said. 'It's all by word of mouth because, like you, I haven't seen anyone from the class since we graduated. Human beings are a little like the fish. They grow as they drift downstream from little creeks to small tributaries to big rivers until they are too big and heavy, too clogged up or age heavy to turn back, before they empty themselves into the ocean, scattered to unknown white shores, strangely always white, to meet with their destiny.'

'Or their deathtiny, death *ti ni,* death kick you,' I said, remembering that it was a pet name given to me by my father when I was a baby but was dropped on account of my mother's strong objection to it. 'What about Zhao?'

'Well, I heard that she'd slept her way to the USA but I do not know where she ended up.'

'Is that what you guys thought of me?'

'Sorry? I don't understand.'

'Did no one think that I'd slept my way to Australia also?'

'Oh, no, come on, what are you talking about? At best, you've only slept your way into English.'

'Ah well, Englishit, perhaps,' Gene muttered to himself, remembering the storyteller.

'You've done the right thing, though.' Dang didn't quite catch that and continued. 'Like Ma.'

'Yes?'

'Ma attended an international English speech competition

in the USA and defected subsequently. I heard that he's running a tourist agency in San Francisco. You can't do any better than that, can you?'

'How do you mean?' I asked.

'You know what I mean after all these decades overseas. After all, it's a language you learn, not a future, less still a fortune.'

'And Liu Ya and Zhenya?'

'I think they've both gone to San Francisco, though I'm not exactly sure.'

'What? You mean together? As lesbian lovers?'

'God, aren't you imaginative! My guess is both of them have married Americans at different stages of their lives and ended up somewhere there, although I am not sure if they are still married.'

'You never know,' I said. 'But I do, my wife is still with me.'

'Who's that?' Dang asked.

'Didn't you know? Deirdre, our Lady of the Southern Hemisphere, remember?'

'Of course, the one who introduced "Broken English" to us, by what was her name, "f" something?'

'Faithful, Marianne Faithful,' Gene said, tolerantly.

'Oh, yes, what a fitting name for your wife! I'm pleased for you that you've still got our teacher in your possession. By now you must have had enough free private English tuition to last you a lifetime?'

'Well, she is okay, I mean, she's really good, faithful, though that's not her surname,' I said. 'What about you? What wind has brought you here?'

'West wind, of course,' Dang replied. 'I am working for a London-based pharmaceutical company. They have stationed me here on a long-term post to gather information on herbal medicine and local insect-based medications. For me, this is the best, getting paid in pounds and working in an environment that is uniquely my own.'

'I can perfectly understand, it and you,' I said, not wanting to pursue him with any more questions. Then, a cloud drifted over, temporarily concealing the sun, staining the canola flowers with large blotches of mud and sand. With that, rose a chorus of roosters calling, something I had not heard since my defection to Australia, to English.

'Are you afraid?' I asked Ash, after we both read what had happened at Songshan in the news bulletin.

He didn't answer but stared straight ahead at a tree, a majestic pine tree, like a random splash of inky cloud against the blue bombshell sky.

'Our fear is our worst enemy,' I remember someone said. Or was it I who said it? 'What if we left? What if we just left?' someone said. I turned around but saw no one except Ash, who was gazing at the tree, smoking a cigarette, the blue smoke slowly disappearing in the wind, leaving traces, of thinking, double thinking, triple thinking.

It must have been a voice issuing from Ash's mind, his heart, I thought.

'I want to be a traveller, going places, and I don't want to be fighting a war, anyone's war,' those words came back to me again. I knew who said them but I didn't want to remember, didn't remember.

'You know,' Ash said. 'In a couple of days' time, we shall reach the bank of the Angry River and our blood will spill, like a pig's.'

'I know,' I said. 'At night I can already hear its thunderous roar accompanied with cries of the dead. What does your mother do?'

'She's a housewife,' he replied. 'Why?'

'Have you ever slept with a woman before?' I ventured.

'Oh yes, many of them,' Ash said, his tone suggesting otherwise.

Where the mountain opens in front of us, it looks like two legs spread open against the pink evening sky with the cluster of trees resembling chunks of hair at the crotch.

'I wish I could do that like you,' I sighed. 'For tomorrow we'll have no more time, for life, for love, for anything.'

'’Cause we would disappear,' he said, 'like the smoke.'

'Disappear,' I said, looking at the mountains surrounding me, one like a soldier eaten clean by the animals, one like two soldiers locked together in each other's arms, one like a head bitten by a jaw and others like bones of all shapes, a smell of sizzling flesh slowly arising.

'Disappear!' Both of us repeated it and almost at the same time we lowered our voice to a whisper, a conspiracy beyond our expectation, beyond our hearts' expression.

At the same time I caught his heart jumping, he caught mine jumping. We'd both detected something in us that chimed together in unison, neither of us willing to admit what it was, even to ourselves.

'The wall has ears,' he said.

'*Ge qiang you er,*' I said.

'What is that?' he said.

'There are ears on the other side of the wall,' I said.

14

Dear Dree, if I must disappoint you, I must, for that's all I have to tell you from my journey. There are other things that have happened on the way but they are not fit for your ears or eyes. Although my dad never told me anything about the Road in his life, I think I know nearly all now and understand why he didn't tell me. A son has to live to his dad's age to understand things unsaid. I'm back to normal now, my dick, too, at least for the moment. I think the song played a large role in their defection or, in my coinage, de-affection or de/affection or even deaffection. Titled, *The Beautiful Shangri-la*, sung by Ouyang Feiying, it became a hit throughout the Chinese-speaking world in the 1940s. Let me translate the last three lines for you from Chinese:

This lovely Shangri-la,
This beautiful Shangri-la,
Is our ideal home …

In search of his voices, their voices, however, I have bypassed 'this lovely Shangri-la' and, perhaps, next time, if ever there is a next time, we shall go in search of it together.

15

On board the plane a woman sitting next to Gene took his breath away. The minute she squeezed past him to settle in her seat by the window, he felt an instant affinity with her. Sitting by her side, he could not gain a full view of her face except for her profile, which was white, and her hair, which was also white.

Feeling the heat of his intense gaze upon her, the woman turned her head to the right and smiled into the gazing eyes of a Chinese man. Gene smiled back and realised that this was the woman he had dreamt of the previous night in Kunming.

'I saw you yesterday,' Gene said, dismissing 'in my dream' as unsayable.

'Where?' the old lady looked puzzled.

'Please,' Gene passed a plastic bag containing an earphone to her.

'Thank you,' the lady said. 'Where are you going?'

'Melbourne. Yourself?'

'Sydney.'

'I thought I saw you in Kunming.'

'Oh, did you?'

'I could be wrong.'

'What did you do in Kunming?'

'I came back from the Burma Road.'

'Oh, did you? I went there also.'

'Which part did you go to?'

'I went only as far as Dali and then I went to Lijiang.'

'What is it like there?'

'You mean Lijiang?'

'Yes.'

'It's wonderful.'

'I knew you must have been there to see your son Ash, who died there many decades ago while travelling with my father', Gene said to himself inaudibly, headwriting.

Their conversation stopped there as the inflight television was switched on, giving safety instructions on where to escape, what to do, how to put on the mask, in other words, how to save yourself in an unsaveable situation.

The white lady did not speak to him again, for some reason, and was engrossed in a thick book. Gene hated to invade her privacy, but he resented her self-obsession. He could barely make out the the title of the book she was reading, but he thought it was *How Euthanasia Can Change Death*.

16

It was a deserted house that Gene returned to. When he pulled the blinds open, he brushed cobwebs. A cockroach scurried back into a dark corner. The kitchen sink was bone dry. On a piece of paper lying on the kitchen table, covered in thin dust, were scribbled these words:

Dear Gene,
I've gone back to Brisbane to stay with Mum and Dad. Call me when you come back. Or simply fly over to join us.
Deirdre

Dear Dre, Gene sighed and smiled, remembering the old joke. Strange, isn't it, that as soon as I set foot here my desire for medications, for madness, returns and the sky recovers its psychiatric-hospital look. I need the medications I chucked out into the rotten river in Kunming. I can see those voices coming together at me, screaming to tear my ears off, my heart out, even though I don't have a heart any more. I can smell those fleshes. Please, please, dear dre. Why did you leave me alone, like a piece of rubbish dumped here where one day feels like a century? Oh yes, I can find something here. Dear Dre, Dear D.S. Jing or Dear D.S. Gene, let me swallow this thing for you called Serenity.

*

At Christmas dinner Gene was surrounded by Deirdre's family, her father, David, and her mother, Margaret, decent true-blue

Aussies who were glad to see their son-in-law back, a good-for-nothing, a stray dog wandering in the land of dead spirits, a weird visionary who claimed to be capable of hearing dead voices and a daredevil devoted to the great cause of spending time for no other purpose than wasting it.

'I've made some *chaomien* specially for you,' Margaret said.

'Did you use butter?' Gene asked nonchalantly.

'Of course she did! What do you think?' Deirdre said. She was not particularly happy about Gene's noncommunication, no emails, no phone calls. Consequently, on their first night, they did not make love. They did try but they didn't succeed because Gene farted and that was like putting a needle into a balloon, puncturing the desire and deflating it.

'Well, then, I won't touch it,' Gene said.

'What do you mean you won't touch it? Don't be silly!' Deirdre scowled at him.

'I said a lot of good things about you to Dang, you know,' Gene said.

'Dang? You mean your old classmate? What's he doing in China now?' Deirdre asked, her voice softened.

'Nothing much, just a *maiban*,' Gene said. 'A comprador.'

'Among your male classmates, I can still remember Xin, the girl-boy, and Bao, the class jester. I wish I'd stayed longer.'

'I know you always resent me for eloping with you before your time,' Gene said.

'Don't start it again, please,' Deirdre said, pulling Gene to her side, the fullness of her breasts suddenly impinged on him. With a rush of primal instincts, Gene began kissing her on the mouth but she pushed him away. Like a spoilt child, Gene felt grumpy. Deirdre whispered something in his ear till he became quiet.

'Here's your chopsticks. Aren't they lovely!' Margaret passed

Gene a pair of white ivory chopsticks that Gene had bought at a local market in Jingxing Street in Kunming. 'Help yourself to anything you like, baked potatoes, pumpkin soup, which I know you like, and …'

'I don't like anything Australians make,' Gene said petulantly. 'Why don't you let me prepare something Chinese for you?'

'You are unwell, Gene,' Deirdre said. 'Or else we would have gladly let you prepare the meal.'

'In that case,' Gene said. 'I'll eat my medications then.'

'You don't eat them, Gene,' Deirdre said. 'You take them.'

'Thank you, my English, teacher,' Gene said. 'But I prefer my Chinese version of *chiyao*, eating medications.'

'Just let him, will you?' David said, as he cut into the turkey with his knife and helped himself to a bunch of steamed bok choy. 'How was your trip, Gene?'

'You don't steam vegetables like that,' Gene said. 'Or else its vitamin structure is all spoiled, no nutrition left, nutrition, you know?'

'Oh, we know what nutrition is, Gene, don't you worry,' came Margaret's placating voice. 'We know what we are doing here, don't we, David?'

'We sure do,' David's voice sounded meaty, mouthful, devoid of any concerns.

'It's so hot here,' Gene said, wiping the sweat from his forehead with a tissue.

'It's just about right,' David said as an understatement, his eyes twice as large through his glasses.

'Can I have some soup, please, Mum?' Gene asked.

'At last,' Margaret sighed, pleased with being called Mum and remembering her son-in-law's refusal for years to acknowledge her presence as a legal parent, a mother-in-law. 'There's plenty of it, the pumpkin soup, and I'll bring you a plate.'

'I'll do that,' Deirdre offered. She had obviously put on weight during his absence, and was wearing a loose dress covered with peacock spots and a pair of rusty iron–coloured clogs, her skin shinily white, which was what Gene liked; he had bought both for her in Hong Kong. His gifts for Mum and Dad were simpler: a long wooden pipe made of water bamboo by the local ethnic Lisu people in Yunnan and a tiny little bottle with a drawing of a bunch of grapes painted inside it.

'I love it!' Margaret said appreciatively. 'Just lov'it!' She turned the bottle upside down and peered inside. 'How did they do this, I mean the Chinese?'

David put his cigarette in the round hole of the pipe head but, finding it hard to fit, squeezed the filter, eventually managing to stuff it in. Still, he could not draw anything out of it.

'Was this a joke or something?' he fumed.

'It has at least a thirty-year-old history, Dad,' Gene said. 'Probably better as a piece of decoration than anything else.'

'All right, if that is the case,' David said, throwing a glance of appreciation to Margaret, the word 'Dad' sounding too good to be true.

'Put that into the rubbish bin,' Margaret whispered into his ear, careful not to let Gene hear it; she didn't like the look of its germ-infested knotty stem.

Gene heard it all right; if it was a dead woman's voice, he could hear it, not to mention a living woman's. He kept silent.

'Is Trevor coming tonight?' Gene asked.

'What are you talking about?' Deirdre said. 'What Trevor?' Sensing that this might be one of his many malapropisms, she ventured, 'Did you mean trevally?'

Gene fell into a silence too deep to be extracted from. It was a boy he had met on board the plane. Waiting outside the toilet, the boy smiled to him and Gene smiled back, and they entered into a short conversation.

'My name's Trevor,' he said.

'My name's Gene,' he said.

'You also going to Cairns to see the rocks?' the boy said.

'No, to see the family,' he said.

'You swim?' the boy said.

'Yeh,' Gene said.

'My dad's taking me to go and catch marlin,' Trevor said.

'Good on ya,' Gene said. 'You eat 'em?'

'I guess,' Trevor said.

'I like fish,' Gene said, and added, 'and fishing.'

'Excuse me,' the boy said when a toilet door opened and he disappeared behind it.

'Give me your glass,' came the insistent voice again.

'You are daydreaming, Gene,' Deirdre said, gently pinching Gene's ear and pulling it towards her.

'No, I'm not but I'm wondering if I could see Trevor again sometime in the future,' Gene murmured to himself.

'Let me pour you a glass of this,' David said, holding a bottle of Martell, branded as 'Fine Cognac', that Gene bought at the airport duty-free.

'You'll end me up in poetryland,' Gene said.

'What's that?' David said. 'Tell me about your trip to China.'

'Oh, that,' Gene said.

'Yes, tell us about it,' Margaret said.

'Last night he told me that he slept around a bit,' Deirdre said.

'Shush,' Margaret said, but David burst into nervous laughter.

'By that I meant I slept a few nights in every new place. That is all,' Gene said.

'Did you say you went to Myanmar?' David asked.

'Yah, just across the river into a small town. That is all,' Gene said.

'And?' All ears pricked up.

'A Burmese guy told me they did not have surnames,' Gene said.

'Is that right? How would they deal with issues of properties and their inheritance then?' David was curious.

'Their system must be a mess,' Margaret said. 'I can't understand how anyone can get around without a surname. What about driver's licenses? Ah, well, they probably don't have cars in the first place.'

'Mum,' Deirdre, being more Asia literate, said. 'They've been living like that for many hundreds of years and are used to it.'

'Mrs Deirdre Gene, you seem to know better than most,' Gene said.

'Don't call me Mrs Gene because I haven't changed my surname yet,' Deirdre responded.

'You know you have a Chinese name that I gave you,' Gene said.

'That's news to me,' Margaret said. 'What is it? Tell me, tell me.'

'Oh, it's nothing and I never use it,' Deirdre said.

'It's Sang Di Li,' Gene said. 'I gave her that.'

'What's that supposed to mean?' David asked.

'Sang comes from Sandringham meaning a mulberry tree. Di and Li is a rough transliteration meaning on the land. So, altogether, it means on the mulberry land. Makes sense?' Gene said, feeling quite exhausted after making such an effort.

'Come on, I hate Chinese names,' Deirdre said without concealing her contempt.

'I would have thought Gene was a perfectly all right surname, though,' Margaret said. 'Sometimes I wish for some ethnic alterations myself.'

'Like what?' David chortled. 'You mean you want to call yourself Mrs Chong or Chua or Ng or Wong? Come on, Marg.'

'Well, a lady in my fitness class did that,' Margaret said. 'She changed her surname to Dong after her third marriage and never looked back.'

'Did I take that to mean that this is also your intention? Mr Wong at the corner milk bar whose wife died in a recent car accident is quite a match for you then.'

'Mind your words, David,' Margaret said. 'We have a guest here today.'

'Guest? Who's that?' Gene asked.

Everyone laughed except Gene.

'Well, I suppose I am one,' Gene sighed. 'I always have been. Wherever I go I seem to be a guest these days. And there's this Burmese guy who wanted me to stay in Myanmar so that I, like him with three wives, could also take as many as I like. Currently, he has got three, you know?'

'With your ability, Gene, you can't even handle one, to say nothing of three,' Deirdre said.

'You are not telling me that, with his medications, he is …' Margaret lowered her voice until words became a trickle of insinuations.

Deirdre nodded her head in painful acknowledgement.

'We don't have sex any more,' Gene confessed. 'We haven't had it for years.'

'What?!' Astonishment on Mum and Dad's faces, induced not so much by the revelation of the fact than by the occasion of the revelation, which seemed highly inappropriate.

'Slap' came an open palm on Gene's left cheek from Deirdre with her raised hand. 'How dare you say that in front of Mum and Dad!'

Gene did not say anything for what seemed an unbearable

length of time, looking straight ahead at a large photograph of him with Deirdre hung on the wall, Deirdre looking so happy. Realising how fake that smile was and overcome with an anger pent up for so long, Gene earthquaked. He stood up and, holding the edge of the table with both his hands, lifted it to shoulder height and, with a tip and a push, sent the whole table laden with food flying all over the floor, spilling the red wine onto the photo, making it see red.

This outburst was beyond the belief of everyone, more so for Deirdre who, in her past years of marriage, always had the upper hand. 'I want to divorce you' was all she could manage to utter eventually.

Without a word, Gene quit the room and was out on the street, leaving the family reunion in tatters.

17

You were reading the first few chapters in a book discussing the essential differences between Western and Chinese notions of what constitutes the ultimate truth in the arts and literature. And you made a comment somewhere along the line by saying: all they are trying to do is pretend they are God doing creations. They think they are superior to nature because they are above nature but below God, a little like Lin Biao, above the nation but below Mao Zedong. To put it in more simple terms, they are Middle God in that sense. You'd rather be a Lower God close to nature with no pretensions. The Western civilisation is founded on this fallacy that somehow the human being is this most beautiful creature on earth who can do anything it wants, even manufacture a truth that is truer than truth. They call that virtual reality. You create something new and think you are superior and progressive but a Chinese comes along and says: we can copy it overnight and make it even better. Now that's the difference. You find having to deal with the Western world in general by producing something astonishing is tedious. It's like expecting an email message from someone who happens to come across your mind and when it does come to you, maybe this minute or in ten years, it is so banal you almost burst into tears. All it says is: Hi, long time no contact. How are things going? Bla-bla-bla. Less than two sentences.

Human beings don't need any communications. They need to be surrounded, excited, moved and epitomised by material things.

You have to press on.

18

The first drop of tropical rain lashed Gene hard on the tip of his nose and made him wince. It felt like a tiny cube of cutting ice. Instinctively, he raised his head and saw the sky overcast with darkening clouds that threatened to bear down on the city. His eyes travelled down to the enormous tree with white flowers. He knew these were not flowers but birds, beings that looked very much like cockatoos, crouching amid yellow-green leaves. He found himself in the square whose name he could not recall but there was a shop he could recognise as a Telstra shop. A black fellow was wandering about aimlessly, seemingly looking for cigarette butts. That reminded him that he had not brought any cigarettes. It was too late to turn back. When the black man came towards him, he had an instinctive fear of him as he thought he might get hurt for some reason. The black man did not look at him but just went past him in the direction of another rubbish bin. At that moment, he saw the first flash of lightning illuminate the gloomy square, flooding it as if with quicksilver. It always gave him the feeling that there was a sky camera taking photos as it pressed its shutter and flashed but he wondered where these massive photos were stored, how they were developed and for whom they were made available. For God himself or herself? The photo, in that instant, would show him and the aboriginal man standing wide apart in a deserted city square, looking totally lost. Then, sheets of darkness fell and a deafening thunder cracked, splitting his ears, followed by rapid-fire rain that seemed to be pouring bucket loads of water directly from the sky, drenching him from head to toe.

'Such four-ocean rain!' he exclaimed, in his exuberant Chinese-English mixture, his face lifted up towards the sky, blinded by the rain whips. The rain stones, reminded him of more than twenty years ago when he was expelled from home by his mother. Or was it by his father or both? Was it related to a woman? Did he tell Deirdre the story about it? The rain whipped him so hard that he appeared to be weeping, crying, although he was actually laughing. But his peals of laughter were drowned by peals of cannon thunder, also laughing. He could not tell whether the stuff running down his eyelids was water or rain or tears, his vision blurred. And he thought of the poem he wrote after that rain, or the rain that he deliberately went out into to experience the marriage of heaven and earth, as he later put it, before they divorced each other again. It would be good if he could find that poem to see what he had written.

Curiously, he felt neither attached to nor hostile towards his new old parents. He felt even less emotional about Deirdre. She was probably feeling that he owed her greatly. It would be unbearable to feel that someone else always owed you something that he or she could never repay. Gene was no longer paranoiac as the rain had washed the last iota of obsession from him, carrying away the remaining medications in all the creeks running throughout his body, his inner city, inner suburbs, shot through with psychosis. He kept his mouth wide open to receive rain drops and quench his burning thirst. It tasted salty, fishy, and mangrove-like. In the distance, he thought he saw the boy on the plane coming towards him in a boat, his hair flowing long behind his back like a horse's mane, and he was shouting in a loud voice: 'Right, right, come along with me and we'll go and catch it!'

He found himself facing the ocean, a spread of foamy waves electrified with energy, fire of lightning everywhere. His shoes were gone, his bare feet felt the cool gritty sand that slightly sucked them in as he stepped out. The boy was somewhere in the distance, too far for him to catch up but too close for him to lose sight of. For a moment, he thought he was the boy looking at Gene from his boat: an aimless and distraught man, abandoned to the elements, a lonely figure cut against the Western sky bent towards hell, twisted out of shape by its own capability to destruct.

19

Deirdre also went to the shore, not on the same night as Gene did, but on a morning as deserted as an empty petrol station. Out from where she was sitting, an expanse of sand stretched till it met the sea, inky under a sky with reddening and yellowing clouds. She listened to the breath of the sea, of her own thoughts and memories. Holding her knees in her arms, she had her right cheek resting against her cold right lap. If someone happened to walk by at this early hour, he or she would see a pale figure perched on a black rock facing the sea. No one would be bothered to take a second look. In China, after Jing told her about Wei's suicide, Deirdre would always shudder to see a lone figure sauntering by the lake after dark. She observed that Jing had a tendency to go out alone at night and she grew quite concerned until she found out about his secret. This sad young man had thought that his future lay in English and, indeed, this white-faced young man had imagined that he had come from English stock or half-English stock. For some reason, she could not help but like him, even love him, or like-love him, as Jing put it. She was five years older than him but Jing said, 'It doesn't matter. As a Chinese saying goes, a woman three years older is like gold to her man. A woman five years older? More than gold, perhaps beyond gold.'

A smile stole to her lips as she raised her head and saw the edge of the sky ringed with, as Jing would often insist, a sliver of *yudu bai,* white fish belly. What a fitting image! She thought of how Gene would only eat three sections of a fish: the head, the tail and the belly, reputedly the best of all from a fish, as the

Chinese would have us believe, and how Gene had described the way a dead fish differed from a dead person in the water, the former belly up and the latter back up. It didn't make sense to her then but she found it hilarious. Now, she couldn't bear the thought of seeing Gene lying face down on the stark beach that night, his back up, exactly the same way as he had described.

She could never understand why such a change had come over Gene. It seemed that everything had gradually reversed for him, day became night, the sun became the moon, what he had once regarded as ideal become hellish, happiness turned into bitterness, English, perversely, had become Chinese. Yes, bitterness was the word. It was almost as if he was Gene of bitterness, gene of bitterness. After a long time living with Gene and observing his Chinese friends, she had come to believe that suffering was what being a Chinese was all about. Take Gene. He was never happy with anything, more so than ever in Australia. He would never go near a cinema. He would refuse to go to a restaurant. He hated to buy new clothes and shoes. It was not that he was miserly. He would never go past a street musician without throwing a one-dollar coin or two into the box. He would never say no to anyone coming to their door for donations. This suffering was more of a heart thing than a materialistic thing. He was born a creature of non-comforts. It was a state of non-happiness that he enjoyed, an inability, it seemed, to come to terms with what Gene called 'the English-instilled Australianness', an antithesis of whatever that was Chinese except for one thing: materialistic pursuit, the mad money instinct.

Waiting for the day to break, Deirdre had found, was like waiting for a pregnancy to come into birth. It was like setting fire to the dead wood of darkness. The flame leapt, tonguing clouds of wave and waves of cloud, with thirst, spreading blood across the sky, first in streaks, then in stripes, and, finally, in tracks of glowing glories. Her heart was lifted as the sun emerged out of the waters, a wet burning disc, as new as a red-hot heat bead on the barbie. With it came the thought that there might still be hope for Gene; she felt sure there was for despite all his bitterness and non-happiness he had a heart of more than mere gold, gold that had no market value. She heard the birds stirring, an occasional riflebird thrashing long whips of shooting. She heard the wind on wavelets. She heard Gene calling: Deirdre, don't leave! Don't leave, Deirdre!

In answer to these calls, imagined or otherwise, she walked home in elastic steps, the first ray of the morning sun flowering in her hair, with this thought in mind, 'Perhaps I can somehow turn the bitter gene into a happy gene, a sweet gene?'

20

Gene's hospital treatment lasted one week before he was allowed out on a community treatment order, given by a panel of medical doctors, one of whom was Mr David Sandringham, Gene's father-in-law. David promised that with the proper administration of medications and family care, Gene would soon be brought back to his 'senses'. As a psychiatrist, Mr Sandringham produced a convincing report on Gene's condition, citing his cultural disorientation and bilinguistic confusion as a major influence on his recent wayward behaviour and his past downward thrusts into darkness a result of a chemically unbalanced mind. To put it in layman's terms, Gene was suffering from what he called a Chinese-English linguistic and cultural conflict, exhibiting such symptoms as a difficulty in switching back into a 'foreign' culture after living in his 'mother' culture for a brief time; a constant need to assert the superiority of his former culture over the present culture in public while unreasonably denouncing his former culture in private; and a perennial sense of victimisation that he did not enjoy full rights as his other fellow citizens did because of his 'wrong' skin colour, his wrong shape of eyes and his wrong gait. He was dogged by the conviction that he was born of foreign-Chinese, possibly English-Chinese parentage, although he was emphatically opposed to a DNA test. From the history Mr Sandringham got out of Gene, there was nothing to suggest that he was born of Chinese-Western wedlock. There was still less evidence to suggest that he was an illegitimate son, possibly of a poor Chinese soldier who had a one-night stand, in Gene speak, One Night Lie, with an American nurse serving on the Burma Road. The only problem seemed to have come from his having learnt English, learnt it as a Chinese. But out of hundreds of thousands of students from Asia who came to this country to learn English, none seemed to have exhibited similar symptoms.

Culturally speaking, Mr Sandringham thought, it was mainly the food. If Gene found all these things hard to swallow, cereals with milk for breakfast, sandwiches for lunch, beef and mutton with potatoes for dinner, and barbecue for holidays, he could always cook his own meals with the stuff he bought at the Chinese market and grocery stores; the country was multicultural enough to provide that type of thing. Indeed, that was what Gene had been doing while residing with Deirdre. David would like to find out a bit more about their sex life but then the thought itself was inherently so incestuous and, potentially ridden with conflict of interest, that he did not get beyond the question of 'How is your sex life going?' Gene's answer to that was classic: 'Why do you want to know, you old dirty bastard? She is your daughter!' He wished that he had heard it wrong but he heard him all right. He did not pursue the matter further but suggested a heavy dose of Zoloft, perhaps out of a vengeful intention to punish his rebellious son-in-law, a good-for-nothing who never earned a cent for himself or Deirdre since he came to this country. With his knowledge and experience, Mr Sandringham firmly believed that he would be able to 'fix' him, to put him right. For the moment, he was not worried about cultural and linguistic significances, consequences, overtones or undertones. Medications were the best weapon. Thinking beyond English and the Australian culture in which he was comfortably situated was not only unnecessary but potentially dangerous. Fixing them with the most advanced technology produced by the Western mind seemed to be the only solution.

Deirdre changed her mind about her proposed divorce. It would be unethical to break off the relationship when Gene was in such a state; one morning after he got out of bed, Gene was so out of his mind that he put a strip of green wasabi on top of his toothbrush to brush his teeth with. To see him sitting on the sofa gazing at a book for hours on end without turning a page was sheer torture. When she removed the book from Gene's hands, she found that he had dozed off. The book was not English. From her limited knowledge of Chinese, she knew it was something related to shamanism. Could it be one of the contributing factors that triggered off the event?

During the day, after he 'ate the medications', Gene grew quiet and docile, like a big old sleepy dog, sitting beside the dining table in the kitchen, a bunch of letters from the past, some of them from her and others from his parents, long dead. He held them in his hand but did not take out the contents to read nor even glance through them. Instead, his eyes were fixed on the addressees' addresses and the senders' addresses as if those were of great interest to him. But Deirdre knew that he wasn't looking at anything in particular by the way his eyes were holding their unmoving blank stare and she guessed that his mind probably didn't even register what he was doing. She moved closer to him, a surge of emotions overcoming her, only for a second, before she took control of herself. It wasn't right for her to leave him like this in an institution for the rest of his life but she had no other choice. 'There's no cure for this kind of thing and relapses are possible every once in a while,' her father's words came back to her.

She had made up her mind to quit her job at the library and stay at home with Gene. She wanted to have sessions with him to find out what really was the matter. Now that she had as much time on her hands as Gene, she could relax and further explore his headwritings.

'Gene, I'm sorry but,' Deirdre began but found it hard to continue, 'is it true that you are determined to separate?'

'Yes,' came Gene's unequivocal answer, his stare now fallen on the television screen, which remained dark, reflecting part of the kitchen as if in a ghost film in which he could see his own tiny head with the tiniest eyes.

'What if I don't want that to happen?' Deirdre asked.

'That's fine with me also,' Gene said.

'Are you sure?' A ray of hope penetrated the room, momentarily.

Silence.

'Gene, you remember the incident you told me in Luoping?' Deirdre enquired, tentatively.

'Which one?'

'The rape flower one,' Deirdre reminded him.

'I know, I know, but it's no more real than my dream,' Gene said. 'Unfortunately, I've deleted it from my headwriting store.'

'Tell me something else then,' Deirdre prompted.

'I know why you don't like me,' Gene said.

'I never said I don't like you,' Deirdre said. 'In fact, you know I do.'

'I come from a family of defectors. My dad hated the war and ran away from it. The consequence he suffered from was the ultimate rejection by China. I hated China and ran away from it but the language I ran into never accepts me. It's not the people. It's the language. It's the most racist of all races. By "you", I don't mean you. I mean the language, the body of this nation, the essence of this race, the colour that includes and excludes, the ...'

'What about the writings you've done with your head?'

'They are done in either or both. What difference does it make? Only people like you make a distinction, a category, a border, a title. But I'll have stop here as I have such a splitting headache and my stomach is all churned up with the pills.'

Deirdre set up the camp bed for Gene to lie down on, a foldaway with a camouflage-covered mattress that reminded him of battlefields.

21

That night, after a long quiet sleep, Gene woke up and said to Deirdre, 'I want to make love. Would you give me a hand?'

Deirdre took a look at him and saw that he was serious, his eyes now fixed on her face, her face with no make-up but with eyes suggestive of the blue sky. She could see that his eyes were fixed on her eyes. Was it the medication or some kind of dream that produced such aphrodisiac effects? He was seldom like this before. Although they had little sex these days, she'd still regularly masturbate Gene until he flooded her hands with fresh cum and she'd ask Gene to masturbate her with his tongue until she uttered small ecstatic cries. It was a taciturn deal struck between them as both seemed afraid of the consequences of childbearing. Penetration into each other's bodies, his penis into her vagina and her tongue into his mouth, was equally conducive to a destructive end through the intermingling of dangerous fluids: a child, who would create endless tasks for them to labour over, a labour of love potentially capable of turning into a labour of hate as Gene once observed of so many people, so many couples. It was simpler to have someone mouthing you or hand relieving you, with the benefit of closing your eyes and letting your mind wander from body to body in a headwriting effort to conquer, to colonise, to even 'creolise', in blind lovemaking, multiple images, simultaneous, spontaneous, promiscuous and globalised, all at once, without yourself moving an inch.

Even in their early days of lovemaking, Deirdre remembered, Gene was never passionate. He was quite passive and had to wait to be aroused, not as aggressive as Dr Wagner, her ex partner.

When she and Gene first had sex, it was in the school toilet on a winter night near Christmas after the evening self-study session. Students had left for their dormitories early as outside a snow had fallen. Inside the classroom under the pale fluorescent light, it was very cold, so cold that Jing offered to give Deirdre his coat, himself paler than the light with the cold.

'You must be joking,' Deirdre said.

'I insist,' Jing said, as stubborn as a tree stump.

'No, you mustn't,' Deirdre said, her eyes intent on his gaunt face, strangely stimulating.

A sudden lull descended in which they could hear the snowflakes fingering the dry leaves and branches like fine sand. Then, the light went out without warning.

With a shudder, they realised that it was past the lights-out time. She did not know how long it was that they remained in their separate seats without moving before she felt his presence, nearing, growing, warm, bookish, bookheavy.

When they finished, she found that they were actually standing in the toilet cubicle between two wooden partitions and her nostrils were assaulted by the strong smell of excrement and urine. She had to use her own handkerchief to dry herself but felt little pleasure. It was like that ever since until they found the way.

Her heart softened by the memory, she reached out and unzipped Gene.

22

Gene got one single card this Christmas. It was from Xin his old classmate, who had not been in touch before. Perhaps Dang had passed his contact details on to him. The card was blank but it held a folded letter in between, which contained just these words:

My Dear Old Friend Jing,
In March next year, I'm going to visit Sydney for the Mardi Gras. Can I call you when I am there?
Let me know,
Yours most sincerely,
Xin

Gene did not know why he should be bothered. The card seemed a painful reminder that, apart from Deirdre, he was left all alone in this world.

*

At night in bed, Gene felt worse than ever. Deirdre could not work out what had happened and she put it down to another attack of depression. Just as she reached over to try to close his eyes staring at the ceiling, he stopped her with his right elbow, which hurt her a little so that she cried out loud, louder than necessary, 'You are hurting me, Gene, what's the matter with you?'

Gene remained still, his eyes still staring as if they could never close again, which was frightening to Deirdre. She turned on her side, facing the other way, muttering.

'I feel sad,' Gene said.

Deirdre did not respond.

'You know what you should do, Gene?' Deirdre said, smiling. 'You've always wanted to be a writer. Why don't you write about them? You've lived your life without a purpose for so long. It's time you started doing something.'

'Stop preaching to me, will you?' Gene said. 'I know how to live my own life without you telling me. I know I have a purpose. My purpose is to live, not otherwise.'

'You know,' Deirdre saw an opportunity for another heart-to-heart session and grabbed it, 'when you told me the other day how you hated China, I thought to myself that I could totally identify with you after sharing a life with you for so long …'

'But I hate myself, not China,' Gene interrupted her impatiently. 'I hate the China within me.'

'Well, that's news to me,' Deirdre was delighted with this revelation.

'Don't you pretend it's nothing new. I hate myself so much for being unwhole, for being a traitor to everything I once held dear, for being unable to resist the temptation to fall into delightful peaces, for the delirium that I have courted.'

'Perhaps we should go back together to live in China?' Deirdre suggested, the prospect firing her imagination; she was even surprised by her own generosity, her courage.

'No, I think not,' Gene said. 'I can't go back to a country where people don't even say "thank you" if you give help to them, where people don't even say "congratulations" to you if you achieve something as if they do themselves a disservice if they say it, where they think generosity means giving money, not kind words, where … well, I can't ever go back to that country

372

of twisted minds, as twisted as mine. In a word, I can't go back to my former self.'

'Then, we shall just stay,' Deirdre provoked.

'Might as well,' Gene said. 'No other alternatives, really, after so long. You still remember that expression that I mentioned in the class years back that goes, *"feiwo zulei, qixin biyi"*?'

'Oh yes,' Deirdre said, a little fazed by its meaning. 'Can I give it a go?'

'By all means,' Gene said.

'He or she who is not of my race has the heart of an alien or … was that right?'

'Too right,' Gene praised, 'but I'd much prefer a direct neither here nor there neither English nor Chinese translation: "Not of my race, the heart must be alien."'

'Good,' Deirdre said, not completely convinced.

'Sometimes you know what?' Gene said. 'I think this should be incorporated into the Australian national anthem.'

'You've got to be joking, Gene,' Deirdre said, aghast.

'You know I am, although it does capture the spirit of this nation in some way,' Gene said. 'Am I not a typical example of this alien ?'

'As far as I am concerned, Gene, I never look at you that way,' Deirdre said, tears coming to her eyes. 'You know when you first said you'd like to come to Australia because China was like a big prison, I took your side and made the biggest decision of my life: to have you as mine and to bring you back to Australia. Since that accident on the hottest day that year – I think it was 1986, am I right – you've gradually changed, for the worse, even though your car was a write-off but you miraculously survived without a scratch. For years I've kept hoping that you would get better so that you could develop your ability as a writer but you never go beyond the level of headwriting.' She sobbed, finding it hard to continue.

'Thank you for reminding me of all this but I've found a new occupation for myself,' Gene said.

'What's that?' Deirdre said,

'I'm sort of tired of the present, both here and in China. I am a bit into the ancient. How do I put it? But I find that I am this long shadow of the past cast over Australia, no, I mean, the square metre of our street, where I can sometimes achieve a communion with some of the ancient poets that I love. For this reason, the other day I found I started translating the ancient poets again, like I did in the class with *Still Night*, remember?'

'Yes, of course I do. You did it in such a unique way, by combining Chinese characters between the English lines or words.'

'I was so weirdly crazy in those days,' Gene said with a wry smile. 'Not anymore. When you are actually crazy, your art becomes sane, like me now.'

'You don't mean to say that when you pretended to be crazy, like in the class, your art was insane?' Deirdre was trying to work out this twisted logic.

'Stop driving me more crazy, Dear Dre,' Gene said. 'I'm not like that anymore for I think it's a great insult to our language and literature …'

'Our? You mean English?'

'Why do you keep interrupting me, Deirdre?' Gene reached over to pretend to cover her mouth up with his left hand but found his middle finger held between her upper and lower teeth, not too forcefully, though painful enough, which, perversely, caused his dick to go harder by stealth. In that moment, Deirdre's hand touched his penis, causing it to raise its head proudly, herself giggling at the same time, sighing a sigh of relief.

Soon, he found himself riding her and looking into her eyes, things of such blue that made him dizzy, feeling as if he were being dragged into the depths of the sea or falling into the sky. But he did not stay in that position for long as Deirdre was afraid that she might get pregnant with his shootings stained with medications and he did as he was told, putting his member between her large firm breasts, rubbing it until it ejaculated onto her face. Then, he licked it clean himself, swallowing the contents and what she ejaculated from her mouth.

Afterwards, they lay side by side, heads on their double pillows, Gene telling her in a husky voice, 'As you probably know, the longer I live here, the more ancient I feel I grow. It's almost as if I were a hermit living in a Taoist temple in the mountain, unknown by anyone except a select few and visited by none. I don't think you can do that anywhere else, can you? True, I can't find mountains and creeks and temples and rice paddies and buffaloes in this corner of the city but I have got plenty of poems that immortalise them, written by my ancient masters, dead thousands of years ago. And that's my secret occupation, didn't you know, turning shadows into realities?'

'What have you done then?' Deirdre said, amazed by his mention of this 'occupation'.

'Nothing, except I have recently attempted to translate one or two ancient poems into English, reviving my old interest but approaching it differently.'

'Tell me what you did?' Deirdre asked. Herself not a passionate lover of poetry, she nevertheless had an artistic side that poetry appealed to.

'I'll recite something I did this morning,' Gene said. 'As follows:

Mountains white, an occasional bird calling
Stones cold, frost about to creep over.

The flowing spring, stained with the moonlight
Turns into a creek of snow'

'Wonderful stuff, Gene,' Deirdre said as she fingered his hair, an act so sexy that it never failed to turn her on. 'I want you to hold me in your arms and whisper it into my ears.'

'You mean ear in its singular form, not plural?' Gene said.

'Now you are getting fastidious!' Deirdre said, remembering something, '"a creek of snow" but who wrote that?'

'A poet living in the fourteenth and fifteenth centuries,' Gene said. 'I can only deal with them; the dead are dear, closer, more alive. Death into life, a condition of dual living.'

23

Each noon after lunch now, you go to bed for a nap. It sometimes lasts half an hour but most often it lasts one hour or two, in which you dream and keep dreaming. By the time you get out of bed, the day is getting old, the sunshine full on your west window, and so you have to draw the curtains up.

Every day you get about one or two email messages and you don't normally answer them. You no longer ring anyone unless someone rings you but someone doesn't.

At night, the house you live in smells of salted fish; salmon it is. And you tell her that it's not as tasty as the one she bought before and she tells you that she did not see the fish there as it obviously had been sold out.

You do not know what the fish is called.

A few words a day and you are content. This unhurried life, in which you read newspapers, sip tea, read a book of poetry, sip tea, read a book of nonfiction, turn on the music, write a poem or two, sip tea, read a book of poetry in another language, eat, piss, read a book of poetry again, sip tea, write a poem, listen to music, wait, see pictures, masturbate, sleep, get out of bed, glance outside through the french door, see flowers, see the sky without a cloud in it, have an idea to write something, jot down the ideas in your narrow and long notebook that you got in Taiwan as a gift from the shop assistant who sold you a suitcase in 2000, put things together in envelopes and put stamps on them and address them.

And this half-forgotten life, in which you write in bed behind a closed door and drawn-up curtains in broad daylight, creating a night for yourself, forgetting them in turn.

24

'I just want to say make senses, in two languages, okay?'

'Fine,' Deirdre said, sullenly. 'But I think it's time you started doing some serious stuff instead of indulging in fantasies about the Burma Road and what not.'

'And I haven't told you about my what not yet. Do you want to know?'

'You'd better shut up, Gene,' 'cause I know what crap you're going to shit on me,' Deirdre said, rolling her eyes.

That was a moment that Gene enjoyed. Looking at her fattened waist and hip lines that he sometimes disliked, he said, 'A woman comes to see me this afternoon. See how good my English has become?'

'Younger than me? I bet she's Chinese,' Deirdre snorted.

'Actually, she's Hong Kongese,' Gene said. 'And she gives me some information about the Church that she thinks I should go to but I think she is nice, quite nice, I mean her eyes sort of, sort of turns me on. Am I getting my tenses right?'

'Your tenses and your fantasies! What are you talking about?' Deirdre was watching *Sex and Mrs X* on Arena when she stopped, 'You're not saying that you wanted to have sex with her?'

'Why not? I sometimes do think it's a good idea because I keep thinking about her eyes after she left.'

'That's the rottenest thing I've ever heard of in my life, and that's the kindest way I could put it,' Deirdre said, fuming.

'I'm sorry,' Gene said, looking worried. 'I only meant that for a joke.'

'It's not funny,' Deirdre said as she switched off the television, her face smeared with her war paint of Beta Alistine Rocket Science Eye-zone, looking like a demi-goddess or demon.

'What's wrong with your face?' Gene asked, noticing her smeared features as if for the first time.

'If you don't like the look of it, lick it clean,' Deirdre said as she made to offer her face for him to lick, causing Gene to run away like a frightened rabbit.

Such harmless skirmishes were now daily occurrences in their shared domestic life, now heading towards an indefinite future over which neither had any control. Unless something drastic happened, it would probably proceed on that basis for as long as they wanted, provided Gene retained his sanity and virility, neither of which he seemed to have at the moment. There was no real conflict. For some, their life looked like a story with no climax, no anticlimax, not even a denouement. It resembled the Murray River that, after some unhindered placid spread, ended its own life undramatically somewhere inland, as Gene wrongly thought it did, like an imagination ending its own life in its source. Still, Gene's inner capacity for trouble or honest *liumang*-ism, a coinage he preferred over larrikinism, would find expression from time to time like dark winds that came from nowhere, sweeping Deirdre off her feet.

'I dislike your growing rotundity intensely,' Gene said one night in bed, a Chinese book in hand, reading by the bed lamp.

'Sorry?' Deirdre could not hear him clearly as she was listening to a CD on her Discman.

'I said I disliked your fat body more and more and you should do something about it,' Gene said, his eyes not leaving the poem he was reading.

'Oh, is that what you were saying?' Deirdre said. 'Do you know what I dislike about you these days?'

'What?' Gene said, pausing with pricked ears.

'If you are not afraid of being hurt,' Deirdre said. 'I can tell you that you are growing idiotic daily, you speak English like Chinese, you speak Chinese like English, you are middle-aged without being middle-class, you leave no one alone and end up being left alone, you stink with the garlic and pickled vegetables you like to eat, the inside of your shorts is stained with shit because you don't clean between your buttocks when you finish shitting and what else? Oh, yes, you think you are a writer, a headwriter to be more precise, but all these years you have not produced one sensible piece of writing and you keep telling me stories that you make up or dream of with no real foundations. You are worse than a good-for-nothing. You are a parasite …'

'And a bad-for-everything, ha? Speaking English like Chinese, is that what you mean, Dear Dree? You are too good for me and I am too bad for you?'

'And you are a racist, too, one of the worst kinds I've ever known because you don't go public but hide it and pretend you're open-minded. Didn't you call me a *guipo* in the presence of a lot of people at a party the other day? Don't you sometimes even call me a *gui* (devil) yourself and say your culture is infinitely superior and that the world will always be dominated by two major centres of civilisation, one Western and the other Eastern, without any compromise, and one will never beat the other, like you and I, and that no one can hold the balance of power?'

'Devil is nothing but "lived" spelt backwards, another way of speaking English like Chinese, ha? Just like your own name, (h)er dried, when spelt backwards? And you should have known by now after having lived with me for so many years that I am a han but, spelt backwards in English, I am nah. My English denies my Chinese. Likewise, my Chinese denies my English. For these many mucking years, they are living together trying to nullify each other, only to manage a coexisting balance, succeeding each other like night and day, cleaning the other only to find itself getting more murky. Like you and me.' Gene erupted, nonstop. 'I'm a genius, don't you know? A sleeping genius, equivalent to your *Sleeping Beauty*, a bad for everything genius, a headwriting genius. Isn't that the very reason you decided to marry me, you *ta ma de*? And play monopoly over me? Did you hear me speaking Chinese like English now, *nigebiaoziyangde*? Are you not racist *niziji* (you yourself)? You talk about the English language as if that was going to be The Language for the whole world but it is not and it's not going to be. It is just an ever-growing and ever-expanding rubbish tip that collects all the linguistic garbage in the world and, you see, that's Wei speaking through me even though he is dead, God, for so many years beyond my *jiyi* (memory). For me, it's nothing but Englishit, as the White Sand storyteller once said. The Hong Mao Hua (Red-haired Speech). You know who I am? I am Wei who killed himself precisely because he did not find the way, the balance.

'Because you married me and brought me to Australia you think at the heart of your hearts, the belly of your bellies, that I should remain grateful for the rest of my life, putting you on a pedestal and kowtowing like a kowtow worm daily prostrate before you as if you were a goddess. And, because of that, you try to turn me into a woman by ordering me around the house, getting me to cook and clean and do all those sorts of stuff that I never do at home in China and you always try to correct my tenses. There are deliberately incorrect tenses, do you know that? You are a disgrace because we are not as equal as you promised we would be before we came out. How could we be ever equal as you don't even speak my language, don't even understand a single fucking character, for example, *fu*, and spent so many years in China without even bothering to learn it? I can now totally identify with the Chinese one hundred years ago when they first came into contact with your red hairs and appreciate what they did: refusing to speak your language and speaking to you only when you learnt to speak the Chinese and when you couldn't they would regard you as barbarians and brutes and they were right.'

Perversely, Deirdre was not upset. On the contrary, she was amused and even turned on. She reached out with her right hand and grabbed Gene by his loins and gently squeezed him as he groaned. The intimate gesture brought a sudden lull in which both fell silent, her unspoken English words somehow in tune with his unspoken Chinese words along sex-surged wavelengths. Or perhaps it was the other way round.

25

At this stage, in mid-age, like in mid-air, Gene paused to consider himself in the mirror. He caught his own eyes when going past his wall mirror on the other side of his bed, one in which he could observe himself and Deirdre, when making love or war in bed, and he was stunned by the cruel unsmiling coldness that they seemed to have acquired over the years. They were no longer Chinese, even if they were shaped like that culture and language. They looked English, very English, especially in the way in which they held people in derision and mock sympathy, although he knew that there was one thing that would remain unchanged and unchanging: he still avoided direct eye contact with anyone, even with himself. He found direct confrontation with himself unsettling. He looked at his mouth and found that its shape had also somehow become twisted through speaking too much English, with its tongue-between-the-teeth 'the's and 'th's, and its constant upwards and downwards movements that strained on his cheeks so that the muscles there had got a little shrunk, making him look austere, like an understatement, and, from a Chinese point of view, not cool, but miserly and ungenerous. He knew that the Chinese never liked the English, from his experience in Yunnan and his readings of the books on the early days when the English explorers went there. On Gene's part, there was neither respect nor contempt reserved for that place once called Red-haired in China, his linguistic link to it as thin as thin, or sin or *xin*, his mind again drawn into this language congee of thousand-year-old eggs with fresh sardines from the Atlantic Ocean.

Deirdre's family, originally from England, had been in Australia for many generations, too many generations to bother about searching all the way back to their roots even though they still had enormous admiration for things British-sounded. At least this was what Gene understood of her family with whom he kept a distant relationship. Similarly, Gene did not bother too much about his own roots. He never wanted to go back again after the trip he had made in search of his dead father's spirits on the Burma Road. If there was no evidence he could find for the existence of an English mother who conceived him after having a love affair with his father, he'd rather regard himself as a fruit born of Jing senior and Lieutenant Ash Kilpatrick's union as they wandered through Gaoligongshan Mountains along those wild rivers among a diverse variety of ethnic peoples, including the Yi, the Buyi, the Naxi and the Bai. Claiming one's ancestry or the purity of one's ancestry was no longer important in this world of increased density of mixtures, least of all for someone who was occupied only with time.

'Write your autobiography,' he heard the voice urging him again. It was first issued from Deirdre's small mouth with tiny sharp teeth as white as her face, whiter. The logic was explained to him a thousand times till it became a refrain, uncompromisingly and shamelessly brutal: As Asians living in a Western democracy, that's the only way out for you. It is where your ability and limit lies and it is what is expected of you by your market. Don't ever try to think in fictive terms. It'll be bad literature that you'll produce because you write bad English. As a non-mother-tongue speaker and user, you ARE inferior to your white brethrens and sisters whose command of the language entitles them to be artists in that language, owners of that language, whereas yours merely keeps you in serfdom, at best an abuser and, at worst, a slave. You do have something to sell of yourself, which is your exoticness, your eyes, for example, and your mouth, in spite of the fact that they are threatening to lose their Chineseness each day you live here. You yourself have said that we as second-language users of the language would never hope to ascend to the status of masters of English.

'It is absolutely true, isn't it?' Deirdre said. 'And it is not racist to say this, you must understand. The same is true of us, I mean how can we ever hope to master your language and become first-rate in it, like your masters? To this day, I still have difficulty distinguishing between *kouyin* and *kouqi* and how to use them properly in Chinese. I do think, though, if you treat our language violently, rape it as you often say you would, that is also fine, as long as you do it in an attractive, proper manner, not by destroying it but by, by, living it and, more than that, twisting it around.'

'You mean speaking or writing English like Chinese?' Gene shook his head. 'I can't believe this but you are harping on your old theory again. I'm Australian, you know that, and by that I mean I am as good as anyone else and value the kind of life I'm living even if it is trash and one of these days I'd even opt for living in the open under the roof of the sky on the bed of the earth, homeless forever, homeless again, with nothing on written record. That is what Australia is all about, isn't it, or originally, aboriginally about?'

'Gene, you are ranting and raging. You are raving mad!' Deirdre said. 'I think you should take your medications now.'

After Bill left Deidre and she had her first miscarriage, and Gene came to stay, her life did change for a time if only because Gene could cook Chinese meals for her, a culinary consolation that meant that she no longer had to go to Chinese restaurants. Everything was prepared for her at home. And they had great sex, too, initially and briefly, as Gene seemed a willing experimenter and enthusiastic participator, his eyes opened by what was readily available in the Australian pornography market. Then, there came the clashes, clashes that were so minor that they were hardly ever noticeable. Even now, she could not remember what they were about, either it was because he waited too long for her outside a bookshop or the other way round, she waited too long for him outside a Chinese grocery. She remembered with a shudder how difficult it was to change his habit of not washing before having sex as he insisted on spontaneity, arguing that by the time he cleaned everything he would have lost the passion. There was also his apparent intolerance of the easy ways in which she dealt with other men of her race, which both amusingly pleased and angered her.

'A little bit of harmless joke cracking is nothing, Gene,' she said to him one day. 'If a male friend kisses me on my cheek, that doesn't mean I'm going to be his lover; it doesn't even mean that I'm going to make love to him sometime in the future. It's just part of our tradition.'

'But I hate the way in which you laugh with them and act so intimately with them, so much so that I actually saw the chap grabbing hold of your hand,' Gene said.

'The chap? Which chap are you talking about?' Deirdre said, quite amazed.

'The chap with a big virile moustache and a row of disgustingly tiny corn teeth,' Gene said bitterly.

'He's Roy, my cousin, Gene,' Deirdre said. 'How can you be jealous of someone who is from the same family and works as a lawyer?'

'And I dislike this girlfriend of yours. What's her name?' Gene said. 'The one with a mane of hair dyed blonde and a face as male as a horse. Such coarse features! She never even speaks to me but acts as if you were the only person existing in the world for her.'

'Are you suggesting we are somehow lovers?' Deirdre went pale at the remark.

'I'm not suggesting anything but it is on your own evidence that you like women more than men. You said so when we made love the other day because you said women would be less violent and volatile.'

'But I was just joking, Gene!' Deirdre said. 'What are you crapping on about? If you keep messing around like this, you may one day find me turned into a bisexual, loving both men and women.'

'It's most unkind of you to say that to me, D.S.' Gene said, looking as if he was going to lose his temper. Then he changed his mind, realising he could retaliate with a similar joke. 'Actually, it might be a good idea for me to pick up a girl, too, someone younger and more sexy than you, like the one who brought me Church information.'

'Come on, Gene,' Deirdre said. 'That's enough. What do you say if I sing "Broken English" for you?'

'Oh, but I think I like her other song better. What's that called?'

'I don't know what you are talking about.'

'The one containing a lot of dirty words, new words or raw words in our lingo.'

'I like "raw words". In fact, I remember you were trying to explain to me in the class that in Chinese you'd never say "new words" but *shengzi*, as if whatever that is new is raw till it is remembered and becomes cooked or *shu*.'

'Don't mention the class, don't ever mention it to me again,' Gene suddenly grew morose and, then, his face was lit up with memory. 'And we have "white word" as well. Do you remember that?'

26

Gene went out for a walk alone. The park was nearby, a mass of summer dry, few trees dotting the groundscape. The high temperature during the day gone, he felt ripples of a cool breeze wafting from nowhere. Grass cracked and cackled underfoot. One or two people were out taking a stroll, one directly coming towards him from the opposite direction, short with a Chinese look, and the other walking from left to right, also with Chinese features, passing in front of him, a dozen metres away. Rarely did Gene ever bump into any Chinese but they, these three including him, did not acknowledge each other's presence, each wending his own way, leaving him alone.

This was Gene's home. He didn't like everything in it but it was his home all right, unlike his other home, which gave birth to him but also reason to leave; this one gave him reason to stay despite his condition. Then he saw this yellow-beaked black bird chirping along, flying a short distance while chirruping, stopping, then flying again. Gene wondered if he knew unhappiness at all. He was amazed by the way in which the bird was not burdened by any possessions. He flew as he sang, his feathers bare of any furniture. He could fly anywhere he wanted. The earth was plentiful in its provisions, his only enemy being Gene and other human beings. It must be the spirit of his dead father for one of his remarks emerged just at that moment:

'The seed of unhappiness is planted in you the minute the two tongues assault each other.'

He kept walking till something dawned on him. The bird was not his father but himself. Like him, Gene had nothing to burden him, physically or spiritually, which didn't mean that he was happier. If he died, all those books that he had been writing in his head would die with him, to which no one, even the best biographer in the world, could gain access. He would die without a name or a record to burden him with, to burden others with; he would die without the shameless audacity to claim to be a worthy human being measured in terms of materialistic possessions. *Ren guo liu ming, yan guo liu sheng,* this Chinese proverb came to him as Gene remembered his university days when he would debate with himself about how he wanted to spend his life, be a recluse or a name on everyone's lips or somewhere in-between. A man passes and leaves a name just as a bird passes and leaves a sound. What an absurdity! A bird certainly does not think that way, only a human being does and he dies irretrievably and irreversibly.

*

Deidre suggested that Gene take up Chinese teaching but Gene wanted none of that. His refusal to teach Chinese and his belief in his own superiority as someone who had graduated with distinctions in English from the English class condemned him to a life of contemplation. It was what Dr Wagner had taught him in China and it was what he had learnt from this country. In his saner moments, he would call this aristocracy: aboriginal aristocracy, not the white strain of exploitation and humiliation. Without knowing their culture, he would regard himself as a spiritual aboriginal because his life was not lived to earn a living but to be at peace with the world and, most important of all, with himself, wandering from place to place in his mind, an eternal exile at heart, an abominable headwriter.

27

You are now divorced. Or imagine you are. Divorced from the reality, which is your large window with white lace curtains, a deserted veranda with a wooden railing outside, a front courtyard that remains empty, grey in the sun for all the years to come if you decide to live and die here. Your mobile and cordless phones lie side by side on your glass tea table next to a mug of hot tea, the tea a friend of yours in Zhejiang bought for you and mailed to you, its postage three times more than its price.

Occasionally, a knocking sound comes from next door where a block of units are being built, breaking the totality of the silence and bringing in bad memories.

You have now entered into a most lonely period of your time, one in which you know if you persist in it without being willing to change its pattern can go on forever until you go. Each morning begins with a lone email message received, garbage not counted in, and your mobile now remains mute for days on end, making you wonder if there is any point going to the agency to change it for a new model with a camera in it. Who is there to take photographs of? And yet you are happy, knowing that you are privileged to be living with you, a talented idiot, to share the life with you and to observe you at the closest ranges possible and to record the most minute details that happen in your life, such as the trouble you had in finding the right spelling for the word 'minute' as you tried 'minuit', 'minite', and 'minuiet' until you sought help from the in-built Dictionary under Tools and the change you have just made to the word minute because you found 'minutest' was highlighted in red by the computer and eventually decided on 'the most minute'.

And you are happy because you have come to the decision that you will devote the rest of your life to being an eye, an I. No, an eye. And after more than a decade you have overcome your opponent: the Australian curse. Or think you have.

28

On a stormy night that seemed to have the power of uprooting all the trees on the mountain and flooding all the houses in the lower regions of Melbourne, Deirdre and Gene, safe in bed in Cheong St, were reading a letter from Dang:

Ah well, I suppose this is life. We probably shall never meet again except perhaps in fiction. What has happened in these many years defies description. To put it in a nutshell, I've since come home in China as you, Jing, are aware, although I did not tell you why. There is no why. It is life. I now use the language truly as a tool, a way of making a livelihood, having given up on believing in it as our saviour, I mean my saviour, something that we can turn ourselves into, something that can turn us into a better being. I would have opted for Australia if I retained an iota of that belief on my return. I have now gone further into the hills and found the real China not in big metropolitan cities like Shanghai, Beijing, Shenzhen and Guangzhou. They are like any other cities in the world, efficient, satisfying, sufficient, liveable, with proper sewage systems. You can call these cities anything and it will not change their nature as a city. The real China is perversely found in the mountains here among the ethnics, in Lijiang, for example, where you can hear the Tang Dynasty in the ancient Naxi music and see it on the black-tiled roofs of all the houses. Tourism is swallowing it up because of that, pushing the boundary further back into the depths of the mountains. That's where I want to go even though I am aware that the process is irreversible. But I want to see what it is like to go against the trend, perhaps a little bit like you. I am sorry but I can't give you any more information regarding other classmates of our beautiful Class except the fragments of the stories I told you while you were in Luoping. Their lives would not be that different from most of the other lives that I have seen lived, either in China by using the language for various purposes or abroad by using it for the same various purposes. It won't make too much difference. As for you, I am sure you'll make good with your great aspirations in school and with your marriage to an English-Australian lady. For others who are married with Chinese, nothing much will change. For you, however, there is a great future, or shall I say, a greater future?

But night is getting deeper and colder here in the mountains and I can hear the wolves howling. What a lovely and welcome sound, actually of wind!

Keep in touch,

Dang from Zhongdian, now Shangri-la

After reading the letter again, they fell silent for a long time, listening to the fingers of rain drumming on the roof, tearing the trees and thrashing the walls, until Gene said,

'Dear Dree, shall I write to tell him that we are going to have a baby?'

29

Jing is no longer there. In his ashes you arise, feeling as inadequate as ever, in search of something dreamable and unrealisable.

All you have managed to achieve is Jinglish.

Author's Note

I wish to acknowledge the following sources consulted during the writing of *The English Class*:

Bai Shan, *xuexian-dianmian gonglu jishi* (Snowline: A Factual Account of the Burma Road). Kunming: Yunnan People's Publishing House, 1992.

Won-loy Chan, *Burma the Untold Story*. Novato, CA: Presidio Press, 1986.

Duan Peidong, *jian sao fengyan* (Swords Sweeping the Wind and Smoke). Kunming: Yunnan People's Publishing House, 1991.

Duan Peidong, *songshan dazhan* (A Battle of the Songshan Mount). Kunming: Yunnan People's Publishing House, 1995.

Tang Zhijie, *menghuan gaoyuan-zhanmusi xierdun yu xianggelila* (Dreamy Plateau: James Hilton and Shangri-la). Kunming: Yunnan Education Publishing House, 2000, p. 51, from which the Ouyang Feifei song is taken for translation into English.

Yang Daiye, *wuhan lüyou mingsheng quhua* (Interesting Talks on Tourist Scenic Spots in Wuhan). Chinese University of Geology Publishing House, 1997.

Zhang Yudan (ed), *Yunnan 18 guai* (Tracking 'The Eighteen Oddities' in Yunnan). Kunming: Yunnan People's Publishing House, 1999.

Zuo Hejin, 'dianmian yuanzhengju yiyuan jishi' (A Factual Account of Interpreters for the Army on the Burma-Yunnan Front), Part 1, *hongyan chunqiu* (Spring and Autumn in the Red Rock), No. 4, 1994, pp. 20-27, and Part 2, *hongyan chunqiu* (Spring and Autumn in the Red Rock), No. 5, 1994, pp. 52-59.

The translated Chinese poem on pp. 375-6 is based on a poem by Yuan Zhongdao, titled, 'Night spring', published in *Overland*, No. 174, Autumn, 2004, p. 123.

The two lines from a Gu Cheng poem, quoted in pinyin and English translation, on pp. 246-7, are so well-known they can be found anywhere online.

Similarly, the poem, 'Gather ye rosebuds while ye may', on p. 229, is also so widely known that it can be found anywhere online.

Ouyang Yu obtained his BA in English and American Literature from Wuhan University and his MA in Australian and English literature at East China Normal University in Shanghai before moving to Australia in early 1991. He has since published 52 books of poetry, fiction, non-fiction, literary translation and criticism in English and Chinese languages. His books include his award-winning novel, *The Eastern Slope Chronicle* (2002), his collections of poetry, *Songs of the Last Chinese Poet* (1997) and *The Kingsbury Tales* (2008), his translations in Chinese, *The Female Eunuch* (1991) and *The Man Who Loved Children* (1998), and his book of criticism, *Chinese in Australian Fiction: 1888-1988* (USA, 2008). Some of his recent publications include *On the Smell of an Oily Rag: speaking English, thinking Chinese and living Australian* (Wakefield, 2008), a book of creative non-fiction, and *The Kingsbury Tales: a novel* (Brandl & Schlesinger, 2008), a book of poetry. In 2009, five of his books were published in China, including a translation into Chinese of *The Masterpiece* by Anna Enquist, a Dutch novelist. The author acknowledges the invaluable support of the Australia Council in the writing and development of his major new novel, *The English Class*. He lives in Melbourne, Australia.

More at: www.ouyangyu.com.au